The
IRISH
NANNY

ALSO BY SANDY TAYLOR

SANDY TAYLOR

The

IRISH
NANNY

bookouture

Published by Bookouture in 2021

An imprint of Storyfire Ltd.
Carmelite House
50 Victoria Embankment
London EC4Y 0DZ

www.bookouture.com

ISBN: 978-1-80019-814-2
eBook ISBN: 978-1-80019-813-5

If I had a flower for every time I thought of you… I could walk through my garden forever.

Alfred Lord Tennyson

Prologue

1941

The morning we arrived in New York was a fine one.

I was woken in the tiny cabin I shared with the baby by the call of the gulls. It had been days since we'd heard any birdsong, and although the caws of the birds were harsh, the familiar sound was like music to my ears.

I knew we must be close to land, so I dressed quickly and changed the baby and wrapped her up in her blanket. I tied a scarf around my head and carried her into the narrow corridor and up the stairs, until I reached the deck level, holding onto the banister with my free hand. Other passengers were making their way up too, anxious to catch the first glimpse of America. There was a buzz in the air, a sense of excitement.

A man held open the door for me and I stepped out into the fresh air. The sea was as huge and grey as ever, mountainous waves swelling and falling around the side of the ship. The air smelled of the sea but it was different now; it had a different texture. I felt salt on my lips and tongue and I could faintly pick out the smells of engine oil and pollen and fried food.

Dawn had broken and the sky was a pale apricot colour, streaked with pink, tinting the tops of the waves.

'Look!' someone cried. 'There it is!'

I followed the direction of their pointed finger and there, hazy on the horizon, was the skyline of New York.

It was a wondrous sight, this silhouette of buildings against the grey sky, one I'd seen in newspapers and on the posters that adorned the walls inside the liner but never in real life and I was filled with emotion.

It was impossible not to feel moved when such a sight as this emerged from the chill of the morning, the buildings gradually losing their haziness and becoming more solid as we approached.

There was also immense sadness because of all that had been lost. I should not have been standing here alone with the baby and I missed those who should have been standing beside me, sharing this moment. I missed them with all my heart.

Ballykillen seemed like a lifetime ago and a million miles away, the faces of my beloved family blurred, as if behind a sheet of glass. When would I hold them again? When would I smell Mammy's roses that trailed across the old stone wall at the back of the cottage? When would I see my home?

I was sailing towards a new country. A new life awaited me: new opportunities, new experiences, new people. But my heart felt like stone and I feared that I would never again feel joy, only sadness and pain. This had been Polly's dream, not mine. It was Polly who had longed for a world beyond the little village where we had grown up. This was not my dream.

The closer we drew to the harbour, the louder the gulls' calls became and the more excited the chatter of those on deck. There were now little boats around us, fishing boats and pleasure craft and ferries.

The baby had narrowed her eyes against the cold air, but seemed entranced by the spectacle before us. She would never remember this terrible journey; she would never remember the people who had been lost and I envied her, for I knew that I would carry their memory with me forever.

PART ONE

Chapter One

1933

I was ten years old when I met Polly Butler and it was a day that I would never forget. I didn't go to school much, because as the eldest of four, I was needed at home. I didn't mind, because I loved Mammy and I was happy to help her with the little ones. I'd only gone to the convent for a couple of years, which wasn't long enough to learn much. It also meant that I didn't have any friends. All that changed the day I was collecting wood for the fire. A few girls ran past me, giggling and laughing.

I watched them until they were almost out of sight and wondered where they were going. I suddenly had a desperate longing to go with them. 'Where are you off to?' I shouted after them.

They kept running. 'Where are you going?' I shouted again.

The tallest girl stopped and turned around. 'What's it to you?' she shouted back at me.

I could feel my face going red. 'I just wondered, is all.'

'We're on a secret mission.'

'What is it?'

'Well, it wouldn't be a secret if we told you, would it?'

'I suppose not,' I mumbled.

'Well, if you must know,' said Finola Dunn, who lived two doors down from me in Cross Lane. 'We're going to get apples from Mulligan's.'

'I didn't know Mulligan's sold apples.'

'He doesn't,' she said, grinning. 'But he has a fine orchard full of them and we thought we'd relieve him of a few. I suppose you can come with us if you want to.'

I knew Mammy wouldn't want me to steal apples but oh, I wanted to join them. I decided I would go with them but I wouldn't pinch any apples. 'Oh, I do,' I said.

'Well, you'll have to be as quiet as a mouse,' she said. 'Or he'll have us up before the judge, miserable old sod.'

'I won't open my mouth.'

'Then you are welcome and mind you keep up.'

I dropped the sticks and started after them. It felt so good to be running through the woods with the girls. I felt a part of something and it felt great, as if I was about to go on some big adventure.

We continued deeper and deeper into the woods, where the trees were so close together that it was getting hard to see in front of us. I tripped over twice but scrambled to my feet, for fear of losing them. We finally emerged into bright sunshine and started running alongside the Blackwater River.

We stopped at the high stone wall that surrounded Mr Mulligan's grand house. He lived alone, for he had neither kith nor kin to call his own. You could feel sorry for him but Finola was right; he was fierce miserable. If we got caught, he would surely slay the backs off us but it would be worth it to be in the company of girls of my own age.

The tall girl put her finger to her lips and we all fell silent. 'Not a word,' she said softly.

'Tuck your dress into your knickers,' whispered Finola, looking at me.

I did as she said and watched as one by one they scaled the wall. I wasn't sure that I would be able to do it and hung back. I was beginning to think that this wasn't such a great idea after all, especially as I had no mind to be stealing apples. 'Don't worry, I'll give you a leg-up,' said one of the girls.

She had two red plaits that bounced off her shoulders and a cheeky grin. I liked her at once. 'Thanks,' I said, smiling. She cupped her hands and I put my foot in them. I was over the wall in a minute and landed in a heap on the other side. I wanted to cry out but remembered that I had to be as quiet as a mouse, so I rubbed my leg and stayed silent.

A basket came flying over the wall, followed by the girl.

We all stood together in a huddle, not moving, just listening, like animals stalking their prey. The only sound was the wind blowing through the trees and the beating of my own heart, pounding in my ears.

'Remember,' whispered Finola again, 'not a word.'

The garden was huge, stretching right down to the river. We skirted the house and crept into the orchard. In front of us were row upon row of trees, heavy with fruit. I wondered why old Mulligan needed all these apples, if he wasn't going to sell them. Wasn't it a sin to let God's own bounty rot on the ground when it could be enjoyed?

'We just take the fallers,' whispered the girl who had hoisted me over the wall.

'What do we put them in?'

'You can share my basket, then we can split them up afterwards.'

'I don't want the apples,' I said.

'Then what, in all that's holy, are you doing here?'

I shrugged my shoulders. I couldn't bring myself to tell her that it was the company I wanted, not the apples.

'Shush,' demanded the tall girl.

We worked silently, spreading out across the orchard, picking up as many of the fallers as we could. I could hear some giggling and Finola telling someone to shut up.

'Leave the rotten ones,' whispered the girl.

My leg was throbbing from the fall but I set to and started filling the basket. Every now and again the red-haired girl smiled at me.

All of a sudden, I heard someone yelling. It was old man Mulligan tearing down the garden towards us.

He was shaking his fist and shouting. 'Ya little barbarians, I'll have you before the judge.'

The girls scattered in all directions. I watched as Finola heaved herself back over the wall but I couldn't move. It was as if I was frozen to the spot. Then I felt someone grab my shoulders and pull me into the bushes. 'Not a sound,' she said.

I looked at her gratefully; it was the girl with the red plaits. We squatted down. I was terrified. Mammy would be disappointed in me and the priest was sure to read my name out at Mass on Sunday. I would bring shame on my mammy and the good name of my ancestors who had gone before me.

I looked at the girl beside me; her shoulders were shaking and she had her hand over her mouth. She must have been crying with the shame she had inflicted on her family. I put my arm around her and it was then that I realised she wasn't crying at all; she was giggling and that made me start giggling.

'Polly Butler,' she said, wiping away the tears that were running down her cheeks.

'Rose Brown,' I said.

We stayed a bit longer, till we were sure that Mulligan had gone back to the house.

'Will we have to climb the wall again?' I asked.

'No, we can cut down by the river.'

'But what about my sticks? I've left them in the wood.'

'Then we'll double back and I'll help you carry them home.'

We held hands and ran along by the river; I could feel my heart bursting with pure joy. I had had the adventure of a lifetime and I had met Polly Butler, who became my best and only friend. I felt like the luckiest girl in the world.

Chapter Two

1937

It was because of Polly that I got the job in Cork. We were sitting on the wall outside the church when Father Luke walked down the path towards us.

'Are you putting the world to rights, girls?' he said, smiling.

'No, Father, just passing the time of day,' said Polly.

'And how's life treating you both?'

'Grand, Father,' I said.

He nodded. 'Is it fourteen you are now?'

'It is, Father.'

'I seems like yesterday that I baptised the pair of you. How did you do in your leaving exams, Polly?'

'To tell you the truth, Father, I didn't do that great. Sister Ignatius said that my calling lay in a different direction to the rest of the class. She just didn't say which direction,' said Polly, grinning.

'Then I hope it's in the direction that our dear Lord has planned for you.'

'I don't know about that, Father, but I have a fine job already lined up,' said Polly.

I stared at Polly. I couldn't believe that she was lying to a priest and now she would have to go to confession and admit that she had lied to him. Jesus, she'd be shamed.

'In the town, Polly?'

'No, Father, I'm off to the city.'

'Then I wish you well. I shall light a candle and ask the Blessed Virgin Mary to keep an eye on you.'

I waited until Father Luke was out of hearing. 'How could you lie to the priest?' I said.

'I didn't lie. I have a grand job in Cork, only waiting for me to step into.'

'Cork?'

'Yes, Cork. I'm going to work in a swanky hotel and I'm saying goodbye to this Godforsaken hole.'

I didn't think that Ballykillen was a Godforsaken hole; I thought it was the most beautiful place in the world and I had no mind to be going anywhere else.

'Why didn't you tell me? How could you get yourself a grand job in Cork without telling me? We tell each other everything.' I could feel my eyes filling with tears. What would I do without my best friend?

'Jesus, Rose, are you crying?'

'And why wouldn't I be crying? You seem quite happy to leave me here on my own and swan off to a swanky hotel in Cork.'

'You daft girl, you're coming with me. You didn't think I'd leave you behind, did you?'

I stared at her. 'And how did we get this job in a swanky hotel in Cork? Don't they want to give us the once-over?'

'My Uncle Pat is the doorman and he recommended me, and I recommended you. He told them that we were two good Catholic girls with nice manners and tidy ways. So, it's all sorted, all we have to do is turn up.'

'Didn't you think to ask me first, Polly Butler?'

'You would have said no.'

'You're right, I would. I don't want to leave Ballykillen, even if you do.'

'There's no work in town as well you know and what little there is, I wouldn't be seen dead doing. Anyway, your mammy is all for it.'

'You've spoken to my mammy?'

'Of course I've spoken to your mammy! She's your mammy and she has a right to know that you're off to Cork to seek your fortune.'

I knew that what Polly was saying was right; there was no work in the town and Mammy needed my wages, but for it all to be decided behind my back was putting me in a sour mood.

'I just think it would have been polite to have been asked.'

'I thought you'd be pleased,' said Polly.

'I'm not sure what I feel right now. It's not easy having your future decided for you.'

'Well, if I'd left it up to you, we'd be shovelling shite up at the slaughterhouse.'

I shuddered. I hated passing the place, all those poor animals, unaware that their days were numbered, but it was the only job going because no one was queuing up to do it.

'So, if you want to shovel shite while I'm working in a swanky hotel in Cork that's up to you and a bit of gratitude wouldn't go amiss, Rose Brown.'

I slipped my arm through hers. 'I know you have my best interests at heart, Polly, it's just come as a bit of a shock, that's all. Did you really tell my mammy?'

'Of course not, ya daft eejit. I just thought you'd make your mind up quicker if you thought she was all for it.'

'Looks like we're going to Cork then,' I said, grinning.

'Looks like it. Now all I've got to do is get my Uncle Pat to put in a good word for us.'

'But you said—'

'Ah, sure it will be no bother at all,' she said, grinning.

As it turned out, Polly's Uncle Pat didn't have as much influence as she thought he had and the pair of us were summoned to Savages Hotel in Cork city for an interview.

'You'll need decent shoes for a start,' said Mammy, looking down at my feet. 'And where in the name of God are we going to find the money for new shoes?'

'I don't know, Mammy.'

'Go across to Mrs Feeny. Orla's just had her Confirmation and she may have a pair of shoes that you can borrow.'

'I'd be ashamed, Mammy.'

'Well, you can't turn up in those, Rose. They'll think it's a tinker that's walking through the door.'

I looked down at my shoes. They were shabby and scuffed, Mammy was right. 'Alright so, I'll ask.'

'Be sure to tell Mrs Feeny that it's just a loan and ask after her bunions.'

'I will, Mammy.'

I walked across the lane to the Feenys' house and knocked on the door. It was opened by Orla.

I'd never taken to Orla Feeny – she had airs about her, not fitting to her station.

'And to what do we owe this visit, Rose Brown?' she said, lounging against the door frame.

'I have business with your mammy.'

'And what sort of business would that be?'

'Not yours, Orla Feeny, so if you would get your mammy, I'd be obliged.'

'Mammy?' shouted Orla. 'It's Rose Brown at the door. She says she has business to discuss with you.'

I waited patiently while Orla stood there staring at me, looking for all the world as if she was sucking on a lemon.

'Well, ask the child in, don't leave her standing on the doorstep,' shouted Mrs Feeny.

Orla reluctantly stepped out of the way, barely giving me enough room to squeeze past her.

Unlike her daughter, Mrs Feeny was a lovely woman. She was feeding her latest baby from her titty.

'You're growing like a beanstalk, Rose Brown,' she said, smiling at me.

I smiled back. 'I have something to ask you, Mrs Feeny,' I said. 'In private,' I added. I didn't want Orla to know my business, for it would be round town before the end of the day that I'd come begging for a loan of her good Confirmation shoes.

'Orla,' said Mrs Feeny, 'take yourself off out of it.'

Orla raised her eyes up to heaven and reluctantly went out of the door, making sure she made her feelings clear by slamming it behind her.

Mrs Feeny took the baby off her breast and put it over her shoulder, patting its back until it gave a huge burp.

'This little feller is an angel, Rose. He burps on demand and he's no trouble at all, unlike that skit of a girl who nearly took the door off its hinges. She takes after her father's side of the family, they're an awful cranky lot. Me knees are only worn out, praying to Our Blessed Saint Jude.'

Mrs Feeny placed the baby in a basket beside the fire. 'Now, what can I do for you, child?' she said, sitting down at the table.

I sat opposite her. 'I have an interview for a job in Cork, Mrs Feeny, but my shoes are a disgrace before God. Mammy wondered whether you had a pair of Orla's shoes that might fit me, just for a loan.'

'Wait there now while I pop upstairs and get her Confirmation shoes and if they fit you, then you're more than welcome to them.'

'Thank you.'

I looked around the little kitchen. It was clean and cosy. The baby was making snorty noises in his basket. I went across to him. He had a round little head and bright blue eyes. There was a trickle of milk running down his chin, so I wiped it away. 'Aren't you a little dote?' I said. 'Aren't you the sweetest feller? Unlike your sister,'

I added. He smiled up at me and gave another huge burp, then he laughed, showing little pink gums, as if he'd done a grand thing.

'You're the cleverest boy in Ballykillen,' I said.

Mrs Feeny came down the stairs and handed me the shoes. 'Try them on, Rose and let's hope they will suit.'

They fitted perfectly. 'They're fine, Mrs Feeny,' I said. 'I'm awful grateful to you.'

'Thanks be to God,' she said, smiling.

'I'll take good care of them.'

'I know you will, Rose. Now tell me about this job of yours.'

'It's in a grand hotel and I'm going with Polly Butler.'

'Your mammy will miss you, child.'

'And I'll miss her,' I said, my eyes filling with tears.

'I'd say your Kathy will step up to the mark. Life has a habit of working out, Rose, and I will be sure to keep an eye on them all.'

'Thank you, Mrs Feeny,' I said, getting up from the table. 'And thank you for the loan of the shoes.'

'You're very welcome, child, I hope they bring you a bit of good luck at your interview.'

'Mammy says to ask after your bunions.'

'I'm demented with them, Rose, but we all have our crosses to bear and God in his wisdom has decided to send me bunions. Thank your mammy for asking, she's a good woman.'

'I will, Mrs Feeny.'

I walked back across the lane, hiding Orla Feeny's Confirmation shoes under my jumper. It all suddenly felt very real and I was terrified. I didn't want to leave home. With a bit of luck, I wouldn't get the job.

I didn't go indoors straight away, I stood outside the cottage that had been my home since the day I was born. All the cottages in Cross Lane looked exactly the same but ours had a ship in a bottle in the window that my granddaddy had made, God rest his soul.

How could I leave this place? How could I leave Mammy and my sisters? How could I do that?

I walked into the cottage, carrying the shoes.

'I have the shoes, Mammy, and they fit as if they were made for me,' I said, smiling.

Mammy took them. 'Now aren't they lovely, Rose? It was good of Mrs Feeny to give you a loan of them. I'd say you will impress those that matter in that grand hotel in Cork.'

Mammy put the shoes on the table and put her arms around me. 'They'll be lucky to have you, my darling girl, even if you were in your stockinged feet.'

'But I don't want to leave,' I said. 'Why can't things stay as they are? Why does everything have to change?'

'Because that is God's plan. We are born and we die and in between, we do the best we can.'

Mammy brushed my hair back from my face and I leaned into her. She smelt of kindness and love and security. She smelt of home.

My mammy was beautiful, with eyes the colour of the sea. Only Bridgy, the youngest, had inherited her eyes and everyone said that she was going to be as beautiful as Mammy when she grew up. My eyes were like the sea as well, only on a grey day, when it was the colour of mud.

My mammy loved roses; that was why she named me Rose. 'As soon as I looked at you, with your little rosebud lips, I knew you were my Rose,' she said.

She had managed to grow them against the back wall, even though we only had a bit of a yard. The neighbours came to admire Mammy's roses and wanted to know her secret.

'You have green fingers,' said Mrs Feeny. 'Like your mother before you.'

When I was a child, I kept watching Mammy's hands, waiting for them to turn green, but they never did. I decided that Mrs Feeny needed her eyes testing.

Life wasn't easy for Mammy. My lovely daddy was a sailor and he died just before Bridgy was born. Someone had left a hatch open on the ship and he'd fallen to his death. I had been too young to realise how heartbroken Mammy was, because she just carried on caring for us. I have since learned that we were almost taken into the workhouse, but the Navy took responsibility for the accident and Mammy was awarded a small pension that was enough to feed and clothe us and to pay the rent on our little cottage.

Just then, my three sisters came into the room.

'Jesus,' said Kathy. 'I'm only sick of school. Sister Concepta is a baggage of a woman.'

'You can't be saying that about a nun,' whispered Agnes. 'She is married to God Himself.'

'Well, I pity God. I don't even think the woman likes children.'

Agnes shook her head. 'Ah, Kathy,' she said softly.

As soon as Agnes started to speak, everyone fell silent, even Bridgy who could talk the hind legs off a donkey. My darling little sister didn't speak much and when she did, her voice was barely a whisper.

I looked around at them all and I knew that if I got the job in Cork, nothing would ever be the same again.

Chapter Three

Me and Polly were out the strand, paddling our toes in the water.
'Orla Feeny gave you a loan of her new holy Confirmation shoes?'
said Polly, amazed.

'Orla Feeny wouldn't give me the drippings off her nose, Polly.
It was Mrs Feeny who gave me a loan of them.'

'Ah sure, she's a lovely woman. How she managed to have a
daughter like that is a mystery. Perhaps she was a desperate sinner
in another life and God decided that Orla was her penance.'

'I have it on good authority that bunions are her penance, Polly.'

'Do you believe in all that stuff?'

'All what stuff?'

'That we've had more than one life? That we've lived before?'

'I'm not sure, but I'm leaning towards the idea. Just imagine,
we might have been royalty in another life.'

'But wouldn't we remember if we'd been royalty?'

'I haven't looked into it properly, Rose, but as soon as I have,
I'll be sure to let you know.'

I couldn't help thinking that if we'd been royalty in another life,
then we must have done something pretty bad to have fallen so low.

I looked across the water at the green patchwork of fields
that tumbled down to the sea and the lighthouse, standing tall
and white further up the coast. I'd spent half my life on this
beach, paddling with my sisters and digging in the sand. I loved
everything about my home town: the main street, the quayside,
the little alleyways and the steep hills. I could walk through the
town with my eyes closed and still know my way home to our
cottage in Cross Lane.

I didn't want to work in a swanky hotel; I didn't want to be in a big city surrounded by strangers. I belonged here amongst my own, amongst the people I loved.

'You're quiet,' said Polly.

'I'm going to miss this place, aren't you?'

'No, I'm not. I can't wait to get away.'

'But isn't there a small part of you that wishes you could work in the town?'

'For God's sake, Rose, Cork city is twenty miles up the bloody road and we'll be back every Friday on the Thrupenny Rush. The train had earned its name because it cost threepence for a ticket and it only stayed in Ballykillen station long enough for us to dash through town and hand over our wages.

'Anyone listening to you would think we were emigrating to America.'

'Shudder the thought,' I said.

'Do you know your trouble, Rose Brown?'

'No, Polly Butler, but I have no doubt that you will tell me.'

'You have no adventure in you, not a scrap. If it was up to you, you'd probably marry some feller from Ballykillen and pop out a baby a year. You'd be happy waiting down the quay for yer man to give you a few pennies for food and be as contented as Minnie Ogg.'

'Is Minnie Ogg contented?'

'She must be, to stay married to that eejit of a man.'

Billy Ogg was desperate, alright. He was the porter on Ballykillen station and the way he strutted around waving his little flag and blowing his whistle you'd be mistaken for thinking he owned the place.

I sighed. Maybe Polly was right; maybe I should look on this as an adventure. After all, I didn't want to end up like Minnie Ogg.

*

The morning of the interview came too soon. I woke up next to Bridgy, feeling like my tummy was full of frogs. I looked across the room. It was barely light outside the little window but I was too nervous to go back to sleep. Why on earth had I let Polly persuade me that leaving Ballykillen was such a great idea?

I'd been dreaming about Billy Ogg, for God's sake. He was standing on the platform dressed as a priest. He was still waving his flag and blowing his whistle. 'I've found my calling, Rose Brown,' he said. 'I'm off to Rome to meet the Holy Father himself.'

I had no stomach for breakfast. I knew if I ate anything, I'd lose it before I got to the end of the town. Mammy wished me well and I left the cottage and walked down the lane, my feet clattering to raise the dead. Polly was waiting for me on the corner.

'This is it then,' she said, grinning. 'The first day of the rest of our lives. Jesus, Rose, you have a face on you like a jug full of sour milk. Couldn't you just show a bit of excitement? You'll never get the job looking like you're about to face a firing squad.'

'I can't help it, Polly, I'm terrible nervous. We have no qualifications to be working in a swanky hotel. They'll take one look at us and send us on our way.'

'You're as good as the next person, Rose, and so am I. They'll be lucky to get us.'

I wasn't convinced.

Billy Ogg was waiting on the platform and I couldn't help but smile as I remembered my dream.

'That's better,' said Polly, grinning at me.

We got on the train and settled down opposite each other. I was still smiling.

'What?' said Polly.

'I dreamt about Billy Ogg last night,' I said, starting to giggle.

'Jesus, that was nightmare, then.'

'He was dressed as a priest and he was off to the Vatican City to meet the Pope.'

We were still giggling as we walked into the foyer of Savages Hotel.

We were met by a girl who was standing beside the reception desk. 'Polly Butler and Rose Brown?' she said, in a superior way.

We nodded.

'My name is Dervla, I'm to take you to see Mrs Mullen and there's no running allowed.'

I looked at Polly and she crossed her eyes, which always made me laugh.

The pair of us could barely keep up with Dervla as she hurried along corridors, down steps, round corners and along another corridor, my shoes tapping with every step. Dervla kept turning around and glaring at me.

'Jesus,' said Polly, 'she should enter the derby, she'd leave the rest of the field behind her.'

I couldn't answer as I had no breath left in me body. Would she ever slow down? Eventually, she stopped outside a door. 'Sit there,' she said, pointing at two chairs, 'and I'll let Mrs Mullen know you're here.'

We sank gratefully onto the chairs and tried to get our breath back.

'Is she on the hard stuff or what?' said Polly. 'Did you notice, Rose? She wasn't even running, she was walking!'

'Who in God's name walks that fast?' I said.

'Those shoes of Orla's are desperate noisy,' said Polly. 'Orla must have sounded like Ginger Rogers, tapping down the aisle of the church.'

I giggled. 'You're funny, do you know that?'

'I do my best,' she said, making a face.

'Aren't you nervous?'

'Sure, what is there to be nervous about?'

'She might not like us.'

'Of course she will, aren't we the two most beautiful girls in Ballykillen? She'll be only delighted with us.'

'You might be the most beautiful girl in Ballykillen, Polly Butler, but I'm certainly not.'

'Yer a hopeless case, Rose Brown.'

I sat there staring at the bare walls, feeling sick to my stomach. Just then the door opened and the racehorse came out. 'Which one of you is Rose Brown?'

'I am,' I said, standing up.

'In you go then, Mrs Mullen will see you now.'

Polly gave me an encouraging smile but I could see that she was now looking as nervous as I was. I could feel myself shaking as I knocked on the door, louder than I meant to.

'Come in,' a voice called.

I opened the door and walked into the room. There was a woman sitting behind a desk and she stood up and held out her hand. 'Rose Brown?' she said.

I swallowed hard and my voice came out in a kind of croak. 'Yes, Missus,' I said.

'You can call me Mrs Mullen.'

'Right, Missus, er, I mean—'

The woman smiled at me. I thought she was very beautiful when she smiled. She looked like a film star, with her dark wavy hair and bright red lipstick.

'Sit down, Rose, and don't look so scared. You're not here for the Inquisition.'

I hadn't a clue what the Inquisition was, but I didn't like the sound of it and I was glad that it wasn't what I was here for.

'I am the housekeeper at Savages, Rose, so I make sure that everything runs as smoothly as it can. That means that the rooms are kept spotless and the beds have fresh linen on them. Do you think that you can do that?'

'Yes, Mrs Mullen,' I said. 'I help Mammy in the house and I can make a bed and dust and wash the floors and get the water from the pump at the bottom of the lane.'

'Well, there will be no need to get water from a pump, we are very modern here and the water comes out of the tap.'

'Well, that's a relief, anyway,' I said. 'For me arms are only hanging off me with the weight of the bucket.'

She smiled again. 'Your uniform will be provided but you will be expected to provide your own undergarments.'

'Undergarments?'

'Your drawers, Rose.'

I could feel my face going red. 'I'm sure we can manage that,' I said.

'And shoes.'

'Oh,' I said.

'Is there a problem with shoes?'

I wanted a hole to open up and swallow me. I nodded.

Mrs Mullen stood up and came around the desk. 'They look perfectly fine to me,' she said.

'They're not mine, Mrs Mullen,' I said shyly. 'They're Orla Feeny's Confirmation shoes. Her mother gave me a loan of them.'

'Well then, we will provide you with new shoes and take a small amount of money out of your wages every week until they are paid for.'

'I'm mighty grateful, Mrs Mullen, and I know me mammy will be too.'

'So, Rose, do you think you would like to work here? You won't be too homesick? We trained the last girl for six months and God love her, she cried every single day of that six months and it upset our guests. She was like a wet sponge. In the end we had no choice but to ask her to leave.'

I thought that I had better be honest. 'I'm not saying that I won't be homesick, Mrs Mullen, because that would be a lie before God. I'll be sure to miss my mammy and my sisters but there's no work in Ballykillen and my mammy needs my money. But I won't cry in front of the guests, I'll do my crying in private.'

Mrs Mullen smiled at me. 'My door is always open, Rose. There will be no need to cry on your own.'

Oh, she was a lovely woman; not just beautiful, but kind as well. I didn't feel so nervous now. 'That's awful good of you,' I said.

'So, Rose, do you think you could be happy here at Savages?'

I smiled at her and nodded. 'Yes, I think that I could.'

'Then I would like to offer you the job, if you have a mind to take it.'

'Oh, I do, Mrs Mullen, and I am very grateful to you. I hope you can see your way clear to taking my friend Polly on as well. I know for a fact she has grand drawers and a fine pair of shoes.'

'I'll bear that in mind, Rose Brown. Now, if you would please ask Polly to come in.'

I opened the door and went back into the corridor.

'Well?' said Polly.

'She's nice. All you have to do is tell her you can make a grand bed and you have a fine pair of drawers.'

'Why is she so interested in me drawers?'

'I haven't a clue but it seemed important to her. Tell her there's frills around the legs, you can confess the lie to Father Luke on Saturday.'

'Thank you for the advice, Rose, I'll be sure to remember what you said. Frills around the legs?'

'That's right, Polly. Frills around the legs and the job's yours.'

Chapter Four

Me and Polly had been working at Savages for five months and although I missed my family, I was enjoying the comings and goings of the hotel. The guests came from all over the world. There were businessmen, in their grand suits; families on their holidays; and newly married couples, who sat at the breakfast table holding hands and gazing into each other's eyes. Mrs Mullen insisted that we put a rose on their pillow. Oh, she was lovely, inside and out. Mostly the guests were nice, except the ones that were so full of their own importance they wouldn't give you the time of day, but Mrs Mullen said that we had to be as respectful to them as we were to the nice ones as they were paying good money to stay there. What we said about them in private was our own affair.

I made sure that I didn't cry in front of the guests who were paying good money to stay at the hotel because I really needed the job but oh, I missed my family. Polly, on the other hand, was only delighted to be out of Ballykillen.

'I've no intention of staying here forever, though,' she said one morning.

'And where would you be going, Polly Butler?'

'I'll be off to England as soon as I can – or America. I can't decide which.'

'What makes you think that England or America will be any better than here?'

'My cousin Alana has a friend who went to England and she says she earns a fortune and the last time she was home, she had a grand fitted costume on her, that had fur round the collar. Alana said she looked like a film star.'

'She must have a mighty job then, to earn all that money.'

'She does,' said Polly. 'She works for a family in London, looking after the children and they take her on holiday with them and she gets to go out in a big posh car that has a man in uniform driving it.'

'I can't see you looking after anyone's children, Polly, you have trouble passing the time of day with your own family.'

'You're right, I do, but that's because they're a load of eejits… but it might be worth it, to have a fine set of new clothes and get to drive around in a swanky car.'

'Well, all I can say, Polly Butler, is that I pity any child that has you as their nanny. You'd scar them for life.'

'Haven't you two got work to do?' said a voice behind us. It was Dervla, the girl who had galloped us down the corridors when we'd come for our interview.

'And what's it to you?' said Polly.

'I have Mrs Mullen's ear, Polly Butler, and she listens to me.'

'I don't care if you have her two legs wrapped round your neck,' said Polly.

The girl's face went red as she glared at Polly. 'I've a mind to go and see her now and tell her you've cheeked me.'

'You can tell her what you like,' said Polly. 'And I'll tell her you mocked her hairstyle.'

Dervla's mean little mouth seemed to shrink in her head as she glared at us. 'But I didn't.'

'It'll be your word against mine and I have a witness,' said Polly, smiling at me.

'She does,' I said, sweetly.

The girl glared at us and raced off down the corridor as if she had the devil himself after her.

'I hope it stays fine fer ya,' yelled Polly after her retreating figure.

'Do you think she'll tell on us?' I said.

'Shouldn't think so,' said Polly grinning. 'The little snitch.'

'How many rooms do you have left to clean?'

Polly sighed. 'Four.'

'I have three, so we'd better get on.'

'I'll see you later,' said Polly.

I made my way up the stairs to room 422, opened the door and walked in.

I stood frozen to the spot as I stared at the man sitting up in bed reading a book. He was naked down to his waist and his chest was a mass of black curly hair. I couldn't stop staring at it.

'Jesus, Mary and Holy Saint Joseph,' I spluttered before I could stop myself.

The man put his book down beside him. 'Sorry to disappoint, but I'm afraid I'm none of those people,' he said, as calm as you like.

'I'm terrible sorry, sir, I thought the room would be empty,' I stuttered.

'Well, I suppose it should be,' he said. 'My fault entirely and I've given you a fright, haven't I?'

My face must have looked like the rising sun, I was that flustered, and I couldn't think of a thing to say. I knew that I was staring at his chest but I had never seen such hair on a man and it fascinated me. I looked down at the floor instead.

'You'll have to forgive me,' he said. 'I lose all track of time when I'm reading a good book and this one is excellent. Have you read Agatha Christie?'

I looked up, trying to avoid the mass of hair, and shook my head.

'Well, you should, she's a great one for red herrings.'

I didn't know what he was talking about; what had this Agatha person got to do with herrings?

'Look, I'll get myself up,' he said, starting to put one hairy leg out of the bed.

'Stay where you are,' I said, in a panic. 'I've other rooms to do. I'll come back later.'

I backed out of the room and leant against the wall. My heart was beating out of my chest. I took some breaths and pulled myself together. For God's sake, it was only a man, I'd seen plenty of men.

My own father was a man, wasn't he? It was just that I'd never seen a bare-chested one before. Mammy had never allowed Daddy to walk around without a vest on. And all that hair… Where in God's name did that come from?

The next morning, me and Polly were helping with the breakfasts.

The dining room was lovely. One wall was taken up almost entirely by long windows, so that when you entered from the dark corridor, you were almost blinded by the light. It was the only room without curtains in the whole hotel. In the evenings you could look out over hundreds of lights, in hundreds of houses, glittering away in the darkness, seeming to cover the city in a blanket of stars.

The tables were round and covered in crisp, white tablecloths. The cutlery shone and the chairs around each table were gold velvet. In the centre of each table was a small vase of seasonal flowers. I thought it was the most beautiful room in the whole hotel.

I couldn't help comparing it to Polly's kitchen in Ballykillen, which was so dark you could barely see what you were eating. Mind you, that was probably a blessing, given Mrs Butler's lack of culinary skills.

'And he had hair sprouting out of his chest?' said Polly when I told her.

'A pile of it,' I said. 'It looked like he had a black cat sitting on him. I nearly fainted on the spot.'

'Now what man sits up in the bed without a good vest on him?' said Polly.

'He's American,' I said.

'Ah, sure, that'll be it then, the Yanks have different standards to the rest of the world.'

'Have you heard of someone called Agatha Christie?' I said.

Polly shook her head.

'Well, she has something to do with herrings.'

'Herrings?'

'That's what yer man said.'

'Well, he sounds like an eejit to me.'

'I don't think he's an eejit, Polly, he seemed nice enough – apart from all the hair, that is.'

'Well, maybe this Agatha woman is a relative of his that works in a fish shop.'

'He didn't look like the type of feller who has a relative that works in a fish shop. Shhh,' I said, as the man walked into the dining room, 'that's him.'

'And he's heading for one of your tables,' said Polly, 'so you'll have to serve him.'

'I can't, all I can see is his hairy chest.' I shuddered. 'All those little black curls, I couldn't take my eyes off them.'

'Then you're a hussy, Rose Brown.'

'I am not.'

'Well, what are you waiting for? Go and get his order,' said Polly, grinning.

I made a face at her and picked up my pad and pencil.

As I got close, I could see that he was reading *The Irish Times*. I cleared my throat. 'Good morning, sir,' I said.

He looked up from the paper. 'Good morn—' he started, then smiled at me. 'We meet again.'

I could feel Polly's eyes boring into the back of my head.

He folded the paper and placed it on the table. 'I'm sorry for giving you such a fright yesterday.'

'Oh, it was my fault entirely,' I said.

'Then we'll share the blame,' he said, smiling.

I noticed, when he smiled, that he had very white teeth. Most of the people in Ballykillen had hardly any teeth left in their heads but his were lovely, all straight and shiny. In fact, I decided, he was altogether very nice to look at.

I licked the end of my pencil. 'Will you be wanting a full Irish breakfast?'

He picked up the menu. 'I'll have the eggs, tomatoes, mushrooms and toast,' he said.

'Do you not want sausage and bacon and black pudding?'

'I don't eat meat.'

I'd never known anyone who didn't eat meat. 'What, none at all?'

He shook his head.

'Do you not like the taste of meat?'

'I prefer my animals to be alive and not dead. I feel we can sustain a healthy diet without eating them.'

I stared at him. 'Really?'

'Really,' he said smiling. 'And it looks as if I've shocked you again.'

'I suppose you have a bit.'

'Well, that's what I'd like,' he said.

I grinned. 'Then that's what I'll get you.'

'My name is David Townsend,' he said. 'And may I ask your name?'

'Rose,' I said. 'Rose Brown.'

'Pleased to meet you, Rose Brown.'

I could feel my face going red. It always happened when I was unsure of something; it was a bloody curse. 'I'll be after getting your breakfast, then,' I said.

I walked back over to Polly. 'Yer man doesn't eat meat.'

'That'll be the Yank in him,' said Polly, as if she knew everything there was to know about Yanks.

'They're all barmy,' she added.

I looked across at him. *Yes, he was very nice to look at, for an ol' feller*, I thought.

Chapter Five

Mr Townsend and meself struck up a bit of a friendship – well, maybe not exactly a *friendship*, but we passed the time of day with each other in a friendly fashion. He asked me about my family and about my life in Ballykillen and I told him about my sisters and my mammy's roses and the people in the town. He made me feel as if our conversations were interesting and that I was worth talking to. I could have chatted to him all day. I loved to listen to him speak, for he had a nice way with words and a lovely accent. He sounded like Gary Cooper in the Westerns that me and Polly liked to watch. I found myself missing half of what he was saying, I was so busy looking at his lovely blue eyes and his shiny white teeth and imagining him riding across the prairie on a horse. I knew that I was being desperate silly but it was nice to be silly sometimes.

'Do you enjoy your job, Rose?' he said one morning.

I hesitated. 'I suppose so, sir. I mean, everyone is very nice and it's better than working in the slaughterhouse.'

'The slaughterhouse?'

'That's the only job going at home and I had no mind to be working there.'

He shuddered. 'I think that would be the saddest job in the world.'

'I think so too – not to mind all the shite,' I added. Dear God, why did I say 'shite'? I'd let meself down but he just smiled.

'I'm going home today, Rose,' he said.

I'd known that he was leaving and I was going to miss our little chats. 'To America?' I said sadly.

'I live in England, Rose. If you ever find yourself in London, do please come and visit. I know that my wife would love to meet you and so would my little boy.'

'You have a son?'

'I do. His name's Raphael but we call him Raffi. He's eight years old and as bright as a button.'

I smiled. 'I think that Raphael is a lovely name; he's one of God's Archangels.'

'You're right, he is. Would you care to see a photograph, Rose?'

'Oh, I would.'

He took a wallet out of his pocket. 'It's a bit creased,' he said, handing me a photo. 'I carry it around with me wherever I go.'

I stared at the picture. There was a beautiful lady sitting on a couch holding a plump toddler on her lap. Mr Townsend was standing behind them, with his hand on his wife's shoulder.

'As you can see, it was taken a few years ago. Raffi isn't a baby any more. My wife's name is Alice.'

'She's very beautiful,' I said, handing the photo back to him.

'She is,' he said, smiling. 'And very special. It's very hard to be away from them both.'

I couldn't help wondering what it would be like to be loved so much. 'It must be,' I said. 'I feel the same way about my family.'

Dervla the snitch was staring at me from the other side of the room. 'I'll say goodbye then,' I said. 'And I wish you a safe journey home to your family and may you one day return to Ireland.'

He stood up and shook my hand. 'Goodbye, Rose Brown, and don't forget, if you're ever in London...'

Well, there was no chance of that, was there? I wasn't going to suddenly find meself in London, was I? But I smiled at him. 'I won't forget, sir.'

*

It was Friday evening and me and Polly were on the Thrupenny Rush heading home to Ballykillen. We didn't have to dash through the town as we had the whole of the next day off and I couldn't wait to spend time with my family.

'You talk about yer man an awful lot,' said Polly. 'Isn't he a bit old for you?'

'Jesus, Polly, I don't think about him in that way! Sure, he could be me father.'

'Only just,' said Polly.

I dug her in the ribs.

'Mind you, he's not so bad to look at,' she said grinning. 'For an ol feller.'

'He was different, Polly, that's all. And I'll miss our little chats.'

'I don't know what you found to talk about, you have nothing in common.'

'He asked me if I liked the job.'

'And why would he want to know that?'

I'd been wondering the same meself. 'I don't know. I suppose he was just passing the time of day.'

'And what did you say?'

'I said it was nice and better than working in the slaughterhouse.'

'You should have said you hated it and everyone was rotten to you and you cried into your pillow every night.'

'And why in God's name would I say that?'

'He might have taken pity on you and whisked you off to England.'

'I have no mind to be whisked off to England, thanks, it's bad enough having to work in Cork.'

'You have no sense of adventure, Rose Brown.'

'And I have no need of one, Polly Butler. I shall leave all of that to you.'

As the train pulled into the tiny station at Ballykillen, I was filled with happiness; we had a whole day off and didn't need to take the Thrupenny Rush back to Cork until Sunday morning.

'I intend to sleep all day tomorrow,' said Polly, yawning. 'And if anyone wakes me, I'll take the head off them.'

'I shouldn't think that anyone would dare go near you.'

'If they want to keep their head on their shoulders they won't.'

As me and Polly stepped down onto the platform, we expected to see Billy Ogg strutting about, full of his own importance, waving his silly little flag and blowing on his whistle but instead it was Jimmy Coyne who was opening doors and helping people with their bags, which was more than Billy ever lowered himself to do.

'Hi Jimmy,' said Polly, smiling at him.

'Hiya girls, off home?'

'Yes,' said Polly. 'Thank the Lord.'

'I'll hold the train for ya, no need to rush back,' he said, grinning.

'That's good of you, Jimmy,' I said. 'But we have tomorrow off.'

'Ah, that's grand, so you'll have a lovely long visit.'

Polly looked around. 'Where's the great and powerful Billy Ogg?'

'He has the gout and it's making him even grumpier than usual. He has to stay at home with his foot up.'

'God forgive me,' said Polly, 'but isn't it a pity that it's not a terminal disease that he has?'

'I'll see you at the church tomorrow then,' said Jimmy.

'What are you on about, Jimmy Coyne?'

'I'd say you'd be needing to go to confession after wishing one of God's children an early demise.'

I left them chatting and wandered out of the station. I walked across the road and breathed in the sweet air, which tasted of salt and warm breeze and home. I gazed out over the sea at the fishing boats silhouetted against the calm, still water. Everywhere was bathed in that golden light that only happens at the end of a fine day. The sun was still burning brightly, a huge globe hovering over the sea, not quite touching it, so that all the waves were capped with light that they carried in towards the shore. The old lighthouse stood tall at the edge of the land as it had always stood my whole life, like a good friend who never changes. The sun had painted its seaward side rose-gold, the colour of the petals of the flowers that my mother so loved to grow, and the glass window at the top blazed as it reflected back the beams. The lighthouse was surrounded by a sturdy dry stone wall and inside the wall, the grass had been cut short, forming a pleasant green area where two rabbits were feeding, without a care in the world. Gulls screamed and wheeled in the sky above me but apart from the gulls, the world was peaceful, lovely, quiet and the bustling city of Cork felt a million miles away. Oh, that I could stay here forever and never leave again.

I watched as the last of the sun touched the horizon and bled into the welcoming arms of the sea. I could almost hear the hiss as it sank below the waves. The day was coming to an end.

Polly was calling my name so, with a sigh, I turned away and joined her on our walk home.

We walked in silence for a bit. It made a pleasant change from dashing through the town, hardly having time to pass the time of day with anyone.

'I said we'd see Jimmy at the dance tonight,' said Polly suddenly.

'What dance would that be? And what makes you think I'd want to be going?'

'It's at the Town Hall and Jimmy says there's a grand showband playing.'

'It will just be the same clodhopping eejits from up country thinking they're God's gift to music and anyway, I'm fit for nothing but my bed.'

'Come on, Rose. Sure, we never have any fun. What does it matter what they sound like? At least we can have a bit of a dance and you never know, this might be the night you meet the love of your life. You can sleep all day tomorrow like meself.'

I sighed. There was very little chance of meeting the love of my life at the Town Hall. Sure, we'd grown up with all the boys from the town and I couldn't see any one of them standing in line to court me, not that I'd be broken-hearted over it. But Polly was right; we had very little time for fun, maybe it would do us both good. 'Okay,' I said.

I left Polly at the end of her hill and carried on home. As I turned into Cross Lane, I could see Kathy and Agnes sitting on the wall outside the cottage. As soon as they saw me, they jumped down and ran to meet me.

'We've been waiting for you,' whispered Agnes.

'We thought you'd never get here,' said Kathy.

'Well, I'm here now,' I said, hugging them.

We linked arms and went into the cottage, where I was enveloped in Mammy's arms. I looked around the little room at the picture of the Sacred Heart above the fireplace and the statue of Our Blessed Virgin Mary on the mantel. A big pan of potatoes was bubbling on the stove and there was the sweet smell of apple cake, cooling on the side. It was my favourite cake and I knew that Mammy had made it especially for me. Oh, it was good to be home and just for tonight, I could forget about the Thrupenny Rush.

It was lovely sitting around the table eating Mammy's delicious stew. Bridgy and Kathy were firing questions at me, and sweet Agnes kept looking up from her plate and smiling, as if she was making sure that I was still there. If only life could always be like this, if only I could find a nice job in the town, I would be content and ask for no more.

I was brushing my hair in front of the kitchen mirror when Polly knocked on the door and walked in.

'God bless all here,' she said, dipping her finger in the holy water font just inside the door.

'Amen,' said Mammy. 'I hear you're off to the dance.'

'We are, Mrs Brown.'

'Rose is hoping to meet the man of her dreams, Mammy,' said Kathy.

'I am *not*, Kathy Brown, and I'd be obliged if you would keep such silliness to yourself.'

'Well, that was where I met your father, Rose, at a dance in the Town Hall, so you never know.'

'I bet you had all the lads after you, Mrs Brown,' said Polly, grinning.

Mammy laughed. 'Well, I don't know about that, Polly, for I only had eyes for himself. The rest of them weren't good enough to wipe his boots and they're still not.'

'Ah, you were lucky, Mrs Brown, for I'd say he was very handsome in his day.'

Agnes came down the stairs and handed me a blue ribbon. 'It's my birthday ribbon, Rose,' she whispered. 'I thought you might like to wear it to the dance.'

I put my arms around her. 'I would love to wear it, Agnes,' I said. 'And I will be sure to take very good care of it. '

'Yer bound to meet the man of your dreams with a blue velvet ribbon in your hair,' said Bridgy.

'And I'll have Agnes to thank for it.'

'T'was Mammy that gave me the ribbon, Bridgy,' whispered Agnes. 'So it's only right that she should get the thanks.'

'Then myself and my suitor will thank you both,' I said, tying my hair back with the ribbon. 'Okay, I'm as ready as I'll ever be,' I said.

'Why can't I go, Mammy?' said Kathy, making a face. She'd had a gob on her ever since she knew where I was going.

'Because you're too young, girl, you have plenty of time for dances and boys,' said Mammy.

'But I'm almost thirteen! I'll be old and grey before I'm allowed to have a bit of fun.'

'Next year, my sweet girl, and even that will be too soon for me.'

Mammy and Kathy were very close. 'Alright, Mammy, I'll bide here with you,' she said, smiling.

The Town Hall was down by the quay and as we got closer, we could see that there was a big ship anchored up. 'I wonder where it's from,' I said.

'I haven't a clue,' said Polly, 'but it's not one of ours. Perhaps the hall will be full of eligible foreign sailors, only dying to get their hands on nubile young Irish girls.'

'Well, they're not getting their hands on me,' I said.

We were laughing as we ran up the steps of the Town Hall. We paid our money and went into the cloakroom. Orla bloody Feeny was standing in front of the mirror smearing rouge on her cheeks. She looked me up and down.

'Well, it's nice to see you are wearing your own shoes, Rose Brown,' she said.

I smiled sweetly at her. 'You are such a wit, Orla Feeny, have you ever thought about going on the stage?'

'But you'll have to be quick,' said Polly grinning. 'For the last one leaves in ten minutes.'

'Go fry yer nose,' said Orla, flouncing out the door.

Polly and me linked arms as we walked into the hall and suddenly, I was glad that I'd agreed to come. Okay, there were the same old guys up on the stage, playing their fiddles and banging on their bodhráns but it was familiar to me; it was what I knew. It was home. I smiled at Polly.

'See,' she said, 'Polly knows best.'

'You do,' I said grinning.

'Gird yer loins, Rose. Tonight is the night we meet our future husbands. I can feel it in me waters.'

Chapter Six

We looked around the hall. The boys were, as usual, on one side of the room and the girls on the other, hoping to be asked out onto the floor. I'd always felt sorry for the lads, having to walk across the empty space and then walking back if they were turned down. Me and Polly never turned a lad down, whatever they looked like, unless they were the worse for drink.

'No handsome sailors then?' said Polly, making a face.

'Maybe yer waters have let you down.'

'My waters never let me down.'

Just then, Jimmy walked across to us. 'Hiya girls. The craic's good tonight, isn't it?'

'Is it?' said Polly.

'Well, I'd say the band's good.'

Polly made a face. 'Is it?'

'Jesus, there's no pleasing you, Polly Butler.'

'Maybe me expectations are higher than yours, Jimmy Coyne.'

Jimmy laughed. 'Well, can I at least interest you in a turn round the floor?'

Polly grinned. 'You don't mind, do you, Rose?'

'Sure, why would I mind? Go and have some fun.'

I watched them walk away and although I said I didn't mind, I felt a bit awkward standing there on my own. I was just thinking of joining the rest of the girls, who were sitting on chairs waiting to be asked onto the floor, when a group of lads burst through the doors. They were laughing very loudly and speaking in a language I didn't understand. They were obviously the sailors from the ship moored up on the quay.

I looked across at Polly, who grinned at me. I made a face back at her.

We'd had foreign sailors in the town before but I suddenly felt uneasy. It was pretty obvious by the way they were acting that they'd hit the bottle before coming to the dance. They were pushing each other and swaying all over the place. I thought I'd escape to the cloakroom, but as I made my way through the dancers, I was almost knocked off my feet by one of them. He caught hold of me before I fell.

'I'm so sorry, miss,' he said. 'Are you alright?'

I looked up and found myself staring into the deep blue eyes of an Adonis. Honest to God, the boy looked like he belonged in Hollywood. Well, I didn't care what he looked like; I could have been laying sprawled out on the floor for all to see. Polly came running across, followed by Jimmy.

'Can I have my friend back?' she said.

'I'm okay, Polly, just a bit shaken.'

'I should think you are. You didn't come in here tonight to be attacked by a stranger in your own town.'

'I really am sorry,' said the boy again.

I couldn't stop looking at him. Jesus, Mary and Holy Saint Joseph, no man had a right to look that beautiful. His hair was blond and oh my God, those eyes. 'No harm done,' I said.

'Let me at least buy you a drink to make it up to you.'

'Alright so, I'll have an orange, please.'

'And you?' he said, looking at Polly.

I stared at her; if she valued her life, she'd say no.

'Yer alright,' she said, grinning. 'I have more dancing to do. Come on, Jimmy.'

As she walked away, she turned around and winked at me.

'Perhaps you could find us a table,' said the boy.

I liked the 'us' bit. 'I will, of course,' I said.

I watched him walk away. He looked very sure of himself as he made his way to the bar. He was so tall and handsome, people sort of made way for him. It was like yer man Moses, parting the Red Sea.

I found an empty table and waited for him to return.

I wondered if I was being a bit brazen, letting a stranger buy me a drink. But sure, he was only being polite, after nearly knocking me sideways. Polly kept looking over at me as her and Jimmy spun round the room. It seemed like a lifetime before the boy came to the table holding two glasses of orange juice.

'Are you not having a beer?' I said.

'I'd say I've had enough for one night and I'm not a great drinker.'

I sipped my orange juice; I was suddenly tongue-tied and didn't have a clue what to say.

Luckily, he broke the silence. 'Are you from the town?' he said.

'I am, but I work in Cork city.'

'Ah, we've docked there a few times.' Then he held out his hand. 'My name is Erik,' he said. 'Erik Larson.'

I took hold of his hand. It felt strong but soft, not like you would imagine a man's hand to feel. My hand felt very small in his. 'Rose,' I said. 'Rose Brown.'

'Well, Rose Brown, I'm glad I bumped into you. I mean, I'm not glad that I *actually* bumped into you,' he said, laughing. 'But I'm glad I met you.'

He was nice, he was, he was nice. Not just to look at but by his manner you could just tell that he was a nice feller – not that I had much experience of fellers.

'You speak English very well,' I said, 'but you're not English, are you?'

'I'm from Norway,' he said, smiling. 'But my mother is English, so I grew up speaking both languages.'

'Well, I'm Irish through and through.'

'And very lovely,' he said, smiling.

I could feel my face going its usual beetroot colour and I felt shamed. Orla Feeny was staring at us from across the room. I bet she couldn't wait to tell the rest of the town that Rose Brown was playing fast and loose with a sailor. Well, I'd tell Mammy as soon as I got home. Mammy trusted me and wouldn't mind one bit.

He stood up and held out his hand again. 'I'm no great dancer,' he said, 'but if you want to chance it?'

I smiled. 'I'm no great shakes meself.'

'Shakes?' he said, looking puzzled.

I laughed. 'I mean, I'm not much of a dancer either.'

'Then we'll both do our best,' he said, smiling.

He put his arm under my elbow and guided me through the dancers and then I was in his arms. He held me firmly but not too tight, just a gentle pressure on my back. It felt nice. I felt safe. He was a good head taller than me but we seemed to fit together easily. We danced all evening and in between dancing, we sat at the table with Polly and Jimmy, drinking orange juice. At one point, Polly kicked me under the table and said she needed to go to the cloakroom so I went with her as that was obviously what she wanted.

Polly got a comb out of her handbag and started teasing her hair. 'Jesus, it looks like a burst mattress,' she said, staring into the mirror. 'A burst orange mattress.'

'Polly Butler, you know very well that half the girls in Ballykillen would only die for your hair.'

She grinned at me. 'God, Rose, yer man is awful handsome. I wish it was me he'd knocked flying.'

'He is, isn't he?' I said.

'But you have to be careful.'

'Why will I have to be careful?'

'Well, you know what they say about sailors? Don't they have a girl in every port?'

'I only let him buy me an orange juice.'

'Ah, but an orange juice can lead to other things and with him looking like he does, you might have your head turned.'

I'd always thought that was a strange saying. I mean, how could you get your head turned?

'Don't worry about me, Polly. My head doesn't turn that easily.'

'You have your reputation to think of. You don't want to end up a fallen woman.'

'Jesus, Polly Butler, will ya stop? Anyway, I'm sure Orla Feeny will have ruined me reputation already.'

'She's an awful baggage.'

'What about you and Jimmy?'

'What *about* me and Jimmy?'

'Well, it looks like the pair of you are getting on great.'

'Ah sure, he's more like one of my brothers – except he, at least, has a brain in his head, which is more than can be said for my lot.'

'Well, the way he looks at you is definitely not very brotherly. You want to be careful you don't get *your* head turned.'

She laughed. 'It'd take more than Jimmy Coyne to turn my head. I'm looking for a rich feller with a grand car, not some young lad who lives in Ballykillen.'

'You could do a lot worse,' I said. 'Jimmy's a nice boy.'

'And I could do a lot better. Come on, or your handsome sailor will be wondering where you are.'

Me and Erik had the last waltz together. It was lovely but I kept thinking that I would never see him again and that made me feel… I'm not sure exactly how I felt. Maybe I felt I was losing something I'd only just found. Maybe that was how I felt.

We walked back to the table and got our coats.

'Can I walk you home, Rose?' he said.

'We can all walk home together,' said Polly quickly.

She was obviously still worried about me reputation.

The streets were almost empty but for a few people walking home from the dance and pitch-black, the only light coming from the moon, which kept disappearing behind the clouds.

We said goodbye to Polly and Jimmy and continued on to Cross Lane. I thought for a minute that Polly was intending to see me to my door.

It was the end of summer and the nights were colder. I shivered and Erik took hold of my hand. I barely knew him; he was a stranger to me but I trusted him and as his fingers closed around mine, I felt safe and warm.

'When do you go back to Cork?' he said.

'Sunday morning,' I said.

'Then can I see you tomorrow, Rose?'

I hesitated. My family would be expecting me to spend the day with them and it was what I wanted, too. It was what I'd been looking forward to. But I knew that I also wanted to see this boy again. I didn't feel ready to say goodbye. He was waiting for an answer.

'Is there a problem?' he said, gently.

'I need to spend some time at home.'

'Of course,' he said.

'I could maybe see you later in the day.'

'Well, if you're sure.'

I nodded. 'Yes,' I said. 'I'm sure.'

'Then if it's okay, I'll call for you tomorrow afternoon.'

'I'd like that,' I said. 'I'd like that very much.'

He leaned down and kissed my cheek. 'Tomorrow then, Rose Brown.'

'Grand so,' I said.

Chapter Seven

Oh, it was lovely to wake up in my own bed, with Bridget's warm little body next to mine. I sat up and looked around the room. I'd missed it so much. Nothing had changed; everything was as it had always been. The uneven walls that Daddy had whitewashed every time he was home. The picture of the Sacred Heart on the wall opposite the bed, with a halo of light around his dear head. The chest of drawers and the closet that held our clothes. There was a little window under the eaves where I could see the rooftops of the cottages that tumbled down the hill. This room made me feel like a child again. I felt safe here; this was where I belonged. This was as much a part of me as the air I breathed.

Bridgy stirred beside me and I gently brushed her beautiful dark hair out of her eyes. 'Hello, sleepyhead.'

'Oh, Rose,' she said, opening her eyes. 'I'd forgotten you were home. I'm awful glad you're home, I've missed you something terrible. It's very hard not having you in the bed with me.'

'Well, I'm here now, my love,' I said, snuggling down and taking her in my arms.

'Was the dance grand altogether, Rose? Was there a band? Did you get asked out onto the floor?'

'So many questions, Bridgy.'

'Well, I have to get in as many questions as I can before you go away again.'

I laughed. 'I suppose you do. So yes, I did get asked to dance.'

'Who was the boy? Do I know him, or was he a stranger?'

'He was a sailor, from Norway.'

'Is that near Kinsale?'

I laughed. 'It's a long way from Kinsale, Bridgy. It's far across the sea and people from Norway speak a different language to us.'

'How did you know what he was talking about then?'

'Because his mammy is English.'

'Well, that's a blessing anyway. What does he look like? Is he desperate handsome?'

'And what would you know about desperate handsome, Bridget Brown?'

'Sure I'm seven years old, Rose and no longer a child.'

'Don't grow up too soon, my darling girl.'

'I'll try not to, Rose, but it just happens. Does yer man have a name? And what was he doing in Ballykillen?'

'His name is Erik and he's a sailor. His ship is moored in the quay.'

'He owns a ship?'

'It's not his ship. Anyway, you'll get to meet him later, he's calling for me.'

'I'll put on me Sunday frock.'

'You do that. Now, I think we should get up and help Mammy with the breakfast.'

'Not yet,' she said, tucking her head under my chin so that her soft hair brushed my cheek. 'Oh, I'm terrible glad you're home, Rose.'

I kissed her forehead. 'So am I, Bridgy, so am I.'

I felt sorry for Erik as he sat in our little kitchen with four pairs of eyes staring at him.

Kathy was trying to look as if she wasn't interested in the handsome sailor sitting at the table. Shy little Agnes looked at him from under her fringe and Bridgy was in her Sunday dress, smiling from ear to ear.

'How long will your ship be in Ballykillen, Erik?' said Mammy.

'Until we unload the cargo, maybe a couple of days, Mrs Brown.'

'And where are you going next?'

'Home,' said Erik, smiling.

'Rose works in Cork, don't you, Rose? You work in a grand big hotel,' said Bridgy.

'I do, Bridgy.'

'Do you miss your home?' whispered Agnes.

Erik hadn't caught what she'd said. He smiled at her. 'Pardon?'

We all fell silent and let Agnes speak.

'Do you miss your home?' she said, softly.

'I did at the beginning. The first few months were the worst but you get used to it and I love the sea, it gets into your blood.'

'The sea gets into your blood?' said Bridgy, looking confused.

We all laughed.

'What's so funny?' questioned Bridgy, looking cross. 'Isn't that what yer man said?'

'You're right, Bridgy, that is what I said but what I meant was that you grow to love it.'

'I love the sea too,' said Bridgy. 'I'm a mighty swimmer. Aren't I, Mammy? Aren't I a mighty swimmer?'

'You are, my love,' said Mammy, smiling at her. 'You put the rest of us to shame.'

Bridgy sat there smiling, feeling very proud of herself. 'I keep telling them that it's really easy. All you have to do is flap around a bit.'

'Right, well, I'm sure Rose and Erik don't want to be spending the afternoon with us,' said Mammy, standing up.

'It's nice, Mrs Brown. I miss my own family, this is nice.'

'You must do. Have you brothers and sisters of your own?'

Erik smiled. 'Three sisters, all older than me, and a younger brother.'

Mammy nodded. 'Family is important and you miss them when they're not there. We miss Rose all the time,' she said, smiling at me.

'And I miss you, Mammy.'

'What are their names?' asked Kathy.

'Leah, Sofia and Anna,' said Erik, smiling.

Kathy let out a big sigh. 'God, they're gorgeous names. Why couldn't you have called me something like that, Mammy?'

'You are called Kathleen, after your grandmother, may she rest in peace amongst the angels, and you should be proud to carry her name,' said Mammy.

Kathy lifted her eyes to the ceiling. 'If someone calls out the name Kathleen, half the girls in the town turn round.'

'Well, aren't you the lucky one?' I said.

'What's your brother's name, Erik?' whispered Agnes.

'My brother's name is Christy and there is only a year between us.'

'Enough of the interrogation, girls, you'll have the lad's brain mashed with your questions.'

'It's only that we're interested, Mammy, and wasn't it yourself that said we should always be interested in the people we meet?'

Mammy laughed. 'What would we do without our Bridgy?' she said.

I stood up. 'We should get going before the chill sets in.'

'Can I come with you?' said Bridgy.

'No, you can't,' said Mammy.

Erik looked at my little sister and smiled. 'I don't mind.'

'There you see, Mammy,' said Bridgy. 'Yer man doesn't mind.'

I looked at Erik. He was grinning. 'Okay,' I said, 'you can come. Would you like to come, Agnes?'

'I would,' she whispered.

'Kathy?'

'I'm meeting Pat Mulcahy, we're off out the strand.'

'Where were you thinking of going, Rose?' said Mammy.

'I thought maybe out the wood road to Temple Michael.'

Mammy opened the pantry door and took out two bowls. 'Then you might as well pick a few berries on the way and I can make a grand pie for your tea.'

'I love picking berries,' said Bridgy.
'We'll all pick berries,' said Erik, smiling.
Oh, he was nice, he was really nice.

Chapter Eight

It was a beautiful day; the heat of summer was behind us and autumn had arrived in all its glory. Summer was lovely but there was something about autumn that lifted my heart. Autumn didn't have to blaze down on you to herald its arrival. You could see it in the changing of the leaves, the way the greens turned to browns and yellows and oranges, the way they drifted down and gathered in secret corners, the way they settled like a carpet of brilliant colours beneath your feet. It was as if autumn was aware of its beauty and needed no fanfare to prove itself. Autumn was my favourite season and I was glad to be sharing this day with my sisters and Erik.

The sun, filtering through the branches, cast long shadows in front of us as we walked through the wood. The girls had run ahead and were busy looking for the best blackberries. I felt Erik's warm hand slip into mine and I felt happy. I had known him such a short time and yet I felt safe with him. It was as if I knew the person he was, the person behind the beauty, as if we already had a history. Some people come into our lives and we just know that they are right for us, like Polly and now Erik.

Bridgy turned around and was running back. 'Erik?' she called. 'Will ya give me a leg-up? There are some lovely fat berries up on the tree but I can't reach them.'

'Can't you just collect the low ones?' I said, smiling at her.

'Mammy says not to pick the low ones because there's a chance that an ol' dog has lifted up his leg and peed on them.'

'Bridget Brown, you know very well that your mammy would never allow such words to come out of her mouth.'

Bridgy grinned. 'Well, those might not have been her exact words, Rose, but it's what she meant.'

'Then you'll have to confess your sin to Father at confession.'

'Do I have to, Rose?'

'You do indeed, for you have besmirched your mother's good name.'

'What does besmirched mean?' asked Bridgy.

I had to think but before I answered her, Erik said, 'It means to sully or tarnish someone's reputation.'

'What does sully and tarnish mean?' said Bridgy, frowning.

I didn't know what they meant either but I wasn't about to show me ignorance.

Erik grinned, then he grabbed hold of her and swung her around, making her squeal with laughter. I could see Agnes watching them, maybe wishing that he would swing her around too, but I knew that she would never ask. She was too shy.

I caught Erik's attention and nodded towards her. He put Bridgy down and said, 'How about a game of chase?'

Agnes's face lit up and she started running.

I sat down on a bit of tree trunk and watched them dashing around. Erik was making a noise like a monster and the pair of them were screaming and laughing, their joy spilling out of them, drifting above the tall trees and into the sky.

Once out of the woods, we followed the path towards Temple Michael, through tall grasses that brushed our legs and swayed in the breeze, as if the whole field was alive. Motes of dust rose into the air and midges danced in the shafts of sunlight and there, in the distance, were the ruins of the old abbey.

'Temple Michael,' I said to Erik.

He stopped walking and gazed at the old grey stones of the ruined temple ahead of us, their starkness standing out against the blue of the sky.

Erik smiled at me. 'It's wonderful,' he said.

I had been coming here since I was a child, playing hide and seek with my sisters, crouching down behind the old grey stones, or chase amongst the crumbling walls and yet today, it felt like the first time because I was seeing it through Erik's eyes. 'Yes,' I said. 'It is indeed wonderful.'

The girls were a long way ahead of us now, as Erik bent down and kissed my cheek. 'Thank you for bringing me here, Rose Brown,' he said.

I hadn't expected the kiss and I could feel my face going red. 'Thank you for coming with me, Erik Larson,' I said, giving him a little smile.

We walked through the old ruins, avoiding the nettles that had been left to run wild over everything. Nothing much remained of the original buildings, only a square tower built of grey stone and the four walls of a church, small and squat with two arched windows on either side. I walked across to them and looked out over the river. All around, big old trees and smaller shrubs had grown up, so that the impression was of a mass of green, with the grey stone peeping through, as if it was almost embarrassed to be there, amongst so much wildness. The graveyard sloped downhill away from the church. Most of the old stones were tilted; it seemed like some playful earthquake had tipped them at different angles. Others lay crumbling and broken on the ground, all of them forgotten, no one left to mourn, no one left to care. All of them covered in lichen and moss, the etchings yellow with age. Some said the place was creepy but I found it peaceful.

Erik picked some grass and rubbed away at one of the stones. 'I think it says Halroyd.'

I walked over to him. 'Most of them do. The Halroyd-Smith family were well-to-do and had a grand big house out in Ballynatray. Most of them were laid to rest here at Temple Michael. They say that this place is haunted but I don't believe in all that stuff.'

'Who haunts the place?' said Erik.

'Well, legend has it that most of the family died in mysterious circumstances. The story goes that during the Great Famine, a poor peasant woman had brought her sick child to the house to seek help and was rejected. She stepped backwards down the thirteen steps at the entrance to the house and cursed the Halroyd-Smiths on every step as she fell. It is also said that is why a lot of the family died on the thirteenth of the month. The last one died in a hunting accident on the thirteenth of September.'

'Is his grave here?'

'It's in the crypt. You can peep into it. He's in there, God rest his soul.'

'This is too fine a day to be peering into crypts,' said Erik.

'Orla Feeny said she saw the ghost of an old monk standing by the ruins, she even got her picture in the paper. Orla could lie her way out of a murder rap, so no one believed her. I don't even think her own mother believed her, she's an awful baggage of a girl.'

Erik laughed. 'There are some words that you say, Rose, that I don't understand.'

'Well, let's just say that if you and her were the last people left on earth, you still wouldn't want to keep company with her. She'd have yer head ruined with all her nonsense; she'd pick holes in The Blessed Virgin herself, if she had no one else to gossip about.'

'She sounds delightful,' said Erik, grinning.

The girls were still happily running round the ruins, so myself and Erik walked down to the river and sat on the grassy bank.

Dappled sunshine fell through the branches of the tall trees that lined the river. It reflected a hundred different shades of green rippling in the shallows at the edge. The trees were always moving, wind whispering through their branches, making the leaves dance, shaking the shadows and in the river, the reflections danced too. Everything moved, everything was alive, everything green. When I thought of Ballykillen, it was the river that I missed the most. Whenever I'd been sad, it was always to the river that I'd come and it had always brought me peace.

'Tell me about your home,' I said.

Erik didn't speak right away; he looked out over the water, as if he was imagining that other place. 'I live in a small fishing village called Reine,' he said, smiling. 'Our house is right on the shore of the Norwegian Sea. As children, my brother and I would wait for the little boats to come back and we would help them unload their catch. We'd arrive home stinking of fish and our mother would make us strip off all our clothes before she would let us into the house. The sea was always calm and the deepest blue you could imagine. Sometimes in the mornings a mist would come down from the mountains, covering the surface of the water like a grey quilt. In springtime the meadows are covered in wild flowers and in the winter the mountains behind our house are covered in snow.'

'It sounds beautiful.'

'It is, and your country is also very beautiful, Rose.'

We sat in silence, watching the river flow by, then he took my face in his hands and very gently kissed me, his lips warm and soft on mine. I knew that I would never forget this moment. It would come back to me every autumn day and I would feel the warm breeze in my hair and the sweet taste of his lips on mine. Down the years it would come back to me and I would remember.

Chapter Nine

'You're quiet,' said Polly as the train sped towards Cork. 'Are you thinking of the gorgeous sailor boy?'

'I am,' I said sadly.

'He must have made a great impression on you, Rose, for he has achieved what no other feller has managed to and believe me, they've tried.'

'You're mistaking me for yourself, Polly, for it's you that has them lining up for your attention. I know for a fact that Donal Mahan puts margarine in his hair to impress you.'

'Well, it doesn't impress me at all, Rose, for it smells rotten and he has half the cats in Ballykillen following him through town.'

'One thing I love about you, Polly Butler, is the way you never exaggerate anything.'

'It's true,' said Polly, grinning. 'And when it's sunny, it drips down the side of his face.'

'You're shameless.'

'I know, it's part of me charm. So, come on, tell me about yer man and don't leave anything out.'

'There's nothing much to tell. We went to Temple Michael and we sat by the river while Agnes and Bridgy ran around picking berries.'

'In the name of God, why did you drag those two along with you?'

'They wanted to come and Erik didn't mind.'

'Then he sounds like a decent kind of chap.'

'He is.'

'If he'd wanted to ravage you, he wouldn't have wanted your sisters along.'

'He's not like that, Polly.'

'Sure he's a man, isn't he? And he's been at sea for months. I'd say he sounds like a decent enough feller, though.'

'He's lovely.'

'And?'

'And what?'

'So, you just sat by the bank like an old married couple?'

'Well, not exactly, we held hands.'

Polly raised her eyes to the ceiling. 'The Lord be praised.'

'And he kissed me,' I said, smiling.

'A proper kiss?'

'I didn't know that there were different kinds of kisses.'

'Well, there are,' said Polly. 'There's the passionate sort and there's the gentle, romantic sort and as it's early days for the pair of you, I'd say it was the romantic sort.'

I thought about the kiss. I thought how soft his lips were and how sweet they tasted, like a newly cut field of hay. No, it wasn't passionate but it was just right.

'And then you had to say goodbye?'

'But he says he'll write to me.'

'Well, don't bank on it, Rose, for he's probably writing to half the pretty girls in the world.'

'I won't bank on it but it would be nice, wouldn't it? Something to look forward to?'

'It would,' said Polly, smiling. 'It really would.'

'And what about you and Jimmy?'

'I like him alright but I told you, Rose, I'm wanting more. If I settle for Jimmy, I'll be saying goodbye to a more exciting life than the one I have here.'

'But you like him, don't you?'

Polly chewed on a strand of hair. 'I like him more than I want to. Now isn't that a desperate thing?'

'It's a shame alright when your heart is set on a fancier life but if you have your mind made up, then I'd avoid Jimmy next time you're home and not lead the poor feller on.'

'I know.'

'Has he exposed himself to you?'

'What?'

'His feelings. Has he exposed his feelings to you?'

'Jesus, Mary and Holy Saint Joseph, Rose. You should be very careful what you're saying.'

'I don't know what you mean,' I said.

'No, you wouldn't,' she said.

*

Spring was welcomed with open arms. Now, people strolled along the streets, stopping for a while to gaze into shop windows instead of hurrying home to the shelter of their houses. They came out into the sunshine like moles emerging from dark caves. They gloried in the warm breeze that ruffled their hair and marvelled at the new life bursting through the rich soil.

There was a park opposite the hotel where Polly and I would sit on the grass and eat our lunch. I cherished these moments with my friend and although we saw each other every day, we never ran out of things to say, mostly about the guests in the hotel and the snitch.

'Have you still not heard from the sailor boy?' said Polly, biting into an apple.

'No, but I didn't really expect to. I mean, what would be the point anyway? He lives on the other side of the world. We were never going to be walking out together, were we?'

Polly sighed. 'I suppose not.'

'The time we had was lovely but that is all it was ever going to be.'

'Don't you think our lives are running away from us?' said Polly, biting into a sandwich. 'It's not that I want to go back to

Ballykillen, I just want to go somewhere different. I want to see new places and meet new people.'

'I know you do but isn't this the life we are supposed to lead? Isn't this the path that God has paved for us? Our mammies are happy enough.'

'Our mammies are old before their time. Jesus, Rose, my mammy is fifty and she looks ninety.'

Well, I thought my mammy was beautiful but I didn't tell Polly, because it's not nice to have a mammy who looks ninety.

Polly was always going on about wanting something different. I'd heard it so many times but I couldn't help her, or even sympathise, because there was nothing to be done. We were who we were and for good or bad, we had what we had.

'This is no life for a young girl, Rose,' Polly went on. 'I don't want to end up marrying someone like Jimmy and having a swarm of kids around my feet.'

I hated Polly talking like this; it made me feel as if the life we had wasn't worth anything.

Chapter Ten

1938

The following July, the change that Polly wanted so much came like a bolt out of the blue. But it didn't come for Polly, who was desperate for it; it came for me.

I was in the middle of cleaning one of the bedrooms when Dervla the snitch came into the room.

'You're wanted,' she said.

I carried on making the bed.

'Immediately. Don't keep Mrs Mullen waiting,' she said, glaring at me.

I stopped what I was doing and walked towards the door.

'And are you not going to finish the bed, missy?'

'It's Rose Brown to you and no, I'm not going to finish the bed. You said she wanted to see me immediately and I can't do both. What do you want me to do first?'

Dervla looked flustered so I pushed past her and left the room. Bloody baggage, I thought as I walked along the corridor. I couldn't think what I had done wrong, because I must have done something wrong for Mrs Mullen to want to see me.

I made my way to her office, feeling a bit nervous as I tapped on the door.

'Come in,' she called.

I turned the handle and walked in.

Mrs Mullen was sitting behind her desk. 'Ah, Rose,' she said, smiling at me. 'Please sit down.'

Well, it didn't look as if I was in trouble, or she wouldn't be smiling.

I sat opposite her and waited to hear what she had to say.

'Do you remember one of our guests by the name of David Townsend?'

'I do, Mrs Mullen, he was lovely.'

'Well, he has written to me about you.'

I frowned. 'About me?'

She nodded. 'It seems you made quite an impression on the gentleman.'

'I did?'

'You did, Rose. In fact, you made such an impression that he is offering you a job.'

I couldn't take in what she was saying. I saw her lips moving but I didn't know what she was on about.

'Rose? Did you hear what I said? Mr Townsend has written to offer you a job.'

'In England?'

'London, to be precise.'

I swallowed. 'Oh, I couldn't do that, Mrs Mullen. I'd be terrible afeared to go to London.'

'I thought that was what you might say but I want you to think about it. It's a great opportunity for you and the pay, quite honestly, is very generous. You would be looking after the Townsends' nine-year-old boy and a new baby, who is due to be born in January. Is that something you think you could do?'

'I could do it alright but I'm quite happy here.'

'And I love having you. You are a good worker and a lovely girl.'

'So, can I stay then?'

'Of course you can but I don't want you to dismiss this out of hand. I am giving you the weekend off so that you can go home and talk it over with your family. Will you do that for me, Rose?'

'I can,' I said, 'but I won't be changing my mind.'

She laughed. 'Don't look so worried, Rose, no one is forcing you into anything. If you decide this is not for you, then we will write to Mr Townsend, thanking him for his kind offer but very politely declining it. Now, I suggest you go and find your friend Polly; I think you need to talk to someone.'

'But I haven't finished me rooms.'

'I'll get Dervla to finish them. Now run along.'

I smiled at her. 'Don't you mean walk?' I said.

She smiled back. 'I think this is a running sort of a day, Rose. And if you see Dervla, could you send her to me?'

'I'd be only delighted to,' I said.

When I got outside, my legs felt like jelly, so I leaned against the wall. London? Mr Townsend wanted me to work for him in London? It was ridiculous. It was out of the question. They must be awful desperate to be wanting me.

Just then, the snitch came round the corner. 'Well, you can finish the room now instead of standing there as if you have all the time in the world and no work to do.'

'As it happens, I *do* have all the time in the world and I have no work to do.'

Dervla gave a smug little smile. 'So, you've been dismissed, have you? Well, not before time. You're a skitty little miss and Mrs Mullen must have taken my advice about you. I told you I have her ear, I make it me business to know everything that goes on in this place. I have me finger on the pulse.'

I was tempted to tell her where to stick her finger but decided against it. 'Oh, go fry yer nose, ya little snipe. Oh, and by the way, she wants to see you. Immediately,' I added.

I eventually found Polly in one of the bedrooms. 'Have you finished already?' she said, looking up.

'No, but I have to talk to you.'

'That sounds serious.'

'It is.'

'Let me just finish here and we'll go up to our room.'

I helped her to finish and then we ran upstairs to the room we shared.

Polly sat on the bed and I stood by the window.

'Okay,' she said. 'Tell me.'

'Do you remember that American gentleman who stayed here?'

'The one you got pally with?'

'Yes.'

'What about him? Has he made a complaint?'

'Quite the opposite, Polly. He's offered me a job. He wants me to work for him in England.'

Polly was staring at me as if I had two heads. 'Why in God's name would he be wanting you to do that?'

'It seems he needs someone to help take care of the children.'

'But why you? There must be plenty of girls in England that would jump at the chance.'

'Mrs Mullen says I made an impression on him.'

'And will you go?'

I sat down next to her on the bed. 'Of course I won't go. I know no one over there and I'm happy here.'

'*Are* you?'

'Aren't *you*?'

'No, I'm bloody not. If I was offered a job in England I'd jump at the chance and if you won't go, I will.'

'Mrs Mullen has given me the weekend off, so that I can talk it over with my family.'

'Jesus, Rose, I'd say you made a great impression on the man if Mrs Mullen is giving you time off.'

'I must have done,' I said.

'I don't want to see you going off to England, for you're me best friend and I'd miss you something terrible but it's a chance to better yourself and chances like that don't come along every day of the week.'

'I'm not like you. I'm quite happy with the life I have.'

'But this could be the start of a *new* life, Rose.'

'I don't want a new life, Polly,' I said.

Chapter Eleven

Me and Polly were on our way to Ballykillen on the Thrupenny Rush. I didn't know how to feel; I'd never been so anxious in my whole life. I didn't want to go to England, I'd made up me mind. It wasn't something that I needed to think about, or talk over with Mammy. Any other time I'd be only delighted to have the whole weekend off but ever since I'd had the conversation with Mrs Mullen me stomach felt as if it was full of frogs and not a morsel of food had entered me mouth.

'Why are you so worried?' said Polly. 'I mean, if you've made up your mind not to take the bloody job, what have you got to be so worried about? You have no decision to make, you've just managed to get an extra day off.'

'You're right and I don't know meself why I feel like this but I do. Am I a desperate eejit altogether, Polly?'

'Well, I wouldn't put it like that but you have had a terrible shock and I think you're still trying to make sense of it all. I mean, it's not every day that you're offered a job in England.'

'Yes, that's it, it must be the shock. I mean, it's up to me, isn't it? No one is going to make me go, are they?'

'I shouldn't think they'd dare,' said Polly, grinning.

I settled back in my seat and watched the familiar scenery rush past the window. It was the same, familiar view that I'd been looking at for years but today even that seemed different.

'I can't believe I have to go back to Cork on me own,' said Polly.

'I'll run back to the station with you.'

'Will you?'

'I will of course.'

As the train pulled into Ballykillen, we saw Jimmy standing on the platform, grinning at us. He held the door open and we stepped down.

'No Billy Ogg?' I said.

'He has a desperate toothache,' said Jimmy. 'Apparently he's roaring with the pain of it and keeping the whole street awake.'

'Ah, God love him,' said Polly, making a face.

'Nobody should have to suffer that sort of pain,' I said. 'However much of an eejit they are.'

'I suppose not,' said Polly. 'But I won't lose any sleep over it.'

'I'll see you later then, girls,' said Jimmy.

'You'll only see me,' said Polly. 'Yer woman here has the weekend off.'

'Well, I'll be sure to hold the train for ya, Polly.'

'Good man you are, Jimmy.'

We ran through the town, passing Brenda Daly, who was pushing a pram along the side of a house. We stopped to look at the baby boy, who practically filled the inside of it. 'He's a dote,' I said, smiling.

'He is, isn't he?' said Brenda proudly.

'And the pram is grand,' said Polly.

'I had it sent down from Dublin,' she said.

'Well, we have to dash,' I said. 'Polly has to get the Thrupenny Rush back to Cork.'

We turned up Cork Hill, where Polly lived.

'This bloody hill,' said Polly holding her side. 'I bet London has no hills at all. I bet it's all wide avenues and parks and if you did live at the top of a hill, you'd be driven up there in a swanky car. If you really don't want to take this job, Rose, would you put in a good word for me?'

I smiled at my friend. 'I will, of course, but I'd miss you if you went off to England.'

I followed Polly into the cottage. It was very dark inside, with only one little window and even that was covered with a bit of cloth. 'God bless all here,' I said, dipping my finger in the holy water font just inside the door.

'Amen,' said Mrs Butler.

The cottage didn't smell so good; it had a clawing aroma of damp about it and I wondered why Mrs Butler never opened the little window to get some air into the place. Three of Polly's brothers were sitting at the long table that took up most of the space in the small, dark room. There was a big bowl of potatoes in the middle and the boys were peeling off the skins and piling them onto their plates. They didn't even look up. Polly said they were a load of clodhopping eejits, who never had any conversation. The youngest boy, John, was sitting in a wooden highchair, grinning at us and stuffing a potato into his mouth, and Finn McCool, Polly's blind little cat, was curled up in front of the fire. Mrs Butler said that it was brain damaged from banging its head on everything, but Polly loved him.

'Have you been home already, Rose?' said Mrs Butler.

'I have the weekend off; I'm running back to the station with Polly.'

'You're a good girl, Rose, and Polly is lucky to have you as her friend. Give my love to your mammy when you see her.'

'She has serious business to talk over with her,' said Polly.

'And what serious business is that, then?' she said, pouring milk into a cup and placing it on John's tray.

'Oh, it's nothing really,' I said.

'She's been offered a job in London, working for a rich family and she'll be getting paid a fortune.'

'I'm not taking the job,' I said, glaring at Polly.

'You do right,' said Mrs Butler, 'for I hear there's all sorts of shenanigans going on over there. I've heard it's rife with white slave traders. You can be going about your business and they just pluck you off the street.'

'Don't talk shite, Mammy,' said Polly.

'I heard on very good authority that a young innocent girl from the town went over there and ended up as a prostitute.'

'Jesus, Mammy,' said Polly. 'She didn't end up as a prostitute, she ended up as a Protestant.'

'Well, that's nearly as bad,' said Mrs Butler, spitting on a bit of cloth and wiping John's face.

'We passed Brenda Daly on the road,' said Polly. 'That baby of hers looks ready for school. Isn't he walking yet?'

'He doesn't get the opportunity,' said Mrs Butler. 'She has the child corralled. Why would he bother himself walking when he gets pushed everywhere in that chariot of a pram?'

'She got it in Dublin,' I said.

Mrs Butler raised her eyes to the ceiling. 'She only bought it for show, you could fit an entire family in it. One of these days he's going to jump out and make a run for it.'

'Anyway,' said Polly, handing her mammy an envelope, 'here's your money and it would be really nice if you spent it on the family and not my gobshite of a father.'

'Ah, you know nothing about marriage, Polly, just wait and you'll be doing the same thing.'

'I will in me eye,' said Polly. 'I'd rather end up an old maid.'

Mrs Butler laughed. 'We'll see,' she said. 'Now give your mammy a big hug and be on your way or the train will be gone.'

'Jimmy is holding it for me; Billy still has the toothache.'

'God love him,' said Mrs Butler. 'I'll be sure to light a candle for him on Sunday.'

'Pity you couldn't see your way clear to lighting a candle under him,' said Polly, hugging her mammy. 'I'll see you on Friday then.'

She kissed John's little head and said goodbye to the boys. This was greeted by various grunts from the table.

'Jesus,' said Polly, as we started down the hill. 'Aren't they just desperate?'

I laughed. 'They're quiet, alright.'

'John has more to say and he can't even talk yet.'

Me and Polly ran through the town and out towards the station. There was a soft breeze coming off the sea, blowing our hair into our faces. Jimmy grinned at us as we walked onto the platform. 'Thanks, Jimmy,' said Polly, smoothing her hair down.

'You're very welcome,' said Jimmy.

I waved to Polly until the train was out of sight, then started to walk away.

'Rose?' said Jimmy, running towards me.

'Yes,' I said, turning round.

He fell into step beside me. 'I was just wondering, does Polly ever mention me?'

'In what way, Jimmy?'

There was a red rash creeping up under his collar and I was beginning to feel sorry for him. 'Well, you know,' he said, scratching behind his ear.

'She's very fond of you, Jimmy, if that's what you want to know.'

'She is?' he said, smiling. 'Umm, do you think she might consider walking out with me?'

'I think that's something you will need to ask Polly yourself.'

'Oh right. I just thought I'd test the waters, you being so close an' all. You didn't mind, did ya?'

'Of course not,' I said, smiling. 'Yer a good man, Jimmy Coyne.'

'And you're a grand girl, Rose Brown.'

I couldn't stop thinking about poor Jimmy as I made my way home. I didn't have the heart to tell him that he was onto a loser, if he thought Polly Butler would step out with him. She had bigger fish to fry. She was after a Yank or an English feller, who had lots of money and a swanky car and that feller certainly wasn't poor Jimmy. Actually, I thought that she could do a lot worse than Jimmy Coyne. Money wasn't going to keep her warm on a cold night but I had a feeling that Jimmy would, given half a chance.

Chapter Twelve

When I opened my eyes the next morning, I felt that familiar feeling of peace that I always felt when I was at home. I looked at little Bridgy sleeping beside me. She was lying on her back with one arm hanging over the side of the bed. Her face was flushed in sleep and her eyelashes were flickering. Bridgy was beautiful.

It was still dark outside the little window and the town was silent. Soon the sun would creep up over the rooftops of the little cottages that covered the hill. I sighed and turned over, pulling the thin blanket around me and Bridgy. It was chilly in the room but at least it wasn't stuffy like Polly's house. It was no wonder she wanted to move away from Ballykillen. I'd want to move away too, if I lived in that dark cottage with those sullen brothers of hers, who never gave you the time of day.

I lay there all warm and snug and thought about Mr Townsend and wondered why he would choose me to look after his children. I mean, he hardly knew me. I suppose he must have liked what he saw and that was nice. I hadn't mentioned the job to Mammy and I saw no need to. I would tell Mrs Mullen that I wouldn't be taking it and to thank Mr Townsend for his kind offer and then I'd put in a good word for Polly. I didn't want my friend to go away but I knew she would be happier in England than I would ever be. With that thought in my head, I drifted back to sleep.

When I woke up again, the room was flooded with light and Bridgy was gone. Instead, it was Agnes who was standing beside the bed. I pushed the hair out of my eyes and sat up.

'Mammy said to tell you that the sausages are cooked if you'd like to come down.'

As always, Agnes's voice was little more than a whisper. She didn't speak much at the best of times but when she did, we all listened very carefully, because it was such a joy to hear her sweet voice.

There was a time when Mammy was worried that there was something wrong with her. I overheard a conversation she'd had with Daddy before he died.

'Mrs Ogg said that there was talk in the town that Agnes is defective,' Mammy had said.

Daddy had only laughed. 'I'd say the only talk in the town comes from her own mean little mouth.'

'But Agnes doesn't say much, does she, John?'

'Has it never occurred to you, love, that the child has nothing to say? And a lot of folk in this town could do well to follow her example. She'll speak well enough when she wants to be heard.'

Daddy had been right. Agnes spoke when she needed to. Mrs Feeny said the child was very sparing with her words but those words were always worth listening to. I liked Mrs Feeny, even though I wasn't so taken with her daughter.

'I helped Kathy carry the water back from the pump and Mammy heated it on the fire, so that you can have a grand wash,' Agnes whispered shyly.

'You're a great girl altogether, Agnes Brown,' I said. 'I'll be right down.'

Agnes stared down at me, smiling. 'I love you, Rose.'

'I love you too, sweetie.'

I could smell the sausages as I walked down the stairs. There was a peat fire burning in the grate and the room was lovely and warm. I went across to Mammy and kissed her cheek. She smelt of the roses that grew in the garden.

I sat down at the table between Bridgy and Agnes and Mammy put a plate of sausages in front of me. They'd smelt so nice as I was walking downstairs but now, I had no appetite for them. I put down my knife and fork.

'I'll have them if you don't want them,' said Kathy.

I pushed my plate across the table.

'Did you not like them?' asked Bridgy.

'They're grand,' I said. 'But I have no appetite.'

'And why would that be?' said Mammy, staring at me.

'Oh, you know.'

'Is there something bothering you, Rose?' she said.

'Not really.'

'So there is something,' said Mammy. 'Have you lost your job?'

'Nothing like that, Mammy.'

'Well, there's something on your mind but I can't help you, if I don't know what it is.'

'Do you have a feller?' said Kathy. 'Is that it? Has he asked you to marry him?'

I gave a big sigh; if I didn't tell them they'd never let up. 'I've been offered a job.'

'But you have a job,' said Mammy.

'In the hotel,' said Bridgy.

'This is a different kind of job,' I said.

'Doing what?' said Kathy.

'Looking after someone's children.'

'And why in God's name would you be wanting to do that?' said Mammy.

'I don't.'

'Then why are you so bothered? For it seems you have made up your mind already. Would it be closer to home?'

'The job is in England, Mammy.'

You could have heard a pin drop as they all stared at me with their mouths open. Kathy was the first to speak. 'England?' she said.

I nodded.

I could see Bridgy's eyes filling with tears. 'But you're not going, are you?'

'No, Bridgy, I'm not going.'

'Promise?'

I nodded. 'Can I leave the table, Mammy? I've a mind to be looking at the garden.'

'You go on,' she said.

I walked outside and sat on the wooden bench that Daddy had made. Daddy was very good with his hands. Mammy had always hoped that he could find work in the town and not have to go to sea. I knew she was lonely without him. A lot of women were glad to get rid of their husbands and only dreading them coming home but not Mammy; you could see that they loved each other very much. Most of the men got straight off the ship and fell into the nearest pub. It was a pitiful sight to see women standing on the quay holding little ones, waiting to get some money off them before they drank it all away. My daddy hadn't been like that.

I felt Agnes's little hand slip into mine. 'Rose?' she whispered.

'Yes, my love?'

'I think you should go to England.'

I turned to face her. 'What did you say, darlin'?'

She looked at me seriously. 'I think you should take that job in England and look after those children.'

'But I've thought about it, Agnes, and I don't want to go.'

'Why?'

'I don't know – a lot of reasons, I suppose. I mean, it would mean moving even further away from you all.'

'Is that the only reason?'

'Maybe I'm a bit scared.'

'I'd be scared too but I think I'd do it anyway; I think I'd take a chance.'

I couldn't believe what was coming out of my shy little sister's mouth. She never had an opinion about anything and here she was telling me that she would go to England if she had the chance.

'I think,' she said, 'that Holy God guides us in the direction that He wants us to go, even if we don't want to go there. I think

He sends people in the form of angels, who take our hands and lead us onto the right path and I think He's wanting you to go to England. That's what I think, Rose.'

Mrs Feeny's words came back to me. *The child is very sparing with her words but those words are always worth listening to.* And Daddy had always said, 'She will speak when she wants to be heard.'

I stood up and took her hand and we walked to the bottom of the garden, where Mammy's roses trailed across the wall. I breathed in the heady scent of them. I knew that wherever I was in the world, the smell of a rose would take me back home.

Mammy walked down the garden and stood between us.

'Rose is going to England, Mammy,' whispered Agnes.

'Of course she is,' said Mammy, squeezing my hand.

Chapter Thirteen

I stood on the deck, looking out over the calm, grey water, and watched as the green hills of my beloved home faded into the mist. I'd asked myself a thousand times, was I doing the right thing? Was Agnes right? Was this the path that I was meant to follow?

Once I had decided to take the job in London, me and Mammy had gone down to the church to see Father Luke.

'And are you sure that this is what you want, Rose?' he'd said.

I nodded. 'Agnes says it's what God wants me to do.'

'That child is a true theologian,' he'd said, smiling.

'She surprises us with the things she comes out with, Father,' said Mammy.

'Ah yes, one of God's little messengers. So,' he said, 'I will write to Mrs Mullen at the hotel and ask her to let me have Mr Townsend's address. I am sure we will all feel a lot happier once we know more about the said gentleman and his family. We must make sure that Rose will be safe.'

'Oh, he's very nice, Father,' I said.

'So, you will leave this to me and I will come and see you when I have some news.'

'Thank you, Father,' said Mammy, standing up. 'It would put our minds at rest to know that she is going to a good family.'

Father Luke dipped his hand in the holy water font and made the sign of the cross on our foreheads.

Me and Mammy walked down the hill towards the quay. We sat on a wall and watched the lads jumping off the groyne and splashing about in the water. Me and Polly used to do the same thing when we were younger and now we were all grown up and

I was going far away from the town that I loved and across the sea to a strange country.

'There will be no shame, Rose, if you change your mind. I'm surprised that Agnes encouraged you to go, for she loves the bones of you, but I'd say that if God was going to speak to anyone it would be Agnes,' said Mammy.

'She said that if she was given the chance to go to England, she would go.'

'She said that?'

'She did.'

'I'd say there is a depth to that child that we have yet to understand.'

'I think so too.'

There was a big ship moored up on the quay and it reminded me of Erik. I hadn't heard from him, but Mammy said it was the same with Daddy. Sometimes it would be months before she had a letter and then she'd get three at once. I often thought about that afternoon we'd spent together at Temple Michael and how much I'd enjoyed his company, but as Polly had said, sailors had a girl in every port and not to be raising my hopes. But something told me that Erik wasn't like that.

I hadn't gone back to Cork; I'd just waited for Father Luke to hear from Mr Townsend. Every Friday evening, I met Polly off the Thrupenny Rush and we ran through the town together.

One evening, we were sitting on the wall before going into her cottage.

'I'm thinking of leaving the hotel,' she said. 'It's not the same without you, and that baggage Dervla is on my case every bloody day. She has me brain mashed.'

'What will you do?'

'Go to America.'

'You can't just go to America, Polly! How will you get there? And what will you do when you *do* get there?'

'Mammy says I have a cousin in Brooklyn who might take me in. It's the first time I've heard of a cousin in Brooklyn.'

'Well, it would have to be a rich cousin, Polly, for how else could you pay the fare?'

Polly sighed. 'If he's related to our lot, he's probably an eejit without a penny to his name but I have to get away, Rose, I just have to.'

'Go and see Father Luke on your next day off. He might be able to help.'

'I'll do that,' said Polly. 'It can't do any harm.'

We went into the cottage and Polly reluctantly handed her wages over to her mammy.

'So, you're off to England, Rose?' she said.

'I think so, Mrs Butler. Father Luke is making sure that the Townsends are a good family.'

'He does right, Rose. For those slave traders come in all shapes and sizes.'

Polly raised her eyes to the ceiling. 'Jesus, Mammy, don't start all that again. Mr Townsend is a very decent man, you could tell.'

'And I'm sure the devil himself could disguise himself into a very decent man. You can always come home at the first sign of any carrying-on.'

'Dear God in heaven, Mammy, won't you just wish the girl well?'

'I do of course but it's better to be warned of the dangers.'

'She's not going to war,' said Polly. 'She's going to England to make her fortune and I wish I could bloody go with her.'

'Ah, Polly, you wouldn't last five minutes in that place; you're awful skitty and being skitty will get you in a whole lot of trouble.'

'Let's go, Rose, before I say something I regret.'

'Goodbye, Mrs Butler.'

'Goodbye, child.'

*

Father Luke had received a letter from Mr Townsend, who assured him that I would most certainly be safe with them and that he'd keep an eye on me. The past few days had been awful; at least someone in the house would be crying, and Polly said it was like a bloody wake in there.

The morning I was leaving, me and Mammy were sitting beside the fire, drinking tea. It was very early and everyone else was still asleep. My suitcase was standing beside the door, reminding us that I was leaving my home and my family.

Mammy stood up and went over to the dresser. She handed me a parcel, inside which was a bible.

'My mammy gave me this just before she died and now I am giving it to you, Rose,' she said.

The tears that I'd been trying to hold back since I'd opened my eyes this morning streamed down my face and I let out a roar that seemed to come from the very depths of my soul. Mammy knelt down in front of me and gathered me into her arms. 'Hush now, my darling girl,' she said, wiping away my tears. 'This will always be your home and your family will always be here, waiting for your return. You are not alone, you will never be alone and if you need me and there is no boat available, I'll swim to England and carry you home with your coat between me teeth.'

I burst out laughing, imagining my mammy swimming the Atlantic Ocean and then Mammy was laughing and our laughter woke my sisters, who stumbled, half asleep, down the stairs and they started laughing even though they didn't know what they were laughing about.

When Father Luke arrived with the car, we were still laughing. 'Well, I thought you'd all be in floods of tears,' he said, dipping his finger in the holy water font and making the sign of the cross.

'And isn't laughter and tears the same thing, Father?' whispered Agnes. 'Aren't they both feelings?'

'I suppose they are, child, I suppose they are,' said Father Luke, smiling. 'And I think that you'll be going straight to Heaven in a velvet lift, Agnes.'

And so, I left my family, not with tears of sorrow on my cheeks, but tears of laughter.

It was chilly on the boat deck, so I went inside to the lounge bar where it was warmer. It was heaving in there, with not a spare seat to be found. Someone was singing 'Danny Boy' in a pure, clear voice and it made me feel like crying. I was just about to go back outside when I noticed a young girl sitting on her own in the corner. I walked across to her. 'Do you mind if I sit here?' I said.

The girl smiled. 'You can, of course,' she said.

I rubbed my hands together. 'It's desperate cold outside.'

She nodded.

Mammy had packed me some sandwiches and apple cake. I unwrapped the parcel but the thought of eating made me feel sad, because all I could think of was home and her making the food for me in our little kitchen.

I noticed that the girl was looking at the food. 'Would you like some?' I said.

'I don't want to take your dinner.'

'Why don't we share it?'

I unwrapped the parcel and handed her a sandwich. I've never seen anyone eat a sandwich so fast, so I gave her another one.

'Are you going to London?' she asked.

'I am,' I said, handing her some apple cake.

She took it eagerly. 'So am I. What part are you going to?'

'A place called Belgravia, how about you?'

'Fulham, to a convent.'

'Are you going to be a nun?' I asked.

The girl smiled. 'No, I'm going to have a baby.'

'A baby?'

'I know. Aren't I a desperate sinner?'

'You must be awful scared.'

'I'm terrified but I've only meself to blame as me father kept telling me.'

'So you couldn't have had it in Ireland?'

'Jesus, no, I'd have ended up in one of the Magdalene homes. I'm lucky that the convent in Fulham is taking me in.'

'So, will you take the baby back home?'

'My father said I'm to come home alone, or not at all.'

'That's awful.'

'He's not a bad man, my father, but he's a proud one. I will have the baby, go home and it will never be mentioned again.'

The girl looked so young and here she was, on her way to a strange country, about to give her baby away, without kith or kin by her side to give her comfort.

'What about the boy?' I said.

'I didn't tell him.'

'But doesn't he have a right to know?'

She shrugged her shoulders.

'Maybe he would stand by you and then you could keep the baby.'

'What in God's name would I do with a baby? I'm only fifteen. No, it will be adopted by a good Catholic family and it will have a better life than I can give it.'

I wasn't so sure that she really believed what she was saying and I felt terrible sorry for her.

'Me name's Mary,' she said. 'Mary Kelly.'

'Rose Brown,' I said.

We slept for most of the journey and it was dark when the train pulled into Paddington station.

'Are you being met, Mary?'

She made a face. 'By a nun.'

Suddenly it all felt very real and terrifying. I just wanted to be at home or working alongside Polly in the hotel. Mary looked just as scared as me.

We took our cases down from the rack and stepped out onto the platform.

I could see two nuns hurrying in our direction.

'Goodbye, Rose,' said Mary, kissing my cheek.

'Goodbye, Mary, and may God go with you.'

She smiled and walked towards the nuns. I watched as she walked away and hoped that she was going to be alright.

The railway station was huge, unlike our little station in Ballykillen; even Cork wasn't this impressive. There were so many people and so much noise. Everyone seemed to be in a hurry and everyone seemed to be shouting. I looked up at the great glass ceiling above my head. What on earth had made me think that London would be like Ballykillen, only a bit bigger? This was nothing like Ballykillen and I was terrified.

'Rose,' said a voice. I looked up to see Mr Townsend walking towards me.

He was just as I remembered him and I have never been more relieved to see a familiar face. 'Hello,' I said.

He grinned. 'Here, let me take your case. I have a car outside.'

I walked towards the shiny black car, thinking that Polly would have called it swanky. Mr Townsend opened the door and I stepped inside. The seats were so soft and it was lovely and warm. I must have fallen asleep and was woken up by Mr Townsend.

'We're home, Rose,' he said.

Home? Well, yes, I suppose this was my home now but not the home that I loved.

Chapter Fourteen

When I woke the next morning, it took me a moment to realise where I was. I hadn't taken any notice of my surroundings last night; I'd been dead on my feet and all I'd wanted was my bed.

I sat up and looked around. I had never been in such a beautiful room. The walls were the colour of forget-me-nots and so was the cover on the bed. The curtains were pure white; they fell in soft folds to the floor and puddled onto the cream carpet. Surely this wasn't my bedroom? Perhaps Mr Townsend had made a mistake and I would soon be moved to the attic but while I was here, I could enjoy the beauty of it.

The door opened and a woman walked in. I'd never seen an angel but if I had, I know that she would have looked just as beautiful. Her hair was so blonde that it was almost white and her eyes were green, with speckles of blue and grey, as if they couldn't make up their mind what colour to be. She was wearing something floaty, in reds and yellows and purples. I'd thought that she looked lovely in the photo that Mr Townsend had shown me but the woman in front of me was even more beautiful. She looked like an angel wrapped in a rainbow.

She sat on the bed and smiled at me. 'My darling child,' she said. 'You must have been exhausted, for it is almost noon.'

'Oh, I'm sorry,' I said. 'I didn't mean to sleep so long, I'll get up.'

'You most certainly will not. You'll stay where you are, until you are well rested.' She smiled. 'Hello, Rose,' she said. 'I'm Alice.'

'Hello, Madam.'

'And we'll have none of that. My name is Alice.'

I could feel my face getting red. 'But I can't call you that, it wouldn't be right.'

'And why wouldn't it be right?'

'Because, well... because.'

She held my hand. 'You see, we are both flesh and blood. We both have hopes and dreams, we are no different. So, you shall call me Alice and I shall call you Rose and we shall be friends, yes?'

'Yes,' I said. 'Oh yes.'

'I hope you like your room, Rose.'

'Is this really my room?'

She laughed, with her head thrown back and her mouth open, showing the whitest teeth I had ever seen. Her laughter seemed to fill the room with such joy. 'Of course it is,' she said.

'I thought...'

'That you would be tucked away in the basement?'

'Well, the attic anyway.'

'Rose, you are a part of our family now and David and I want you to be happy with us.'

I gazed at this vision sitting on my bed and smiled. 'I know that I will,' I said, and I meant it.

'So, I shall leave you now and when you feel ready, I will introduce you to Raffi. He is beside himself with excitement. He's been drawing you a picture and he can't wait to give it to you. If he'd had his way, he would have been waking you up at the crack of dawn.'

Alice was very slim but I could see a slight swelling beneath her floaty dress. If the baby was due in January that would make her four months pregnant.

'You must be looking forward to your baby being born.'

She frowned. 'My baby?' she said.

'Yes, it's an exciting time, isn't it?'

A shadow seemed to pass over Alice's face; her beautiful smile was gone. She walked over to the window and stared out into the garden. She just stood there, not saying a word. I'd upset her but I didn't know why, except that it was something to do with the baby she was carrying.

Suddenly she turned around and smiled her lovely smile. 'Yes, I suppose it is.'

I stared at Alice. Something felt wrong but I couldn't think what it could be. I had mentioned the baby and that should have been a perfectly normal thing to talk about but it was very obvious that Alice didn't want to and I wondered why.

'Now then, you must be hungry, so come downstairs when you are ready and we shall have some food together.'

At the door she turned around. 'Darling Rose,' she said, smiling, 'you and I will have such fun.'

Then she was gone, and the light in the room seemed to fade with her leaving. I lay in the comfy bed and tried to understand what had just happened. I had never met anyone like her in my whole life and I couldn't easily explain to myself how she made me feel. Mammy would have said that I was being fanciful and that she was just a person like the rest of us but she wasn't. It was as if she had just been born, still all shiny and new, like nothing bad or unclean had touched her. She reminded me of someone but I couldn't think who and then it came to me: Alice reminded me of Bridgy, she reminded me of a child.

I got out of bed and walked across to the window. The smooth green lawn sloped away from the house, down to a row of tall trees. There was a fountain, with some sort of statue in the middle of it, and I knew that if I opened the window, I would hear the water splashing into the stone bowl. I thought about the little yard in Cross Lane and wondered what Mammy would think of this beautiful garden. I could hear her saying, 'The good Lord has given me enough space to grow my roses and they will be as beautiful against a stone wall as anywhere else.'

*

It turned out that Raffi wasn't as excited about my arrival as Alice had said he was. He was very polite when we were introduced but as soon as his mother left the room, he glared at me.

'I don't need a nanny,' he said. 'I'm not a baby.'

'I can see that,' I said, smiling. 'The thing is, Raffi, I'm only fifteen. I'm far too young to be anyone's nanny.'

For a minute he looked confused. 'What are you here for then?' he said, scowling.

'To help your mother with the baby. I can see that you are too old to need a nanny but perhaps I could be your friend.'

He stared at me. 'I don't need a friend. Alice is my friend and I don't need another one.'

I was a bit shocked. 'You call your mother Alice?'

'It's her name, why shouldn't I? After all, she calls me Raffi. What's the difference?'

I didn't know what to say. For God's sake, he was a nine-year-old child and he had me completely dumbstruck.

'What do you call your mother then?' He said it as if he had thrown out a challenge.

'I call her Mammy.'

Raffi laughed but it wasn't a nice laugh. 'Isn't that what babies call their mothers?'

'Where I come from, everyone calls their mammies Mammy, even the grown-ups.'

'What's her name, this mammy of yours?'

'Her name is Christina.'

'Why don't you call her Christina then, if it's her name?'

'It wouldn't be respectful, Raffi.'

'Are you saying I'm not respectful?'

'No, I'm saying that in my country it wouldn't be respectful.'

'Alice said that you are from Ireland. I've never been there.'

'Oh, you'd love it, Raffi, it's a very beautiful place. The town I live in is called Ballykillen and it's on the banks of a beautiful river. We have woods and fields and we have a haunted abbey.'

That seemed to catch his attention. 'A haunted abbey?' he said. 'You must tell Alice, she likes ghosts. We both do.'

'And what about your father? Does he like ghosts?'

'David thinks it's nonsense but he goes along with Alice.' Raffi stared at me. 'We both go along with Alice.'

I was lost for words. I was just imagining what Polly would say about this child that spoke like a man. It made me smile.

'What's so funny?' said Raffi.

'I was thinking about my best friend Polly. Do you have a best friend, Raffi?'

He turned his back and walked over to the bookcase. 'I don't have any friends,' he mumbled.

I wasn't surprised; this child was strange, or maybe English children were different to Irish ones.

'What about your schoolfriends, don't they come round to play?'

Raffi turned back to me. 'I don't have any schoolfriends.'

'Why not?'

'Because I don't go to school. I have a tutor that comes to the house. You ask an awful lot of questions.'

I laughed. 'You should meet Bridgy,' I said.

'Who's Bridgy?'

'My little sister.'

'I nearly had a sister and before you start asking, I'd rather not talk about it.'

'That's alright. So why don't you go to school?'

'Because Alice doesn't want some stranger filling my head with nonsense. She wants me to make my own mind up about things. She wants me to be a free spirit like her.'

I had a feeling that perhaps Raffi didn't really agree with his mother about this, but I didn't say anything.

'So, shall we be friends, Raffi?' I said.

He stared at me for what seemed an uncomfortably long time and then he said very solemnly, 'Yes, Rose, we shall be friends.'

I grinned and Raffi grinned and I knew that we were going to be okay.

Chapter Fifteen

Besides the four of us there was a woman that came in every day to cook our meals. Her name was Mrs Berry and she looked just like you would expect a cook to look. She was as round as she was tall, she had a ruddy complexion and she always seemed to be in the middle of something very important, like the butcher sending chops instead of pork loin, or the baker delivering bread that she suspected was yesterday's. Actually, I think she enjoyed all the drama and would be at a loss for conversation if she didn't have some problem to tell us about. It was very noticeable how fond she was of Raffi and she delighted in making him his favourite foods.

One afternoon, when Alice was resting and Raffi was reading to her, I walked down the garden and sat on a wooden bench. There was a cold wind moving the branches of the tall trees that surrounded the lawn. I was happy here, I was, but I was missing home. I was missing my sisters and Polly but most of all I was missing Mammy. Home seemed such a long way away. There was an ocean between me and everything I loved. My eyes burned with tears but I blinked them away. I knew that if I started to cry, I would never stop.

I liked the family, I liked them a lot, but there were some things that were puzzling me. It was October now and the baby was due soon and yet no one talked about it. It should have been the main topic of the house and yet it was as if it wasn't happening at all. Even Mrs Berry didn't mention it. Alice was now six months pregnant and big with child. The coming baby was hard to ignore and yet they all managed to.

There was always someone in Ballykillen who was pregnant and however many children they already had, it was still something to be celebrated, for every birth was a gift from God and a joyous occasion. Candles would be lit in the church and prayers said for the baby's safe arrival. I wondered what Mammy would say about this. I wished I could talk to her about it, for my mammy was wise and I valued her counsel. Polly would probably say that the lot of them were mad and God forgive me but I was beginning to think the same thing meself.

'Ah, there you are,' said David, walking towards me. 'I thought we'd lost you.' As he came closer, he looked at me and said, 'And I think that perhaps you *are* a little lost, Rose. Am I right?'

'I'm missing home but I'll be alright, I will, I'll be alright.'

David sat down beside me. 'This must all seem rather confusing to you, Rose. Even I am aware that our family may seem a bit unusual to those who don't really know us.'

I took a deep breath. 'Can I ask you something?'

'Of course.'

'I don't want to pry but…'

'Go on,' he said. 'You can ask whatever you want.'

'It's about the baby.'

'Ah yes,' said David.

'No one seems to mention it.'

'We are waiting for Alice.'

'To do what?'

'To acknowledge it. To be interested in its arrival. Because you see, Rose, that when she does, you, Raffi and myself can spring into action and what a joyous day that will be. Alice just needs time.'

I couldn't help thinking that Alice had had plenty of time but I didn't say so. 'You said in your letter that the baby is due in January, is that right?'

He was quiet for a while, gazing out over the garden, and I wondered if I had been wrong to ask. 'Yes, Rose, our little girl will be born in January.'

'But how do you know that it will be a girl?'

'It has to be, Rose, for that is what Alice wants.'

I couldn't help thinking that Alice might want a girl but it was up to the good Lord to decide this and not Alice.

'You see, four years ago, Alice gave birth to a sweet baby that we called Martha after her beloved aunt. Our beautiful little girl only lived for an hour and died peacefully in Alice's arms. My darling Alice never recovered from the pain of losing her. She was ill for a very long time and no one could reach her, not even me and Raffi. She was lost to us, Rose. She slowly came back but she remained, and still remains, very fragile. In many ways, Raffi was denied a normal childhood. He had only just started school, which he loved, but he refused to go back. He wouldn't leave her side. His childhood seemed to end the moment that baby died. I want Raffi to have a childhood. I want him to have friends of his own age. My son carries too much responsibility for one so young, especially when I have to go away. Alice is a wonderful woman, Rose, she is so full of joy that it shines out of her, but she also has dark days when she shuts herself away from us but we have learned to be patient, for she always comes back.'

My eyes filled with tears. 'That is so sad,' I said. 'So terribly sad.'

'We had everything prepared for the baby coming home but sadly that wasn't to be. I cleared the nursery while Alice was in the hospital and she was almost hysterical when she saw the empty room. I thought I was doing the right thing, I thought it would ease her pain but it made everything worse. I don't think that I ever forgave myself for that.'

'You did what you thought was right.'

David shook his head. 'But I couldn't have been more wrong.'

'Do you still have the baby things?' I asked.

'They are in Martha's house in Brooklyn. We left them behind when we moved here. There were too many memories in that house, too many hopes and dreams had died there and a piece of Alice had died there too.'

'Didn't Alice have a mammy that could have helped out?'

'Alice's parents died in a train crash when she was four years old and she went to live with her Aunt Martha, who loved her like her own. You would love Martha, Rose; she is eccentric and full of fun and a little bit mad and she was just what Alice needed. Martha said that Alice's parents travelled a lot and often left the little girl with strangers. She said that they were so in love with each other that they had no time for the child. Isn't that sad, Rose?'

'It is,' I said. 'It's terrible sad.'

'Even Martha couldn't reach our darling girl when the baby died, so we left America and came here.'

'And is she happier here?'

'It took time but yes, I would say she is happier here. In fact, her mood seems better since you arrived, so thank you for that, Rose.'

'I'm glad.'

'I have at least done one thing though. I've hired a nanny for when the baby arrives. Her name is Helen. She's Irish, like you, from Kerry.'

I didn't understand. 'But isn't that why I am here?' I said. 'To take care of the children?'

David was staring down at his feet as if he couldn't look into my eyes and then he began to speak.

'To begin with it was, because I knew that Alice would need help but I think that what our darling girl needs more than a nanny is a friend. And she likes you, Rose, things have been better since you came. If we were still in America she would have had her Aunt Martha but here she has no female companionship and I think that is what she needs.'

'So, you want me to be her friend?'

'Not just her friend but Raffi's, too. He worries about his mother, much more than a young child should. Alice is fragile and Raffi feels the need to protect her. I suppose we all do. I want you to help us take care of her. Does that scare you, Rose?'

I thought about it. 'I don't think so,' I said.

'Because if it does, I will understand. I truly didn't mean to lie to you.'

'It was only a white lie,' I said, smiling. 'I tell them all the time. I'm forever up in the confessional box asking God to forgive me. My friend Polly is worse than I am.'

'And does He forgive you, this God of yours?'

'Of course he does. A couple of Hail Marys and a Glory Be and I'm grand again. It's a great feeling.'

'And that's why I chose you.'

'Because I tell white lies?'

David laughed. 'What I saw in you, dear girl, was wisdom, kindness and compassion. I knew you were the right one. Was I wrong, Rose?'

I didn't need to think about it this time. 'I'd be honoured to help care for Alice,' I said, 'because I have never laid eyes on such a beautiful person.'

'So, it will be the three of us against the world.'

'I'll guard her with my life,' I said.

David smiled. 'Well, that makes me very happy but hopefully it won't come to that.'

Just then, Raffi came running down the lawn towards us. He was grinning. 'Did you ask her, David?' he said. 'Did he ask you, Rose?'

'He did,' I said, smiling.

'And will you do it, Rose? Will you help us take care of Alice?'

'I will.'

'Do you promise?'

'I promise, Raffi, and I never break a promise.'

'And will you rescue her, even if it means putting yourself in danger?'

David laughed. 'For heaven's sake, Raffi, you'll have her packing her case and running for the next boat home.'

But Raffi was deadly serious. 'Will you, Rose?'

I put my hand on my heart. 'I promise.'

Raffi sat down on the grass and leaned against my legs. 'I think that three is much better than two, don't you, Rose?'

I very gently stroked his hair. 'I do, Raffi, I do.'

Chapter Sixteen

Alice held out her hand. 'Come with me, Rose,' she said.

I followed her upstairs to her bedroom.

'I have something to show you. Sit, sit.'

I sat on the bed and waited.

Alice opened a cabinet and took out a box, then she sat down beside me. Inside the box was something wrapped in a cloth. She unfolded it and poured the contents onto the bed until the quilt sparkled and gleamed with the most beautiful stones I had ever seen.

'These are my treasures. Aren't they lovely?'

I was mesmerised by the colours; the blues and greens and whites and purples. Some of the stones seemed to hold all these colours within them. A thin, wintry sun had found its way into the room, catching the brightness of the stones and reflecting pools of colour onto the walls. I had never seen anything so beautiful in my whole life.

'These stones are crystals, Rose, and each of them has a special role to play.'

'They are beautiful,' I said.

Alice placed a creamy-coloured stone in my hand. 'This is a moonstone crystal. It is a symbol of love and fertility. It was given as a gift between lovers and is believed to arouse passion. Some say it changes colour and appearance to reflect the phases of the moon, hence its name.' She pointed to a pale blue stone. 'This is called angelite and is the stone of awareness. It helps you to speak your own truth. And this,' she said, picking up a beautiful yellow stone, 'is a citrine. It is an energising stone and promotes happiness, courage, hope and warmth. It is said to hold the energy of the sun.'

Alice put the stone down and picked up a beautiful blue one. 'This is my favourite,' she said. 'This beautiful turquoise stone protects and balances the body. It is widely thought of as a good luck charm. I carry this one with me wherever I go.'

'They are all so beautiful,' I said.

'But which one speaks to you, Rose?'

'Speaks to me?'

'Yes. Look at the stones, take your time and you will know which is the one for you.'

I felt a bit silly staring at the crystals, waiting for one of them to speak to me.

'Have patience,' said Alice. 'It will happen.'

I wanted to pick the pretty pink one or the bright blue one but I felt myself being drawn towards a pale green stone. I looked again at the pink one and again my eyes went back to the pale green stone. I held it up to the light and realised it wasn't just green, it had threads of grey and blue running through it. It was the colour of the sea; it was the colour of Alice's eyes.

'What's this one called?' I asked.

'That is aquamarine. It is known as the stone of courage and is believed to be the treasure of mermaids. It is linked to water and the sea, and will protect you from those elements. It also encourages a lover to return and helps two people of different lifestyles to live together in harmony.'

I looked at the little green stone in my hand. 'It does all that?'

'So they say and who am I to doubt it?'

It made me think about Erik. We certainly had different lifestyles. Could it have worked, even with the distance between us? I put the stone back on the bed with the others.

'No,' said Alice. 'You must keep it.'

'Oh, I couldn't.'

'It chose you, so take it, it's yours.'

I looked again at the little green stone. 'Thank you, I will treasure it always.'

Next, Alice handed me a black shiny stone. It felt smooth and cool in my hand but it wasn't pretty like the others. 'This is called obsidium,' she said. 'It is named after the man who discovered it. It is a natural, volcanic glass and it is said to bring courage, wisdom, sincerity and truth. When David first talked to me about you, I just couldn't envisage the girl that he wanted to come and live with us. "Why this girl?" I said. David took my hand and said, "Imagine the obsidium, Alice, for that is Rose Brown."'

I smiled. 'How lovely.'

Alice wrapped the stones in the cloth and put them back in the box. 'Now,' she said, 'you shall read to me.'

She picked up a book that was on a table beside her bed. 'Have you read *Alice in Wonderland*, Rose?'

I stood there, staring at her. I felt frozen to the spot and I didn't know what to say. I could feel prickles of sweat forming under my arms. I had only gone to school for a very short time. I had learned my letters but hadn't got beyond the baby books that the nuns had given me.

'Oh, you will love it. My mother named me after the little girl in the book, who fell down a rabbit hole and found Wonderland. Wouldn't you love to find Wonderland, Rose?'

I was finding it hard to breathe. What was I doing here with all this talk of crystals that gave you courage? And a girl called Alice, who fell down a rabbit hole? I didn't fit in, why did I think that I could? I couldn't become someone that I wasn't and I didn't want to try. I was Rose Brown from Ballykillen and that is who I would always be. This was another world; I didn't belong here. I belonged at home with my own kind.

'You shall read it to me, Rose. I love to be read to, don't you?'

I was staring at the carpet; I could feel beads of sweat on my forehead.

'Rose?'

I looked up. 'I'm sorry,' I said softly.

Alice smiled her beautiful smile. 'Sorry for what, my dear girl?'

'I can't. I'm sorry but I can't read.'

Alice stopped smiling and her eyes filled with tears, then she took my hand and we ran downstairs. We went into a room I had never entered before. The heavy velvet curtains were closed, shutting out the light. Alice walked across to the window and pulled them back, causing motes of dust to fly around the room. I wondered why she had brought me here. The whole of one wall was filled with books, reaching from the floor up to the ceiling. Rows and rows of books were stacked haphazardly on the shelves, some leaning against each other and others scattered on the floor beneath the bookcase. Alice ran her fingers along the books as if she was caressing them.

'I could never get rid of a book, Rose, it would be like turning my back on a good friend.' She lifted one down from the shelf and held it up to her face and sighed. 'It smells so delicious that I want to gobble it up, every page and every word so that it is part of me forever. Wouldn't that be wonderful? Wouldn't that be the most wonderful thing? Oh, how I envy you, Rose.'

I didn't know what she was talking about. Why in all that's holy would Alice envy me?

'Why?' I said.

'Because there is a world of wonder waiting for you, my darling girl. See all these books? They will take you anywhere you want to go. You will have adventures that you only dreamed of. You will find your very own Wonderland between those pages.'

Alice gently brushed away the tears that had started to run down my face. She smelt of sunshine and lemons and new beginnings.

I could feel something bubbling up inside me and suddenly I was laughing and Alice was laughing, that beautiful laugh that I loved so much. She took my hands and we spun around the room until we both fell to the floor in a heap. Then she gently cupped my face and said, 'I shall teach you to read, darling Rose. I shall teach you to read.'

Chapter Seventeen

As the weeks went on, I slowly started to make sense of the letters I had learned as a child. Alice and I read every morning, mostly in the library, curled up together on the window seat. When the day was warm, we would sit on a bench in the garden. Sometimes Raffi would join us but when the tutor came to the house, it was just me and Alice. I grew to love these times. I missed my family and still had moments of overwhelming homesickness. I'd heard desperate stories of girls being treated badly in England but I had grown fond of this family and that helped. It also helped when I received letters from Agnes; it made me feel part of what was going on at home. I would read Agnes's words and I would hear her voice telling me about Mammy and my sisters and any gossip going on in the village and I would feel less sad.

I loved listening to Alice read. She had the most beautiful voice, so soft and clear. I think that she enjoyed those times too. The first book that she picked for me was called *Winnie-the-Pooh*.

I looked at the dark green cover of the book. 'Is this a children's book?'

'What makes you say that?'

'It has a picture of a boy and a bear on the front.'

'It's an any-age book,' said Alice, smiling. 'That boy is called Christopher Robin and the bear is Pooh.'

'Pooh?' I said, grinning.

'Yes, Pooh, and he is very wise and very funny. You will love getting to know him, Rose.'

I traced my finger under the name at the bottom. 'A,' I said. 'A Mm… i… l… n. A.A. Milne?' I said.

Alice clapped her hands. 'You clever girl, you clever, clever girl. And soon you will meet all of Pooh's friends. There's a very sad and gloomy donkey called Eeyore but everyone loves him all the same. There is a wise owl who knows everything about everything, a rabbit and Kanga with her baby, Roo.'

'Kangaroo,' I said, laughing.

'Exactly,' said Alice. 'And then there is Piglet, who is very small but one morning he discovers that even though he has a very small heart, it can hold a rather large amount of gratitude. Don't you think that is the sweetest thing, Rose?'

'Oh, I do,' I said, 'I can't wait to meet them all.'

'And you will and I hope that you will love them as much as I do.'

Every day I was falling a little more in love with Alice, even though she still remained a bit of a mystery to me.

I couldn't stop thinking about the coming baby, though. One morning, after I'd finished my lesson, I spoke to Raffi about it.

'Isn't there anything we can do, Raffi?' I said.

He shook his head. 'We have to wait for Alice.'

Raffi has spoken the exact same words as his father and I wondered how much he was influenced by this and what his own thoughts were.

'Couldn't we at least find a room in the house that would make a good nursery?' I said.

Raffi was silent for a while and then he nodded. 'I suppose there would be no harm in that.'

'Let's do it then,' I said. 'Let's find a nursery.'

'It can't be on the same floor as Alice,' said Raffi.

'Why ever not?'

'Because its crying will disturb her sleep.'

'But won't she want the baby close to her?'

'I just told you, Rose, it will disturb her sleep. When we talk about Alice, you must listen, because David and I know her best.'

This was getting stranger by the day and I was beginning to feel uncomfortable about the whole thing. I began to wonder whether all this protecting of Alice was a good thing. David and Raffi were forever whispering about her; they would decide if she was having a good day and if they decided she wasn't, they hardly left her side. They were almost telling her that she was ill, when in fact I couldn't see any change in her at all. If she was happy and laughing and full of joy, they took this as a sign that all was not well and if she was a bit quiet, they would encourage her to lay down and Raffi would read to her. I thought a nice walk in the park would do her more good. As Mammy used to say when one of us was a bit under the weather, 'Get yourself outside and blow those cobwebs away.'

The room we decided would be the most suitable for a nursery was on the top floor and even better, there was a room next door for Helen. The long window looked out over the back garden. It was bright and sunny and I thought it would be perfect for the baby. Now all I had to do was suggest it to Alice and I wasn't looking forward to that at all.

I found her in the library, curled up on the window seat, reading a book. She smiled as I went in.

'What are you reading?' I said.

Alice passed me the book. 'It's called *The Railway Children*,' she said. 'Such a wonderful story. I have read it so many times but I never tire of it. One day you will read it, Rose, and then we shall discuss it.'

I passed the book back to her. 'I hope so.'

'Oh, you will.'

'Can I show you something?' I said.

'Is it a surprise, Rose? I do so love surprises.'

I supposed it was a surprise in a way but maybe not the sort of surprise that would make her happy. 'I hope so,' I said.

As we walked upstairs, I wasn't sure that she was going to love this one. I opened the door to the little room and Alice followed me in.

She walked across to the window. 'What a marvellous view.'

'That's what I thought,' I said.

'Do you want to change bedrooms, Rose? If you want to sleep up here then you shall—'

I interrupted her. 'I'm very happy with my room, Alice, I don't need to move up here.'

She frowned. 'Then what is this about? Why have you brought me here?'

I took a deep breath. 'I thought it would make a lovely nursery.'

'A nursery? What a funny thing to say, Rose.'

'For the baby, Alice. I was thinking that we need to prepare for the baby coming.'

Her eyes filled with tears as she walked back to the window. She stood gazing down at the garden below. She stayed like that for a long time, just gazing out. I didn't speak; I'd said what needed to be said, now I just had to wait. Eventually she turned around and gave a sad smile. 'I'm scared, Rose,' she said softly. 'I'm scared.'

If this had been someone at home, I would have taken them in my arms and comforted them but I didn't want to crowd her and I didn't want to make it into a big drama.

'I'm scared that I won't be bringing this baby home, Rose.'

I walked across and gently placed my hand on her tummy, just as the baby kicked. We both laughed. 'Your baby is strong, Alice, and God willing, your baby will come home.'

'I really want to believe that. I want to believe that with all my heart.'

I nodded. 'So, what do you think?'

Alice looked around the room. 'I think the walls should be yellow and the curtains white and there should be pictures, lots of pictures and teddy bears and— Oh, Rose, we will make it beautiful! We will create Wonderland for little Sarah!'

'Sarah?'

'Yes, don't you think that is a lovely name?'

'I do, but…'

'It will be a girl; I know it will be a girl.'

'But it might be a little boy, Alice.'

'Then I hope he won't mind being called Sarah.'

This made me laugh and it made me happy, because Alice was acting normally.

'Have you heard of Sarah Bernhardt, Rose?'

I shook my head.

'She was a very famous French stage actress and she was magnificent. My Aunt Martha modelled herself on her. We would dance around the room, adorned in floating scarves and Aunt Martha's jewellery. We would pick flowers and entwine them in our hair. We would spin around with such sheer abandonment and joy and for those few moments, we were Sarah Bernhardt.'

'That sounds wonderful,' I said, smiling.

'Mind you, Sarah was a bit strange.'

'What was strange about her?'

Alice sat on the floor, with her back against the wall. She patted the place beside her and I sat down.

'Well, she had this fear of being buried alive, so she bought a coffin and furnished it in the very best silk and satin and she slept in it.'

'She slept in a coffin? Why in God's name would she want to do that?'

'To get used to death. And that's not all: she had read somewhere that it was a sin to die rich, so she spent all her money so that she would die a pauper. And it doesn't stop there. She had a box for her letters that was made out of a human skull. The jaw moved up and down and it is said that the teeth glowed white as snow. She called the ghastly thing Sophie. Don't you think that is an absolute hoot, Rose?'

I shuddered. 'I think she sounds a bit odd.'

'But aren't we all a bit odd? My Aunt Martha used to say that she would rather die at the hand of a jealous lover than be thought of as ordinary.'

I laughed. I liked the sound of Alice's aunt already. She put me in mind of Polly, for this was the sort of thing she would have said. I smiled, thinking about my dear friend.

'Oh, Rose, I wish you could meet Aunt Martha. When I was a child, I thought her the most glamorous person in the world. She lived in Paris for a while, in an attic room overlooking the Seine, where she kept company with artists and musicians, gigolos and Bohemian sorts, and she had lots of illicit affairs with handsome men and glamorous women.'

'Women?' I said.

'Darling Rose, I've shocked you, haven't I?'

'A bit.'

Alice laughed, that high-pitched laugh that seemed to fill her entire mouth. 'Aunt Martha would find you so amusing, Rose, and very bourgeois.'

I hadn't a clue what that meant but I was guessing it wasn't a compliment and yet I sat there, mesmerised by Alice's memories of her aunt. God forgive me but I couldn't get enough of it.

'In the evenings,' Alice went on, 'she would sit on the windowsill with her legs hanging over the ledge, drinking French wine and smoking Turkish cigarettes in long ivory holders. She had a wardrobe full of beautiful couture gowns and she let me wear them, even though they probably cost a fortune and were far too big for me. Aunt Martha said that she despised money. She said it stopped creativity; that you had to have a hunger in you, and passion and money made you lazy. She is magnificent, Rose.'

I couldn't help thinking that you had to be awful rich to despise money, because surely the poor would be only delighted to have a few shillings in their pockets.

Alice took my hand and we stood up. We looked around the room that would soon have yellow walls and white curtains and pictures and, God willing, a baby girl called Sarah.

'Thank you, Rose, thank you,' said Alice.

Then she took my hand and we ran down the stairs like two children.

From that day, there was a change in Alice and because she was happy, we were all happy. I hadn't realised until then how much Alice's mood affected the rest of us. Even Mrs Berry smiled more. It was as if we had all been holding our breath waiting for Alice, always waiting for Alice.

Chapter Eighteen

We were going on an outing to buy everything that was needed for the baby's arrival and I was as excited as the rest of them. I could hear Raffi shouting, 'Are you ready, Rose?'

I picked up my coat and ran downstairs. 'I'm coming,' I called back.

When I got to the bottom of the stairs, Alice and Raffi were waiting for me, with big smiles on their faces.

'David is bringing the car round,' said Alice. 'Are you excited, Rose? Aren't you just bursting with happiness?'

I laughed. 'Yes, Alice, I'm bursting with happiness.'

'Do you have the list, Raffi?' asked Alice.

Raffi put his hand in his pocket and took out a piece of paper. 'Of course, I have it.'

'You wrote it all down, didn't you, dear? You didn't forget anything?'

'I wrote down everything you told me to write down, Alice, now stop worrying.'

I still hadn't got used to Raffi calling his mammy by her first name. It seemed to put them on the same level and that didn't seem right to me. In fact, there were times when Raffi seemed to be in charge of Alice; she became the child and Raffi the grown-up. Perhaps if her son called her 'Mother', she might become that person, she might even begin to believe that she *was* a mother and take some responsibility. As it was, she just didn't take on the role of mother at all. She was more like a sick child that everyone tiptoed around.

We heard David beep the car horn and we went outside. 'Harrods, ladies?' he said, opening the doors. Alice sat in the back with me and Raffi sat in the front, beside David. Surely Alice should be in the front next to her husband?

I had to stop thinking about it all; it was hardly my place to be having an opinion on the way this family was run and for all I knew, Alice liked it.

I stared out of the window, watching the world go by.

'Shall we go the scenic route, David? Shall we show darling Rose the sights of London? You'd like that, wouldn't you, Rose?'

'I'd love it, if it's no trouble.'

'No trouble at all,' said David.

Raffi started pointing things out to me. 'Buckingham Palace,' he said, as we passed a grand building with guards at the gate. I'd never seen anything like it in all my life.

'Who lives there?'

'The King,' said Raffi. 'George the Sixth, with his wife and the two princesses, Elizabeth and Margaret Rose.'

'Wouldn't you love to be a princess, Rose?' said Alice.

I thought of home and Mammy and my sisters and how happy my childhood had been. We might not have lived in a palace or had the things that the two princesses had, but I wouldn't have swapped my life for theirs. 'I don't think so,' I said.

'But doesn't every little girl want to be a princess? Margaret Rose even has your name.'

'But I wouldn't be free, would I? I'd have to be on my best behaviour all the time and people would be following me around. I would rather be free than be a princess.'

Raffi turned around in his seat. 'Good decision, Rose,' he said. 'One princess in the house is enough.'

Alice laughed her beautiful laugh. 'Oh, Raffi, darling, how lovely. Are you talking about the new baby?'

'No,' said Raffi. 'I'm talking about you.'

'Did you hear that, David? Raffi thinks I'm a princess.'

'You're *our* princess, my beautiful girl,' he said.

I stared out of the window. I'd got that same feeling, that all this was a bit strange.

Maybe Polly had been right; maybe it was just an American thing. No one talked like that at home, it would be seen as giving yourself airs and graces that were above your station.

Raffi pointed out the Houses of Parliament and Nelson's Column and Tower Bridge. There were crowds of people everywhere and buses and swanky cars, Polly would have loved it. We crossed over a river. 'The Thames,' said Raffi. I looked down at the water beneath us; it was grey and oily, nothing like my beautiful Blackwater. London was indeed an amazing city but it wasn't fit to kiss Ballykillen's boots.

Alice's cheeks were pink with excitement as we stopped outside a big store.

'Harrods,' she said, grabbing hold of my arm.

A stout gentleman in a grand uniform with gold braids on his shoulders opened the door for us and gave a small bow as we walked inside. I struggled to keep the smile off my face. Nobody had ever opened a door for me like that. I could just imagine this happening to me and Polly; we'd be killing ourselves laughing. Stepping inside the store was like crossing into a different world. As soon as the door closed behind us, the cold and dark and the noise of the London streets disappeared and instead we were in a place of soft golden light, of warmth, of air that smelt sweet, of hushed voices and thick carpets and people that wanted to help.

I gazed about me, trying to take it all in. A grand staircase rose up in front of us and to one side was the shop itself, the ceilings higher than the roof of our little house in Cross Lane and huge lamps casting a wonderful warm glow all about us. Women were examining different fabrics laid out on enormous tables, feeling the quality between their fingers. Other women moved quietly around them, all wearing the most beautiful hats, the loveliest coats. The place was so quiet, with only the murmur of voices, sounds as gentle and expensive as the slip of silk against velvet. The whole magical effect, I realised, was increased by the mirrors – mirrors everywhere, so that the lights were reflecting the colours and wonderful sights. I saw my reflection and I was ashamed. The young girl looking back at me was just a country girl, a girl that didn't belong here. It occurred to me that Polly and meself wouldn't even have been allowed in.

A man dressed like a butler approached and asked if he could help us find what we were looking for.

'We'd like to buy some items for the baby,' said Alice, smiling her beautiful smile.

I could see the man almost dissolve at the sight of such beauty. He cleared his throat and said, 'Please follow me, Madam,' and set off up the stairs. Alice and I exchanged a small smile and then, feeling like the princess that I never wanted to be, I reached my hand for the banister and took the first step up the grand staircase that would lead into something like Wonderland for babies.

Chapter Nineteen

David had booked my boat ticket home and I would be leaving in two weeks' time. I couldn't wait to go home for Christmas. I ached to hold my family in my arms. I even missed the Thrupenny Rush, how daft was that? Living here in London didn't feel real and there were days when I wasn't even sure who I was. I had lost myself in this strange family and longed to be amongst my own kind, even if it was only for a short while. The only time I felt truly at home was when I was at church. The smell of incense, the Stations of the Cross hung around the walls, the statue of the Blessed Virgin Mary and Jesus himself on the cross – it was all familiar to me; it was what I had grown up with. It was home and childhood all wrapped in love.

The priest's name was Father Tom and he was lovely. He knew that I missed my home and always took the time to talk to me.

'I know how you feel, Rose,' he'd said. 'When I first arrived in England, I thought I was going to die of the homesickness and missing the potatoes, sure I was all for getting the next boat back to Kilkenny but I had to trust that this was where God wanted me to be, so I made the best of it and I'm glad that I did, for I am needed here.'

'I'm not sure this is where God wants me to be, Father. My sister Agnes convinced me that it was, she said Himself was pointing me down the right path but sometimes it doesn't feel like the right path at all.'

'The people you are working for, are they kind to you, Rose?'

'Oh yes, Father, they are very kind.'

Father Tom smiled. 'But they are not your own?'

I shook my head. 'They are not my own.'

'Well, my door is always open, Rose, and you can talk to me about anything. I might even get my housekeeper to bake us a bit of a cake.'

'That would be grand, Father,' I'd said, smiling.

On Sunday morning, I put on my good coat and shoes and I was just about to open the door when Raffi appeared in the hallway. He had a habit of suddenly appearing out of nowhere and I found it unsettling.

'Where are you off to, Rose?' he said.

'To Mass,' I answered. 'As you very well know.'

'I'd like to come with you, if you don't mind.'

'Of course I don't mind, Raffi. The company will be nice. Don't you need to tell your mother?'

'Alice is resting, I've left a note.'

So, it seemed that he had already decided to come with me, whether I wanted him to or not. It wasn't that I wasn't fond of Raffi, I just wished he would act more like a nine-year-old boy. It made it difficult to get close to him. I wished I could find the child underneath all this protecting of his mother.

The Catholic church of St Peter's was a short walk across the park and I always enjoyed the walk. It was nice to get out of the house and be alone with my thoughts. The house was indeed very beautiful but sometimes I found it hard to breathe; it seemed to close in on me, making me long to escape even for a short time.

It was a blustery day but dry. The tall trees surrounding the park were swaying in the breeze and brown crinkled leaves danced around us. I didn't own any gloves, so I put my hands in my pockets.

'Have you always been a Catholic, Rose?' said Raffi.

'Since the day I was born,' I said.

'So, it wasn't your choice?'

I thought that was an odd thing to say but then Raffi was always coming out with odd things. I shrugged my shoulders. 'I don't suppose it was.'

'So how do you know it's the right religion?'

I stopped walking and looked at him. 'How do you know that you like chocolate?'

'I just do,' he said grinning.

'So that's the answer to your question, Raffi. I just do.'

Raffi seemed satisfied with my answer and we carried on walking.

St Peter's was a lovely old church, built of warm yellow stone with high arched windows. There were a few people walking ahead of us through the wooden gate. We followed them along the path between old gravestones, some leaning over and others cracked and broken on the ground and almost completely covered in green moss and weeds.

As we entered the church, I dipped my fingers in the holy water font and made the sign of the cross.

Raffi was staring at me. 'What are you doing?'

'Making the sign of the cross,' I whispered.

'Why are you whispering, Rose?'

'Because this is the house of God.'

'So, you're not allowed to talk?'

'Jesus, Raffi, will you stop asking questions? You'll have me brain mashed.'

'Alice said I should always ask questions if I don't know about things. Alice says that is the best way to learn.'

'Going to school would be the best way to learn,' I snapped.

'Alice says that school is very bourgeois and I happen to agree with her.'

'What in all that's holy does that mean?' I said.

'Now who's asking questions?' said Raffi, grinning.

'Clever dick,' I said.

We walked down the centre aisle and I knelt in front of the Blessed Sacrament, before taking my seat. 'Don't ask,' I said to Raffi.

'Wasn't going to,' he said.

I knelt down on the little cushion and joined my hands in prayer. Out of the corner of my eye I could see Raffi copying me. I prayed to God to allow Raffi to be a child again and to lift the burden of his mother from his young shoulders. Then I made the sign of the cross and sat down. It was chilly in the church but I didn't mind; this was where I felt at peace. The smell of incense and musty old prayer books and the beautiful statue of the Blessed Virgin smiling down at me took me back home to my own church in Ballykillen. I just wished Polly was beside me. I wished that when Mass was over, we could walk out on the strand and sit on the flat rocks and listen to the waves rattle the shingle on the shore. Oh, how I longed to be home.

Father Tom was standing at the church door as we left, shaking people's hands. 'So, who do we have here?' he said, smiling at Raffi.

'I'm Raphael Townsend,' said Raffi, holding out his hand. He might be a bit on the odd side but the child had lovely manners.

'God's archangel,' said Father Tom.

'So, I've been told,' said Raffi.

'Quite a name to live up to,' said Father Tom. 'He was quite a feller, our Raphael. One of the Lord's favourite angels. He was a great healer and he watched over the traveller and gave him protection.'

'I know that,' said Raffi. 'Alice told me.'

'A friend of yours?' said Father Tom.

'My mother, actually,' said Raffi.

Father Tom looked at me and I nodded.

'Well, I hope to see you again, young man, and you, Rose.'

As we walked back home across the park. I felt his hand slip into mine and it made me smile. For all his questions I had enjoyed his company. 'Maybe you can come to church with me again, Raffi.'

'Rose,' he said, looking up at me, 'if I had understood one bloody word of it I might.'

'Raffi,' I said, shocked, 'you swore.'

'You're right,' he said grinning. 'I did.' Then he started running. 'Race you home,' he shouted.

Raffi looked like any other nine-year-old boy as he raced across the grass. Maybe God in His holy wisdom had granted my prayer.

Chapter Twenty

I wanted to let my family know that I would be returning for Christmas but although my reading was getting better every day, I didn't yet feel confident enough to write a letter home. I found Raffi in the lounge, sitting beside the fire, reading a book.

'Raffi? Would you write a letter for me?'

He closed his book and smiled at me. 'Of course I will, Rose. Who are you writing to?'

'My family.'

'Let me just get a paper and a pen and then you can tell me what you want to say and I will write it down.'

Raffi left the room and I stood by the window looking out over the garden. There had been a frost overnight and the lawn sparkled under a thin sun that was nudging through the grey clouds. I was hoping that it would snow. Ireland got very little snow but I'd heard that England got tons of it.

'Do you think it might snow?' I said, as Raffi came back into the room.

'I think it is too cold for snow – at least that is what David said when I asked him the very same question. I have a wooden toboggan in the basement and I'm longing to have a go on it. You can have a go too, Rose.'

'Let's hope your father is wrong then and we can go whizzing down the hill.'

'David is very rarely wrong, Rose.'

'Well, I shall pray for snow at Mass on Sunday.'

There was a small wooden table in the room where Raffi and David played chess.

'Let's sit at the table,' said Raffi.

We sat opposite each other and Raffi picked up the pen. 'Okay, tell me what you want to write.'

'Dear Mammy, Kathy, Agnes and Bridie,' I began. I waited until Raffi had written it down.

'Go on,' he said.

'I am writing to let you know that I will be coming home for Christmas.'

Raffi dropped the pen, which fell to the floor and rolled under the table. I bent down to pick it up.

'Leave it,' he screamed, glaring at me, his face as pale as the frost on the lawn.

'What on earth is wrong?' I said.

'You know very well what's wrong.'

'No, I don't.'

'You tricked me into writing a letter, instead of telling me,' he shouted.

'You have me confused, Raffi. What in God's name are you talking about?'

'Don't you know that you can't leave us? Don't you know that? Or are you stupid?'

'Don't speak to me like that, Raffi.'

'Are you just a stupid little Irish girl, who can't read and breaks promises? You said that you would help us take care of Alice.'

'And I do, but I want to see my family, can't you understand that? I'm very fond of you all but you are not my family, any more than I am yours.'

'Well, you can't go and that's that.'

I could feel myself getting angry. 'Well, I'm sorry you feel like that, Raffi, but I am definitely going home for Christmas. Alice doesn't mind and neither does your father.'

Raffi's eyes filled with tears and I immediately softened. He was just a child, an unhappy child. He glared at me and walked across to the window. His hands were clenched and his whole body was rigid.

I followed him and tried to take his hand but he pulled away, so I sat down on the couch and waited.

Eventually, he turned around; the tears were running down his face now but he didn't wipe them away. 'You don't understand,' he said quietly.

'But I'd like to,' I said.

Raffi walked across to the couch and I patted the place beside me. I held his hand as we sat quietly together. He wiped his nose on the sleeve of his jumper. I had always thought that was a desperate filthy thing to do. It was what the boys at home did, but somehow seeing Raffi do it made me feel happy. It was such a childish thing to do that it pleased me.

We stayed like that for a long time. We said nothing but it didn't feel awkward and I didn't want to push him into telling me anything that he wasn't ready to tell me. Then he started to speak.

'Alice's baby died four years ago, on Christmas Eve. We haven't had a proper Christmas since then. No tree, no decorations, Alice doesn't even get out of bed, she just cries and cries. The whole thing is miserable. You can't leave us.'

'Your father will be with you; you won't be alone and anyway, I have a feeling that this Christmas will be different. Alice is happy and this baby is strong, she is looking forward to bringing this baby home.'

'But what if the same thing happens again? How do you know that it won't?'

'Well, I don't, but wouldn't it be a very sad if we were always waiting for something bad to happen?'

'I wish we had never left America, Rose.'

'You were happy there?'

He nodded. 'I went to school for a while.'

'Did you enjoy school?'

'Yes, I did. I had lots of friends and there were parties and I enjoyed myself, but then Alice lost the baby and everything changed. I never went back to school. I couldn't leave her, you see. I still got to see my friends though and I could help Aunt Martha to take care of Alice. Then I was told that we were leaving Brooklyn and coming to England. No one asked if it was what I wanted to do. Nobody asked if I would miss my friends or Aunt Martha, they just told me we were leaving and they tried to make it sound like a big adventure. David said that Alice would stop being sad if we came to London but she hasn't, has she?'

'Some days she's happy,' I said.

'But don't you see, Rose? That's worse. If she was sad all the time then I'd know what to do. I'd read to her and bring her tea. But there are days when she is laughing and she never says what she's laughing at and she puts horrible loud music on the gramophone and wants me to dance with her and it frightens me and I want to go home.'

I put my arm around his thin little shoulders and he leaned against me. 'It would frighten me too.'

'I'm sorry I said you were stupid, Rose.'

'I suppose when we're angry, we all say things we don't mean.'

Raffi smiled. 'Do you?'

'I did once. You see, my daddy died and I was very angry and I didn't know what to do with all my anger. I wanted to hurt someone because I was hurting. I couldn't hurt God because He's God and He died on the cross to save us, so I took my anger out on poor Mrs Hogan the baker's wife.'

'What did you do?'

'I told her that I thought it was high time she shaved off her moustache.'

'The baker's wife had a moustache?'

'A big, hairy, black one.'

'I thought only men had moustaches.'

'Well, Mrs Hogan had one.'

'Was she very angry?'

'I don't know because I ran out of the shop. I ran all the way home and I cried all the way, because I had been unkind to a good woman who had never been unkind to me.'

'So, what did you do then?'

'I told Mammy what I had done.'

'Was she cross?'

'No.'

'Why not?'

'Because she knew that I was not an unkind girl. She wiped away my tears and took me down to the end of the garden where the roses grow and she picked a bunch of them and told me to give them to Mrs Hogan.'

'And did you?'

I nodded. 'I gave her the roses and I said that I was terrible sorry and that she had a very nice moustache.'

'And did she forgive you?'

'Yes, and do you know why?'

Raffi shook his head. 'Because she knew that I was not a bad girl, just an angry one, because I had lost my daddy. That's why I'm not angry with you, Raffi, because I know that you are not an unkind boy, just an angry one.'

Raffi started to giggle.

'What are you laughing at?' I said.

'Poor Mrs Hogan's moustache.'

Then I started to giggle, until we were laughing so much that I got a pain in my tummy. That's when Alice came into the room.

'What on earth is causing such hilarity?' she said, smiling.

Raffi could hardly speak. 'Mrs Hogan's moustache,' he managed to blurt out.

'Well, you can tell me all about it on our way into town to get a Christmas tree.'

Raffi ran to Alice and flung his arms around her. 'Did you know that Rose is going home for Christmas, Alice?' he said. 'But don't worry, she'll be back.'

Alice and me smiled at each other over Raffi's head.

'Of course she will,' said Alice. 'Rose will never leave us, will you, Rose?'

'No, Alice, I will never leave you,' I said, crossing my fingers behind my back.

Chapter Twenty-One

My heart was bursting with joy as the green fields of home emerged through the mist. I breathed in the smell of Ireland. I gazed at the criss-cross of fields and the humble cottages dotted around the hills. I wanted to gather it all up in my arms and never let it go.

My fingers closed around the pendant that Alice had given me for Christmas. The stone felt cool in my hand.

'This beautiful aquamarine will keep you safe on the water, Rose,' she'd said. 'For this is the crystal that chose you. And the crystal that will bring you back to us.'

I couldn't match her present but I handed her the turquoise heart that Raffi and I had found in a tiny little shop not far from the house. Alice's eyes had filled with tears as she ran her fingers across its smooth surface, then she closed her eyes and held it to her cheek.

'I know it's not much,' I'd said.

'Oh, darling Rose, it's everything and it's everything because you gave it to me. I shall keep it with me always and whenever I look at it, I shall think of you.'

Raffi had given me a book. 'Someday you will be able to read it, Rose. It's called *Treasure Island* and it's wonderful. Aunt Martha gave it to me and now I'm giving it to you.'

'I can't take this, Raffi,' I'd said.

'Yes, you can and one day we shall read it together. So you see, you have to come back. You *will* come back, won't you, Rose?'

I didn't answer his question but I took him in my arms and kissed his cheek. 'I shall light a candle for you at Midnight Mass, Raffi. Now off you go while I pack my bag.'

Raffi had stood in the doorway staring at me. 'We need you, Rose. Me and Alice, we need you.'

'I know,' I said gently.

It had been a rough crossing but David had booked a cabin for me and the motion of the big ship had rocked me to sleep. I had come up on deck early, because I was desperate to see land, *my* land. As the ship got closer to Cork, people were waving from the banks, welcoming their people home. There had been no welcome when I'd sailed into Wales, no waving from that other place.

As the ship sailed down the River Lee and into Cork harbour, I went back to my cabin and collected my things. I was home.

I wasn't expecting anyone to meet me but there on the dock was Father Luke, waving and smiling. I joined the queue of people struggling down the gangplank with cases and children, all looking happy to be home this Christmastime amongst their own people.

Father Luke was at the end of the gangplank and he immediately took my case.

'It's good to see you, Rose,' he said, kissing my cheek.

'Thank you for meeting me, Father. I wasn't expecting to see anyone here.'

'Well sure, I had a meeting up here in the convent yesterday, so I decided to stay with the nuns, so that I was able to meet you this morning.'

'Well, it was good of you, Father, and it's lovely to see a friendly face.'

At last we reached the outskirts of the town. We passed the lighthouse, standing tall and proud, looking out over my beloved Blackwater. We passed Minnie's ice cream shop, where me and Polly would go when we had a few pennies. We passed the Gardai station and the Presentation Convent where we had gone to school.

I smiled as we passed the end of Polly's hill and then at last, we turned into Cross Lane.

They were all waiting for me at the door and as soon as I got out of the car, they threw themselves at me. We were laughing and crying as they almost pushed me into the cottage. And there was Mammy, my beautiful mammy, with her arms open and tears running down her cheeks. Oh, to be in her arms again and to know that I was loved. 'I'm home, Mammy,' I said, looking into her beautiful eyes. 'I'm home.'

'God is good,' she said. 'For He has brought you back to us.'

Mammy had put on a grand spread and we tucked into sausages and eggs and bacon and black pudding. Everyone was talking at once, they all wanted to know about England and what the family were like and were they good to me. A thousand questions and oh, it was lovely.

'Will you give the girl some peace to eat her food,' said Mammy, laughing.

'Oh, I don't mind,' I said. 'It's just grand to be home, ask away.'

Mammy was smiling at me. 'You look well, Rose; I'd say that England is suiting you.'

I didn't know what to say, because in many ways I loved being with Alice and Raffi and David but there was a part of me that felt out of my depth, as if I was acting a part, because I didn't think that the real me was good enough.

They were all staring, waiting for me to say something. 'It's different,' was all I could manage.

'But they're good to you, Rose?' whispered Agnes, looking worried.

'Oh, they are, love, it's just not home.'

'Ah well,' said Mammy. 'It would be strange alright, if you weren't missing your home.'

'What's the boy like?' said Bridgy, biting into a sausage.

'Don't speak with your mouth full, Bridgy,' said Mammy.

'Sorry, Mammy. But what's the boy like, Rose?'

'Raffi is like no other boy that I ever met.'

Bridgy waited until she'd finished her mouthful of sausage. 'What's wrong with him then, Rose?'

'I didn't say that there was anything wrong with him, he's just not like the boys round here. He has an old head on young shoulders.'

'Jesus, Rose, where did he get that old head from?'

This made us all laugh. Bridgy always made us laugh.

'You're a tonic, Bridgy Brown,' I said.

'Have you met any decent lads?' said Kathy.

'I'm sure she is too busy with the family to be meeting lads, decent or not,' said Mammy.

Kathy made a face. 'Isn't that an awful shame.'

'Mammy's right though,' I said. 'I don't have time for boys.'

'But you must have time off,' persisted Kathy.

'I suppose I must.'

Kathy lifted her eyes up to heaven. 'You mean you don't know?'

'Well, as long as Alice is alright, I can pretty much do what I like.'

'Alice?' said Mammy.

'The lady I work for.'

Mammy looked shocked. 'You call the mistress by her name?'

'I didn't want to, Mammy, I thought it was disrespectful, but she insisted. I couldn't get used to it at first, but now it just seems natural.'

'Well, that's the oddest thing I ever heard.'

'Is it because they're Yanks?' said Kathy.

'Maybe.'

'I think it's lovely,' whispered Agnes. 'For aren't we are all God's children, created in His image?'

'Well, if you ask me,' said Bridgy, 'they all sound a bit odd.'

'But aren't we all a bit odd?' whispered Agnes.

'I'd say you're right, love,' said Mammy, smiling.

'And some are odder than others,' said Kathy. 'That gobshite Orla Feeny across the lane for one.'

'You say you can't go out unless she is alright? Is the woman ill?' said Mammy.

I didn't know what to tell them. I didn't want them worrying and fretting about me and anyway, there was nothing wrong really. I could feel my eyes getting heavy. I'd been travelling since yesterday morning. Mammy noticed.

'Enough now, girls,' she said. 'Rose needs to rest.'

'I'm afraid I do,' I said, unable to stifle a yawn.

'Away with you then,' she said.

The little room was chilly, so I got under the blanket fully clothed. My head was still spinning from the motion of the boat. Oh, but it was so lovely to be home. Alice, Raffi, David and London seemed like a lifetime away, as if it had all been a dream. I looked at the picture of the Sacred Heart on the wall and I closed my eyes and slept.

When I woke up, it was dark outside the little window and I had no idea what time it was. I hurried downstairs. 'Am I too late to meet Polly off the Thrupenny Rush?' I said.

'You've plenty of time, love, and I'm sure she'll be delighted to see you.'

'Not as delighted as I'll be,' I said, running back up the stairs. Oh, I couldn't wait to see my friend again. Thrupenny Rush, here I come.

Chapter Twenty-Two

I hurried through town. I wanted to be waiting there on the station when the train pulled in.

The wind coming off the sea was bitterly cold. I unwrapped the scarf that Mammy had put around my neck and covered my ears with it instead.

Billy Ogg was pacing up and down the platform, rubbing his hands and stamping his feet.

'You're home then, I see,' he said. 'London not good enough for you then, Rose Brown?'

'London is grand, Billy Ogg.'

'Well, I hope it stays fine fer ya.'

'I'm sure it will, Billy.'

There was no shelter on the station, so when it rained you got soaked and when it was sunny, you nearly scorched to death.

'The bloody train's late again,' said Billy. 'So, I'll be sending it back early. I have a schedule to stick to.'

'Yer all sunshine and roses, aren't ya, Billy?'

I was mightily relieved when the train came rattling down the rails.

'Stand back, stand back,' he yelled at me.

'Where do you want me to stand, Billy, on the beach?'

Billy glared at me and waved his little red flag.

Jesus, he was a baggage of a man and the biggest fool in Ballykillen.

The train chugged into the station and there, amidst a cloud of white smoke, was Polly. She started running towards me. We fell into each other's arms, laughing and crying.

'Oh, it's good to see you, Rose,' she said. 'I've missed you something terrible.'

'I've missed you too, Polly, oh I have. I suppose we'd better start running.'

'We don't have to. I told Mrs Mullen that you were coming home and she gave me the holiday off, so that we can spend it together. Dervla the snitch is taking my place. If looks could kill, I would have been dead and buried.'

'Poor Dervla,' I said.

'Poor Dervla, me eye! She's the devil's spawn. She has me brains mashed with her goings-on.'

'But you have to feel sorry for the girl,' I said.

'Jesus, Rose, has England turned you into a saint?'

'I hope not, but it *has* taught me a lot about people and what makes them the way they are.'

'We have to meet up tomorrow, Rose, and then you can tell me everything. I'm only dying to know.'

We held hands and started to walk home.

'I'm frozen,' said Polly. 'It's colder here than in Cork.'

I nodded. 'That will be the sea, but who cares? We're home and it's Christmas and tomorrow we can go to Midnight Mass together.'

As we walked through the dark streets of this town I knew so well, people were calling out to us, welcoming us home. It was lovely to be back amongst my own kind. This was where I belonged. This was where I could truly be myself.

I left Polly at the bottom of her lane and walked on to my house. Orla Feeny was leaning against a wall, chatting to a boy.

'Yer home then,' she said, sneering at me.

'Very observant, Orla,' I said.

'Get you, Rose Brown, in England five minutes and you're already posing mad and using fancy words.'

'Go fry yer nose, ya little snipe,' I said.

I was smiling as I went into the cottage; my rise to sainthood hadn't lasted long.

It was warm and cosy in the little room, with a bright fire burning in the grate and holly decorating the fireplace.

'What about the letter, Mammy?' whispered Agnes.

'Oh dear God, I forgot,' said Mammy, standing up and going over to the dresser.

'You have a letter, Rose,' said Agnes softly.

'Who would be sending me a letter?'

'I'd say it's that sailor you were canoodling with,' said Kathy, grinning.

Thinking about Erik made me smile. We had been together for such a short time and yet I felt a connection with him that I had never felt with any other boy. I hadn't heard from him, so I was thinking that he hadn't felt the same. I suppose that sometimes you have to let things go but I would never forget him, or that special day we spent together.

Mammy handed me a white envelope. The writing on the front was all swirls and loops.

'He has a lovely hand, doesn't he?' said Mammy. 'I'd say the lad had a good education.'

Agnes whispered in my ear. 'Do you want me to read it to you, Rose?'

'I would, Agnes,' I said, smiling at her. 'Shall we go upstairs?'

'But we're only dying to know what he has to say,' said Kathy, making a face.

'You mean *you're* dying to know,' said Mammy. 'Let the girl have a bit of privacy.'

'Don't worry, Kathy, I'll let you know,' I said.

'Well, don't be long.'

Me and Agnes sat on the bed and I opened the envelope. I recognised Erik's name at the bottom of the page.

'Kathy's right,' I said, smiling. 'It's from Erik.'

'How do you know that?'

'Alice is teaching me to read, Agnes. I don't know many words yet but I know the sounds.'

'Oh, that's wonderful,' she said. 'Do you want to try?'

'No, I will be too slow and I want to hear what he has to say.'

We lay close together on the bed and Agnes started to read.

Dear Rose,

I hope this letter finds you safe and well. Even though we had so little time together, I find myself thinking of you constantly. That one beautiful day we spent at your haunted abbey comes back to me as if it were yesterday. I remember your two delightful sisters running around picking berries and you and I sitting together beside the lovely Blackwater River.

I don't know if, or when, I shall see you again but if I ever find myself in Cork, could I perhaps come and see you at the hotel where you work? Savages, wasn't it?

Please remember me to your lovely family.

With love,
Erik xx

'That was a lovely letter, Agnes, don't you think so?'

'I think it was a very loving and respectful letter.'

'Yes, I think so too.'

'Will I read it again, Rose?'

'Yes, please.'

Chapter Twenty-Three

The next morning, I went to call for Polly. I dipped my finger in the holy water font just inside the door.

'God bless all here,' I said.

'Amen,' said Mrs Butler. She was stirring something in a big pot over the fire that smelt like roadkill. Mrs Butler wasn't known for her cooking skills. I hoped she wasn't going to invite me to dinner.

'Ah, Rose,' she said. 'It's grand to see you home for the holidays.'

'It's lovely to *be* home. Where is everyone?' I said, looking around.

'The boys are off down the woods gathering holly, as we're lacking a bit of festive cheer in the house. Sean is asleep and the ole feller is propping up the bar at Cohan's.'

'Where's Polly?'

'She hasn't risen from her bed but God love her, it's not often she has a bit of a lie-in, so I'm leaving her.'

'Shall I come back later?'

'No, you go up, she'll eat the face off me if I tell her you were here and I let you go.'

I was smiling as I went up the narrow staircase and into Polly's bedroom. All I could see was a lump in the bed and Polly's beautiful hair, spread out across the pillow.

'Polly?' I whispered.

The lump in the bed didn't move.

'Polly?' I said a bit louder.

'Jesus, Mammy, will you let me sleep,' she mumbled.

'It's me, Polly, it's Rose.'

Polly poked her head out from under the blankets and grinned at me.

'I thought you were Mammy.'

'Your mammy said she was leaving you to sleep.'

Polly pushed herself up the bed and leaned her head against the wall. 'Get in with me,' she said, shifting over.

The bed was tiny but I managed to squeeze myself in beside Polly.

'So, tell me everything and don't leave anything out.'

'Don't you want to go for a walk?'

'No, I bloody don't! I'm happy to stay here all day.'

'We could go to the hotel for a cup of tea and a bun.'

Polly sighed. 'Well, by the smell of what's coming from downstairs, I won't be eating anything here, that's for sure.'

'I'll go and talk to your mammy while you get ready.'

'Grand, so.'

'Is she awake?' said Mrs Butler, as I walked downstairs.

I nodded. 'We thought we'd take a walk out the strand.'

'Are you mad altogether, Rose Brown? You'll freeze to death out there.'

'We wanted some fresh air.'

'It'll be fresh, alright.'

Polly came running down the stairs. 'We'll be off then, Mammy,' she said.

'I'll save you both a grand bit of stew, it will be something for you to look forward to after your walk.'

'I'd rather gouge me eyes out than eat that stuff,' said Polly as we walked down the hill. 'Even the bloody dog has the sense not to eat it.'

'The boys eat it though, don't they?'

'As long as they have something hot and deceased on the plate they're delighted.'

I laughed and linked my arm through hers. It was so lovely to be with my dearest friend, walking through the town that I had missed so much.

'Isn't this grand?' said Polly, smiling at me.

'I wish I could stay here forever and never have to leave again.'

Polly stopped walking and stared at me. 'Really?' she said. 'You'd rather be here in this one-bit town than living in a swanky house in London? You must be losing what little brain you had, Rose Brown.'

'Maybe I am,' I said.

We started walking again. The wind coming off the sea was bitterly cold. 'Shall we run?'

'Let's,' she said, grinning.

We ran the rest of the way and were soon outside the hotel.

'Shall we sit on the rocks before we go in?' I said.

'Are ya mad? It's bloody freezing.'

'I've missed the sea, Polly.'

'Jesus, couldn't you get someone to take a picture of it?'

'It wouldn't be the same, you can't smell a picture.'

'Well, just for a bit then, but I wouldn't do it for anyone else, Rose Brown.'

We linked arms and ran across the road. The sea was rough and grey with little white tips on the tops of the waves that rolled into the shore but oh, it gave me such joy. This was what I'd missed. The flat rocks were damp and as cold as ice, so we stood up. Polly was stamping her feet and blowing on her hands.

'If you had a stack of money, what house would you live in?' said Polly, turning around and pointing to the row of beautiful houses that ran the length of the strand and looked out over the sea.

This was where the rich people lived. The girls all went to the Loretto, which was the posh school at the edge of town. They wore brown gymslips and yellow blouses and they wouldn't give you the time of day if they passed you on the street.

'Sure, I'd never have the money to live in one of those and neither would you.'

Polly sighed. 'But just say you did, which one would you choose?'

I knew exactly which one I would choose; I'd been looking at it for years. 'The pink one with the balcony,' I said. 'So that every morning when I drew back the curtains—'

'The velvet curtains,' said Polly, butting in.

'Okay, when I drew back the velvet curtains…'

'The pink velvet curtains,' said Polly, grinning.

'Jesus, Polly, it will be meself that's living there and I'll choose me own curtains, thanks very much.'

'Just trying to help but don't you think that pink velvet curtains would be the height of elegance?'

'Well, my curtains would be blue and every morning when I drew them back, I would be looking at nothing but the sea. I'd have a little chair on the balcony and I'd sit there with me cup of tea and thank God for the bit of money He'd given me and for the wonders of His universe. Which would you choose?'

'The one with the big iron gates.'

'Why that one?'

'Because it's the poshest. Now, let's go to the hotel before me ears fall off and I hope Mary Coyne has lit the bloody fire.'

We walked in and were immediately enveloped in the warmth coming from the big fireplace in the corner of the room.

'Ladies?' said Mary, who was sitting behind the desk. Mary was Jimmy's sister. Me and Polly had gone to school with her and she was great craic. 'Are you booking into the executive suite?'

'No,' said Polly. 'We're meeting Clark Gable for a cup of tea.'

'You do right,' said Mary, grinning. 'Sit yourself down by the fire and I'll bring it over.'

'Yer a grand girl, Mary Coyne,' I said.

'And a couple of apple cakes,' said Polly.

'Certainly, madam,' said Mary, grinning.

We stood in front of the roaring fire, our hands stretched out towards the flames.

'Heaven,' said Polly, sighing.

Mary came across with the tea and buns and we sat down at the table.

'England suits you, Rose,' she said. 'Yer looking grand.'

'That's what Mammy said.'

'No one's ever told me that Cork city suits me,' said Polly, making a 'poor me' face.

'That's because you always look gorgeous, Polly Butler.'

Polly grinned. 'That'll be it then.'

'I'll leave you to catch up then, girls. Give me a shout if you need a fill up.'

'Thanks, Mary,' I said, smiling at her. 'She doesn't change, does she?' I said to Polly.

'Ah, she's a lovely old slob of a girl,' said Polly, biting into the bun. 'Always has been. She's doing a line with Liam Cokeley. I'd say it's serious; they make a lovely couple.'

'Ah, they would, Liam has always been a nice lad.'

'Anyway, I don't want to be talking about the goings-on in Ballykillen. Tell me about London. Tell me all about Mr and Mrs Townsend.'

'Alice and David are lovely to me.'

'Alice and David?'

I nodded.

'You call them Alice and David?'

'Mammy thought it was strange as well and Bridgy said it was awful odd.'

'Well, I'd agree with the pair of them.'

'I didn't have a choice in the matter, Polly, because that's what they told me to call them.'

'Mind you, they are Yanks.'

I didn't speak right away.

'Is there something you're not telling me, Rose?'

'They're hiring a nanny, for when the baby is born.'

Polly frowned. 'But isn't that why you're there? Why would they be wanting a nanny?'

'It turns out I'm not there to look after the children.'

'But that's what you were led to believe.'

'I know it was.'

'So, what in God's name are you doing there?'

'I know this sounds strange, Polly, but I'm there to help look after Alice.'

Polly frowned. 'What's wrong with her, then? I mean if yer woman's ill, that feller should have told you, yer not a bloody nurse. He got you there under false pretences.'

I knew it would be hard for Polly to understand but it was such a relief to talk to someone about it.

'I suppose he did.'

'There's no suppose about it, Rose, you've been taken advantage of and my advice to you is, don't go back.'

'Alice isn't sick, not the kind of sick where you have to stay in bed.'

'Is she in a wheelchair?'

'No.'

'Then why does she need looking after?'

'It's hard to explain, Polly.'

'Give it a try.'

'She's fragile and sort of childlike, she doesn't seem to know how to think for herself.'

'Is she like the unfortunates up at the Workhouse?'

'Oh no, nothing like that. Alice is like no one I've ever met before. David and Raffi feel it's their job to protect her. I think I am there to support Raffi when David is working.'

'But what exactly does she need protecting *from*?'

I thought about what Polly had just said. 'Herself, I think.'

'Herself?'

'She had a little girl after Raffi. The baby only lived for a short while. She died in Alice's arms.'

'That's desperate sad, Rose.'

'I don't think she has ever got over it and now she's expecting again and David and Raffi are watching her every move.'

'I do feel sorry for her, Rose, of course I do, but look how many women in the town have lost babies and children and they just have to get on with things.'

I'd been thinking the same thing myself but of course I could never say anything.

'The thing is, Polly, there's something about Alice that makes you want to look after her, like it's a privilege. Maybe women like Alice are not as strong as the women we know.'

'She's kind to you, though?'

I nodded. 'She's teaching me to read.'

'Well, for all her oddness, she seems to be good to you.'

'They all are.'

'Then I'll stop worrying, for I'd say that you have enough sense to work it all out for yourself.'

I rummaged in my bag and handed Polly the letter. 'Guess who?'

'The Adonis?'

'The very man.'

Polly took the letter out of the envelope and read the single sheet of paper.

'Ah, that's a lovely letter, Rose, very polite and not a bit flowery, that would put you in the awkward position of having to declare yourself.'

'I thought so too.'

'Will you write back?'

'I haven't mastered the writing bit yet but Agnes will do it for me, I just have to tell her what to write.'

'Do you think you'll ever see him again?'

'I shouldn't think so.'

'No, I suppose you're right, so is there any point in keeping up the correspondence?'

'Well, I'm thinking that it can do no harm to have a penfriend and then when I learn the writing, it will give me someone to practise on.'

'That's a sensible way to look at it, Rose, as long as you don't give the poor feller false hope and stop him from walking out with someone closer.'

I nodded. 'He was lovely, though.'

'And easy on the eye,' said Polly, grinning.

'Agnes would say to leave it in the hands of the Lord, so I think I'll do that.'

'Well, let's hope the Lord isn't too busy, then.'

'I'm asking Him for a special intention at Mass tonight.'

'That should do the trick, Rose. I'd say Himself would be duty-bound to listen to a special intention and if you're really earnest about it, it might even take you to the top of the list.'

'Well, let's hope he's not too busy, it being his birthday an' all.'

'Let's hope,' said Polly.

Chapter Twenty-Four

Oh, I loved Midnight Mass. Every year the church would be so packed that people would have to sit on the steps outside. Even the ole fellers staggered out of the pubs and put in an appearance. They might still be holding pints of Guinness and swaying all over the place but God love 'em, they were there and I'm sure God thought no less of them.

I met Polly outside and we made straight for the front, where we had a good view of the nativity scene. I knelt down and gazed at the baby Jesus laying in the manger, with Mary and Joseph smiling down at him. It was the same figures that I had been looking at all my life. When we were younger, me and my sisters used to help set it up. Agnes and Bridgy still did. The stable, with the star overhead, guiding the wise men to where the baby Jesus lay in the manger, the shepherds and the angels – they were all there, just as they had always been, every Christmas Eve of my life.

I turned to Polly and we exchanged smiles. What was it about the church on Christmas Eve? That sense of excitement and hope, the feeling of community that was strongest at this time of year?

We had to budge up on the pew to make space for more people. Everyone was happy and smiling and wishing each other blessings of the season, it was as if I'd never been away. I was glad to see their welcoming faces, glad to exchange words with these people I had known all my life. After a while I stopped looking around me and sat quietly, opening my heart up to the magic of this Midnight Mass.

Candles burned on the altar amongst the holly and ivy and swathes of pine, cut to decorate the sloping stone ledges in front of the beautiful stained-glass windows. The dark reaches of the church flickered in the candlelight: the vaulted roof, the shadows behind the pillars, the secret, sacred places where church business took place. Behind me I could hear the murmur of a multitude of voices and then suddenly, as if by magic, those voices fell silent and a single voice rose up into the darkness, clear as the sound of glass being struck by a knife.

'Once in royal David's city…'

And we were lost in the magic of Christmas.

Once Mass was over, me and Polly knelt in front of the statue of the Blessed Virgin and lit a candle for the poor souls in Purgatory and the dead babies in Limbo. I didn't actually know where Limbo was, but I didn't like the sound of it. I mean, it wasn't the baby's fault that it had died before being baptised, was it? I wasn't that keen on the sound of Purgatory either but apparently if you prayed hard enough, Jesus would let one of them out. Perhaps he'd see his way clear to let a few of them out as it was his birthday.

I looked up at Mary's beautiful face smiling down at me. Something about her reminded me of Alice, perhaps it was the pure innocence of that smile. I hoped that the Townsends' Christmas would be as wonderful as mine. I hoped that Alice would find peace and I hoped that Raffi could find the child in him as Christmas morning dawned. I wished only the best for them all.

I looked back at Mary and was reminded of that other Mary, the young girl I'd met on the boat. I closed my eyes. 'Have pity on her, Jesus, in her time of trouble, for she is one of your own, and didn't you say yourself, "Suffer the little children to come unto me" and Mary Kelly is but a child who has lost her way.'

We walked slowly back through the dark streets of the town; we were in no hurry to end this beautiful night. The sky above the cottages shone with a million stars, like a blanket of diamonds covering our heads.

'I don't want to go home yet,' said Polly.

'Neither do I.'

We held hands and walked down to the quayside and sat on a bench, overlooking the river. It was so quiet; the only sound was the splashing of water against the old stone wall and the movement of the boats tied up on the quay. The water was inky black, the only light coming from the lighthouse further up the coast.

It was cold but I didn't mind. Even Polly wasn't complaining and she hated the cold.

'Remember when we used to watch the boys jumping off the wall?' she said.

I laughed. 'It was *you* that used to drag me down here. I had no interest in watching boys jumping off the wall.'

'You always came, though.'

'I couldn't say no to you, Polly Butler, you were the only friend I had.'

'Wouldn't you love to just go back to those days?'

I looked out across the river. 'I don't think we can go back, Polly. I think we have to keep moving forward and learning and growing.'

'Do you know what, Rose? I think that England is changing you.'

'Maybe it is and maybe that's not such a bad thing. I mean, what's the point of discovering new things if it doesn't change you in some way?'

'Well, I'm learning nothing in that bloody hotel except an urge to commit murder on a daily basis.'

'You're learning how to make a bed,' I said, grinning.

'That pair of bloody eejits that are my brothers could learn how to do that.'

I laughed. 'Ah sure, they're not so bad.'

'It's easy for you to say, Rose, you don't have to live with them.'

We sat quietly together, watching the river flow by. Twinkling lights from the cottages on the far bank cast patterns of colour on the black water.

'When are you going back?' said Polly.

'Tuesday, so I'll have St Stephen's Day at home. What about you?'

'The same. I'll be on the bloody Thrupenny Rush at six o'clock Tuesday morning. I want something different, Rose, but I haven't figured out what it is yet.'

'Would you like to work for a family in London?'

'Well, that would be a start.'

'I could ask the parish priest, Father Tom, if he knows anyone who wants a girl.'

'Will you?'

'I will, of course.'

'We could see each other,' said Polly, smiling. 'Now wouldn't that be grand?'

'That would be wonderful,' I said. 'I wouldn't miss home so much if you were there.'

'Are you definitely going back, then? Because I sense you have doubts.'

'You sense right. I have had my doubts but what will I do if I come home?'

'Is there any other reason you don't want to go back? Other than the fact that they all sound a bit cracked?'

'I suppose it's because I don't really know my place there. My only job seems to be to look after Alice and I'm not sure she always needs looking after. I'm always afraid of saying or doing the wrong thing and then Raffi gets very cross.'

'The boy?'

I nodded.

'But he's a child, why would you care what he thinks?'

'He says, "You have to listen, Rose, you have to protect Alice."'

'Jesus, Mary and Holy Saint Joseph, are you telling me that the boy calls his mammy by her name as well?'

'I know, I couldn't take it in either.'

'Trust you to land up with a family like that.'

'Let's forget about them, eh? It's Christmas Day tomorrow and I'm going to enjoy it.

'I'll come up to you after I've had me dinner. In fact, could you ask yer mammy to save me a bit, as God only knows what the mammy is going to put on the table.'

'I will, of course.'

I left Polly at the bottom of her hill and walked home under a sky that twinkled in the darkness of this perfect Christmas night.

Chapter Twenty-Five

'The fat man's been,' said Bridgy, shaking me awake.

I pushed myself up the bed and smiled at her. 'You must have been a good girl, love.'

'I've been an awful bold girl, Rose, but I went to Confession and I've had all me sins forgiven. I've a clean slate till I do something else.'

'Well, I'm pleased to hear it, Bridgy Brown.'

'I feel sorry for people who aren't Catholic, don't you, Rose? They have no one to forgive them and they're doomed to spend the rest of their lives lugging around all those sins. It must be a mighty burden to be carrying around.'

'Bridget Brown, what on earth would we do without you? Now, go and wake Agnes up!'

'What about Kathy, Rose? Will I wake Kathy?'

'Unless you want the face eaten off ya, I'd leave her be.'

'I'll not wake her then.' Bridgy stopped at the door. 'Happy Christmas, Rose.'

'Happy Christmas, Bridgy.'

I lay in bed, staring up at the ceiling. There was a damp patch in the corner that Agnes said looked like an angel but I'd always thought looked more like a rabbit.

I was awful confused about what to do. My heart was telling me to stay here at home and go back to work in the hotel. It wasn't so bad there and Mrs Mullen liked me, so I might be able to work my way up to a better position. I would see Polly every day and my family every Friday. It would be easy enough to get Agnes to write a letter to the Townsends, telling them that I was needed at home.

Just then, Agnes and Bridgy ran into the room and jumped up on the bed.

'I have me stocking, Rose,' whispered Agnes. 'Did yer man leave one for you?'

I laughed. 'I'm too old for stockings, Agnes.'

'Then you can share mine,' she said, squeezing in beside me.

'And mine,' said Bridgy, not to be bested by her sister.

'Yer good girls altogether,' I said, hugging them both.

Mammy had put the same things into the stockings as she put in every year and yet, as the girls poked around in the knobbly old socks and pulled out oranges, coloured pencils, little notebooks and new ribbons, these lowly gifts were greeted to the same oohs and ahs as if they were worth a million pounds.

'Shall we go downstairs?' said Bridgy, jumping off the bed.

Agnes's warm little body was cuddled up beside me and I didn't want to move. 'We'll be down in a minute,' I said.

'You can have my pencil and notepad,' whispered Agnes. 'So that you can practise your letters.'

'Thank you, love, but I don't know whether I'm going back.'

Agnes sat up and looked at me. 'But you said they were nice and that they were kind to you, why wouldn't you go back?'

'They *are* nice – in fact, they're lovely – but they are troubled.'

'Maybe that's why God sent you to them.'

'But I can't fix them.'

'Maybe you're not supposed to, maybe just being there is enough. People aren't always looking to be fixed. Some things can't be fixed; sometimes you just have to accept them. If people were always fixing things for you, how will you learn to fix them yourself? I've always thought that quiet acceptance is more healing than words.'

I smiled at my little sister. 'You have more wisdom than all of us put together, Agnes.'

'I listen a lot,' she whispered, smiling her sweet smile.

'Raffi says I don't listen enough.'

'Or maybe you're not telling him what he wants to hear. You will be okay, whatever you decide to do, Rose, for God will take care of you.' She pointed up to the ceiling. 'See that angel up there?' she said.

I looked up at the rabbit. 'Yes.'

'Well, I think that she has always taken care of you, even when you're not at home, like your very own guardian angel.'

I smiled to myself. It was comforting to know that I had my very own guardian angel, even if she did look like a rabbit.

Christmas dinner was magical. I looked around the table at my family, laughing and joking and enjoying just being together and I felt blessed. Mammy had placed white candles around the room and beside the statue of the Infant of Prague. The flickering light shone on his red cape, showing up where the bits of plaster had peeled off over the years. He had also lost one of his eyes along the way. Mammy had tried to paint a new one for him and Polly said it made him look cross-eyed, leaving his one good eye following you around the room like a demon but he had been there forever and home wouldn't be home without him.

Before eating, we prayed for our daddy, who should have been here beside us. A single tear ran down Mammy's face, which she quickly brushed away. She looked so beautiful in the candlelight, her hair a mixture of reds and browns and golds, like an autumn tree in all its glory. Her beauty made me think of Alice and I hoped that she too had found peace and happiness on this wonderful Christmas day.

After the dinner was cleared away, we sat on the floor around Mammy and opened our presents. It was almost dark outside the window, making it feel even cosier inside our little cottage. The peat fire burned merrily away in the grate, filling the room with its own special smell. Mammy rattled it with the poker and sent sparks flying out onto the rug.

We settled down to open our presents. Bridgy had drawn us all a picture of a donkey. 'Because I like donkeys,' she said, grinning and making us all laugh.

'And didn't Jesus ride into town on a donkey?' whispered Agnes.

'He did,' said Mammy. 'He did.'

We each had a grand bar of chocolate from Kathy and a medal each from Agnes. Mine was a St Christopher medal. 'He will keep you safe while you are away from us, Rose.'

Mammy had been secretly knitting scarves for us all and we pranced around the little room as if they were the Crown Jewels we had around our necks. It reminded me of Alice's Aunt Martha and Sarah Bernhardt.

I ran upstairs to the bedroom and took the presents out of my case. I hoped they would like them and not think that I was showing off with my English gifts. I had got them all a crystal on a chain. Not the real thing, of course, but the glass looked pretty.

I watched as they unwrapped them and I could see that they were only delighted with them and not a bit offended. 'These are your birthstones,' I said.

'Bridgy, your birthstone is sapphire, for September, and it means truth.'

'She'll have to work on that a bit then,' said Kathy, grinning.

'It's true,' said Bridgy, not in the least put out.

'What does mine mean?' said Kathy.

'Your stone is peridot for August and it means beauty.'

'Oh, I'm delighted with that and I shall tell everyone I meet, whether they want to hear it or not.'

When I had discovered Agnes's birthstone, the beautiful purple amethyst, I could hardly believe it.

'And yours, Agnes,' I said, putting my arm around her, 'is amethyst and it means wisdom.'

'It's beautiful,' she whispered.

I handed Mammy her brooch. 'This is pearl, the birthstone for June, and it means love.'

She gently touched my hair. 'Oh, Rose,' she said, 'you'll have me weeping again and this is not a day for tears.'

I looked around at my family and I realised that all the crystals in the world would never shine as brightly as these people that I loved so much.

Chapter Twenty-Six

Once dinner was over, I met up with Polly and we decided that even though it was chilly, we'd take a walk out the wood road.

It was one of those beautiful winter days when the frost sits on the branches of the trees like cotton wool and the ground crunches beneath your feet.

Our breath streamed in the cold air behind us as we walked. A little robin followed us, hopping from twig to twig, his red breast a brilliant flash of colour in a world that was silver, black and white.

We walked close together for warmth, our hands stuffed deep in our pockets, and I felt myself coming alive at the sight of this beautiful Irish countryside. The green patchwork of fields on the far bank were now covered in a silver frosting, like a Christmas cake. I hadn't realised until this moment how much I had missed it all, from the tall dark trees with their empty branches and twigs all frosty, sparkling in the thin winter sunshine, to the nettles and brambles that trailed along the side of the path, dead now but still beautiful in their frozen state.

It was a different kind of cold to the cold in London. It was a cold that was familiar, one that was in my blood.

We walked in silence until we came to the bridge, then we continued along the river bank.

The river changed with the seasons and every change held its own beauty. Today the water was calm and grey under this wintry sky. I looked further down the river and started giggling.

'What?' said Polly.

'I can just see the roof of old Mulligan's house and it reminded me of the day we went scrumping apples, the day I met you.'

'You were such a timid little thing, I felt I had to take you under me wing.'

'I'm glad you did, Polly,' I said, smiling at her.

'I'm glad I did too.'

We sat on some old logs beside the river.

'I can't sit here long,' said Polly. 'Me backside is only frozen.'

'Stand then,' I said, grinning at her.

Polly didn't move and I continued to watch the grey water flowing by. The river always gave me peace.

'Are you looking forward to going back, Rose, or are you dreading it?'

'Neither, really.'

'Well, you must feel something.'

'Of course I do. I've loved coming home but it makes going back really hard.'

'But you like it there? They're good to you?'

'They treat me like one of the family. They're different, that's all.'

'Then I'd fit in fine,' said Polly, 'because they couldn't be any more different than my bloody lot!'

I laughed. Polly always managed to make me laugh and I suppose it was laughable in a way; perhaps I was taking the whole thing far too seriously.

'I'm just not sure if I'm actually helping them. There are problems and I don't know how to fix it for them.'

'You shouldn't have to. Isn't it up to them to fix whatever's wrong themselves?'

'That's kind of what Agnes said.'

'Then I'm in good company, for your little sister is a wise dote of a girl.'

I smiled, thinking of my quiet little sister. 'She is.'

'Look, why don't you stop trying to make things better and just go along with it? I mean, what harm can that do? Then she can teach you to read and she can take you shopping in the swanky car and maybe even take you to a show. Now that's not so terrible, is it? Then if the three of them have yer brain mashed, you can come home.'

'So, I just stop trying?'

'Yes, that's all you have to do. Anyway, you have to go back.'

'Do I?'

'You said you'd ask the priest about a job for me.'

I linked my arm through hers. 'So, it's all about you then, is it?'

Polly grinned. 'And why wouldn't it be?'

'Why indeed?' I said, smiling at her. 'Listen, Mammy has invited a few neighbours in tonight, nothing special, just a bit of a do, will ya come?'

'Anything to get out of the house. Of course I'll come. I'll wear me Christmas jumper that the mammy gave me, it's only gorgeous. It's the first time she's ever bought me anything that wouldn't look better on Minnie Ogg. Are they coming?'

'I'm afraid so.'

'Well, let's hope that Billy doesn't get blathered with the drink.'

'We can only hope,' I said, grinning.

As it turned out, we all had a lovely time. Polly looked beautiful in her Christmas jumper, which was the colour of summer trees. It set off her red hair and pale skin and I felt proud to be her friend. Mammy had placed the last few roses of winter in a blue stone jug in the middle of the table. Agnes had lit candles beside the Infant of Prague and underneath the picture of St Francis of Assisi that had hung on the wall for as long as I could remember. The flame from the candles cast long shadows across the white plaster walls of the cottage. The room smelled of peat and Billy Ogg's pipe and the faint smell of roses.

Father Luke sang 'The Rose of Tralee' and we all joined in. Mrs Feeny recited 'The Lake Isle of Innisfree'. Orla, who was leaning against the door, raised her eyes up to heaven, as if her mother had shamed her. It was about time the skitty girl copped onto herself. Then, to everyone's surprise, Minnie Ogg got up, as casual as you like, and sang 'Danny Boy' and her beautiful clear voice had us all in tears. Who would have thought that such a sweet sound could ever come out of Minnie Ogg's mouth? The pair of them had always been a bit of a joke but I think that Christmas night, we all looked at Minnie in a different way. We gave her a thunderous applause when the last note faded away and she sat down as casually as she'd got up.

'Jesus,' said Polly, 'she has the voice of an angel! Where in all that's holy has she been hiding that all these years?'

'Life's full of surprises, Polly.'

'The woman could be on the stage with a voice like that.'

'Well, she'd have to change her name. She'd have a hard time conquering the musical world with a name like Minnie Ogg, however beautiful her voice was.'

'You'd think if God in his wisdom had chosen to give her such a gift, he'd have stopped her marrying Billy Ogg and ruining her career.'

'You'd think so, wouldn't you?'

It was very stuffy in the little room. What with the blazing fire and Billy Ogg's pipe, you could hardly draw breath. 'Let's go outside,' I said.

We walked to the end of the yard and sat on Daddy's bench. There was no moon, just a deep black sky that twinkled with a million stars.

Polly linked her arm through mine. 'So, what are you going to do?'

'I've been thinking about what you said and you're right. It's not my job to fix them, is it? I'm sure they coped perfectly well before I arrived.'

'And if they have yer head mashed, you can come home,' said Polly.

'I can, can't I?'

'I'm sure Dervla the snitch would be only delighted to see you back at Savages. I'm sure she's been on your mind.'

'Day and night, Polly, day and night.'

We sat in silence on the bench until the cold had seeped into our bones and we could sit no more. As we walked back up the path, Polly stopped and put her arms around me. 'I shall miss you, Rose,' she said.

'And I shall miss you, my darling Polly.'

Chapter Twenty-Seven

On St Stephen's Day, I was woken up at the crack of dawn by Agnes, who was whispering in my ear.

'Look out the window, Rose, look out the window.'

'Jesus, Agnes, it's the middle of the night! Will you let me sleep?'

'You can't sleep, Rose, for something wonderful has happened.'

'Have you woken anyone else up to see this wonderful thing that has happened? Or is it just me?'

'Just you, Rose.'

Bridgy stirred beside me and rolled over onto her tummy. I waited until she had settled, then reluctantly dragged myself out of the warm bed. 'Well, aren't I the lucky one?' I said.

'I knew you'd feel like that, Rose, that's why I woke you first. Look out of the window.'

I shivered as my feet touched the cold floor, then I pulled back the curtain and looked out; it was still barely light and I could see nothing wonderful. Was Agnes sleepwalking? 'What in God's name am I supposed to be looking at?'

'Keep looking, Rose.'

I peered out onto the lane until my eyes grew accustomed to the darkness. A pale wintry sun struggled through the dark sky, rising up behind the rooftops, rooftops that were as white as the driven snow. I felt a tingle in my tummy, like every Christmas morning of my life. I felt like a child again.

I grinned at Agnes. 'Put your warm coat on,' I said.

'Yes, Rose,' she said, disappearing out the door.

I ran downstairs and put a coat on over my nighty, pushed my feet into my boots, took two warm scarves from off the back of the door and waited for Agnes.

She came running down the stairs and I wrapped a scarf around her neck. We opened the back door as quietly as we could, so as not to raise the rest of the house and stepped out into the yard, catching our breath as the cold hit us. Neither of us said a word as we stared at the winter wonderland before us. The snow had fallen and covered everything in a soft white blanket that rounded the corners of roofs and walls and made hats on the fence posts. Everything was hidden beneath a layer of pristine white that made gentle shadows and sparkled in the moonlight.

We wrapped our arms around ourselves, turned and shared a smile. Our breath gathered around us before it melted into the air. The snow fell still and silently, flakes as big as my fingertips catching in our hair and on the shoulders of our coats.

The ground was pure white, like a blank page waiting to be written on. Snow covered the winter skeletons of Mammy's roses and the top of the old brick wall. I remembered how excited we used to be when we were children and the first snow came, with all the fun it promised. I had always loved our home at this time of year.

There was peace and stillness all around us. It was as silent as that other silent night so many years ago.

Agnes sighed and dropped to her knees.

'What are you doing?' I said, looking down at her.

'I'm thanking God for this wonderful gift, Rose.'

'Well, you can thank him standing up, Agnes Brown. Do you want to catch your death of cold and send your poor mother to an early grave?'

'I wouldn't want to do that, Rose.'

'Then get up off yer knees. I'm sure that God will make an exception and anyway, he'll be only delighted with you for thanking him. I don't suppose he gets thanked that often.'

I felt my sister's cold little hand slip into mine. 'I love you, Rose,' she whispered. 'And I will never forget this moment. I wish I could place it in a box and keep it forever.'

'You can place it in your heart, my sweet girl. It will be safe there and when you find yourself missing me, this snowy day will come back to you, down the rails and roads of your life.' I grinned at my little sister. 'Shall we?'

'Oh yes, Rose,' she whispered.

And so we lay in the snow and moved our arms up and down. We stayed like that until our teeth chattered and our fingers were numb. 'Bed now,' I said, getting up.

At the door we looked back and smiled at the two angels, laying side by side.

'It was wonderful, wasn't it, Rose?' whispered Agnes, as we climbed up the stairs. 'I was right to wake you, wasn't I?'

'Yes, my darling, you were right to wake me and yes, it was wonderful.'

Later, I called for Polly and we joined the rest of the kids up on the hill behind the graveyard. We thought ourselves far too grown up to be sliding down the field on a tin tray but oh, how we wanted to.

Polly linked her arm through mine. 'To hell with trying to be adults. Dermot!' she yelled, across the field.

'What?' shouted a dark-haired boy.

'Will ya give us a loan of yer tray?'

'What's it worth?'

'I'll give you twopence for sweets.'

Dermot walked across to us, carrying a tray. 'Make it threepence and it's yours.'

'You'll make a great business man one day, Dermot Casey,' said Polly, grinning at him.

The boy grinned back at her. 'You can have it for an hour.'

And so, on my last day home, me and Polly took turns sliding down the hill and screaming at the tops of our voices. Perhaps we hadn't quite put childish things away and oh, how wonderful that felt.

*

Our evening meal was a sad little affair. Mammy kept getting up from the table, saying she had to get something, but we all knew that she was crying. I got up and went across to her. 'Don't be sad, Mammy,' I said, putting my arms around her shoulders. 'This is my home and this is my family and I will always come back. I promise that I will always come back, for this is where my heart is.'

Mammy dried her eyes on her apron and brushed my hair back from my face. 'Of course you will, my darling girl, I don't doubt that for one moment and we will always be here waiting for you, but I will miss you, my Rose.'

'And I will miss you, Mammy, but let us have a nice meal, all of us together and let that be the memory I take away with me.'

'Shall we say a prayer?' whispered Agnes, as we sat back down. We held hands. 'Can I say the prayer, Mammy?' said Bridgy. 'I'd say Agnes has His ear more than you do, Bridgy Brown.' 'Ah sure, let her,' I said.

Bridgy closed her eyes. 'Dear Jesus, Kathy said you won't listen to me but I think you will, for didn't I help put the nativity up in the church and didn't I put a penny in the box for the brown babies?'

'Jesus,' said Kathy, 'yer man knows what you've done, you don't have to bend his ear!'

Bridgy glared at Kathy. 'I'm just jogging his memory.' She cleared her throat. 'Thank you for the snow and the lovely presents and thank you for sending Rose home to us and take care of her on the journey back to England.'

At which point, she burst into tears, starting the rest of us off.

Chapter Twenty-Eight

As the ship pulled away from the dock, I waved at the families lining the quayside. People around me were crying and calling out the names of loved ones that they were leaving. It was the saddest thing. It seemed that the children of this beautiful land were destined to forever leave its shores and yet the green hills of home always drew them back again.

It was freezing up on deck and I didn't want to see my homeland disappear into the mist so I went into the lounge bar. It smelt of beer and cigarettes but it was grand and warm. I got myself an orange juice and sat down beside a woman who had a baby on her lap.

The baby was dribbling and its chin looked red and sore.

'He's teething,' said the woman, 'and I'm not looking forward to the teeth coming through.'

I looked down at the baby and realised that he was one of God's special little angels. There was a little girl in the village who looked just like him. He gave me the sweetest smile, which lit up his little face.

'Oh, he's lovely,' I said.

The woman gently wiped his chin 'The priest says he's a blessing from God,' she said, 'but…'

I didn't know what to say. I couldn't trot out some words of wisdom because whatever I said wouldn't change anything and I was sure she'd heard all the wise words she wanted to hear and she was only sick of them, so I just touched her hand and she smiled, a smile that didn't quite reach her eyes.

'Would you take him for a minute?' she said. 'I'm desperate for the toilet.'

'Of course,' I said, reaching for him. 'What's his name?'

'Anthony, his name is Anthony.'

'Don't worry, I'll take good care of him.'

She nodded and made her way across the room.

The baby felt warm and heavy in my lap. 'Hello, Anthony,' I said. I stroked his hair, which was fine and almost white. He smelt of wee and sour milk but I thought that he was beautiful. 'You're beautiful,' I said. 'Do you know that? And special, very, very special.' He smiled up at me and then, seeming to like what he saw, snuggled into my arms, tucking his head just under my chin. I watched as his eyes closed, his fair lashes resting on his plump little cheek. I hoped that God would protect him from any sadness. I hoped that he would bless him and allow him to lead a happy life and that no one would ever take advantage of his innocence.

I watched the woman walking back towards me. She looked defeated and worn out but she smiled as she got close.

'Listen,' I said. 'I have a cabin that I have no use for. I would be delighted if you would take it, so that the pair of you can rest.'

'Oh, I couldn't, cabins cost a lot of money. It's very kind of you but I couldn't.'

'If it makes you feel better, I didn't pay for it, the man I work for did and as I'm not going to use it myself, it would be a shame if no one does.'

'Well, I *am* tired.'

'So, take it.'

'I will then and thank you, you are very kind.'

I handed Anthony to her and she smiled down at him.

'Goodbye, Anthony,' I said. 'Sleep tight.'

I got up and walked back on deck. I leaned over the rail and stared down at the grey water beneath me, the same grey as the sky above it. The waves were tipped with white foam that Mammy said were called white horses and I supposed they did look a bit like horses galloping for all they were worth across the sea. A trail of froth and bubbles trailed in the wake of the big ship before running into the choppy water.

I hoped that I was doing the right thing; I hoped that I could really be of some help, otherwise what was the point of going back? Polly's words came into my head. 'Just go along with it, Rose, and if they have yer brains mashed, you can just come home.' Yes, that was what I would do and if it didn't work out, then at least I would have tried.

If my reckoning was right, Alice's baby was due to be born in about three weeks' time. Raffi had said that Alice was very ill in her mind after she lost her little girl and I hoped that in this child, she would find peace and joy. That was what I hoped, but it would all depend on whether David and Raffi actually allowed Alice the space to become the mother she needed to be. I hoped that they would treat her like a young mother and not an invalid.

It was the middle of the night when the train finally chugged into Paddington station. I was so tired, I could barely stand up. I could still feel the movement of the ship beneath my feet, which made me very light-headed.

As I stepped down from the train, my eyes scanned the platform for David. What if they'd forgotten that I was coming back today? What if I was left here all night? I felt a burning sensation behind my eyes. I was exhausted and everything felt worse than it really was. *Cop on to yourself*, I thought, *you're not a baby. You're Rose Brown, Rose the brave, Rose the beloved daughter of Christina Brown.* I straightened my shoulders and wiped my eyes, just as I heard my name being called. I looked around and there was Raffi, tearing across the station, with the biggest smile on his face. He flung himself at me and as we hugged each other, I realised that

I'd actually missed him. Perhaps I even loved this strange little boy who carried such a burden on his young shoulders.

'Oh, Rose,' he said. 'I'm so very glad to see you. I thought that maybe you wouldn't come back and nothing would ever be the same without you here. That nanny has arrived and she's awful. She stays in bed all day and when she's not asleep, she's crying and wailing.'

Raffi seemed to have stored up all his words for the past five days; it was as if they'd been hovering on the tip of his tongue and now, he was spewing them out and hardly stopping for breath.

'I expect she's homesick, Raffi,' I said, smiling at him.

'I'm sure you were homesick, Rose, but you didn't expect the whole house to listen to you crying and weeping. I wish she'd go back to where she came from. Alice needs her rest, the last thing she needs is wailing Helen from Kerry.'

'I'm sure she'll be grand once she calms down, just be patient with her, Raffi.'

'Oh, I'm so glad you're home, Rose, everything will be better now.'

'Well, I'm here and all I want is my bed.'

Raffi laughed and picked up my case. 'We'll soon have you home. David is outside with the car, I wanted to be the one to meet you.'

I smiled at him. 'And I'm glad you did.'

'Are you, Rose? Are you really glad to see me?'

'And why wouldn't I be?'

Raffi shrugged his shoulders. 'I don't think I'm to everybody's taste.'

'Well, you're to *my* taste, Raphael Townsend, and the rest of them can go fly a kite.'

Raffi laughed. 'I'm glad,' he said, taking my hand.

I didn't ask about Alice as we walked out of the station. I didn't want anything on my mind that would stop me from sleeping. Tomorrow would be soon enough.

Chapter Twenty-Nine

I was sitting beside the fire, facing Alice. Her hands were resting gently on her belly and she looked happy and contented. Raffi had put a blanket over her knees, even though the heat from the flames made the room warm enough.

'We've missed you, Rose,' she said, smiling her beautiful smile.

'You look well,' I said.

'I am well, I really am, and it's all because of you, my darling girl.'

'Me?'

'Yes, you. You talked about the baby, which David and Raffi couldn't. You made me believe that I really could be a mother this time. You gave me hope, Rose, and I shall always be grateful to you.'

'You've nothing to be grateful for, in fact it could have been awful. You might have been angry with me for asking you to face something that you weren't ready to face. You might have thought I'd forgotten my place.'

'Have you learned nothing about us, Rose? Your place is wherever you want it to be. We are the same, you and I, and I will not have you speaking about *place*.'

I grinned at her. 'Well, that's telling me.'

Alice laughed, that amazing laugh that was so full of joy. If we were in a room filled with people, I would still know Alice's laugh. 'I hope so,' she said, trying to look cross but failing miserably, which made us both giggle.

'And what's all this merriment about?' said David, walking over to Alice and kissing the top of her head.

'We have Rose back, my darling, isn't it wonderful?'

'It is indeed and she makes you happy?'

'She makes me very happy, David.'

It was strange, because they were talking about me as if I wasn't there and it was making me feel strange again and then I remembered Polly's words: '*Why don't you stop trying to make things better and just go along with it?*'

'It's lovely to be back,' I said, smiling at them both.

'Shall we do some reading, Rose?'

'As long as you're not too tired.'

'I have all day to rest, I want to spend some time with you.'

'That would be grand, then.'

I hadn't been practising my letters while I'd been home and I struggled with some of the words.

'I'll tell you what,' said Alice. 'I'll read the page first and then you read it. It will give you an idea of what the story is about.'

This proved to be a great success and as the days passed, the black scrawl became words and the words became a story. My eyes filled with tears as I looked up. 'I'm reading,' I said. 'I'm actually reading.' I looked at her beautiful face. 'Thank you, Alice.'

She took me in her arms and we were laughing and crying. 'My clever, clever Rose,' she said. 'My clever, clever Rose.'

I hadn't seen the weeping nanny, I'd only heard her. She seemed to be nailed to her bed and expected Mrs Berry to take all her meals up to her room on a tray.

'Three flights,' said Mrs Berry. 'Three bloody flights because she's too lazy to shift herself. Am I her servant or what? I've a mind to let her starve.'

'You won't though, will you?' I said, smiling.

'I suppose not, I wouldn't want it on me conscience.'

Anyway, I decided it was time to make meself known; perhaps she wasn't as bad as everyone said she was. I ran up the stairs and listened for some movement but there was no sound coming from behind the closed door. I opened it as quietly as I could and stepped inside.

There was someone in the bed. I sat down and stared at the arm resting on top of the quilt. It was very white and covered in freckles, so I guessed the rest of her would be too. I coughed, but she didn't move an inch. It was after noon, so I thought it was time she was up and about. How on earth was she going to manage with a new baby to look after? I coughed again, louder this time and a sharp little face sprang up out of the covers. Her hair was bright ginger; it looked like a burst mattress. There are two kinds of Irish ginger, one kind was beautiful and romantic like Polly's and then there was the other kind. Helen Casey was unfortunate enough to have the other kind.

She pulled herself up the bed and I was right; every piece of her that was visible was covered in freckles. Some of them were joined together, like orange blobs as if someone had thrown a can of paint on her.

Her face was neither round, square nor heart-shaped. It was in fact oblong and yet her mouth was huge, seeming to take up most of the space. I could almost hear Mammy's voice: '*God love her, here's one that won't have the lads queuing up at the door.*'

I smiled at her. 'You must be Helen,' I said. 'I'm Rose.'

'The darling of the house,' she sneered and then she yawned and I thought she was in danger of swallowing the pillow.

I chose to ignore what she'd said and kept smiling. 'How are you settling in?'

'I'm not,' she spat.

'I was homesick when I came as well.'

'Who said I was homesick?'

'I just thought…'

'Well, you thought wrong. I couldn't wait to get away from the place.'

I didn't know what else to say to her.

'They're all mad here, I've landed in a madhouse.'

I suddenly felt very protective of this little family; she didn't know them well enough to make such an assumption. 'They may be different than you are used to, Helen, but they're not mad. They are, in fact, the kindest people I have ever known.'

'Well, she might be okay but that boy gives me the creeps.'

'Raffi?'

'Well, there's no other boy in the house, is there?'

I decided that I didn't like this girl and I didn't want her looking after Alice's darling baby.

'He stands at the door and stares at me,' she said. 'Doesn't say a word, just stares. Don't tell me that's normal.'

'It depends what you call normal, doesn't it?'

'Well, I can see you're well and truly in their camp.'

I'd had enough of this baggage and stood up. At the door I turned around. 'This isn't a camp, it's a family, and you should be down on your knees thanking God for bringing you here.'

'Well, I hope it stays fine fer ya,' she said, disappearing back under the bedclothes.

When I got back on the landing, Raffi was leaning against the wall, grinning.

'Ghastly?' he said.

'Absolutely ghastly.'

'She has to go?'

'She has to go.'

'I've got an idea,' said Raffi.

We ran downstairs to the kitchen. Mrs Berry was standing in a haze of flour, pummelling a lump of dough as if her life depended on it. Her round face was red and sweaty.

'Hello, Mrs B,' said Raffi. 'We need your help.'

'Ask away.'

'Do you have a pot with a lid that we could borrow?'

'I'm sure I have,' she said, rubbing her hands down her apron and going across to the dresser.

She rummaged round and took a tin pot down from the shelf. 'Will this do?'

'Perfect,' said Raffi, kissing her cheek.

'Are you two up to no good?'

'Absolutely,' said Raffi grinning. 'And now you're an accessory.'

'Well, if it has anything to do with that lump of compost in the bed, I'd be glad to be an accessory.'

I still didn't know what Raffi had in mind as we went into the garden until he said, 'Are you scared of spiders, Rose?'

'Our house is full of them, they're like part of the family. So, no, I'm not.'

'Great, start collecting them.'

'You really are up to no good, aren't you?'

'Well, let's hope it works.'

We crept into the bedroom as quietly as we could but when I looked at Raffi, I just knew that I was about to giggle, so we had to creep back out again. We ran down the stairs and leant against the wall. I was laughing so much that tears were streaming down my face and Raffi was holding his stomach. When we eventually calmed down, we sat on the stairs and tried to compose ourselves.

'We have to think of something sad,' said Raffi.

I sat and thought. 'Polly had a pet pig once and her mammy had it slaughtered for Christmas dinner. Polly wouldn't touch a bite of it and cried for weeks. It made me sad to see my best friend so sad.'

'Okay, you think of the pig.'

'How about you?' I said.

'Leaving Aunt Martha.'

I took a deep breath. 'Okay, we can do this, because it's all in a good cause. She has to go. Think of it as a Holy Crusade.'

I thought about Polly's pig and by the look on Raffi's face, he was thinking about leaving Aunt Martha.

Polly's pig, Polly's pig, I thought, as we crept across the carpet. All of a sudden, the lump in the bed turned over and made a snorting sound. Me and Raffi froze. I had a desperate urge to giggle again. *Polly's pig,* I thought, *Polly's pig.* We waited until she was still, then

Raffi emptied the pot of spiders all over the bed. We crept back out of the room and waited on the landing.

'How can anyone sleep this long?' said Raffi.

'God alone knows,' I answered.

At least another half hour passed before the screaming started. And then she flew out the door like a banshee. Her face was bright red, which wasn't a great match with her hair.

'This was you, wasn't it?' she yelled, glaring at Raffi. 'You're wrong in the head, you should be locked up in an asylum!' Then she lunged at him and slapped him hard across the face, just as Alice was coming up the stairs.

'Pack your bags, Helen,' said Alice, calmly. 'David will arrange your passage home. You are no longer welcome in this house.'

'I haven't been made welcome since I got here and don't bother about my passage home. I have a cousin in London, I shall go to her. At least she's not mad, like you lot. I'll be glad to see the back of you.'

'Likewise,' said Alice, smiling her gentle smile. 'Are you alright, darling?' she said, going to Raffi.

Raffi was rubbing his face where Helen had hit him. 'It was worth it,' he said, grinning.

'You naughty, clever boy,' said Alice, holding him.

Raffi looked at me and winked and I winked back.

Chapter Thirty

Trafalgar Square was crowded; people of all ages had come together to welcome in the New Year. It was freezing cold but everyone was happy and smiling. Strangers were hugging strangers and wishing them happiness on this special night.

An old man was sitting by the fountain playing a fiddle and people were dancing. Young women were being carried aloft on young men's shoulders and everyone was having a great time. Oh, how I wished Polly was here; she'd have loved it and so would my sisters. I was suddenly overwhelmed with a longing to be home but I wasn't going to spoil this magical night for anyone.

Alice's baby was due any day and I worried that she would get jostled by the crowd but she had wanted to come so badly that none of us had had the heart to say no to her.

I looked across at Raffi and it touched my heart to see the excitement on his face. There wasn't enough excitement in his young life. He looked relaxed and carefree; the permanent frown that he'd carried for so long wasn't there. It may not last but oh, I was glad that for this one night, he looked like a child.

There was a hut selling hot drinks and sandwiches, and David and Raffi went to get some for us. I managed to make my way through the crowd so that Alice could sit down on the low wall surrounding the fountain. Some young people had started to jump into the water, laughing and splashing about like children.

'You're getting wet, Alice,' I said. 'Perhaps we should move.'

She didn't answer. She was bending over, holding her stomach. 'Are you in pain?'

She nodded. 'Please get David, I need David.'

I didn't want to leave her, so I called over a couple of young girls. 'Could you please sit with Alice while I get her husband?'

'Well, it's your lucky night,' one of them said, 'because we're nurses. Don't worry, we'll look after her.'

The girls sat next to her on the wall and one of them held her hand. 'Okay, Alice, just breathe through the pain, you are going to be alright,' she said, gently.

Satisfied that Alice was in good hands, I pushed through the crowd towards the hut, calling David's name as I ran.

He must have seen by my face that something was wrong. He put the coffee down and ran to me, followed by Raffi, who'd gone as white as a sheet.

'Is it the baby?' said Raffi. 'Have you left her alone? Is she scared? Oh, Rose, is Alice in pain?'

I grabbed Raffi's hand. 'She's with two nurses and she's going to be alright.' Then I smiled at him. 'She's going to have a baby, Raffi.'

David and Raffi helped Alice towards the car.

I sat in the front with David, as Raffi had insisted that he rode in the back with Alice. He was suddenly so calm; he spoke softly to her, as you would to a child that was hurting.

'We'll soon be there, dearest Alice,' he murmured. 'There's nothing to worry about and I won't leave your side. I won't ever leave your side.'

'I know, my darling, I know.'

David drove to the hospital through streets packed with revellers. Some were the worse for drink and were weaving all over the road and singing at the tops of their voices. He had to keep beeping the horn for fear of hitting them.

Suddenly Alice gave a piercing scream.

I turned around. She was clutching her tummy and she looked terrified. Her eyes were large and filled with pain, her face was sweaty.

'Breathe, Alice,' I said. 'Just breathe.'

'We're nearly there,' murmured Raffi. 'Squeeze my hand tight.'

'You'll soon have Sarah in your arms, my darling,' said David.

I wished he hadn't said that because no one could be sure that it was going to be a girl. Would she love a little boy? I hoped so.

I had never seen David look so scared, his knuckles were white from gripping the steering wheel. I wanted to say something, to reassure him, to tell him that everything was going to be alright but I doubted that he would even hear me. We pulled into the hospital, just as Alice let out another scream. He started beeping the horn, which immediately brought a nurse running out to the car, followed by another one with a wheelchair. They waited until the contraction had passed, then helped her gently out of the car.

David was holding her hand as Alice was wheeled into the hospital.

'I'm scared,' she said.

'Don't worry, love,' said the nurse. 'You're in good hands now.'

'Her name is Alice,' said Raffi.

The nurse looked at Raffi. 'That's a nice name,' she said.

'You have to take care of her,' he said.

'Don't worry, son,' said David. 'Don't worry.'

We hurried after the nurses as they sped along endless corridors, then stopped outside a pair of double doors.

'There's a waiting room around the corner,' said the nurse.

'But she can't do this on her own,' said Raffi. 'I have to be with her, she'll want me with her. I promised I wouldn't leave her side.'

'I'll be alright, Raffi,' said Alice.

Raffi put his arms around her and David kissed her cheek. 'We'll be right here, my brave girl,' said David.

'It's time to leave her with us now,' said the nurse. 'I promise we'll take good care of her. If you go back to the main entrance you can get a cup of tea and something to eat.'

None of us wanted to eat, but a cup of tea would be very welcome.

Raffi didn't want to leave the waiting room, so me and David went to get the tea.

'She'll be alright, won't she, Rose?' said David.

'Of course she will and you will soon be holding your son or daughter. Have you both decided on a name in case it's a boy?'

'It can't possibly be a boy.'

He sounded so sure that I started to laugh. I thought the next thing he was going to say was, 'I won't allow it.'

I was still laughing. 'I don't think you have a choice, David.'

And then he smiled. 'You're right, Rose Brown, it's a good job that someone in this family has some sense.'

'I think you all have sense, although perhaps it might sometimes be a bit misplaced where darling Alice is concerned.'

'Right again, dear girl, right again.'

As we started walking back to the waiting room, Raffi was running towards us.

'What's wrong?' shouted David.

'Nothing, but she needs her crystal. She has to have her crystal, Rose. We have to go home for it.'

'No, we won't,' I said. 'She always carries it with her. It will be in her coat pocket.'

'Oh, you are clever, Rose,' said Raffi. 'I'll tell the nurse.'

David smiled. 'Raffi seems a lot calmer now, don't you think?'

'Yes, he does, he really does.'

'I think it's time he went to school, Rose. What do you think?'

'I think that is exactly what he should do and if he can see that Alice is being taken care of, I don't think he will put up any objections.'

'Do you know what, Rose?'

'What?'

'Everything is better since you came to us.'

I didn't know what to say.

'You know, if Raffi hadn't taken to you, he wouldn't have let you anywhere near Alice. You gained his trust with your gentleness and kindness of heart. You have shared the burden he has been carrying round for so long and for that, I can't thank you enough.'

'You don't need to thank me, David, you have all become very special to me.'

'All of us?' he said, grinning.

I laughed. 'All of you.'

We stayed in that waiting room for hours, sitting on hard wooden chairs, which meant we had to keep standing up and walking around. We heard Big Ben chime twelve and the three of us hugged and wished each other a happy New Year. We could hear fireworks going off outside and people cheering and singing. It seemed we would have a New Year's baby.

Raffi eventually fell asleep. David put his coat over him and I folded mine under his head.

'I wondered how long it would take for him to give in,' said David, smiling.

At last, a nurse came into the room carrying a bundle. 'Congratulations, Mr Townsend,' she said, handing him the baby. 'You have a beautiful daughter.'

'And my wife?'

'She's been a star.'

'She *is* a star,' he said.

I gently shook Raffi. 'You have a little sister,' I said.

Raffi rubbed his eyes. 'Is Alice alright?'

'Your beautiful, amazing mummy is fine.'

The three of us stared down at the baby. She was beautiful and she looked like Alice. Her little hands were like two tiny starfish, worrying at the blanket that she was wrapped in.

'Your little sister is strong, Raffi,' said David, lifting her into Raffi's arms.

Raffi kissed the baby's forehead. 'Hello, Sarah,' he said. 'I'm your big brother.'

'Nineteen thirty-nine is going to be a wonderful year,' said David. 'It will be full of peace and filled with happiness. I just know it will.'

'Oh, I do hope so,' I said.

Chapter Thirty-One

Winnie Tuttle was lovely and fitted into the little family perfectly. She took care of Sarah as if the baby were her own. She came from a big family in a place called Poplar, in the East End. She was sweet and kind and funny. Alice said she was so tiny that she reminded her of a little bird. Her hair was almost black and she wore it in a neat plait that almost touched her bottom.

'Me mum says we might as well laugh at life or we'd be bloody crying. Sorry about the language, Miss Rose.'

I grinned at her. 'You don't have to call me Miss.' And then I said what Alice had said to me, 'We're the same, you and I.'

'Oh, we ain't, miss,' she said. 'We ain't the same at all and that's only right and proper. Me mum says I must always respect me betters.'

'I'm not your better,' I said. But I knew that I was wasting my breath and I had to accept that Winnie Tuttle was going to call me Miss Rose, whether I wanted her to or not.

'Me mum said, "Winnie," she said, "you must never forget yer place. If you do that, you'll never find yer way back." Our neighbour's middle girl, Shirley, went to work in a hotel on the Isle of Wight and she never come back. Me mum said it was 'cos she lost her way. But I think it was 'cos they slept seven to a bed and she wanted a bed of her own, that's what I fink, anyway.' Winnie paused as if she was deep in thought. 'Course I could be wrong, I'm wrong a lot.'

'I'm wrong a lot too, Winnie, but we won't worry about it, eh?'

'Yer real nice, Miss Rose,' said Winnie, grinning.

'You're real nice too.'

Winnie couldn't bring herself to call Alice by her first name either and always referred to her as Miss Alice, so Alice and I decided to call this sweet girl 'Miss Winnie'.

Winnie thought this was the funniest thing she'd ever heard. 'Wait 'till I tell me mum,' she said, giggling. 'She'll think I've joined the gentry.'

To my surprise, Alice wanted to feed Sarah herself. I had always thought that rich people hired a wet nurse but Alice would have none of it. 'I fed Raffi,' she said, 'and I shall feed Sarah.'

Of course, this caused a lot of discussion between David and Raffi, who thought that she was too fragile and that it might cause her to spiral down into another depression. I decided to forget my place and speak out.

'Alice was depressed because she lost her baby,' I said. 'But Sarah is thriving. You only have to look at Alice to see how happy she is, she's glowing with happiness.'

'Is Rose right?' said David, smiling. 'Are we both a couple of old fusspots, Raffi?'

Raffi grinned. 'Rose is right, Rose is always right.'

'I don't know about that,' I said. 'I'm just saying what I see.'

And so Alice, with all our blessings, fed her little girl and was happy.

For most of January, London was covered in a blanket of snow. One morning, Alice appeared in the kitchen, where me and Raffi were eating our breakfast. She was all smiles and she looked beautiful.

'Who's up for sliding down a hill?' she said.

Mrs Berry started laughing. 'Well, you can count me out.'

'I'm up for it,' said Raffi.

'And Rose?' said Alice. 'Is Rose up for it?'

'Of course she is,' said Raffi, before I could answer.

Alice was so excited that you couldn't help but be excited too. She just sort of caught you up in her happiness.

Sometimes when I looked at Alice, I thought she was far too beautiful for this world. Winnie adored her and joined our little circle of protection. 'She's like an angel, ain't she, Miss Rose? She's like a proper angel, come down to earth, to give us poor buggers somfin' nice to look at.'

'I think you're right, Winnie,' I said, thinking back to the first time I'd seen her.

'Okay,' said Alice, 'warm coats, boots, scarves and gloves and Raffi, the sledges are in the basement.'

David poked his head around the door. 'So, are they up for it, my darling?' he said.

'Of course they are. It's a snowy day and snowy days are made for sliding down hills and rainy days are made for books.'

Raffi came upstairs dragging the yellow wooden sledges behind him.

'What about Miss Winnie?' he said.

'But Winnie has to look after Sarah, darling,' said Alice. 'The baby is too young to be going out in this weather.'

'I don't mind staying,' I said, 'if Winnie would like to go.'

'No, Rose,' said Raffi. 'You have to come with us.'

'Not if she doesn't want to,' said Alice, frowning.

'Of course she wants to. Don't you, Rose? You want to come with us?'

When Raffi was anxious, he had a habit of lifting his shoulders so high that they almost reached his ears and that's what he was doing now.

'Of course I want to be with you, Raffi, I can't think of anything I'd rather do.'

'You can all go,' said Mrs Berry. 'I've made a big pot of soup for lunch, so I've nothing else to do. I'd love to spend some time with that little angel.'

'I'll tell Winnie,' said Raffi.

Winnie was delighted to be joining us and kept thanking Alice. 'It's awful good of ya, Miss Alice, thinking of me like this.

Me mum says I've proper landed on me feet here and she's right, I proper have.'

'Well, we're proper glad to have you with us, Miss Winnie,' said Alice, smiling.

Winnie laughed out loud. 'I still can't get used to you calling me that. Miss Winnie, indeed! Whoever heard the like?'

To everyone's surprise, Raffi had really taken to Winnie. When it wasn't too cold, the pair of them would wheel the pram down to the bottom of the garden and sit on the bench, chatting. I had worried that Raffi would be jealous of the new baby but that seemed never to be the case. Sarah was such a happy little girl and I think this was why he could love her. Had she been a whingy little thing, Raffi would have resented her for upsetting Alice and as for Winnie, I think her gentle nature posed no threat to Raffi's relationship with his adored mother.

Winnie loved to sing and she especially loved to sing to the baby. Songs she knew from her life in the East End.

'They're mostly songs me ole man sings when he's had a few,' she said. 'Sarah's favourite is "Roll out the Barrel". She loves that one.'

I thanked God that we'd got rid of the gruesome Helen. If we hadn't, things would not have been as happy and peaceful as they were. This was a very different house to the one I had arrived in.

David drove carefully through the snow. Everywhere looked so clean and bright, as if the city of London had been painted white. The snow was still falling softly, drifting past the windows of the car like soft feathers and landing gently on the ground.

'Ain't it lovely?' said Winnie, sighing. 'Ain't it just bloody lovely? Me mum always told us that it was God shaking out His pillows.'

'You're priceless, Miss Winnie,' said Alice. 'Utterly and beautifully priceless.'

'Ta, Miss Alice.'

'You are very welcome, Miss Winnie.'

'Are we going to Parliament Hill, David?' said Raffi.

'Well, that's the best place I can think of, for sliding down hills.'

'You'll love it, Rose,' said Raffi.

'It sounds wonderful,' I said.

David parked the car and he and Raffi hauled the sledges out of the back. There were lots of people on the hillside, whooshing down the snowy slope on all sorts of makeshift objects.

The four of us trudged up to the top of the hill and looked out over the city.

'It's like the top of the bloody world,' said Winnie.

'It is,' said Alice. 'It really is.'

We spent the morning taking turns on the sledges, laughing and screaming as we sped down the hill. Alice was not able to join us but she was happy watching the rest of us.

By midday the snow was coming down in thick white flakes and the wind was picking it up and blowing it, helter-skelter, across the hillside and over the city, like some mad dance.

David, Winnie and Raffi were still racing down the slope and I was alone with Alice at the top of the hill, staring out over the white rooftops of London.

Alice slipped her hand in mine. 'Do you feel it, Rose? Do you feel the magic of it all?'

I nodded.

'But doesn't it scare you a bit too?'

'I don't think so.'

'But don't you think that moments like this are just too beautiful to last?'

I sort of knew what she meant, because it was how I often thought about Alice; that she was too beautiful for this world. I sometimes thought the same thing about Agnes. It wasn't so much a perfectly beautiful face, it was an inside beauty that shone out of them both, a beauty that might only be given to us for a short time, as if they were on loan from God, to show us what true goodness was like, that we might strive to copy it.

'It does scare me a bit,' I said, shivering in my thin coat.

'Shall we go home, Rose?' said Alice.

Home, I thought, and felt something change inside me, something warm, something real, seeming to melt the freezing snow that was drifting all around me.

'Yes, Alice, let's go home,' I said. Because that is what it felt like now. It felt like home.

Chapter Thirty-Two

Spring, when it arrived, was only slightly better than winter. It was a spring that seemed reluctant to be there. New life struggled to push through the hard ground, only for it to wither and die in the frosty earth.

On warmer days, Winnie and Raffi would wheel Sarah to the park in the beautiful pram. Sarah at three months old was beautiful and sunny and we all adored her. She was full of smiles from the moment she woke up to the moment she went to sleep.

'I ain't never known such a good baby, Miss Rose,' said Winnie as she got ready to take her out one day. 'I've got eight brothers and sisters and every one of them arrived with their gobs open, yelling their bloody heads off. All except poor Lizzie of course, but Lizzie's not right in the 'ed. But we loves her just the same, Miss Rose.'

'Of course you do,' I said. 'For isn't she one of God's special children? And He must have had His reasons for sending her to you.'

'Me Auntie Pat said that Mum should put her away in an institution. Mum told her to bugger off and never darken the doorstep again.'

'And did she? Did she darken the doorstep again?'

'Well, she left it about a month, then turned up with a new hairdo and an apple cake, as if nuffin' had happened.' Winnie laughed. 'She's proper nice to Lizzie, though.'

'I bet she is,' I said, grinning.

I watched them from the doorway. As they walked down the street together, I could hear their laughter drifting back to me on the breeze. I was glad that Raffi had found a friend in Winnie and that he felt happy to leave Alice in my care. Winnie had brought something to this little family that was hard to explain. Maybe it was her acceptance of them all. Whereas Gruesome Helen had said they were all mad, Winnie just loved them and she let them know it, every day.

I had made a promise to Polly that I would ask Father Tom about a job for her and I felt bad that I hadn't asked yet, so I set off across the park towards the church. Today it was warm; today it felt like summer was on its way. Some brave little snowdrops had managed to survive the frost and gathered around the foot of the trees like a ballerina's tutu. Oh, it was lovely. I was in no hurry, so I sat down on a bench to take it all in. A warm breeze lifted the hair on the back of my neck. I lifted my face to the sun and thought about my family. It had been so long since I'd seen them and Christmas felt like a million years ago. Maybe I could go home again in the summer. I knew that Raffi wouldn't mind, as Alice was happy with Sarah and had Winnie's help. So much had changed for the better, the house, which was full of warmth and laughter, and Winnie's singing. Even Mrs Berry seemed happier. But it was in Raffi that the change was most apparent. Slowly, he was shedding the weight of responsibility that he had been carrying for so long, he was becoming freer and lighter every day and the invisible cord that had tied him to Alice was beginning to loosen. I knew that it wasn't going to happen overnight but there was hope and that made me happy. David was looking for a good school.

With this in mind, I got up and carried on to the church. If Father Tom could find a job for Polly, it would make being away from home so much easier. We could go to the cinema together and maybe walk around the shops. I had begun to think that my life was pretty small as I spent most of my time in the house. There were days when I longed for company of my own age and I felt Raffi did too. If Polly moved to London and Raffi made friends at school, maybe it could happen for both of us, now wouldn't that be wonderful?

I opened the wooden gate and walked down the path between the old gravestones.

Just then, I heard someone calling my name. I turned around to see Father Tom wheeling his bike up the path behind me.

'Ah, Rose,' he said. 'Have you come to visit the dead or myself?'

I laughed. 'Yourself, Father.'

'Then sit there on the bench and I will get Mrs Baxter to bring us some tea.'

I sat down and looked out over the graveyard. I had always found graveyards to be very peaceful places and nothing to be frightened of at all. There was something very unhurried about them. Now I know that's a daft way to describe a graveyard, because there was no one here about to hurry anywhere but that was how it made me feel; all calm inside, somewhere you could just sit and think and, well, just be. My own daddy was buried in the graveyard at the back of our wall at home and I'd often sit beside him and have a bit of a chat and smell the roses that Mammy always put there. I could be there at night and I wouldn't be a bit scared. As Mrs Butler was fond of saying, 'It's not the dead you need to be afraid of, Rose, it's the bloody living.'

Polly had wanted to bury the remains of her pig there but Father Luke had said that he understood how she felt but if he made an exception for the pig, the place would be full to bursting with the town's pets. 'But if it makes you feel better, Polly,' he'd said, 'bring the remains to me and we'll give him a Viking funeral befitting a grand pig.'

So, once everyone had had their fill of the pig, Polly had scraped the plates into a tin can, gravy and all, and taken them to the presbytery, where herself and Father Luke burned him like a Viking. Polly said to me afterwards that the ceremony had been very dignified, given that there wasn't much of him left, on account of the fact that her brothers were more pig-like than the pig.

Father Tom came and sat beside me. 'I think my cycling days are over, Rose,' he said, rubbing his back. 'These old bones aren't up to it anymore.'

'Sure, you're not old, Father.'

'I'm old enough, my young friend, I'm old enough and these busy roads of London don't give me the pleasure that the boreens of home used to give me.'

I nodded.

Mrs Baxter came out with a tray of tea and apple cake. 'It's Father's favourite,' she said.

'And that is why I have to cycle the roads when I'd rather be reading a good book.'

'All that reading is bad for the eyes,' she said as she walked away.

'Now, Rose, did you want to talk to me about something?'

'I do, Father.'

'Then fire away.'

'I have a friend, Polly, who lives in Ballykillen and she has a great desire to work over here. I was wondering if you knew of a family that's wanting a girl.'

'I'll ask Mrs Baxter, Rose, because she knows what's going on before the people involved do themselves and I'll put a notice up in the church.'

'Thank you, Father,' I said, getting up.

'It's always a joy to see you, Rose. God bless you now and as soon as I hear anything, I will let you know.'

On a blustery day in June, David came home from work early, which was unusual for him. He looked worried and upset. He and Alice were in the bedroom for a long time, while me and Raffi hovered in the hallway. Eventually he opened the door and asked us to come in.

'I have been called back to America,' he said. 'We have a problem in the New York office and it seems serious enough for me to be there.'

'Are we all going?' said Raffi, looking hopeful.

'No, darling,' said Alice. 'Sarah is too young for the journey.'

'I will come back as soon as I can, but I have to sort this out. I'll be back before you know it.'

We were all sad the morning he left. David was holding Alice in his arms and Winnie and Mrs Berry were dabbing at their eyes. The house seemed a quieter place once David had gone and it wasn't because he was noisy; it was because he wasn't there and we all felt his loss. Mrs Berry seemed to think that the best remedy for sadness was food and was determined that even though our hearts were empty, our bellies would be full.

A few weeks turned into a month, then two months. It was now August and I wondered when he would be home. Letters arrived for Alice but she never shared them with me and why would she? I wasn't family and it really wasn't my business. But I felt the responsibility of caring for Alice beginning to weigh heavily on my shoulders. I didn't know David in the same way as I knew Alice and Raffi, although I liked him and he was always kind to me and I could tell he cared about how I was feeling, but he had a steadying influence on Alice and the house and without him, I felt there were days when we were all floundering a bit. I would be glad when he was back.

Winnie had been home for a few days, as her sister Lizzie had been taken ill, and we all missed her. We missed her singing and her laughter and… well, we just missed Winnie. When she came back, she looked worried and not like her usual happy self. There was no singing coming from the nursery and I was worried about her.

I went upstairs to see what was wrong.

Winnie was standing at the widow and she turned around as I came into the room.

'Is something worrying you, Winnie?' I said, gently.

'There's trouble afoot, Miss Rose. Real proper trouble.'

'At home? Is it Lizzie?'

No, Miss. Lizzie just has a weak chest but me mum covered her in goose fat and she's fine now.'

'What, then?'

'There's this geezer in Germany, Miss Rose, what's causing all sorts of 'avoc. My ole man says if that Hitler bloke don't stop causing 'avoc, we'll 'ave to do somfin' about it.'

'Winnie, it's happening a long way away. There has been lots of talk but I'm sure that's all it is, so stop worrying about something that is never going to happen.'

'Well, it's what me ole man says.'

'Well, he's wrong and I don't want this sort of talk around Raffi and Alice.'

'Oh, I won't say nuffin', Miss Rose. I'd rather cut me own tongue out than upset that lady, I would, really, I would.'

'There's no need for that,' I said, laughing. 'You wouldn't be able to sing without your tongue and we would all miss your singing.'

'I won't say a word, Miss Rose. I'll be sure to keep me bloody gob shut.'

'I shall hold you to that, Miss Winnie.'

'Every time you calls me that, it makes me wanna laugh me socks off.'

'Well, you call me Miss Rose, so why shouldn't I call you Miss Winnie?'

Winnie frowned. 'Whatever you say, we ain't the same, are we?'

'Where do you think I come from, Winnie?'

'I dunno, somewhere posh.'

'My daddy died when I was a child,' I said. 'I had to help Mammy care for my three sisters. I lived in a humble cottage in

Ireland. I hardly ever went to school because I was needed at home. When I came here, I could barely read or write.'

Winnie had tears in her eyes. 'So, we're not so different then, are we?'

'No, we're not but I think we're alright, don't you?'

Winnie grinned. 'Yeah, I think we're alright.'

'Why don't you pop downstairs and have a cup of tea with Mrs Berry? I'm sure she'll be glad of the company. I'll keep an eye on Sarah. And Winnie?'

'Yes, Miss?'

'No more talk of war.'

Winnie grinned. 'Cross me heart and hope to die.'

After Winnie had gone, I walked across to Sarah's cot and looked down at her. She was a beautiful child. Raffi looked like David but there was nothing of David in Sarah, she was all Alice.

It was stuffy in the room, so I opened the window. Winnie didn't like fresh air in the nursery; according to her mum, it carried all sorts of germs.

I looked out at the long garden; the grass was so green and the flowers in the borders, that Alice tended so carefully, were beautiful. I could see the branches moving gently in the breeze and hear the birds twittering as they flew from tree to tree. Next door's black cat jumped over the wall that separated the two houses. I watched as it moved slowly across the lawn, then settled in a shady spot under a tree. Everything was so peaceful. Surely Winnie's dad was wrong? It was ridiculous to think that there would be a war. I wouldn't give it another thought.

Chapter Thirty-Three

As it turned out, Winnie's dad had been right when he said that the geezer in Germany was causing havoc. A shadow was hanging over England as talk of war became more than just idle gossip.

Winnie stopped singing and even Sarah became fractious, as if she knew what was ahead.

Every day, Raffi was becoming more like the anxious little boy that I'd first met.

'Do you think there'll be a war, Rose?'

'I don't know, Raffi, I hope not.'

'How will I be able to protect Alice if there's a war? How am I supposed to do that?'

I'd hoped that once Alice had the baby, Raffi would stop feeling so anxious about her. She was happy and strong and as far as I could see, she really didn't seem to need protecting.

'Raffi,' I said, 'why do you think Alice needs to be protected? What does she need protecting from?'

Raffi glared at me. 'You're not listening, Rose. I told you when you came here that you have to listen to me.'

'I am listening, Raffi, I'm just not sure what I am supposed to be listening to.'

'You're here to look after Alice, you're here to help me look after Alice. You know that's why you're here. You're not here to look after me, you're not here to look after the baby, you're here to look after Alice.'

'Has it occurred to you that your mother may not need looking after now?'

Raffi's voice was getting louder. He was almost shouting at me. 'You're not listening, Rose, you're not listening! Are you stupid? Of course she needs looking after. It's your job, just do your job.'

'I think that you should calm down,' I said. 'I won't be spoken to like that. I can see that you are worried, we all are, but I think you owe me an apology.'

Raffi took some deep breaths. 'Alright, I'm sorry.'

'You're forgiven, young man, but don't speak to me like that again or I'll be on the next boat home.'

Raffi's eyes filled with tears. He brushed them away with the back of his hand. 'You won't leave us, Rose. Say you won't leave us.'

'Come on,' I said. 'Let's get some fresh air.'

He nodded and we went out into the garden. It was a beautiful day, too beautiful for talk of war.

'I wish my father was here, Rose, don't you?'

I was so used to Raffi calling his father David that it sounded strange on his lips. It made him seem more vulnerable in a way, as if the mask of trying to be a grown-up was slipping.

I wished David was here too. I was worried about this anxious young boy and the responsibility that suddenly felt too heavy for me. I put my arm around his shoulder. 'You're not alone,' I said. 'If you think that Alice needs our protection then we will do it together.'

Raffi smiled at me. 'I really am sorry I spoke to you like that.'

'We won't mention it again.'

I was sitting on the window seat with Alice, having my lesson. I was now able to read simple children's books but Alice thought I was ready to try something more challenging. She stood up and walked over to the tall bookcases, where she knelt down and started taking out books from the bottom shelf.

'Here,' she said, handing me a book. 'I think you'll like this.'

I looked at the picture on the front. There were boats and a river and children and dark woods. I thought it looked gloomy and not very interesting. 'What's it about?'

'It's a wonderful story, Rose. It's about one magical summer in 1929 in the Lake District. It's about freedom and adventure and bravery and loyalty and growing up. Raffi loves this book. Perhaps we should all have a holiday in the Lake District and sail a boat on the river. We shall be Swallows and Amazons, yes, that's what we shall do. Do you think that Sarah is too young for such an adventure?'

I didn't know how to answer her. Everyone was talking about war and here was Alice talking about a holiday in the Lake District. 'But…' I began.

'Yes, of course you are right, Sarah is far too young. How lucky we are to have you, Rose, for you always know the right thing to do.'

I didn't always know the right thing to do or the right thing to say. In fact, most of the time, the things I really wanted to say would probably lose me my job and if I was honest, I wasn't even sure what my job was anymore.

Surely Alice couldn't be entirely ignorant of what was going on in the world? 'Have you been listening to the news at all, Alice?' I said, hopefully.

'Heavens, no! It's all doom and gloom and why should we all be gloomy?'

'Raffi isn't happy, Alice, he's very worried.'

Her eyes seemed to glaze over; it was as if I hadn't spoken. 'I'm feeling tired, Rose,' she said. 'I think I will lie down for a while.'

I watched her walk across the room.

'I just don't understand why everyone can't just be happy,' she said in a dreamy voice, as if she was talking to herself. Perhaps the gruesome Helen hadn't been so wrong when she'd said that they were all mad, because God forgive me, I was beginning to think it meself.

That night in bed, I couldn't get the conversation out of my head. I had told Alice that her son was worried and she didn't seem to care. In fact, I got the feeling that she wasn't happy that I'd mentioned it at all.

I was missing my home and my family; I had a desperate need to talk to Mammy. Mammy may not have been educated like Alice but she was blessed with a wisdom that went beyond a swanky education and she knew her children inside and out. We didn't have to tell her when we were sad or worried or anxious, or even holding something back from her that we were ashamed of. She knew us and our worries were her worries. We may have been poor, but we knew we were loved. We had a wise mammy who always put our needs before her own.

I wondered what she would make of Alice but I had a good idea. I could almost hear her voice.

'She's a spoiled child who doesn't want to grow up, Rose.' And suddenly it all became clear. I sat up in bed. That was it: Alice didn't want to grow up; she wanted to be shielded from anything that wasn't perfect, as you would shield a child. As long as we allowed her to do this, her flame burned bright. All of us, in our own way, were keeping the flame alive and as long as we continued to do that, our reward was her beautiful smile and we could happily bathe in its warmth.

I felt a stinging behind my eyes. Poor Raffi, he hadn't been protecting Alice at all, he had been begging for her attention. If he kept her warm when she was cold and cool when she was hot and agreed with everything she said, he would gain his mother's approval. Raffi yearned for her love. And David? I realised that it was the same for him. You can only love an angel from a distance because they very rarely came down to earth and even if they did, would they survive?

If *we* knew about the threat of war, then surely David knew too, so why didn't he come home? He must know that we needed him to be here.

The next morning, I found Alice sitting on the bench in the garden, reading a letter that I guessed had come from David. She looked up as I approached.

I sat beside her. 'Alice?' I said gently.

She smiled. 'Don't you look pretty today, Rose?'

'Thank you.'

'But worried. Is something worrying you?'

I nodded.

'Then share it with me, I'm sure it can't be that bad. We can sort it out together. Would you like that?'

'Yes, I would.'

'Then tell me and I shall listen.'

'Can I ask you something?'

'You can ask me anything you like,' she said, smiling.

'I don't want to speak out of turn and I don't want to pry into something that is not my business.'

Alice laughed, that laugh I loved so much. 'How serious you sound, Rose.'

'I'm sorry but I've been wondering why David is still in America.'

'Oh, Rose, is that all? You don't need to worry, it's all just a silly misunderstanding. Darling David will be home before you know it.'

'So, he's coming home soon?'

'Not yet, he says, not yet but soon, Rose, very soon.'

I should have felt relieved but I feared there was more to it than Alice was telling me.

My silence paid off and she began to speak. 'Just a silly misunderstanding, nothing for you to worry your little head about. David wants to come home, he misses us dreadfully but he can't, you see, because he's not allowed to.'

'I don't understand.'

'His company is being investigated for some sort of fraud. How ridiculous is that? As if David would do anything underhand! He's the most honest person I know. But there you are; he's not allowed to leave the country until it's all sorted out.'

'I had no idea.'

'Well, now you know, so you can stop worrying. David assures me that everything will be alright and he will be home as soon as he can, so you see there really is nothing at all to worry about.'

I looked at Alice sitting there without a care in the world and I wished I could feel the same but I didn't.

Chapter Thirty-Four

At eleven o'clock on the morning of the third of September, everyone except Alice was in the kitchen, sitting around Mrs Berry's wireless.

'Shouldn't Alice be here?' I said.

'Don't be silly, Rose,' said Raffi.

'I got an 'orrible feeling about this 'ere speech of Chamberlain's,' said Mrs Berry. 'I think we're in for a shock and no mistake.'

'A bloody big shock if you ask me,' said Winnie.

'Well, nobody is,' snapped Raffi.

'Shush,' I said as the wireless crackled into action.

'Give it a thump,' said Winnie. 'That's what me dad does.'

Mrs Berry turned a few knobs and Mr Chamberlain's voice came out loud and clear, making Winnie jump and filling us all with dread.

I am speaking to you from the cabinet room at 10 Downing Street. This morning the British ambassador in Berlin handed the German government a final note stating that unless we heard from them by 11 o'clock that they were prepared at once to withdraw their troops from Poland, a state of war would exist between us. I have to tell you now that no such undertaking has been received, and that consequently this country is at war with Germany.

Mrs Berry turned the wireless off and made the sign of the cross. 'God help us all,' she said softly. 'God help us all.'

Winnie started to cry, big noisy sobs that filled the little kitchen. 'What we gonna do, Miss Rose? Do you think them bombs are on their way? Are we all gonna die?'

'A cup of tea, I think, Mrs Berry,' I said.

'Right away, Rose,' she said, filling the kettle with water.

'And Winnie, stop putting the fear of God into us all.'

'I'm sorry, Miss Rose, but me nerves are at me.'

The blood seemed to have drained from Raffi's face but he hadn't said a word. Winnie was still bawling and I felt dead inside.

'I want me mum,' sobbed Winnie. 'I just want me mum.'

I put my arm around her. 'I want mine as well, Winnie.'

I looked around the room. 'We must tell Alice,' I said.

Raffi stood up. All the colour seemed to have gone from his face. 'No, we don't, we don't.'

'She needs to know, Raffi.'

'Tell me one good reason why you think she needs to know. And tell me one good reason why you think it's your decision to tell her.'

'You didn't ought to be talking to Miss Rose that way,' said Winnie, sniffing. 'You really didn't.'

'Keep your nose out of it, Winnie, it has nothing to do with you.'

Mrs Berry put the cups of tea on the table. 'Whether you like it or not, Raffi Townsend,' she said, 'your mother is not a child and she has to face this, the same as the rest of us.'

'She's not like the rest of us,' shouted Raffi.

'She's exactly like the rest of us. I'm no Bible-basher but I think I heard somewhere that He made us all in his own image and likeness. He didn't make the posh ones one day and then use the bits that were left over to make the rest of us. Now drink yer tea. We've got be brave and strong, including your mum. Can you do that?'

'Mrs Berry?' said Raffi.

'Yes, love?'

'Will you tell her? Will you tell Alice?'

'If you want me to.'

'I do.'

'Then I'll go directly. And don't you worry, I'd say your mum is tougher than she looks and she will want strength around her and not gloomy faces.'

Raffi put his arms round Mrs Berry's ample waist. 'Thank you,' he said.

'And haven't you something else to say, young man?'

Raffi looked across at me. 'Sorry, Rose. You won't be getting the next boat home, will you?'

I didn't answer him.

'I'll take her up a cup of tea, shall I?' said Mrs Berry.

'I think that would be a very good idea,' I said.

Winnie was dabbing at her eyes. 'Me mum says tea soothes the soul, or was it water?'

'It was neither,' said Raffi. 'It was music, not tea and it wasn't the soul, it was the savage beast. Music hath charms to soothe the savage beast.'

'I prefer me mum's version,' said Winnie.

Raffi smiled at her. 'I was rude to you too, Winnie, and I'm very sorry.'

'That's alright, Master Raffi, I forgives ya.'

'Well, thank you, Miss Winnie.'

I wanted to be on my own, so I went into the garden.

A warm breeze brushed my face and the sun dappling through the bare trees cast long shadows across the lawn. We were at war with Germany and it was hard to take in. I felt as if the whole weight of this family was sitting firmly on my shoulders.

I knew what Polly would say. 'They're not your responsibility, Rose.' Oh, I wished I was with her now. There would be no war at home and home was where I longed to be, home was where I would be safe, but how could I leave them?

My feelings for Alice were changing and that made me feel sad because I had grown to love her. She had shown me nothing but kindness and like everyone else, I had wanted to protect her from a world I had thought she was too fragile to deal with but now it was Raffi I wanted to protect and I couldn't help but blame Alice for that. I even blamed David, though I knew it wasn't his fault that he wasn't here.

I felt the need for some peace and decided that the one place I would find it was in God's house. I went back indoors and let Mrs Berry know where I was going.

It was cool inside the church and the familiar smell of incense took me back to my childhood and my home. There were quite a few people there, which was unusual for this time of the day but I suspected they were also in need of comfort. I lit a candle below the statue of Our Blessed Lady, her beautiful face smiled down at me and I felt at peace.

Suddenly, a group of children filed down the middle aisle, led by Father Tom. They settled themselves in the choir stalls and Father Tom turned to face us. He made the sign of the cross and started to speak.

'This is a sad day,' he said, 'and we must call on Our Lord Jesus Christ to give us the strength to be brave in our hour of need, as he himself was brave in the face of his enemies. I believe that there is nothing more beautiful than the voices of innocent children raised in song, so let us join together in praise and sing our hearts out to his glory.'

The strains of the organ filled the church as the children began to sing one of my favourite hymns, 'Sweet Heart of Jesus'.

As I listened to the song, I heard a door slam behind me. I turned around to see who was coming into the church and saw it was Raffi. His face was flushed. He walked down the aisle and stopped at the end of the pew.

'You have to come home, Rose,' he said. 'You have to come home now.'

'Shush,' I said.

'Listen to me, Rose, listen to me,' he shouted.

The singing stopped as everyone stared at us.

I stood up, genuflected in front of the altar and made the sign of the cross.

'Get up,' Raffi screamed. 'You have to come home now.'

Father Tom walked towards me. 'What's wrong, Rose?'

'Something has happened at home,' I said. 'I don't know what.'

Father Tom looked at Raffi. 'Can you tell me what's wrong, lad?'

'No, I can't,' said Raffi rudely. 'Come on, Rose.'

'I'm sorry, Father,' I said.

Father Tom touched my shoulder. 'Let me know if I can be of any help.'

I followed Raffi outside. He was walking in front of me and I pulled his arm back.

'I can see that you're upset, Raffi, but what right have you to speak to a man of God like that?'

'Why should I care about him? And why should you care about him when Alice needs you?'

'You haven't even told me what's wrong.'

'What does it matter what's wrong? Isn't it enough that I'm telling you that you're needed? That's your job, isn't it? To be there when you're needed.'

'Jesus, Raffi, you'd test the patience of a saint.'

I heard the screaming as we neared the house. I ran up the steps and pushed open the door.

Winnie was sitting on the bottom of the stairs with Sarah in her arms. She was as white as a sheet and tears were running down her face.

'How long has she been like this, Winnie?'

'Since Mrs Berry told her that we're going to war.'

I ran upstairs to the bedroom, with Raffi right behind me. Alice was cowering in the corner and Mrs Berry was rocking her in her arms as if she was a child.

'Raffi,' I said, 'go downstairs and get some whisky.'

Raffi looked relieved to be doing something. 'Yes, Rose,' he said meekly.

I sat on the floor in front of Alice and held her hands. I didn't know what to say or do, so I thought about Mammy, who always found the right words and always made things better.

'Now what's all this about?' I said gently.

'She hasn't said a word since I told her,' said Mrs Berry. 'She just started screaming, so I sat with her, I didn't know what else to do.'

Alice's screams were piercing and I could barely hear what Mrs Berry was saying.

I took Alice's face in my hands and forced her to look at me. '*Stop, Alice!*' I shouted. '*Stop!* You're frightening the baby, you're frightening Sarah.'

Alice's eyes widened as she stared at me and then at Mrs Berry as if she'd just realised that we were there. The screaming stopped and she started sobbing and shaking.

'Help me get her into bed, Mrs B, and then ring for the doctor.'

Raffi was standing in the doorway, a glass in his hand.

'I can ring the doctor, Rose,' he said. 'I've done it lots of times.'

I wondered just how *many* times he had witnessed his mother in this state. More times than I cared to think about and my heart went out to him.

'You're a grand lad,' I said, smiling.

As he opened the door, he looked back at me. 'I'm glad you're here, Rose.'

'So am I,' I said.

Chapter Thirty-Five

Wind and rain battered the pavements that winter and Christmas was a sorry affair. No tree in the hallway, filling the house with the scent of pine. No candles lighting up the rooms and none of us bothered to scour the shops for presents. Mrs Berry had knitted a little pink rabbit for Sarah but that was about it. Winnie had gone home to spend the day with her family, so it was just Mrs Berry, Raffi and myself at the kitchen table. Alice ate her Christmas dinner in her room.

It wasn't just the war that had made us all miserable, it was Alice, who never got dressed or came downstairs anymore. You see, it had been Alice who had brought joy to the house, Alice who we had all wanted to please, Alice who could fill the greyest day with sunshine but who could just as quickly overshadow it with the darkest of clouds.

Without her, the sunshine had disappeared and the heart had gone out of the house.

Alice seemed calmer but she still took no part in family life.

On New Year's Eve, I sat alone, watching the fireworks exploding over London and I thought back to this time last year, when Sarah was born. How happy we were, sitting there in that waiting room, gazing down at the miracle that was Sarah. I remembered David saying, 'This will be a wonderful year, Rose, full of peace and happiness, I just know it will.'

Well, he couldn't have been more wrong, could he? This year had turned out to be the worst year of our lives. I pulled the heavy curtains across the window and went to bed.

In February, another letter came from David. It was addressed to Alice so I took it up to her bedroom. She was sitting in a chair, looking vacantly out of the window.

'I have a letter for you, Alice,' I said, smiling. 'I think it's from David.'

I put the letter on her lap, but she didn't even touch it. I watched it slide onto the floor.

'Don't you want to know what it says?'

'Give it to Raffi, Rose.'

I was beginning to feel angry and I knew that my anger wasn't going to help. 'The letter is for you, Alice, not Raffi,' I said.

She turned to face me. There was no expression on her face at all. I stood there holding the letter, feeling stupid.

'I said, give it to Raffi.'

'I heard what you said, Alice, but I really think that you should read it. Don't you want to know what your husband has to say? He might be letting you know that he is coming home.'

'Why don't you read it, Rose, if you are so interested?' Her voice was flat, no bitterness, no anger, just nothing.

I picked up the letter and left the room. I had grown up surrounded by people who loved me, people I could go to when I had a problem. I had never felt more helpless, or more alone in my life. I felt like getting on the next boat home. I could almost hear Polly saying, 'Get yourself out of that place and don't look back, Rose, for they're all mad.'

I looked at the letter. It wasn't my place to read it and if Alice wouldn't, then Raffi would have to. I went slowly downstairs to find him. I thought he might be in the kitchen but it was just Mrs Berry and Winnie.

'Ah, Rose,' said Mrs Berry, smiling. 'Have you been with Miss Alice?'

'I've just left her. I'm looking for Raffi.'

'Come here, girl, you look in need of a hug.'

I was enveloped in Mrs Berry's large arms and ample bosom. That would have had me laughing at any other time but her kindness had me roaring crying, which started Winnie off.

'Tea, Winnie,' she said, lowering me down into a chair.

'Right away,' said Winnie, filling the kettle.

Mrs Berry knelt down in front of me. 'Now what has brought all this on?'

'I think that Alice is sick.'

'What sort of sick?' said Winnie, putting three cups on the table.

I took a deep breath. 'I'm not a doctor but I think that she has given up. I think that her mind is so full of fear, there is no room for anything else.'

'But we're all afraid, aren't we?'

'I take Sarah to see Miss Alice every day but she barely looks at her. That darling baby has a right to a mother's love. It would break your heart, the way she ignores her own child.'

'It's not your place to judge the mistress, Winnie,' said Mrs Berry, frowning.

'But it's not right.'

'I think that Miss Alice's fear goes a lot deeper than ours,' I said.

'Why?'

I shook my head. 'I've yet to figure it out.'

'Well, I think that her husband should know what's happening here,' said Mrs Berry. 'It's him that should be taking care of his wife, not you, Rose.'

Mrs Berry was right; the responsibility of this broken family was beginning to weigh heavily on my shoulders. I was only seventeen but I felt like an old woman. They were all looking to me for guidance and I had none to give them. I was as bewildered as they were. Polly's words of wisdom were no use to me now. I had returned after Christmas because she had said to just ignore their goings-on and learn to read and go out in the swanky car. Well, my lessons had stopped and no one else could drive the car.

'It's like living in a morgue, it proper is,' said Winnie.

Just at that moment, Raffi came into the kitchen. 'And what would you know about living in a morgue?' he snapped. 'Is that where you live, Winnie Tuttle? In a morgue?'

Winnie burst out crying and ran out of the room. Mrs Berry followed her.

'It's just a saying, Raffi,' I said. 'Why do you have to be so mean?'

'Because I feel mean.'

'That doesn't give you the right to hurt people.'

'Why can't she try? Why can't she at least try? Why can't she get out of that bloody bed? It makes me angry and I'm sick of feeling angry.'

Raffi looked so lost standing there that my heart softened. He was just a child, a very sad child.

'Let's take a walk,' I said. 'I think it's stopped raining.'

We wandered aimlessly through the streets and ended up at the church. We didn't go in but we sat on a bench overlooking the graveyard.

'Great idea, Rose, this is just the place to cheer us up.'

'Well, at least it's peaceful,' I said.

'Of course it's peaceful, they're all dead.'

And then we were laughing and we couldn't stop and although our laughter seemed out of place as it echoed across the old gravestones, it was a release that we both needed.

'Can you think of anything that would make her happy?' I said, wiping my eyes.

'She needs David. I don't think we're enough for her, Rose.'

I put my hand in my pocket and took out the letter. 'This came today,' I said.

Raffi took the letter from me and looked at the writing on the envelope.

'It's addressed to Alice,' he said.

'She won't read it, Raffi, so I think you should.'

'It's from David, isn't it?'

I nodded.

'And you think that I should open it?'

'Well, someone ought to and it's not my place.'

I waited patiently as Raffi read the letter. When he'd finished, he folded the sheet of paper and put it back in the envelope.

'Well?' I said.

'He wants us all to come to America.'

'And do you want to go?'

'Of course I do,' said Raffi. 'I want to be with my father and Aunt Martha. I want to be with them more than anything.'

We sat quietly together, each with our own thoughts. Then Raffi said what I had been thinking.

'Alice won't go, will she?'

'I don't know, Raffi.'

It had started to rain again, that thin hazy rain that soaks you to the skin in minutes, but we took our time walking home because neither of us wanted to be there.

Chapter Thirty-Six

Mrs Berry went upstairs to read the letter to Alice, while me and Raffi waited in the kitchen.

'Do you think she'll agree to go, Rose?' said Raffi.

I shrugged my shoulders. 'Do you?'

'I hope so. I think she will get better once she's with David and Aunt Martha. I wish we'd never come here, Rose.'

'I know you do, love.'

'I'm tired of it all.'

To hear a child say something like that was so sad. I wished I could take him home to Ballykillen, where he could run the fields and hills, with no worries except what was for dinner. I'd have loved to see him jump off the quay with the other boys and come home wet and muddy and happy. Oh, how I wished that for him. He deserved to feel that sort of freedom. Not just for his body but for his mind.

I looked up as Mrs Berry came into the kitchen. 'We'd have to knock her unconscious to get her on that ship,' she said. 'I did my best but she wouldn't even consider it, I'm sorry.'

Raffi stood up and left the room.

'I hate to say it, for I love that sweet lady but she's thinking of no one but herself and it makes me angry.'

'You're allowed to feel angry, Mrs B. It's Raffi I feel for. He wanted to go back. I think he felt safer there and isn't it every child's right to feel safe?'

'It is, Rose, it is.'

Children were being evacuated to towns and villages outside London and the war became very real. Food was being rationed and Mrs Berry thought it was a personal attack on her. 'How am I supposed to make a meal out of two eggs and a couple of slices of ham? Not to mention the lack of sugar! Am I a magician or what?'

'You're doing wonderfully,' I said.

She grinned. 'Well, I'm glad someone appreciates me.'

'We all do, Mrs B.'

Winnie's brothers, Stanley and Frank, came to the house to help Raffi construct an Anderson shelter at the bottom of the garden. I loved to hear their laughter as they struggled to lift the six panels of corrugated iron into place. I had never seen Raffi so happy and it brought joy to my heart to see him joking with the two boys. They worked all day under the hot sun, sleeves rolled up and faces covered in dirt. Mrs Berry and myself kept them going, with fresh lemonade and homemade cakes.

The next day, we lifted sandbags on top of the shelter. Yesterday's sunshine had turned to driving rain and we laughed as we saw each other caked in mud. Life was still going on, but without Alice.

One morning, I went into her room and sat on the bed. 'Are you awake, Alice?' I said softly.

There was no movement. 'Alice?' I said louder.

She turned away from me, so I went around to the other side of the bed.

'Alice, you have to talk to me.'

She opened her eyes. I had never seen such sadness; her eyes were dull and full of pain and as always, my heart went out to her.

I held her hand. 'Please, Alice,' I said.

She nodded and I helped her to sit up. 'We all miss you; the house is not the same without you. Don't you miss us? Don't you miss Raffi and Sarah?'

Alice smiled but it was a sad smile. 'What good am I to them, Rose? What good am I to anyone?'

'You don't have to be good,' I said. 'You just have to be there; you don't even have to get dressed if you don't want to. We just want you to be with us. Can you do that, Alice? Can you just come and sit with us for a while?'

'You miss me?'

'Of course we miss you, we all miss you.'

'And you think I should come downstairs?'

'I do, I definitely do.'

'Then I shall come and sit you with you for a while.'

I helped her into her dressing gown. She seemed so fragile. 'Shall I brush your hair?'

She touched her hair as if she was surprised that it was there. 'Yes, please, Rose.'

I walked across to the dressing table and picked up the beautiful silver brush.

Alice's hair, once so immaculate, was dry and tangled and it smelt musty. Alice would have hated this if she'd been in her right mind but sadly, she wasn't. I brushed her hair as best I could without hurting her. 'There now,' I said. 'Doesn't that feel better?'

She touched my hand. 'How kind you are, Rose.'

'Would you like me to wash it for you later?'

'Would that be a good idea?'

'I think so.'

'Such plans you have, Rose, such adventures.'

Well, I wasn't sure that washing her hair was an adventure but Alice seemed to like the idea.

Mrs Berry had been waiting outside the door in case I needed any help. I called her and she came into the room.

'Well, Miss Alice,' she said. 'How nice to see you up and about. Are you coming to join us?'

Alice smiled. 'Yes, I think I am, Mrs B.'

'Then this is a wonderful day indeed. Wouldn't you agree, Rose?'

'Oh, I would,' I said. 'A wonderful day indeed.'

*

Slowly she came back to us and even on the gloomiest of days, her smile brought warmth back into the house.

In the evenings, Raffi would read to Alice and Sarah would toddle around the room. Sometimes Winnie would join us and they were such happy times. Alice wasn't completely herself; there were times when she seemed to go back to being a child and there were times when we lost her completely but we learned to let her be because at least she was with us and not in her bedroom.

We didn't mention the war to Alice and as she didn't go outside the house, she didn't see the giant barrage balloons floating over the rooftops or the red pillar boxes that had been painted yellow, to enable the wardens to detect gas, or the sandbags piled up outside shops and public buildings.

We did our best to coax her into trying on a gas mask but she would have none of it, so we gave up.

Besides, apart from the rationing, there was no sign of a war anyway. In fact, it was being called a 'phoney war'. Children who had been evacuated to the countryside were now returning to London. We'd heard that people were beginning to use the Anderson shelters to store their coal.

In August, the first bomb fell on London. We couldn't get Alice into the air raid shelter. I stayed with her and insisted that Winnie, Raffi and Sarah ran for shelter.

There was a cupboard under the stairs and I managed to get her in there.

I had never seen Mrs Berry so angry when she heard about it. 'That must never happen again, Rose,' she said.

'But I couldn't leave her alone.'

'In that case, I shall move in here and if I have to, I shall drag her bodily down the garden. I'll not have you risking your life because of her contrary ways. I won't have it, Rose. You go above and beyond your duty to this family, without laying down your life for them.'

I laughed. 'I think you would as well.'

'You can depend on it, Rose Brown.'

The word 'depend' gave me peace because for so long there had been no one that I could depend on, but now I could share the responsibility with Mrs Berry and I felt like crying with the relief of it.

On the afternoon of September 7th 1940 bombs started falling on the city and I was so grateful that Mrs Berry was with us because, true to her word, she coaxed and encouraged Alice to safety. We spent almost every night in the shelter as bombs rained down on us. Millions of people lost their lives and thousands were made homeless as the city was reduced to rubble.

In October, a wire came from David. Whereas in his letter he had encouraged Alice to make the journey, this time he insisted.

Chapter Thirty-Seven

David had arranged passage on a ship from Southampton to New York. I would miss working for this family but I had been thinking that it was time for me to go home and now I wasn't going to be letting them down.

Winnie had been crying on and off since she was told the news.

'I'll miss that little baby, Miss Rose. She feels like me own, she does really.'

'And you've been wonderful with her, but she will be safer in America and that's what you must think of and be happy for them.'

'I'll try, Miss Rose, but this is the best job I ever 'ad, I'll never find another place like this one. Miss Alice has been so kind to me, treated me like family, she 'as.'

'I think your family will be happy to have you home, Winnie, especially now.'

'Why can't life just stay the same? It's all that bloody 'itler's fault.'

'Maybe we should just accept that life never stays the same. It will do what it wants, whether we like it or not.'

'I 'ope you'll be happy in America, Miss Rose.'

'What an earth makes you say that?'

'I just hopes you'll be 'appy, that's all.'

'But I'm not going to America, Winnie. I'm going home to Ireland.'

'Perhaps you'd better tell that to Raffi, 'cos he told me you was going with them.'

'Well, he's wrong, are you sure you heard right?'

'Yep, that's what he said, plain as ya like, cross me 'art and 'ope to die. He said you was going with them to take care of the baby.'

'Well, I'm not. Do you know where he is?'

'He's with Mrs Berry.'

I ran downstairs to the kitchen. Raffi was sitting at the table eating cake that Mrs Berry had managed to make from powdered eggs, carrots and apples from the garden.

'Can I interest you in a bit of apple sponge, Rose? Fresh out of the oven.'

'No, thank you, Mrs Berry, I need to speak to Raffi.'

'Just let me finish my cake,' he said.

'The cake can wait, Raffi. I need to speak to you now.'

Mrs Berry must have noticed how angry I was.

'I'll make meself scarce,' she said.

'Well?' said Raffi.

'I just want to get one thing straight,' I said. 'I don't know where you got the idea that I would be coming to America with you but you've got it wrong. I most certainly am not.'

Raffi glared at me. 'Of course you are. How can I take Alice all the way to America on my own?'

'You are not taking your mother to America; she is taking you.'

Raffi's face was bright red and sweaty; his shoulders were hunched up, the way they always were when he was upset. 'I refuse to listen to you, Rose, because you don't listen to me, you never listen to me. You are coming to America with us and that is that.'

I took a deep breath. 'I always listen to you, Raffi, but what you don't like is that I'm not doing what you want me to do.'

I knew I had to calm this down; we were shouting at each other now and neither one of us was going to back down.

'We won't go then. We won't go unless you come with us. We'll stay here and get bombed and probably die and it will be all your fault.'

And suddenly he was crying and screaming and gasping for breath.

'Mrs Berry,' I shouted, hoping she was nearby.

She rushed into the room and took Raffi in her arms. He tried to twist away from her but her strong arms held him tightly to her. She was speaking to him in a soft voice, soothing him with her gentle words. 'Now what's this all about, my sweet boy? It can't be that bad.'

'Tell her,' he screamed. 'Tell her.'

'Tell Rose?'

His voice was high-pitched and screechy. 'Tell her she has to come to America with us.'

Mrs Berry looked across at me. I shook my head.

'I know you're upset, Raffi, but you must calm down so that we can talk about this sensibly.'

'I don't want to be sensible. I don't, I don't! You have to make her listen, you have to.'

Mrs Berry took Raffi's hand and led him to the table. 'Take some deep breaths. That's right, some nice deep breaths. Rose, would you get Raffi a drink of water?'

My legs felt so weak, I could hardly stand. I was shaking as I filled a glass with water. I had seen Raffi's temper before but never as bad as this.

Mrs Berry was still holding him to her. 'Are you feeling calmer?'

Raffi nodded.

'So, you want Rose to go to America with you and she doesn't want to?'

'I'm sorry, Raffi,' I said, 'but I have my own family and I can't go halfway across the world with you, however much you want me to.'

Raffi didn't answer. He just laid his head on the table and sobbed and sobbed.

It was then that I realised just how troubled this young boy was. I felt responsible for his happiness and it was breaking my heart. Could I go to America just because he needed me? Didn't my own family need me just as much as he did? I sat beside him and put my arm around his shoulder. I could see Mrs Berry shaking her head.

'No,' she mouthed.

'I'll have to let my family know,' I said quietly.

Raffi jumped up from the table and flung his arms around me. 'Oh, thank you, Rose, thank you.'

'Will you help me write a letter to me mammy?'

Raffi was finding it hard to look me in the eye.

'Well?'

'It's all sorted, Rose. I went down to see Father Tom and he's writing to your priest, who'll let your mother know.'

I was trying to look cross but there was laughter bubbling up inside me and I couldn't hold it in. And then the three of us were laughing.

Rose Brown from Ballykillen was going to America.

I'd spoken to Mammy from the phone in Father Tom's house, next to the church and Mammy was speaking from the vicarage in Ballykillen.

It was a hard conversation, not least because her voice kept fading out and I couldn't hear what she was saying but I could tell that she was crying and it broke my heart. In the end we just said goodbye and that we loved each other. Tears were running down my cheeks as I replaced the receiver.

Father Tom put a cup of tea in front of me. 'I've shovelled the sugar in,' he said. 'Now, are you really sure about this, Rose? For there will be no shame if you change your mind.'

He was giving me a way out and at that moment I wanted to grasp it with both hands and run for my life. 'I'd be lying if I said I was perfectly sure, Father.'

'How can any of us be perfectly sure, child? Most of us just muddle our way through and hope for the best. How can we ever be sure about anything? Even our dear Lord Jesus must have made the occasional mistake.'

I was shocked at what Father Tom was saying. I had never heard anyone criticise Jesus before, especially a priest. 'But wasn't he perfect?'

'God sent his only son into this world in human form, Rose, and as a human, he had all the frailties that the rest of us have. He might have bodged up the odd job when he was a carpenter.'

I wasn't sure that Father Tom should be talking about Jesus as if he was an ordinary man. I'd say it was verging on blasphemy but he was a priest, ordained by God and I had no right to be judging him.

I knelt down and Father Tom made the sign of the cross on my forehead.

'I wish you God's speed on your journey, Rose. Send me a letter when you are settled. I shall keep you in my prayers.'

'Thank you, Father,' I said.

Saying goodbye to Winnie and Mrs Berry was heartbreaking; the three of us were up all night, crying. They were desperate sad to be leaving the house and the family that they had grown to love and worried about finding new jobs. I was terrified of what lay ahead for me. Was I mad altogether to have let Raffi persuade me to go to America? But it seemed that he always got what he wanted even though he was but a child.

'You don't have to go, Rose,' said Mrs Berry. 'Raffi might be angry but he'd get over it soon enough and what will you do when you get there?'

'I don't know, Mrs Berry, but I can't go back on my word.'

'Yes, you can. This is your life we're talking about and your life belongs to you, not Master Raffi Townsend. There will be nothing for you to do there, girl, you won't be needed. This Aunt Martha that Raffi keeps going on about can take care of Miss Alice and Miss Sarah. You'll be a spare part in a strange country, wondering what in heaven's name you are doing there. Go home to Ireland where you belong, go home to Ireland, Rose.'

Chapter Thirty-Eight

I didn't take Mrs Berry's advice. I couldn't, I had promised Raffi, but as I stood looking up at the great dark ship, I wished I had. Oh, how I wished I had.

It was blowing a gale and you could hardly see a hand in front of your face. Even the ship we were about to board was almost in darkness. A young sailor took our cases and helped us up the gangplank. He reminded me of Erik, I hoped he was safe in these terrible times.

'There are a few lights on down below,' he said. 'But once we set sail, they will be dimmed.'

'Why?' I said.

'Well, miss, we don't want to be drawing attention to ourselves, do we?'

I looked down at the inky black water and felt frightened. It just hadn't occurred to me that this journey to America could endanger our lives. I didn't want to be here; I didn't want any of us to be here. How careless I had been with my promises. I looked across at Alice, who was holding Sarah. She'd heard what the sailor had said and yet she smiled back at me as if she was on a day trip.

I took a deep breath and smiled back. 'Just think, Alice,' I said. 'You will soon be with David.'

She stared at me and didn't answer.

I turned to the sailor. 'Thank you for your help,' I said.

Raffi was ahead of us. He looked back and glared at me. 'Come on, Rose,' he shouted.

I settled Sarah down and went back up on deck. I leaned on the railings as the ship slowly pulled away from the dock. I could hear people calling out names in the darkness. It reminded me of when I left Ireland and that felt like a million years ago.

It was really happening; I really was going to America. I hoped to God that I was doing the right thing. I knew that this was what Raffi wanted, to be back with his Aunt Martha, and Alice would be back with David. As for Sarah... well, she would never remember this journey to the other side of the world.

The young sailor came and stood beside me. 'I hope you've brought your sea legs with you, miss,' he said. 'I'd say it's going to be a rough night.'

'I'll be grand,' I said. 'I'm from a seafaring family.'

'Most of us are,' he said. 'My own father was in the Irish navy. The name's Billy,' he said. 'Billy Tandy from Cavan.'

I smiled at him. 'Rose Brown from County Cork.'

'Well, Rose Brown, I wish you a comfortable journey.'

I watched as the lights of Southampton grew dimmer, then went back down the stairs. We had three cabins. They were small but comfortable. Sarah's cot was beside my bed and Alice and Raffi had the other two cabins. As night fell, we were plunged into darkness, just as Billy had said we would be. As the great ship pitched and heaved beneath us, I thanked God for my sea legs.

I lay awake for ages, even though I was tired. I tried to imagine what America would be like and whether I would be happy there. I hoped that once Raffi was back with his beloved Aunt Martha, he would relax and maybe even go to school. I thought about Mammy and my sisters. I wondered what they would think about me travelling so far from home. It had been Polly's dream to have a new life in England or America and yet it was me that would be living a dream that had never been mine.

I wondered how long the war would last. I wondered how long it would be until I would be back home in Ballykillen with my family and Polly. I saw each one of their dear faces and I felt as though my heart was breaking in two. It seemed to me that there was a price to pay for loving and this one wasn't cheap. My pillow was wet with my tears as I closed my eyes and slept.

When the explosion happened, I thought that I was dreaming and then I heard the screaming and knew that it wasn't a dream at all. Something was very wrong. My heart was thumping as I jumped out of bed and ran towards Alice's cabin. I met Raffi in the corridor. He looked terrified.

'We've been attacked,' he screamed.

People were spilling out of their rooms in different stages of undress. Children were crying and men were looking bewildered. I went into Alice's cabin. She was standing there like a statue and looking to me for direction, so I said the only thing I could think of. 'Put some warm clothes on, Alice, the warmest clothes you have. You too, Raffi, I'll see to Sarah.'

But Alice hadn't moved. 'Must I?' she said, calmly.

'Yes, Alice, you must. Do it now and hurry.'

I went back to my cabin and looked down at Sarah, who was fast asleep. I threw some clothes on and lifted her from the cot. She looked at me through sleepy eyes as I wrapped her up in the blankets from the bed.

Then a voice boomed out, 'This is your captain speaking, I have to inform you that this ship has been torpedoed by an enemy submarine. Please make your way up on deck, where lifeboats are being made ready. I ask you not to panic. There are plenty of lifeboats for everyone. We are currently off the coast of Northern Ireland and help is on the way.'

I stepped into the corridor. People were running past me and I was nearly knocked off my feet. When I went into Alice's cabin, poor Raffi was helping to dress her. I handed the baby to him and took over. 'We'll be alright, Alice, you heard what the captain said? There are lifeboats for everyone and help is on its way. We will soon be rescued.'

She didn't say anything but allowed me to dress her in the warmest clothes I could find.

'What shall I do?' said Raffi.

'You don't have to do anything,' I said. 'We just have to get up on deck, like the captain said, that's all we have to do.'

Alice still hadn't moved and it made me feel angry. 'Alice!' I said sharply.

She looked at me and smiled. 'Yes, Rose?'

'We have to go. We have to go now. Raffi, help your mother.'

There was water running down the stairs as we stepped out into the corridor.

'We're sinking,' someone screamed.

Alice was clutching onto the rail as people pushed and shoved past her. A woman in front of me fell and people were just stepping over her in their panic to get up on deck. I gave the baby to Raffi and helped her up. Was this what happened when people were scared? Did they lose all sense of humanity? They were like a bunch of animals, trying to save their own skins, with not a thought for those around them.

'I think we should go back to the cabin,' said Alice, calmly. 'I think it would be better if we did that. Don't you think so, Rose?'

Jesus, Mary and Joseph, I wanted to hit her and I'd never struck another person in my whole life. 'No, Alice, I don't. We have to go and we have to go now.'

I unclenched her hands from the rail and half pulled, half dragged her up the stairs.

Raffi was glaring at me. 'What do you think you are doing, Rose?'

'I'm trying to save her life; what do you think I'm doing?'

As we stepped outside, the wind nearly took my breath away. Sarah had started to whimper, so I took her from Raffi and pulled the blanket over her head. She immediately snuggled into me. 'Hush now,' I said, softly.

There were people everywhere: women holding onto their children's hands; men with their arms around their wives, trying to look brave but looking totally bewildered; all of them waiting to be told what to do.

Someone shouted, 'Woman and children first.'

The night was black but clouds were scudding in front of a bright half moon which lit up the mountainous waves that kept rolling towards us. Nothing would stop them, I knew that. They would keep coming until they'd battered the ship and brought it down, pulling it down into the deep. The ship was at an odd angle; it no longer rode the waves but smashed against them. The air was full of spray. I tasted salt in my mouth and my skin stung each time droplets hit it. The deck was slippery and kept tilting violently so that it was almost impossible to stay upright. If there hadn't been so many people around, I would have fallen, or worse, dropped the baby. I kept imagining myself slipping forward, Sarah in my arms and the two of us sliding under the barrier, falling, falling into that black sea. I imagined the shock of the cold, wondered if I'd be able to hold onto her if we fell. I looked up at the sky, hoping, praying for some calm, but the clouds that held the moonlight were huge and sullen, full of violence, clenching their thunderous fists as if they too were waiting to lay into the ship and claim her for their own.

A young sailor touched my shoulder, 'You have to go, Miss.' I could tell that he was trying to remain calm but I saw the panic in his eyes.

'Come on, Alice, come on, Raffi,' I said, thanking God that Raffi was still a child and would be allowed into the boat.

I took Alice's hand but she snatched it away. 'Alice, we have to get in the lifeboat.'

'No,' she said, in a calm voice. 'I have to get my crystal.'

'No, you don't,' I said grabbing her arm. 'You have to get in the boat. We can buy another crystal.'

'Don't be silly, Rose,' she said, smiling and walking away.

I didn't know what to do. I had to get Sarah and Raffi into the boat, they were my priority and God forgive me, but I couldn't risk their safety because of Alice.

'Quick, Rose,' said Raffi. 'We have to go with her.'

'No, Raffi, we don't, we must get into the boat now.'

He started pulling at my sleeve. 'Listen, Rose, you have to listen, we have to protect Alice.'

'I have to protect Sarah and I have to protect you. Alice will get in another boat; there are plenty of boats.'

Sarah started to cry as people banged into us, not caring that I was holding a baby, caring only for their own survival, desperate to get off the ship. Men were hurrying their wives and children towards the safety of the lifeboats.

A sailor touched my arm again. 'You have to go, Miss.'

'Please, Raffi, I'm begging you, we have to leave the ship. You have to come with me now.'

'You promised, you promised,' shouted Raffi. 'I can't be left alone with Alice.'

People were pushing past him but he kept yelling at me. 'You have to listen, Rose; you have to listen. David is paying you to look after me, not Sarah, don't you understand? Don't you understand anything?'

'And who's to look after Sarah?'

'Give her to someone.'

I held Sarah closer. 'No,' I said. 'I'm sorry, Raffi.'

'Miss?' said the sailor again.

Raffi glared at me. 'I hate you, Rose; I hate you.' And then he was gone, lost in the crowd.

I turned to the sailor. 'Please, please make sure that they get on a boat. They are in cabin nine. Alice and Raffi Townsend, can you do that?'

'I'll try, Miss, but I'm sure they will be fine, try not to worry. The crew will make sure that no one is left on board.'

'May God keep you safe this night,' I said.

'And may He keep you safe too, Miss.'

I held onto Sarah as the lifeboat was lowered slowly into the water. It hit the rough sea with a splash. A woman screamed and I held Sarah closer. As we were being rowed away, I looked up at the ship, towering above us, my eyes searching, hoping to see them. I tried to stay calm and to tell myself that they would be safe but Raffi's words echoed in my head. 'I hate you, Rose; I hate you.'

PART TWO

Chapter Thirty-Nine

BROOKLYN

1941

There was a fierce wind blowing in from the sea as I walked down the gangplank towards my new life. Sarah was asleep. She wasn't a tiny baby anymore and I was struggling with the dead weight of her in my arms. I was still hoping that somehow Alice and Raffi had survived and would be waiting there to welcome us. Father Devlin in Northern Ireland had contacted David and told him that his wife and son were reported missing, but I still had hope. My heart sank as David ran towards me and I was enveloped in his arms. He touched Sarah's cheek as tears ran down his face. There was no Alice or Raffi. They hadn't made it home. He held me tightly but he couldn't speak, and neither could I.

Standing apart from us was a woman who I guessed must be Aunt Martha. I handed Sarah to David and walked towards her. She was smiling through her tears as she held me close. Her cheek was soft against mine and she smelt of flesh flowers. It was like being held by Mammy. I couldn't speak, my heart was full, and my throat ached with all the sadness that I had been holding back for weeks. I wasn't alone anymore; I wasn't responsible for Sarah anymore.

We were both crying as Aunt Martha stepped back and held both my hands in hers. 'Thank you for looking after Sarah. We shall be forever in your debt, Rose, and now we will look after you for as long as you need us.'

'I couldn't help them,' I said, wiping away the tears. 'I tried but I had to leave them, I had to keep Sarah safe.'

'And you did, my brave girl, you did.'

'I had hoped that they would be here.'

'We all hoped,' she said. 'We still hope but Sarah deserves more from us than tears and long faces and so we shall hide our sorrow and surround her with our love. Isn't that what Alice and Raffi would want?'

I nodded. 'It is.'

Sarah was reaching out her little hands to me. I took her from David, and she buried her face in my coat. Her father and her aunt must have seemed like strangers to her. For so long, it had just been the two of us; she hadn't let me out of her sight. We had gone through something momentous together, her and I, something that had bonded us as nothing else could, but I knew that here, she would be surrounded by love. I knew that she would be alright. I also knew that I would miss her need of me.

'Let's go home, Rose,' said David.

Another home, I thought. *Another home that wasn't mine.* Yet, as I looked at David and Aunt Martha and the baby, who had felt like my own, I could feel a warmth slowly spreading through my body. Perhaps I could be happy here.

When I went to bed that night in Aunt Martha's beautiful white house, I felt as if I could have slept for a million years. I was desperate for sleep. I was desperate to forget. My body was exhausted but my mind was full of the sounds and images and horror of that night. As I lay my head down on the softest of pillows, it all came flooding back to me again, as it had every night for months. I could hear the howling wind, feel the bone-chilling cold and see again the terrifying blackness of the water as the lifeboat plummeted into the sea. I hadn't paid attention to Raffi screaming that he couldn't be left alone with Alice. I should have listened; Raffi was always telling me that I didn't listen. Alice wasn't just childlike, and Raffi wasn't desperate for her attention. Alice was mad and Raffi was afraid of her. I had let him down. I should have dragged

that beautiful boy onto the boat, instead I had turned my back
on him and let him go.

I'm so sorry, Raffi, I'm so terribly sorry.

The next morning, it took me a minute to remember where I
was. I pulled myself up in the bed and looked around the room.
The walls were painted in the palest blue and the long curtains were
the colour of dew-soaked primroses on a spring day. A cool breeze
drifted through the open window and lifted the curtains into the
room, like a ship in full sail. It was the sort of day that me and my
sisters would walk out the wood road to pick berries. The sort of
day that I had spent with Erik at Temple Michael. I felt safe and
at peace. I hadn't a clue what time it was, but I didn't care; it was
the first time in weeks that I had woken naturally and not been
dragged from sleep by the urgent cries of the baby. I found myself
looking forward to what the day would bring and maybe even a
little excitement. I was in America, I had made it, I had survived.

I got out of bed and walked across to the window. Sarah was
toddling around the garden with Aunt Martha right behind her in
case she fell. She was beautiful, just like Alice. *Oh, Alice, there is not
a day goes by when I don't think about you and darling Raffi.* I hoped
that somehow you would just show up with that beautiful smile
and say 'What's the fuss?' But I know in my heart that you won't.

If David had told me the truth about Alice, would I still have
stayed? Yes, I probably would, because like Raffi, I had fallen under
her spell.

I washed and dressed and went into the garden. I called Sarah
and she tottered towards me. I picked her up and spun her around
and her laughter filled the air. 'You are beautiful, do you know
that?' I said, kissing her cheek. 'You are beautiful and I love you
so very much.'

Sarah put her chubby little arms around my neck. I breathed
in her baby smell and my heart melted. She touched my face.
'Mamma?' she said.

I could feel a stinging behind my eyes, she had never said this before.

I pointed to myself. 'Rose,' I said. 'Can you say Rose?'

'Mamma?' she said, laughing.

Chapter Forty

David was pleasant to me but the loss of Alice and Raffi had changed him. He seemed detached from everything; even his beautiful little girl seemed to bring him little joy. The investigation into fraud had been resolved and the manager had been arrested. David was cleared of all wrongdoing. This man had been one of his closest friends, he had trusted him to take care of his business while he was in England and he felt betrayed. I felt so sorry for him but there was nothing I could do to make things better. Aunt Martha was worried about him too. She cooked the food he loved and barely ate. He would disappear for hours, walking the streets of Brooklyn long after we had gone to bed. The hardest thing is to watch someone you care about in such pain and that was all Martha and I could do.

'He just needs time, Rose,' said Aunt Martha. 'The poor man is racked with guilt. He says that if he hadn't insisted that you all come to America, Alice and Raffi would be alive today. He needs to grieve and we must give him that time but he will come back to us, we just have to be patient.'

I took Sarah out most days, pushing the pram through unfamiliar streets, past unfamiliar landscapes. I loved Aunt Martha but I longed for a friend of my own age, someone to talk to and be silly with. Someone like Polly.

Sometimes when I looked at Aunt Martha, I smiled to myself, remembering all the things that Alice had told me about her. She was old now and it was hard to imagine her as she had once been, sitting high up on a window ledge with her legs dangling down the wall, drinking French wine and smoking cigarettes in a long ivory holder and yet sometimes, I saw glimpses of that young free-spirited girl that she once was and when she laughed, I saw Alice.

Oh, how she loved Sarah! Perhaps in this beautiful little girl she still had something of Alice and Raffi left; they were not entirely lost to her. She cared for Sarah as if she was her own child and although it was hard to let go, I knew that this was the way it was meant to be. Hopefully this war wouldn't last long and I could go home without worrying about her and the pain of losing her wouldn't be so hard.

It had been winter when we'd arrived and now and it was spring. The new season should have been a time of hope and new life and new beginnings but I almost preferred those dark days when I could tuck myself away and nothing was asked of me. The strange thing was that all those months after being rescued, I'd had to be strong. I'd had Sarah to look after; I was needed. Her eyes still lit up when I entered a room but now it was Aunt Martha that she followed around, and it was to Martha that she turned when she needed comfort. I was no longer her Mamma and although that was how it should be, I mourned the loss of her need of me. Now she called me Rose – well, her own baby version, which was 'Wose'.

One morning, as I was settling Sarah into her pushchair, David walked into the kitchen.

'Would you girls like some company?' he said.

I looked across at Aunt Martha, who was stirring something on the stove. I could see that she had tears in her eyes as she turned around and smiled at me.

I smiled back at her. 'That would be nice, David,' I said. We walked towards the park, with Sarah talking her baby talk all the way.

'Car,' she said, pointing to the road.

'You clever girl,' said David. 'Clever and beautiful, like your mummy.'

This was the first time he had mentioned Alice since I'd arrived and it brought joy to my heart. When we got to the park, I sat on a bench and watched him playing with his daughter. He held her up and spun her around, making her giggle. In the bright sunshine it looked as if there was a halo of light around the two of them. Wise Aunt Martha had been right; he had needed time to come to terms with the loss of his beloved wife and son. He was coming back to us just as she had said he would.

From then on, when he wasn't in the office, he would join us on our walks. We were easy with each other and I loved his company. Those times spent with David became precious to me and I found myself missing him when he wasn't there.

Mrs Berry had been right when she'd said that there would be nothing for me here. I needed to do something, yet I was not quite brave enough to venture too far into this strange new world I found myself in. There were days when I didn't want to get out of bed. There seemed no point and the more I went into myself, the less brave I became, until I hardly knew who I was, let alone where I belonged.

'Get yourself out of the house, Rose,' said Aunt Martha one day as I stood in the kitchen watching her cook. 'You're wandering round the place like a lost soul. There's no bogeyman out there, child, there's nothing to be afraid of. Walk the streets of Brooklyn and grow to love it as I do.'

'But Sarah is asleep,' I said.

'Go on your own, Rose, there is more to this beautiful city than the park. Sarah will be fine here with me.'

At first, everything seemed overwhelming and I was desperate homesick and wanted to run back to the safety of the house but as the days went by, I grew braver. And I found that I was enjoying myself. I wandered past the big stores and gazed in the windows at the mannequins, wearing the latest dresses and hats. Swanky cars pulled up outside the doors and beautiful ladies stepped out onto the pavements, dressed in fine furs, their feet encased in delicate little shoes. Oh, I wished Polly was beside me. She would have loved all this. It was at times like this that I missed my darling friend.

The streets teemed with people: workmen with flat caps and brawny arms who smiled at me as I went by; boys selling papers on every corner, yelling out the latest news at the tops of their voices; and still more boys kneeling on the pavement as if in prayer, polishing shoes.

The houses that lined the streets were like nothing I had ever seen before. Aunt Martha said they were called brownstones. They were at least three stories high, plus a basement. Steep steps let up to double doors and stone pillars. What I loved most about them was that the steps were a gathering place for families, friends and neighbours. Children of all nationalities ran between them and jumped down off the steps, with whoops of joy. They all played together and it didn't seem to matter at all that they each spoke in a different tongue. I thought it was wonderful and their closeness reminded me of my home.

Everything about Brooklyn was exciting, alive and busy. This place had a heart that throbbed with life and I grew to love it. London had been okay but Brooklyn felt like home. I decided I must tell Polly when next I wrote to her to forget England; it was America that she would love.

Father Tom had said that there was an Irish pub on every corner and he was right. Sometimes I would hear a song from my homeland as I passed the door and it made me smile. There was nothing in London that reminded me of home but Brooklyn touched my heart like England never had.

One day, on my wanderings, I found the Catholic church of Saint Rosalia. Aunt Martha said that there were as many Catholic churches here as there were Irish pubs. Saint Rosalia seemed like a sign, as it reminded me of Mammy and her roses, so I walked up the steps and went in. I was immediately enveloped by all that I knew: the smell of incense, the silence, Jesus hanging on the cross, his poor body bathed in the soft beam of light streaming from the beautiful stained-glass window above his head. I walked down the aisle towards the side altar, where the statue of the Blessed Virgin Mary smiled down at me. I lit a candle and knelt in front of her. 'Please take care of my family, sweet Mary, as you took care of your own son. Keep them safe until I can return home to them.' I made the sign of the cross and stood up to leave when a priest came out of the vestry. Tall and slightly stooped, he had a head of white hair and he looked well fed. He walked towards me, smiling.

'I don't think we've met,' he said. 'I'm Father Paul, parish priest of Saint Rosie's.'

'Saint Rosie's?' I said, smiling.

'That's what we call this old place. It's what the priest before me called it and the priest before him and… Well, it has been known as Saint Rosie's from time immemorial.'

'That's nice,' I said. 'Friendly.'

'I think so too.'

'My name is Rose Brown. I'm new to Brooklyn. I'm new to America.'

'Well, it looks as if the good Lord has led you to the right place and you are very welcome. Can you sing?'

'Not very well,' I said.

'That's a shame, for we have a shortage of voices in the choir. We had some grand singers in the boys until their voices broke. I try to catch them young,' he said, grinning. 'It's not all boys who want to be seen singing in front of their friends. I have to bribe them with a few cents for sweets.'

'I'm sorry I can't help. My mammy has always said that I sound like a dying cat, caught in a trap. My sister Agnes has a lovely voice but the Good Lord didn't see fit to bless me with one.'

'So, would your sister like to join?'

'My sister is back home in Ballykillen, Father.'

'Ballykillen, you say?'

'Yes, Father, it's in County Cork, beside the Blackwater River.'

'Sure, I know it well.'

'You do?'

'My family are from Waterford and we would often visit Ballykillen. I am still in touch with your parish priest, Father Luke. We studied at the same seminary.'

'You know Father Luke?'

'I do, he's a grand fellow and back in the day he could do great things with a hurling stick.'

'You don't sound very Irish, Father.'

'I've been here longer than I was in Ireland, so I guess New York is in my bones now. So, I will see you at Mass on Sunday?'

'You will, Father.'

'God bless you, Rose Brown.'

I walked out into the late summer sunshine and almost immediately a girl fell at my feet. As I helped her up, I could see that she was not a girl but a woman, a very small thin woman.

'Are you hurt?' I said, helping her up.

She rubbed her knee. 'Smashing,' she said.

'You've smashed your knee?'

She smiled at me and I realised that she didn't understand what I was saying.

'Home?' I said, smiling. 'Can I help you home?'

She pointed across the street.

'Is that where you live?'

She nodded.

'Okey-dokey.'

I held onto her arm as we crossed the busy road. We turned a couple of corners and then into a narrow lane, where there were some boys kicking a ball against an old brick wall.

'Good day, Mrs Lyn,' said one of them.

'Smashing,' she said, smiling at them.

I could hear their laughter behind us as we walked away.

Further down the street, she stopped outside a small shop. There were bales of material in the window all piled on top each other. I assumed that it was a tailor's shop. On the door was a sign that made me smile, it said: DON'T STAND THERE SHAKING, COME IN AND HAVE A GOOD FIT.

Underneath that was a sign that said: GIRL WANTED

'Home?' I said.

She smiled up at me, joined her hands together as if in prayer and bowed. 'Come,' she said.

I followed her into the shop. It was small and dark and it smelt of dust and must and something sweet that I didn't recognise. There was a young girl halfway up a ladder. She immediately jumped down and went to the woman. She put her arms around her and said something that I didn't understand.

'She had a fall,' I said. 'Outside the church.'

'And you brought her home?' said the girl in perfect English – well, perfect American.

'Yes.'

'Please come into the kitchen.'

I shook my head. 'I should go home.'

'Please, my father will want to thank you.'

'Just for a minute, then.'

In the room was a man sitting in front of a sewing machine.

'Mamma had a fall, Papa, and this girl kindly brought her home.'

He helped the woman into a chair and spoke to her gently in a language which I later discovered was Japanese, then he did the same as the woman had done earlier. He joined his hands together and bowed. This time I bowed back.

'Thank you,' he said. 'Thank you for bringing my wife home.'

'You are very welcome,' I said, smiling.

'You must stay for tea,' he said.

'Oh no, I really should get home.'

'You shall have tea with us, you will be our guest.'

That day I took a mouthful of the worst tea I had ever tasted in my whole life. It was also the day I got a job in the tailor's shop.

Chapter Forty-One

I was happier now. The tailor's shop had given me a purpose and even better, I had found a new friend in Hanna Lyn and I didn't feel so alone.

Hanna was born and brought up in Brooklyn. She was beautiful, with shiny hair as black as night that she wore in a thick plait down her back, and almond-shaped eyes that were almost as black as her hair. Hanna and I were the same age and we had become instant friends. I hadn't forgotten Polly, who would always be my very best friend, but oh, it was nice to have found someone like Hanna in this new country. We started spending time together, just going for walks and window shopping, but it was nice. I think that Hanna had been lonely too. She did the bookkeeping for her parents and had little time to meet friends or have a social life of her own. Mr and Mrs Lyn were lovely but very strict, which caused friction between them. Hanna, like all young girls, wanted her freedom but her parents wanted to shield their daughter from a world that they still didn't understand. They had been in America for eighteen years and yet they wanted to bring Hanna up in the old ways. She would stay home, meet a nice young Japanese boy, get married, have children and make them proud.

'I have my own life to live,' said Hanna. 'I can't live theirs. I'm not like them. I didn't grow up in Japan, in fact I've never even been there and quite honestly, I don't want to. I like America, I want to live like an American girl. Is that too much to ask, Rose? Or am I an ungrateful daughter who doesn't listen to her parents?'

'You're a lovely daughter, they just want to protect you.'

'From what? Life? I have to find my own way, Rose. I have to make my own mistakes and I probably will, but how else will I learn if I don't experience it?'

Listening to Hanna was like listening to Polly in that they both wanted more than they had. I had always been contented with my life and never yearned for more than the little village and the love of my family.

'They shouldn't have come to America,' she went on. 'They should have stayed in Japan, maybe then they would have a daughter they could be proud of. I can't be what they want me to be.'

'Then we'll have to put our heads together and find a solution.'

Hanna looked doubtful. 'One that won't hurt them?'

'Yes, one that won't hurt them. Leave it to me. I promise I will think of something.'

At home that evening, I talked to Aunt Martha about it.

'Now that's a hard one, Rose,' she said. 'Because no one should come between a child and their parents, for they generally know what's best for them.'

'But she's not a child, she's a young woman and she wants to have some fun. Didn't you have fun at her age?'

Aunt Martha grinned. 'I had more fun than I care to admit, Rose.'

'Well then?'

'Hanna comes from a different culture, one we don't really understand but must respect. She may want to have the freedoms of an American girl, but she is still a Japanese girl and that will always be her heritage.'

'I promised that I would help her.'

'And what grand plan do you have in mind?'

I made a face. 'I don't,' I said.

'Well, you'd better come up with one then, hadn't you? A promise is a promise; you have given your word and a man's word is sacrosanct.'

I sat quietly and tried to think how I could fulfil a promise so rashly given.

'Well, there's a film on at the Carlton. If I can assure her parents that she will be safe with me, they might let her come.'

'What's the film? '

'*Rebecca*, starring Laurence Olivier and Joan Fontaine.'

'I wouldn't mind seeing it myself, Rose. I've read the book by Daphne du Maurier and found it to be very atmospheric. I can just see Laurence Olivier playing the part of Maxim de Winter, for he is very brooding, but I shan't tell you anymore because I don't want to spoil the film for you.'

'Well, I'm only going to go if Hanna can come with me. I'd be terrible scared to walk into a cinema on my own, I wouldn't know who I'd be sitting beside.'

'You're right to feel scared, girl, for there are some very odd men about that wouldn't think twice about playing fast and loose with an innocent young girl like yourself.'

'I'd give them a good dig if they tried,' I said, laughing.

'I'm sure you would, my darling girl.'

'I went to the pictures with Mrs Dempsey while I was in Belfast,' I said. 'We saw *King Kong*; it was desperate sad. This poor gorilla was nothing but kind and they killed him. We were only roaring crying when we came out.'

'People don't like what they don't understand, Rose.'

Aunt Martha was quiet for a moment as if she was remembering something and then she spoke.

'Not everyone understood darling Alice. I did my best to protect her, but I was always worried that someone would take advantage of her naivety. She was an innocent in so many ways but I'm sure you know that already. When David came along, it was like a blessing from God. I knew she would be safe in his hands and she was.'

I nodded. 'Yes, she was.' I wanted her to say more, I wanted to understand more but Alice was gone now and sure, what did it matter anyway? I would remember the good times: her laughter and her beauty; the way her smile could light up a room; and the way she treated me like family and taught me to read. That's what I would remember, the good times.

'You have never talked about your time in Belfast, Rose. Were you unhappy there? Is that why it's hard for you to talk about it?'

Aunt Martha was right; I hadn't wanted to talk about it, because if I did, I would have to go to that dark place that I wanted to forget. It wasn't Belfast that I didn't want to talk about, it was the hours before we were picked up from those freezing waters.

The sea had been rough that night, as only the Irish Sea could be. The small boat pitched and tossed in the huge waves that battered its sides and I feared at any minute we would be thrown into the icy grey water. I feared for Sarah, who shivered in my arms. I started to take off my coat, to give her an extra layer of protection, but an older lady stopped me. 'Your baby needs you to survive, you have to live for her. What good will it do her if you die of the cold?'

I didn't tell her that Sarah wasn't mine but what she said made sense. I couldn't leave her, she had lost enough already. I had to get her back to her father.

The sailor who was rowing the boat had pointed to a box on the floor. A man opened it and inside was a sheet of tarpaulin that he handed over to me. I gratefully covered the baby with it and hoped that would be enough to keep her alive.

Aunt Martha was waiting for me to speak.

'We were picked up by the Irish navy and taken to Belfast,' I said. 'It was the middle of the night and yet there was a crowd of people waiting to offer what help they could. We were taken to a hospital first and once they were sure that we were alright, the Protestant church settled us with families.'

'That was good of them, Rose.'

I nodded. 'Sarah and I were taken in by a lady called Kate Dempsey. She was a widow, who had two children of her own. She fed us and clothed us, even though she had barely enough money to feed her own family.'

'We will repay her kindness, Rose.'

I nodded. 'That would be wonderful.'

'It's the very least we can do.'

'She was so kind to us. She took care of us as if we were her own, as we waited for another ship to bring us here. I was scared to get on that boat. I never wanted to get on another boat again as long as I lived. And God forgive me, Aunt Martha, but I even thought of just taking Sarah home to Ballykillen, where we would be safe.'

'You didn't though, did you, Rose?'

'No, I didn't. I couldn't. It helped that I could share my worries with Kate and we became friends. I'd always been told that Protestants were to be feared – not by Mammy, but by the people of the town. The way they talked about them, you'd swear they had horns and a tail, but the people I met in Belfast were good people and no different to my own kind.'

'Sometimes I think we'd all be a lot better off with no religion at all.'

'But don't you believe in God?' I said, shocked.

Aunt Martha smiled, her eyes full of mischief. 'When I was younger, I worshipped at the altar of Hedonism.'

'Is that a religion?'

'Not as such, no,' she said, laughing.

'What is it, then?'

'I'd say it's the pursuit of pleasure, a kind of self-satisfying indulgence and most definitely the privilege of the young. We used to go around quoting Aristippus and believing ourselves to be the bright young things of the day.'

'Who in God's name is he when he's at home?'

Aunt Martha laughed. 'He was a student of Socrates.'

She said it as if I was on nodding terms with yer man but I let it go.

'He believed,' she went on, 'that the art of life lies in taking pleasures as they pass and that the keenest pleasures are not intellectual, nor are they always moral.'

The Catholic Mass was in Latin but even that made more sense than this load of baloney.

'And do you still believe that stuff?'

'Oh no, I did that awful thing: I grew up. Now I let people believe what they want to believe and listen to my own good sense. With age comes wisdom, Rose, and I don't need any man-made religion to dictate how I should think, or what I should believe. I have my own set of morals and if I am to be judged by anyone, it will be myself.'

I was beginning to understand why Alice loved Aunt Martha so much. I thought she was magnificent and like no one I had ever met.

'And I think it's time to drop the Aunty bit. I'm not your aunty and it will get in the way of our friendship.'

'That's grand then,' I said, hugging her.

Chapter Forty-Two

The beads tinkled, glass on glass, as I pushed back the curtain between the shop and the Lyns' kitchen.

'I'm off now, Mr Lyn,' I said.

'Ah, Rose,' he said. 'Good day today, yes?'

'Yes, Mr Lyn,' I said, smiling. 'A very good day. Two suits and a day dress. I've booked them in for a fitting.'

'Two suits, Rose? That's good, that's very good.'

Mr Lyn measured the gentlemen and Mrs Lyn measured the ladies and I became a kind of translator.

Mrs Lyn was sitting at the table with her little boy, Simmy, on her lap. She spoke very little English and I spoke no Japanese but we managed somehow to understand each other. Mrs Lyn managed to get the words *smashing*, *okey-dokey* and *darlin'* into all her very limited conversations.

'I'm off now,' I said, smiling at her.

'Home? Smashing.'

'Yes, home. I'll see you tomorrow.'

'Smashing,' she said, smiling at me.

Just then, Hanna ran down the stairs. 'I'll walk home with you, Rose.'

'Mr Lyn?' I said.

He looked up from the sewing machine. 'Yes, Rose?'

'There's a film I want to see at the Carlton cinema.'

'A movie?' he said.

'Yes, a movie, but I don't want to go on my own and I wondered if Hanna could keep me company.'

'You want Hanna to go to the movies with you?'

I nodded.

Mr Lyn said something in Japanese to his wife, who shook her head.

'No movie, no movie.'

'I promise that she will be safe, I will take good care of her.'

Mr Lyn repeated what I'd said to his wife.

'No movie,' she said again.

Mr Lyn stood up and walked over to his wife, put his arm around her and spoke gently.

'You will bring her home straight after the movie?' he said.

I smiled. 'Of course I will and thank you, thank you both.'

'Mrs Lyn?' I asked.

'Okey-dokey,' she said.

Once Hanna and I were outside, we held hands and ran down the street, laughing.

'A movie?' said Hanna.

'I thought that might be a good start.'

'I can't believe that I shall be going to the movies like a proper American girl. Oh, I love you, Rose Brown, and I'm so glad that my mother fell at your feet. I mean, when you think how many pairs of feet there are in Brooklyn, wasn't it a spot of good luck that it was your feet she fell at?'

'Now is that the sort of thing a good Japanese girl should be saying about her mother?'

'I guess not,' she said, grinning, 'but she would have fallen anyway.'

'Will you come in for a drop of tea?' I said as we neared my home.

'I'd better not push my luck; besides, your tea tastes like poison.'

'I'll see you tomorrow then,' I said, laughing.

'The movies, eh?'

'You haven't even asked what's on.'

'I don't care what's on,' she said, walking away.

When I walked into the kitchen, Martha was feeding Sarah at the table.

'Hello, my lovely girl,' I said.

Sarah clapped her hands and grinned at me. 'Wose,' she said.

'Can you say Rose?'

Sarah giggled. 'Wose.'

'R-r-r Rose,' I said.

'W-w-w WOSE,' she said, laughing.

'Close enough,' I said, kissing her sticky cheek.

'This child would live on pancakes and maple syrup if I let her,' said Martha. 'Do you not have that in England? For she can't seem to get enough of it, bless her little heart.'

'She's had pancakes alright,' I said. 'But in England, she had them with sugar and lemon.'

'A pancake is not a pancake without the syrup. It's a good job you came here when you did and got yourself introduced to the real thing.'

'I'll give Sarah her bath, if you like,' I said.

'I'd appreciate that, Rose. For some reason I'm bone-weary this evening.'

Martha was getting old, perhaps too old to care for a toddler, who was into everything. Should I stop working at the shop? Should I be here to help her? Is that what I should do? I didn't know. I decided I would talk to David about it.

Sarah splashed and squealed in the warm soapy water until I was soaked. Her slippery body shone like silk and I wanted to scoop her up and hold her forever. She picked up a little boat and plunged it into the bubbles again and again, laughing as the water splashed over her face.

Alice would never see this beautiful little girl, she would never be there to share her adventures, she would never be there to watch her grow into a young woman and saddest of all, Sarah would never know Alice, or her big brother.

I didn't want to feel sad, I was too young for all this. Why was I here at all? I wanted to see Mammy and my sisters. I had grown to love this place but I didn't belong here. I wanted to go home, oh, how I wanted to go home.

Sarah picked up the little toy. 'Boat, Wose? Boat?'

'Yes, it's a boat, you clever, clever girl. Wose loves you, Wose loves you very much, do you know that?'

'Boat,' she said again.

Chapter Forty-Three

Me and Hanna held hands in the cinema as we watched *Rebecca*. It was awful scary and we just didn't know what was going to happen next. Mrs Danvers was a baggage of a woman, who bullied poor Mrs de Winter and who reminded me of Dervla, the snitch at Savages. It had a happy ending, thanks be to God, and we came out happy.

Hanna sighed. 'Don't you think that Joan Fontaine is the most glamorous woman you ever saw?'

'She's beautiful, alright,' I said. 'But I'm happy being who I am, for didn't God Himself make me? I'd be awful ungrateful if I was wanting Him to have made me more like Joan Fontaine.'

'I suppose you're right,' she said, linking her arm through mine.

We walked home through the dark streets of Brooklyn and even though it was late, there were still people sitting on the steps of the brownstone houses, their laughter shrill against the silence of the night. We stopped in front of a family that Hanna knew. The woman had a fat baby lying across her lap. The baby was fast asleep, its head almost touching the stone step. The woman hitched him up over her shoulder and said something to Hanna in Japanese, which made her laugh.

We said goodbye and started walking home.

'What did she say?'

'She said that the baby is eating her out of house and home.'

'He's like Brenda Daley's baby from the town; he's an old slob of a boy and you could just eat him but he's desperate fat, God love him.'

'Slob?' said Hanna.

'You know, he's a dote.'

'A what?'

I laughed. 'He's cute.'

'Oh right, some of the things you say make no sense to me at all, Rose.'

'It's the Irish blarney,' I said, grinning.

'Well, I like it, whether I can understand it or not.'

'I'm glad you enjoyed the film, Hanna.'

'Oh, I did and I want to go again, if my parents will let me.'

'Well, we'd better get a move on, or they'll blame me for keeping you out too late.'

We held hands and started running for home.

Every evening, Martha and myself would sit beside the wireless and listen to the desperate news coming from England. People were spending nights in the tube stations and children were being evacuated to the safety of the countryside again. I thought of all those children leaving their homes to live with strangers and mothers having to say goodbye to their babies, not knowing when they would see them again.

Our journey to America had been terrible. We had lost Alice and Raffi, but I was so thankful that me and Sarah were here right now and not in London.

When the British air force conquered the Germans over the skies of Britain, everyone was hopeful that this would bring an end to the war and for a while, we thought it would and maybe soon it would be safe for me to return home.

Germany continued to attack England, with massive air raids on major towns and cities. The loss of lives and homes left myself and Martha in floods of tears and I feared for Winnie Tuttle and Mrs Berry. I couldn't bear to think of them dead or injured.

When David came home that evening, he found us sobbing in each other's arms.

'Now what's all this?' he said, gently.

'Bloody men and their bloody wars,' said Martha. 'Have they nothing better to do than to bomb innocent people who deserve to keep themselves and their children safe? Just because some maniac wants to rule the world.'

'Maybe you should turn the wireless off,' he said.

'And what? Pretend it's not happening, while we sit in our safe little houses? Is that what you think? It's not our war, so why should we care? Is that your advice?'

'Come on, Martha,' said David. 'You know I care every bit as much as you but your tears aren't going to stop what's happening, so why upset yourself by listening to the news every evening when there is nothing we can do?'

'And weren't you the one that said information is knowledge? Or am I thinking of some other smart Alec?'

David looked shamefaced. 'You are right of course, Martha,' he said. 'But then you always are.'

'I think I'll take myself off to bed,' she said. 'I can't bear to listen to any more of this.'

'You do that, dear,' said David gently, 'and let us hope that tomorrow will bring us better news.'

'Well, it couldn't be much worse,' she said, walking out of the room.

'Tea?' said David, standing up.

I shook my head and started crying again. 'It's all so awful, why can't people live in peace?'

David knelt in front of me and took my hands in his. 'Oh, my dear girl,' he said. 'My dear sweet Rose.'

As I sat there with David's hands in mine, something happened. A spark of joy crept into my heart, a bubble of excitement filled my tummy. I wanted to stay like this forever. I wanted to hold onto David forever.

He wiped away my tears. 'Oh, my dear, sweet girl,' he said. 'My very dear Rose.'

Time seemed to stand still as we gazed into each other's eyes. I wanted him to kiss me so badly, I thought I would go mad if he didn't. Very gently, he took my face in his hands and then his lips were on mine. It was the sweetest, softest kiss I had ever known and I knew in that moment that I was lost and whatever happened from now on, this night would live in my heart forever and I would always be grateful for it.

When I went down to breakfast the next morning, I could barely look at David but he smiled at me and then I knew that we were going to be alright.

'I was just saying to David,' said Martha, 'that he should take you to Coney Island.'

'Would you like that, Rose?' said David.

'What's Coney Island?'

'The seaside. Would you like to go to the seaside, Rose?'

I'd missed the sea; I'd missed my own beautiful strand and the lighthouse. I'd missed looking out over the water to the humble houses scattered across the hillside and the church tower, further along the coast. I felt a lump in my throat as I thought of Polly and how we would sit on the rocks and watch the waves tumbling the pebbles. I smiled when I remembered us running barefoot across the wet sand and the delicious feeling as the coldness of it squelched between our bare toes.

I tried not to think too much about Ballykillen because if I did, I'd go mad with the longing to be there. The only thing that brought me peace was knowing that Ireland was not part of this awful war and that Polly and my family were safe. Yes, I wanted to go to the seaside and I wanted to go there with David.

Chapter Forty-Four

I stood at the water's edge, holding Sarah's hand, as the waves trickled over our toes. David joined us and took Sarah's other hand in his.

'Shall we jump the waves?' he said, smiling down at her. 'Would you like that?'

'I think she would,' I said. 'I think you would, wouldn't you, my angel?'

I tucked Sarah's dress in her knickers and David rolled his trousers up above his knees. His legs were very white and covered in black hairs, which reminded me of the first time I met him. I smiled as I remembered Polly saying, *'Now what man sits up in bed without a good vest on him?'*

We waded a bit further into the sea and as a wave rolled towards the shore, we lifted Sarah high into the air, making her squeal with laughter.

'Again, Wose,' she said. 'Again.'

'We should have brought costumes,' said David.

There was no way that I would let David see me in a swimming costume, just the thought of it made me blush.

'Maybe another time,' he said, laughing.

Coney Island was nothing like the strand in Ballykillen – for a start, the beach was very crowded; you could hardly see a grain of sand for people of all ages, enjoying a day out by the sea.

It didn't remind me of home at all and for that I was grateful.

'Ice creams?' said David, scooping Sarah up into his arms.

'Lovely,' I said.

'You get them, Rose, while I fetch a blanket from the car.'

As I walked back to the beach with the three ice creams, I could see David spreading the blanket down on the sand. A couple of pretty girls were looking at him and giggling. Yes, David was a fine-looking man and not just that, he was kind. I thought of how lovely he was with Sarah and Aunt Martha and how gentle he had been with Alice. He must miss Alice and Raffi so much, yet here he was, taking me and Sarah for a day out at the beach.

As we sat together, leaning against the wall, Sarah fell asleep beside us, her ice cream still in her hand, dripping onto the blanket.

'Thank you for today,' I said.

'I'm glad it has pleased you. I owe you so much more than a day at the seaside.'

I closed my eyes, enjoying the warm sun on my face and listening to the waves tumbling towards the shore. I felt happy and contented, then I felt his hand cover mine, so gently I barely felt it, but I knew it was there. It was warm and soft, as warm as our kiss had been and it filled every part of me with happiness. I wanted this day to never end.

'I don't know what I would do without you, Rose,' he said softly.
I don't know what I would do without you, I thought.

As summer turned to autumn, David and I would take Sarah to the park. Autumn was my favourite season of the year and this one didn't disappoint. I watched as they jumped into the piles of fallen leaves. The colours were so dazzling, they took my breath away. Deep greens, lime greens, reds and faded yellows flew up all around them. Their laughter carried on the soft breeze and for a split second, I wished that Alice and Raffi could be with us to share this beautiful moment. We were making memories, but were they ours to make? If Alice had survived there would be no 'us'. I wondered if David felt it too. It was almost a year since we had lost them and it felt like yesterday. Alice's laughter was as clear in my head as if she was beside me and Raffi's anger still crept into my dreams, filling me with guilt.

I started living for our evenings together. Aunt Martha would go to her bed early, leaving David and me alone. I couldn't wait to finish work; I knew that what I was feeling was wrong but I cherished these times. David taught me how to play chess, we talked and were easy with each other and I wanted nothing more than to be near him. Sometimes we spoke of Alice and Raffi and I was glad, because I could see that talking about them made David happy. I had never wanted to mention them before as I thought it would make him sad.

David and I hadn't kissed again. Maybe it was only friendship he felt for me and gratitude for bringing Sarah home to him. If that was the case then friendship had to be enough. I never allowed myself to hope for more, because if I did, I would be lost.

We listened to music and he introduced me to the great jazz musicians and singers, names I had never heard of before: Duke Ellington, Dizzy Gillespie, Charlie Parker and Glenn Miller. One evening, he selected a record and put in on the turntable.

'Close your eyes and listen to this, Rose,' he said.

I did as he said and then the room was filled with the most beautiful voice I had ever heard. The words touched my heart. They were everything I was feeling; it was as if she was singing just for me.

As the last strains of the song ended, I felt my eyes fill with tears for everything I felt but could never have.

'That's how I felt when I first heard her voice,' said David.

I wiped my eyes. 'Who is it?'

'The wonderful Billie Holiday,' he said. 'What does she make you feel, Rose?'

'She makes me feel…' I started. 'She makes me feel as if she was singing just to me.'

'And is it a happy feeling?'

'No.'

'I guess that's why they call it the blues. Not something to listen to if you are sad or troubled. Are you sad, Rose?'

I couldn't tell him what I really felt, so I put a big smile on my face. 'Well, I wasn't until I heard that,' I said.

'Then I'm sorry I made you sad, Rose Brown. I shall try never to make you sad again.'

'Thank you, Mr Townsend. I'd appreciate that.'

We had both stopped smiling as we stared at each other.

'I mean it, Rose,' he said. 'I never want to make you sad.'

But you will, I thought, *because I love you. I love you and you will always make me sad.*

Chapter Forty-Five

I was still enjoying working in the little tailor's shop and me and Hanna enjoyed spending time together. The Lyns now trusted me and we saw as many films as we could. There were dance halls in Brooklyn but those were out of bounds for Hanna and it made her question her parents' rules.

'Have you ever been fond of a boy who's not Japanese?' I asked her one day.

Hanna nodded. 'His name was Joe and we met at school. We were only friends but I think it could have become something else. He was smart and funny and kind and very creative; he wanted to be an artist. He painted beautiful pictures for me but of course I couldn't take them home. I know my parents want the best for me but surely, I should be the one that knows that.'

I didn't know what to say to her. In my heart, I was sure that I would feel the same but I remembered Martha saying that you couldn't come between a child and its parents. But maybe Martha was wrong? Maybe I should support my friend and let her know that what she was feeling was what most young girls would feel.

Hanna was a good daughter; she would probably have loved to have taken Joe's paintings home and maybe put them on her bedroom wall but she didn't because she knew her parents wouldn't approve. She put their needs before her own.

'So, what do I do?' she said. 'Hide things from them? Tell them what they want to hear, lie to them?'

'I think that if you find the right boy, the one that you love with all your heart, then my advice would be to fight for him. Your parents love you and they wouldn't want to lose you, so live the life you want, Hanna, and leave the rest to whatever God you believe in.'

Hanna and I had never discussed religion because it didn't matter to us what the other one believed in, but I was suddenly curious. 'What do you believe in, Hanna?'

'We believe in the teachings of Buddha.'

'And I believe in Jesus. Maybe one day you can tell me about your God and I'll tell you about mine.'

Hanna smiled at me. 'Thank you for being my friend, Rose.'

'Thank you being mine,' I said.

One evening, after putting Sarah to bed, I was sitting on the couch with Martha, reading the *Little House on the Prairie*. I could read pretty well by now but I still struggled with some words and Martha was there to help me.

'Your reading is really coming on,' she said.

'I shall always be grateful to Alice, for teaching me.'

We sat quietly for a while.

'I think I see her every day,' said Martha. 'Running around the garden with little Raffi. I know she's not there, but in my mind I see her and I want to run down the garden and join them. Those were such happy days, Rose.'

I wished that those were the memories I had of Alice but mine were much darker. Mine were clouded with panic and noise and that inky black water that I still dreamt about. I tried to block these thoughts from my mind. I tried to remember the happy times, when we danced around the room, and when we stood on top of Parliament Hill in the snow, looking out over London. I wanted to remember her kindness and her laughter but however hard I tried, the black water would come and wash all those lovely memories away.

'Have you given up hoping, Martha?' I said, gently.

'I have to for my own sanity. I don't want to, but I have to accept that they are gone. Is that wrong of me?'

'Oh no, Martha, don't ever think that.'

'I know it's painful for you, Rose, but can you tell me how it happened? I think I'm ready to know, I think it's time.'

And so, I went back to those last, horrible moments when Alice and Raffi refused to get into the lifeboat. 'She went back to get her crystal,' I said, 'and Raffi refused to leave her. There were plenty of lifeboats, so I thought that they would be alright. I prayed that they would be alright. I was angry with her, Martha, and God forgive me, but I wanted to hit her. I did; I wanted to hit her. I'm sorry.'

Martha nodded. 'From a child, Alice marched to no drum but her own. I was proud of her for that, I thought it would stand her in good stead, for a world that was too often ruled by men. I wanted her to be able to think for herself and not cling to someone else's philosophies. I wanted her to believe in herself and not to allow anyone to tread on her dreams. I fear that I indulged her. She had had such a sad childhood, Rose, and I wanted to make it up to her. I wanted her to be happy every day of her life and I felt that was a privilege, but life has a way of tossing your dreams up into the air and leaving them in pieces at your feet. That is what happened to my darling girl, when she lost her sweet baby and I could do nothing but stand by and watch her fall apart. All the love I had in my heart couldn't save her.'

'She had happy times, Martha. She was full of love and joy and she made everyone around her happy. How could she have given all that love if she hadn't known it? I don't think you can feel love if you've never been shown it.'

Martha had tears in her eyes. 'You're a good girl, Rose.'

'Am I? Sometimes I think that I am a very foolish girl.'

Martha leaned across and took my hand in hers. 'I think that love, whatever form it takes, can only be a good thing and in the end, love is the only thing that really matters.'

That was when I realised that however hard I had tried to hide it, Martha knew what was in my heart. I also knew that there was no safer place for it to be.

Martha dried her eyes. 'We shall make this a wonderful Christmas for Sarah. The best Christmas she's ever had.'

'We should get a tree,' I said, smiling.

'We'll all go together and find the finest tree that money can buy.'

'Do you have decorations?'

'I have a box of them in the attic that haven't seen the light of day since the family went to England. I had no heart for Christmas once they'd gone.'

'Well, we'll have to change all that, won't we?'

'We will, darling Rose, we will. We shall have a tree and baubles and candles and…'

'A big fat turkey,' I said, grinning. 'And crackers.'

'Oh yes, we mustn't forget the crackers,' said Martha. 'We shall bring life and joy back into the house and we shall have such fun doing it.'

In that moment, Martha sounded so like Alice. I remembered the day she'd walked into the room and announced that they were going to get a tree and his smile as he hurled himself at her. Yes, that was a lovely memory; maybe in time I could allow these happy times to replace the sad ones.

'It's you and Sarah that have brought the joy back, Rose.'

Just at that moment, the door opened and David came into the room. We knew at once that there was something terribly wrong. His face was drained of colour as he sank down onto the floor and covered his face with his hands and wept.

Martha rushed to his side. 'What's wrong, my dearest? What's wrong?'

I just stood staring at the two of them on the floor. I didn't know what to do. I felt helpless at the sight of this strong man, struggling to speak. I took a deep breath, sat down beside him and gently took his hand away from his face.

'What's happened, David?' I said, softly.

Tears were running down his cheeks as he looked at me.

'They've bombed Pearl Harbor, Rose. Those bastards have bombed Pearl Harbor.'

Chapter Forty-Six

More than two thousand men were killed on that dreadful day and hundreds were injured. Twenty American naval vessels were destroyed and three hundred planes. The USS *Arizona* sank with more than a thousand men trapped inside. There had been no warning, David said they were sitting ducks. On December eighth, President Roosevelt declared war on Japan.

Not only were the American people in mourning, they were angry and their anger was aimed at innocent Japanese families, living in their towns and cities.

One morning, I arrived at the little tailor's shop to see Hanna standing on a ladder cleaning the shop window. Someone had thrown paint all over it.

'Oh, Hanna,' I said. 'Let me help.'

She didn't say anything, she just looked at me with such hopelessness in her eyes. I was suddenly scared for this lovely family who had done no harm to a single person in their lives.

It took us all morning to get rid of the paint and not one customer came anywhere near the shop.

'We've probably just wasted our time,' said Hanna. 'They'll do it again.'

'But you're American citizens! You and Simmy were born here, this is wrong.'

'I fear it's only the beginning,' she said, sadly.

Hanna was right. Doctors, lawyers and teachers were targeted, their only crime being that they were of Japanese descent.

Everyone was talking about the war. Men aged between twenty-one and thirty-five responded to the country's call to arms. The queues outside the recruitment offices reached right around the block. Young lads, who looked too young to fight, were singing 'The Star-Spangled Banner' at the tops of their voices. These were boys who wanted to be men, who wanted to prove themselves and fight for their country. As I looked at their fresh young faces, I wondered if they knew what was ahead of them, or did they think it would be a game of toy soldiers? I wondered how many of them would survive this war. I wondered how many would come home.

David was thirty-six and I thanked God for it. I knew it was selfish of me but I didn't care. The thought of him going to war scared me; the thought of him dying terrified me. If he died, a part of me would die with him.

Hanna stopped leaving her house after a group of boys spat at her as she pushed Simmy to the park. There were no more outings to the cinema. There were no more walks around town. I was sad and worried for the Lyns. The little tailor's shop was struggling to survive; orders dried up as people were scared to be seen going through its doors. Friends tried to help but the odd alteration wasn't enough to keep them going. Mrs Lyn cried a lot and Mr Lyn smoked a lot. His friends would gather in the small yard behind the shop and they would spend hours speaking in Japanese. I think it helped them to be together and to share their fears for an uncertain future.

I knew they couldn't afford to keep me on but I continued to go to work every day and I refused any payment. Having a job had never been about the money, it had just given me something to do and I had loved it.

'Do you think that they would like to spend Christmas with us, Rose?' said Martha one day as I was telling her about the worrying situation they were in.

'I'll ask, but they are frightened to leave the shop. One of their friends had a brick thrown through their window. It's not fair, Martha, they have done nothing to deserve this.'

She nodded. 'Young boys with too much testosterone. It's a game to them, it makes them feel big in front of their friends. They have no idea of the harm they are doing to these poor families; it makes me sick and it makes me angry.'

'It makes me angry too.'

'I fear for you too, Rose, going there every day. You'll be tarred with the same brush, they may start on you.'

'Don't worry about me, I can take care of myself. I'll give the skitty little eejits as good as they give me.'

'I have no doubt about that, Rose, no doubt at all.'

On a cold Christmas Eve, David insisted that he came to Midnight Mass with me because he didn't want me out in the dark on my own. As we neared Saint Rosie's, we could hear the bells ringing out into the dark night, welcoming in a Christmas that for some, would never be the same again. The sweet voices of the choir filled the church with the hymns of my childhood, 'Away in a Manger' and 'O Little Town of Bethlehem'. If I closed my eyes, I could imagine that I was at home, with my mammy and sisters beside me. I would light candles in front of the baby Jesus as I had done every year of my life for as far back as I could remember. I longed to go home and although the odd letter was coming through, it wasn't enough; I needed to see my family and Polly. But going home would mean leaving David and leaving Sarah, who I had grown to love as if she were my own and anyway I was going nowhere until this war ended.

Father Paul prayed for peace and called on God to put an end to the war. He prayed for our brave boys, that they would come safely home to us. We bowed our heads as he read from the Bible.

Do not be afraid, do not be discouraged.
Be strong and courageous. This is what the LORD will do,

to all the enemies, you are about to fight.
When you pass through the waters
I will be with you and when you pass through rivers
They will not sweep over you
When you walk through fire, it will not burn you.

When Mass was over, we thanked Father Paul and walked outside to a winter wonderland. A thin blanket of snow had covered the ground and clung to the bare boughs of the trees and the rooftops of the buildings. It glistened in the glow of the lamplight and swirled this way and that in the wind as if it couldn't make up its mind where to land.

We walked slowly home, savouring the magic of this Christmas night.

'Oh, David, isn't it beautiful? Isn't it the most beautiful thing?'

He stopped walking. 'I have something to say to you, Rose.'

'Is it "Happy Christmas"?' I said, smiling.

But David didn't return my smile and I knew at once what he was going to say. I wanted to run as far away from him as I could, so that I wouldn't have to hear his words, the words that would surely break my heart.

'You're going away, aren't you?'

He nodded.

I walked a little away from him. 'You can't,' I said.

'Would you have me sitting in my safe little office while men and young boys are dying? Is that what you would have me do? Is that the sort of man you think I am?' he shouted after me.

By now, tears were running down my cold cheeks and into my mouth. I turned around, glaring at him. 'Yes, that's exactly what I want you to do. I want you to sit in your safe little office. You don't have to go to war, you don't have to.'

David walked towards me. 'Yes, I do, Rose.'

He held my face in his hands. 'I have to say something and I want you to know that I say it with no hope or expectation. I love you, Rose. I know I have no right to, but I do. There, I've said it and I shall say no more.'

'You love me?'

'With all my heart.'

And then I was in his arms. I was laughing and crying as we held each other and then as the snow fell around us, we kissed and I felt as if I had come home.

Chapter Forty-Seven

David lifted Sarah up so that she could put the silver star on the top of the tree. Her chubby little legs were hanging down and she was giggling. One of her socks was missing and my heart overflowed with love for her.

I had been right when I'd said that the Lyns wouldn't leave the shop and I prayed that they could find some joy on this Christmas Day.

My thoughts were all over the place. I missed my family and I missed Polly but my heart was full of joy because I was loved by the dearest man in the world. I still couldn't quite believe it and I wouldn't let myself think that having found him, I could lose him.

The snow continued to fall all morning, dancing and swirling across the lawn and over the trees and into the secret places. Sarah stood at the window, her little face squashed against the glass, watching the big fat flakes falling outside. After dinner, me and David wrapped her up and took her into the garden.

At first, she just stood there, her eyes wide with excitement.

'It's snow, my darling,' I said.

'Snow, Wose?'

'Yes, snow, just for you.'

'My snow?'

'Yes, all for you because you are the best little girl in the whole world and you deserve snow on Christmas Day.'

We held her hands and jumped into the soft, powdery whiteness of it. Sarah threw handfuls of it up in the air, giggling as they fell about her face. Every so often, David and I would look at each other and smile. My heart felt as if it would burst out of my body with happiness as our hands touched, while attempting to build a very wonky snowman. Martha watched from the window, waving and smiling.

I wondered what she was thinking. I wondered if she was wishing it was Alice and not me that she was looking at.

On New Year's Day, we had a birthday party for Sarah. I couldn't believe she was three years old. Every day she looked more like Alice. Her hair was as blonde as her mother's and her eyes were the same greeny-grey that changed with her mood, just as Alice's had done. There was nothing of David or Raffi in her. She was her mother's daughter and there were times when, God forgive me, I wished she wasn't. Alice and Raffi could still be alive and there were days when I felt that I had betrayed them, for if Alice was alive somewhere, then a piece of me would die. I was only now learning that love could make you selfish and I was ashamed.

Martha had made a birthday cake and we had hung balloons about the room. I bought Sarah a rag doll that she loved. She carried it around everywhere, holding it by one arm so that it dangled down her leg.

'What do you want to call her?' I said.

Sarah frowned and looked very serious as she thought about this.

'What about Peggy?' said David.

Sarah shook her head.

'Polly?' I said.

'No.'

'Such a big decision,' said Martha, smiling.

'Bill,' she said, with a huge grin.

I laughed. 'But Bill's a boy's name.'

'Bill,' she said again.

David picked her up and swung her around. 'Bill it is, then! Happy birthday, my beautiful girl.'

I remembered the day she was born. We had been so happy, little knowing what lay ahead. I knew that Martha was feeling the same. David was leaving us and alongside the joy of this day, we were terrified of what was to come.

For the whole of January, it rained, turning the white snow to a grey slush that piled up beside the sidewalks and gathered in mounds around the trees and in the corners of the steps that led down to the garden. The wonky snowman's head had got smaller and smaller as its body puddled onto the wet grass. Each day we woke to grey skies and howling winds. The shop was only a short distance from the house but every day I arrived at work soaked to the skin and Mrs Lyn would take my coat and make me sit beside the fire. They feared going to the shops for food, so Martha made sure that they had everything they needed. We were also concerned that they may be running short of money, with so little business coming in, but we both knew that they would be too proud to ask for help.

'She smashing lady,' said Mrs Lyn. 'She okay woman.'

'She is,' I said.

There was nothing much for me and Hanna to do, no customers for me and no books for her to see to, so we spent most of our time in her bedroom. The room was chilly, so we wrapped the blankets around us and sat back against the pillows.

'I wonder if they will still hate us when the war ends,' said Hanna. 'I wonder if our lives will ever be the same again.'

I wanted to tell her that everything would be alright but I didn't know that it would and I wondered what would become of these kind people and all the other families of Japanese descent. They were being treated as if they were the enemy, even though most had been born here and considered themselves to be American.

'It's not fair, what they are doing to you. It's just not fair and it makes me so angry.'

'I can't even take Simmy out.'

'I could. I could take him out.'

'Rose, Simmy looks Japanese and anyway, my mother won't let him out of her sight.'

'I'm sorry, I didn't think.'

Hanna sighed. 'I suppose everything has an ending and one day people will forget.'

'I pray for it.'

We were silent for a while and then I said, 'David has enlisted in the army.'

'When is he leaving?'

'In a couple of weeks.'

'Oh, Rose, I'm so sorry. You'll miss him, won't you?'

I nodded.

'Rose, forgive me if I'm wrong, but have you grown fond of him?'

I could feel my eyes filling with tears. 'I don't know what I will do without him.'

Hanna put her arm around me and allowed me to cry. It felt good to let out all the feelings that I had been keeping from her.

'And has he grown fond of you, Rose?'

'Yes, yes, he has.'

'I think that is beautiful.'

'You don't think badly of me?'

'Is that why you haven't told me? Did you think I would judge you?'

'I didn't know, I'm sorry.'

'Oh, Rose, there is so much hate in the world right now, how can love be wrong?'

'But Alice could still be alive.'

'Then enjoy what you have and if she is alive, I know that you will face it with grace and dignity and you will be brave, for you are the bravest girl I have ever met.'

I dried my eyes and smiled at her. 'Thank you, my friend, thank you for understanding.'

'Always,' said Hanna. 'Always.'

Chapter Forty-Eight

It was a warm day as I walked to work, the first warm day for a long time. I was enjoying the sun on my face, reminding me that spring was on its way after this long cold winter.

As I neared the shop, I could hear yelling and shouting. My heart was pounding in my chest as I ran down the street. I just knew that something bad was happening. To my horror, I saw Mrs Lyn cowering outside the shop, holding Simmy in her arms. She was surrounded by a mob of men who were shaking their fists and screaming at her. I tried to get through the crowd but I was pushed back. Mr Lyn and Hanna were carrying boxes out of the shop. I was shouting Hanna's name but with all the noise, she couldn't hear me.

Mrs Lyn started screaming at a big burly policeman, who seemed to be enjoying every moment of this family's terror.

'Not take Hanna,' she pleaded. 'She real American girl, she smashing.'

He went up to her, almost touching her. 'She's a dirty little Jap, like the rest of you,' he shouted.

The crowd parted as a truck came down the street and stopped outside the shop.

I took my chance and elbowed my way to the front and ran to Hanna. She dropped the boxes and fell into my arms. 'They're taking us away, Rose.'

'Taking you where?'

'I don't know, they just turned up and told us to take what we could carry, then they ordered us out of the house.'

The policeman was pushing Mrs Lyn towards the truck. Mr Lyn ran to her and stood between them.

'This is my wife and my son, you do not touch them,' he said very calmly.

The man sneered and pushed him to the ground. Hanna was at his side in a second, yelling at the man and pushing him away from her father. 'Leave him alone, you great bully! What has he done to you? Think you're a big man, do you, with this mob of idiots around you?'

As the policeman went towards her, I saw David emerge from the crowd. 'You touch her and I'll see you behind bars.'

The policeman hesitated. 'Who the hell do you think you are?'

'A better man than you are,' said David.

'Well, I've got a job to do, so if you'll just step out of my way.'

'Have you no sympathy, man?'

'Where was their sympathy when they bombed the hell out of our lads?'

There were mumblings of support from the crowd, which caused the eejit of a man to continue his rant, knowing the mob were behind him. He was delighted with himself as he egged them on. 'Looks like we've got a Jap-lover amongst us, folks,' he shouted.

I feared for David as the crowd moved nearer but he was unmoved.

He walked closer to the police officer, who took a step backwards.

'You may have a job to do, sonny, but a bit of compassion wouldn't go amiss. Although I doubt you've even heard of the word.'

The man started to speak but David cut him short. 'You are the very worst of humanity and you're an idiot with it.'

'You can't talk to me like that, I'll have you arrested for interfering with an officer in his line of duty.'

'You can certainly try,' said David, smiling. 'I'm sure that my good friend Chief Ryder will be very interested in what you have to say.'

The policeman's face paled. 'Chief Ryder?'

'In fact, if you don't apologise to these good people in the next two minutes, I shall make it my personal business to see you thrown out of the force and that, my fat friend, is not a threat, it's a promise.'

You could see that the eejit didn't know what to do. If he apologised, he would lose face and if he didn't, he could lose his job.

'One minute,' said David, looking at his watch.

The policeman looked defeated as he walked towards the Lyns. 'Sorry,' he mumbled.

'I'm afraid we can't hear you,' said David.

'Sorry,' said the man, louder this time.

Mr Lyn joined his hands together and bowed. 'Thank you, sir,' he said.

I had never seen such dignity, such acceptance, in the face of such ignorance. I was so proud to know these beautiful souls.

As the crowd started to drift away, I went across to Hanna. We hugged each other and cried.

'Don't worry about us, Rose,' she said. 'We will be okay, we have each other and one day we will come home.'

'Goodbye, my friend,' I said.

'Goodbye, Rose.'

I would miss my good friend and I feared for her and her family. Tears were running down my cheeks as I watched the truck turn the corner and disappear.

A young policeman put his hand on my arm. 'They are not being punished,' he said, gently. 'Your friends are being removed for their own safety; they will not be harmed.'

'Thank you,' I said. 'I needed to know that.'

'We're not all like him,' he said.

As we walked home, I held David's hand and I didn't give a fig who saw us. 'Do you really know Chief Ryder?'

'Never met him in my life,' he said, grinning.

'Then you should be in the movies,' I said. 'For that was a fine piece of acting.'

'I'm sorry about your friend, Rose. You'll miss her, won't you?'

I nodded. 'Will they be alright?'

'Yes, I think they will be alright and maybe safer than they would be if they remained here.'

'They don't deserve this.'

'No, my love, they don't.'

We continued walking but not towards home. 'Where are we going?'

'I need to speak to you, Rose.'

We walked to the park and sat down on a bench. There were signs of spring everywhere: pure white snowdrops in clusters around the base of the still bare trees; yellow and purple crocuses, pushing through the soil, vying for attention. Each new little flower bringing with it hope of new beginnings and reminding me of the wonders of God who created it all. We sat close together, and I could feel the warmth of his body next to mine. I loved him so much and the thought of him leaving terrified me. How could I say goodbye when my heart was screaming, 'Don't leave me, oh please don't leave me.'

We sat quietly as I waited for him to speak.

'You won't want to hear what I have to say, Rose, but it has to be said.'

His words and the look on his face was scaring me.

'We have to face something, my darling girl, that I know we would rather not face.'

'Face what, David?'

'I may not come back.'

'You will, you will, you *must*.'

David put his finger gently to my lips. 'I may not come back and we can't pretend that is not a possibility. Better to talk about it now and get it out of the way. Can you do that, my brave Rose?'

I could feel a stinging behind my eyes. 'No,' I said. 'I don't want to be brave; you have to come back.'

David put his arms around me and I sobbed. 'Please, Rose.'

'Alright,' I said. 'But keep holding me.'

'I will never let you go. Even when we are separated, I will carry you in my heart.'

'And I shall carry you in mine.'

'I have opened a bank account for you and you are to use it for whatever you want – a new hat, a new dress, toys for Sarah, chocolates for Martha, anything, Rose. It is there for you and it is in your name.'

'I've never had a bank account.'

'That is why I will give you the name of my lawyer, who will help you with anything you need to know. His name is Bruce Carty and he knows all about you.'

'Thank you,' I said.

'There is something else I need to say, something I need to ask you.'

'You can ask me anything.'

'Martha is too old to bring up a child. If I don't make it home, will you take care of Sarah? It's a lot to ask of you, I am aware of that. You are young and deserve a life and a family of your own but I have to know that Sarah will be alright and there is no one I trust more than you to take care of her.'

'Oh, David, of course I will but you will come home and we will care for her together.'

'I hope so, my darling, I hope so.'

We tried to make our last evening with David special but it was hard. Martha made all his favourite food – steak, mashed potatoes, corn and baby peas, followed by apple sponge and cream.

'I'll never fit into the uniform,' he said.

One of us would have said something funny at this point but we couldn't. The thought of him in a uniform made joking impossible. The delicious food stuck in my throat and Martha was pushing hers around the plate. Only Sarah was tucking into it, abandoning the spoon for her fingers.

'Good decision, Sarah,' said David, grinning and putting down his fork. 'A much more civilised way of eating.'

We picked up handfuls of mashed potato and peas and bit into the steak, almost choking with laughter, laughter that we had never expected to hear on this awful night.

After we had eaten, I put Sarah to bed and Martha retired early. I knew that David's leaving was as hard on her as it was on me, and yet she allowed us to have this last night alone. Martha was one of the strongest, kindest women I had ever known; she reminded me of Mammy.

David walked across to the desk and handed me an envelope.

'Open it when I've gone, Rose,' he said.

He took my hand and we went upstairs. We spent the night holding each other and talking about a future that we hoped and prayed would be ours.

Oh dear God, please let it be ours.

Morning came too soon but we tried to be brave as we waved him off.

'He needs to remember us with smiles on our faces, not tears in our eyes,' said Martha.

I waved until the bus was just a dot in the distance, then slowly climbed the stairs to my room. I sat on the bed and opened the envelope. It was a single sheet of paper and not just a letter but surprisingly, a poem.

Tears were running down my face as I read it.

My darling Rose.
I was broken and you put me back together.

I was lost and you showed me the way home.
I am a better man because of you.

CASTLES IN THE SAND

One day I will build a house by the sea,
If I showed you the path, would you share it with me?
If I built a dream into every door
would you turn the lock and stay evermore?
If I coloured the walls in shades of the sun,
would it warm your heart when summer had gone?
If I planted a memory, sprinkled with dew,
would you stay by my side and watch as it grew?
If the key to my heart fits the house by the sea
would you take it, my love, and live there with me?
Am I asking too much? Well then, I'll understand
And for now, we'll build castles in the sand

Until we meet again
Love David xxx

PART THREE

Chapter Forty-Nine

BROOKLYN

1945

I waved until the yellow school bus turned the corner and was out of sight.

I'd found a small private school that had been recommended to me by David's lawyer.

'My own children went there, Rose,' he'd said. 'They thrived, not only academically but emotionally. The school motto is "Kindness above all else". I'm sure Sarah will be happy there.'

I'd wanted to keep her with me, I'd wanted to keep her safe but she was six years old and I knew that I had to let her go. All she had known was me and Martha, she needed friends of her own age.

I had cared for her since she was a baby, and I couldn't have loved her more if she had been my own, but I knew that I couldn't keep her at home forever. Alice had been protected all her life and she had never really grown up. She had never had a chance to become the woman she was meant to be and I was determined that, however much I loved Sarah, I wasn't going to let that happen to her. Love isn't about owning someone, love is about guiding them to a place where they can discover who they are, not who you want them to be.

I now looked after Sarah full-time as Martha was becoming frail and was only able to do the lightest of tasks.

I was only twenty-two years old and there were times when I felt much older. The responsibility of these two people I loved often weighed me down and I wondered how I had ended up in this place, so far from home and with no one to take care of me.

Each letter that arrived from David assured me that he was still alive and that with God's help, he would one day come home to us. I kept the letters under my pillow and read and reread them over and over. I touched the paper that he had touched, I held them up to my face and inhaled all the love that they carried. I prayed every night for his safety, to a God that I believed wouldn't be so cruel as to take him from me.

On a beautiful day in March, my dreams were shattered. It had been an ordinary day. Martha was in in the kitchen, baking Sarah's favourite cookies and I was in the garden, weeding the flower beds. It was one of those perfect spring days that made you feel glad to be alive and I was enjoying working outside in the sunshine. The warm breeze picked up the hair on the back of my neck and it felt like a caress. I could hear the chirping of the birds as they flew between the branches of the trees. I could feel damp grass under my knees. I felt more at peace than I had felt for a long time and I was smiling as I eased the weeds out of the soft ground and put them in a pile beside me.

I was so absorbed in my task that I didn't see the man walk up the path. I dropped the little trowel as he stood beside me. I was aware of the brown earth under my fingernails. I was aware of the soldier's shiny boots but the world had gone silent: no birdsong, no movement, no breeze. Everything was still, the world had paused. Then I heard the screaming and David's voice being called over and over again.

The noise brought Martha hurrying towards me and that was when I realised the screaming was coming from me. It was coming from the very depths of me. I sounded like an animal caught in a trap from which there was no escape. I was gasping for air. Martha knelt down beside me and took me in her arms. She felt solid, the only solid thing in this world that had disintegrated around me. I thought I would die from the pain that filled every part of me. I couldn't breathe. I didn't want to breathe. I didn't want to live – how could I live without him? Where was this God, who I prayed to every night? Why had He abandoned me? I hated Him, I hated Him.

The soldier who held out the telegram towards Martha was young, too young to be given this task. Martha took it from him.

'I'm sorry for your loss, ma'am,' he said softly.

Martha nodded. 'I know you are, lad. I know you are.'

Once he had gone, Martha helped me to my feet and I held onto her. This frail old woman had somehow found the strength that I lacked. I felt thin and empty, as if my insides had been ripped out and I was left with nothing but bones that were too weak to hold my body. I clung to Martha as we walked slowly into the house. She had become my rock. I was lost and she had become my compass.

I was shaking as she eased me down onto the couch. She wrapped me in a blanket and smoothed my hair as if I was a child. I leaned into her, needing to touch her. She was the only thing that was real, the only thing that made any sense to me. The telegram lay on her lap as if it was a live thing, waiting to spew its contents into the room, as if it couldn't wait to destroy our lives with words we didn't want to hear.

I could sense that Martha was waiting for some sort of sign from me. I took a deep breath and nodded. I watched as she opened the envelope, I watched as her eyes scanned the words. She let it slide onto the floor and took my hands in hers.

'He isn't dead, Rose,' she said, as the tears streamed down her cheeks. 'It doesn't say that he is dead, it says he is missing and missing isn't dead. Missing things can be found.'

I wanted to believe what she was saying but I knew in my heart that he had gone. I'd known as soon as I'd seen the soldier.

*

Martha collected Sarah from the school bus and she burst into the house, full of the tales of her day.

Sarah loved school; she was happy there and I knew that we had made the right decision to let her go.

'Tommy Evans stuck gum in Rachel Cohan's hair and he had to stand in the corner all morning,' she said, grinning.

'Well, that wasn't a very nice thing to do, was it?' said Martha.

Sarah looked thoughtful. 'Well, Rachel Cohan's not a very nice girl, she snapped my pencil in half. That's why Tommy stuck gum in her hair.'

'I like him already,' said Martha, smiling.

'So do I,' said Sarah, grinning. 'He asked me to marry him.'

'Really? And what did you say?'

'I said I'd think on it.'

'Wise decision, darling,' I said.

Our hearts were broken but we couldn't let Sarah see our tears. We'd made the decision to keep the news from her. She was too young to understand that she may never see her daddy again.

We would have to tell her one day, but not today.

It was a relief to put her to bed. It was hard to keep up this pretence when all I wanted was to shut out this world that had become too painful to live in. The future we had planned together was gone and I didn't know how to live without him.

Chapter Fifty

I had never felt so alone in my life. Everything seemed pointless. I wanted desperately to go home. I needed my family; if I could be with them, then maybe I could make some sense of this life that made no sense at all.

It was Sarah that kept me going, because however hopeless I felt, I had to take care of her. Sarah's welfare was more important than my own and I had to keep going for her sake. I even thought of going home and taking Sarah with me but Martha needed me too, now more than ever. I couldn't just abandon her and she was too old for the long journey, even if she wanted to come with us, which I knew she wouldn't. Of course she wouldn't. This was her home, this was where her memories were. This was where she danced with Alice, in flowing scarves and long dresses, pretending to be Sarah Bernhardt. This was where Raffi was born and this was where baby Martha had died. Ballykillen held nothing for her, my little town was a world away from all she knew and loved. Her memories were all she had left and I knew she would never leave them behind.

One morning, I woke feeling ill. I ached all over, it felt like I was swallowing knives and I was shivering with cold. Sarah came running into the room and jumped on the bed.

'Get up, Rose,' she said, pulling at the covers as she did every morning. This was my cue to start tickling her, but I could barely lift my head off the pillow.

'Can you get Martha, darling?'

'Are you poorly, Rose?' she said.

I nodded.

'Are you poorly in your belly? Tommy was poorly in his belly and he was sick all over his desk, he had to go home.'

'Just get Martha, there's a good girl.'

Sarah jumped off the bed and ran out of the room. My head felt as if it was splitting in two, I couldn't remember when I had last felt this ill.

Martha came hurrying into the room. 'What's wrong, Rose?'

'I don't know, I think I must be going down with something. I feel desperate ill.'

She put her hand on my forehead. 'You're burning up, girl!'

'But I'm so cold.'

'I'll fetch another blanket, then I'm phoning the doctor.'

'I don't need a doctor, it's probably just the start of a cold.'

'Let's be on the safe side, eh? It will give the old goat something to do.'

I managed a smile. The old goat was Doctor Williams. Martha said he had one foot in the grave and another on a banana skin and was as old as God.

'His only saving grace is that he's as blind as a bat, so I never worried about him looking at my lower regions as I was confident in the knowledge that he saw everything through a reassuring haze.'

I started to laugh, which turned into a cough that tore at my chest.

'That's more than a cold, Rose. Now try and rest, while I give Sarah her breakfast and get her off to school.'

I lay there wondering what a doctor who was as old as God and blind as a bat could do for me, but I felt so bad that I was beyond caring.

I managed to sleep and was woken by Martha touching my hand. Behind her was a young man, who walked towards me.

'My name is Doctor Williams,' he said, smiling.

Well, he didn't look old and his eyes looked fine.

'It's Rose, isn't it?' he said.

I nodded.

'Let's see what's going on, shall we?'

He looked down my throat, took my temperature and listened to my heart. 'I'd say you have the dreaded flu, Rose. There's a lot of it about, they're dropping like flies in the neighbourhood. My father and I are run off our feet. I will give you something to bring that temperature down and something for that throat.'

'She'll be alright?' said Martha.

'Plenty of fluids, soup and rest is the order of the day, Martha.'

'Oh, I can do that, Doctor.'

'Ring me if you are concerned about anything, but I think it will just run its course. Goodbye, Rose.'

'Goodbye,' I said.

After he'd gone, Martha came back upstairs. 'Will you be alright if I pop to the drugstore for your medicine? I'll be as quick as I can.'

'I'll be fine, all I want to do is sleep.'

She stopped at the door and turned back to me.

'Well, I won't be calling *him* out if I have trouble down below,' she said, grinning.

Darling Martha, I thought, as I closed my eyes.

I slept for four days, waking only to take sips of water and a few mouthfuls of soup. Martha took such good care of me but I felt so guilty lying there, while she had to take care of Sarah and run up and down the stairs to see to me. One morning, I felt better but when I tried to get out of bed I nearly collapsed and would have fallen, if Martha hadn't caught me.

'You're not ready yet,' she said, settling me back into bed. She plumped the pillows up behind me. 'Shall I read to you, darling?'

'Oh yes, please.'

She got a book and lay down beside me. '*Pride and Prejudice* by Jane Austen,' she said. 'Have you read it?'

I shook my head. 'No.'

'It's a great romance, as are all of Austen's books. I think you will enjoy it, Rose.'

I closed my eyes and listened to the story of Elizabeth Bennet and her family. They put me in mind of my own family, although Mammy had never tried to marry us all off to rich men – mind you, she would have been hard pushed to find any rich men in Ballykillen.

I gradually began to get better and sat downstairs most afternoons. I felt so sad and so lost. What was I supposed to do with this life of mine? Where did I fit into a world without David? The future we had planned together had gone the moment the soldier walked up the path. My world that had been so full of colour was now a dark place and all my hopes and dreams had become nightmares.

I missed Hanna; we could have talked and she would have helped me make sense of it all but she was gone too and I had to find my way through this without her. I thought about her often and prayed she was alright and that the family were being treated well. How could such happiness turn into such sadness?

When Martha became ill, I had to stop thinking about myself. It was my turn to take care of her now, as she had taken care of me.

The flu hit Martha harder than it had hit me and I was worried sick. I couldn't lose her too, I just couldn't.

Young Doctor Williams came in every day and he looked as worried as I was.

'She will be alright, won't she? I got better.'

'You are young, Rose; it will take Martha longer to get over this.'

'But she *will* get over it?'

He didn't answer. 'I will come back tomorrow but if you are worried before then, ring me.'

'I will and thank you.'

'She's a tough woman and I'd say she still has some fight in her. A strong spirit is a wonderful thing and Martha certainly has plenty of that.'

'She has,' I said.

I didn't have time for my own worries now that I had Martha and Sarah to care for.

'Is Aunt Martha poorly like you were, Rose?' said Sarah.

'I'm afraid so, darling. Will you help me take care of her?'

'I will,' she said very seriously. She picked up her doll. 'Do you think she would like to cuddle Bill? Do you think Bill will make her happy? Bill makes *me* happy?'

I kissed the top of her head. 'I think that is a splendid idea and very kind.'

'Aunt Martha is very kind to me.'

I felt my eyes fill with tears. 'She's very kind to me too, Sarah, so we must help her to get well again.'

'I'll take Bill up to her then, shall I?'

'She might be asleep.'

'Then I shall put her on the pillow.'

I smiled as I watched her running up the stairs, the doll dangling down beside her. She was such a sweet little girl; Alice would have been so proud of her. *I* was so proud of her.

Chapter Fifty-One

Martha didn't get better. The flu turned to pneumonia and the doctor said the time had come for her to be taken into hospital, but Martha would have none of it.

'If I'm to die, I will die in my own bed,' she insisted.

'But they can care for you in the hospital, Martha. They can make you better.'

She raised her eyebrows. 'We both know that is not true, don't we?'

Tears were running down my cheeks. 'Sarah needs you; *I* need you.'

'You will be fine, Rose Brown. You are strong and you are brave and I am at peace, knowing that Sarah couldn't be in better, kinder hands than yours, but I don't intend to spend my last moments on this earth in a hospital bed surrounded by strangers.'

'Have you always got your own way?'

She smiled. 'Mostly.'

'Then it will be the way you want it.'

'Can I speak to you of something that has been on my mind?'

'Of course, you can speak to me about anything.'

'Have you thought about what you will do when you return home?'

'What do you mean?'

Martha started coughing, so I held the glass of water up to her lips.

'Please don't tire yourself, Martha, we can speak another time.'

'There may not be another time, Rose.'

'Oh, please don't say that, I can't bear it.'

'I've faced it and so must you. Sit beside me.'

I sat on the bed and waited for her to speak.

'The young girl that left Ballykillen is not the same girl who will return.'

'I'll be older, I know that.'

'It is not about age, Rose.'

'Then what?'

'From what you have told me of your early life, your family were poor and you led a very simple existence, am I right?'

'We didn't have much money, if that's what you mean, but we were happy and I was loved.'

'I have no doubt about that, you wouldn't be the wonderful girl you are if you had not known love.'

'Then, I don't understand.'

'For the past six years, you have experienced a different way of life; you have known privilege and I wonder if you are prepared for that. I wonder if you have even thought about how you will fit back into that life. You have grown in ways that you would never have grown if you had stayed in Ireland.'

I didn't know what to say.

'And Sarah? Have you thought about how she will fit in? For she has also known privilege.'

'Are you saying I shouldn't go home?'

'That is not what I'm saying. David wanted you to take Sarah back to your family, if anything happened to him. I just want to prepare you for something that might not be as simple as you think it will be. You need to take off those rose-coloured glasses and face the reality of yours and Sarah's lives in Ballykillen.'

I frowned; was she right? Would I not fit in at home? That wasn't possible, was it? And yet I could see some truth in her words. How could I expect Sarah to live in the humble little cottage in Cross Lane after the grand houses she had been accustomed to? Why hadn't I thought of that? Was I a fool or what? Well, I was going to have to think about it now, wasn't I?

'Have I hurt you, Rose?'

'Of course you haven't, and it's making me think.'

'And that was my intention,' she said, closing her eyes.

Every night, I slept in a chair beside Martha, listening to every tortured breath, not wanting her to suffer and yet selfishly dreading the moment when her suffering came to an end. I wasn't ready to let her go. I wasn't ready to say goodbye to this wonderful, astonishing woman, who had become as dear to me as my own family. Alice had called her magnificent and that was exactly what she was.

After a particularly bad day I considered going against her wishes and making arrangements for her to be taken into hospital. I felt helpless; I didn't know what to do for the best and I had no one to ask.

I stayed awake all that night just watching her sleep. I picked up her hand and held it in mine. I gently stroked the blue veins running across the pale, wrinkled skin. I'd never really noticed her hands before and I'd never really thought of her as old but these were the hands of an old woman.

I remembered Alice once saying that Martha would rather die at the hands of a jealous lover than be thought of as ordinary. Well, I couldn't arrange the jealous lover but I could at least honour her last wishes and let her die in her own bed.

Martha had had the sort of life that the rest of us could only dream of. I closed my eyes, imagining the young Martha, living in an attic room in Paris, mixing with artists and musicians and gigolos. I would never sit on a windowsill with my legs dangling over the edge, smoking Turkish cigarettes and drinking French wine and there would be no illicit love affairs for me. Ballykillen wasn't the sort of place where you could easily have an illicit love affair.

I dozed on and off through that night. The chair was uncomfortable and I was aching all over. I decided that from now on I would sleep on the floor with some pillows and blankets.

I woke early. It was dark in the room and so quiet. I went across to the window and pulled back the curtains. Thin rays of sunshine dappled through the trees and across the lawn.

'It's a beautiful day, Martha,' I said softly. 'Too beautiful to die.' I walked over to the bed and knelt beside her. She looked so peaceful lying there, as if she was in a deep sleep. I held her hand; it was icy cold. I took her in my arms and kissed her cheek. 'Goodbye, my darling friend,' I said. 'Goodbye.'

Chapter Fifty-Two

David's lawyer, arranged Martha's funeral. She had no religion that I knew of, she'd never spoken to me of her beliefs, but I remembered her saying that she didn't want Alice to cling to someone else's philosophies and that the world would be better off without religion. I couldn't imagine Martha kneeling at the altar of any God.

The funeral was a sad little affair, with only Bruce, Father Paul, Sarah and myself at the graveside and yet I knew that this was probably what Martha wanted – no fuss, no fanfares and definitely no hymns. I held Sarah's hand as the coffin was lowered into the ground and I cried for this kind, wonderful woman, who I had grown to love and would never forget.

It had been hard to tell Sarah that her beloved Aunt Martha had died. How did you tell a child of six something like that? She'd never even had a pet that had died, did she understand the meaning of death?

She had frowned as I was telling her. 'Where is she, then?'

'She's with Jesus and all the angels.'

'And where do they live?'

'In heaven,' I said.

'Can we go and visit her?'

I shook my head. 'I'm afraid not, my darling.'

Sarah was throwing Bill up in the air and then catching her. I wondered if she had understood anything at all.

'So, Martha won't be living here anymore, Sarah, do you understand?'

'Because she's too far away to visit us?'

'That's right.'

'Rose?' she said.

'Yes, my darling?'

'Why haven't I got a mummy?'

My eyes filled with tears for this little girl who had no one but me.

'I told you about your mummy, have you forgotten?'

Sarah shrugged her shoulders.

'Her name was Alice, Aunt Martha showed you a picture of her when she was a little girl.'

'Was that my mummy?'

I should have spoken more about Alice; I should have kept her memory alive for Sarah but I hadn't. 'Your mummy was beautiful,' I said. 'The most beautiful person I ever met. Her hair was the colour of gold, just exactly like yours and her eyes were the colour of the sea. Your mummy was kind and funny and full of joy. She loved you very much, Sarah, and she would be so proud of you.'

She stared at me, as if she was trying to figure something out.

'Why did she go away, then?'

I wished Martha was here; she would have been so much better at this than I was. What could I say? That a piece of stone was more important to her than her daughter? 'Aunt Martha loved you, didn't she?'

'Yes.'

'But she had to go away because she became ill, even though she didn't want to leave you?'

Sarah nodded.

'Well, your mummy didn't want to leave you either.'

'Was my mummy ill, like Aunt Martha?'

'I think perhaps she was, my darling.'

Sarah climbed onto my lap. It was lovely to feel her solid little body in my arms. She smelled of lemons and I breathed her in. I couldn't get enough of her. 'We will take care of each other now,' I whispered, brushing her beautiful hair out of her eyes.

'Rose?' she said.

'Yes, my darling?'

'Is my daddy in heaven as well?'

My eyes filled with tears but I didn't want to cry in front of Sarah. 'I'm not sure, darling, but I think that wherever he is, he will be watching over us and so will your mummy and Raffi and your Aunt Martha.'

'You won't go to heaven, will you?'

'No, Sarah, I shall stay here with you.'

Sarah never mentioned Martha again and I found this strange, because Martha had been like a mother to her and before she'd started school, they had spent every day together. Maybe it was part of being a child, this ability to accept things, even sad things and just move on. I wished I could do the same.

After the funeral, we went back to the vicarage, where Father Paul's housekeeper had put on a spread for us. I didn't feel much like eating but I didn't want to offend her after all the trouble she'd gone to.

Father Paul kept rabbits, so Sarah went into the garden to pet them.

'What plans do you have now, Rose?' he said.

'I haven't any plans, Father. I just wish this war would come to an end so that I can go home.'

'And what about Sarah?'

'I shall take her with me.'

'You'll take Sarah back to Ireland?'

'I think that is the best thing to do. My family are there and they will help me to raise her, I won't be alone and I think that David would understand.'

'I'm sure that he would.'

'That little girl has lost so much in her short life, she needs to know that there is someone she can trust, who isn't going to just disappear one day.'

'I was going to mention the convent, who would take her in and care for her but I can see that you have made up your mind and so I shall say no more.'

We walked outside and stood watching Sarah playing with the rabbits.

'And I forgot to say that I love her like my own and she loves me.'

Father Paul smiled. 'And didn't I know that already, Rose? I just wanted you to know that there was an alternative.'

'I know you meant well, Father, but I could no more leave her in the convent than fly – and as God in His holy wisdom hasn't fitted me with wings, I shall be taking her back to Ballykillen.'

'You haven't been to Mass for a long time, Rose.'

'No, Father.'

'Have you lost your faith, child?'

I didn't answer him.

'I'm thinking you may find some peace here, even if you don't want to attend Mass. Our door is always open. Saint Rosie's would welcome you back with open arms and I'm sure God won't be judging you.'

I nodded. 'Thank you, Father.'

'God bless you, Rose.'

Sarah and myself walked slowly back through the streets. There was no rush, no one was waiting to welcome us home. No one would even know if we didn't come home. I had never needed my family more than I needed them now.

What on earth was I supposed to do, living in that big empty house, bringing up a child that wasn't my own? Could I even give her the life she deserved? I felt trapped in a country that wasn't mine and in a house that had become a prison. I was desperate to go home but it was still too dangerous to travel. Sarah was my responsibility and I had to keep her safe. I was lonely, for the first time in my life.

Chapter Fifty-Three

I hated being alone in the house. I could feel the presence of Martha and David in every empty room and it was killing me. Most days, after seeing Sarah onto the school bus, I would go back to bed and stay there until she got home. I couldn't be bothered to eat, or wash, or tidy the house. I cried a lot and I screamed at a God who had broken my heart. Didn't I go to Mass every Sunday? Didn't I go to Confession every Saturday? Didn't I put pennies in the poor box? And didn't I light candles to His mother? And for what? For Him to abandon me when I needed him most? I might just as well have been a bad person, for all the good it had done me. I hated my life.

The only thing that gave me comfort apart from Sarah was reading the letters from home that I had received over the years. I'd kept them all in the little cabinet beside my bed. I read and re-read them over and over. It was a piece of home that warmed my heart. I would hold the letters up to my nose and imagine that I could smell Mammy's roses. I lived through those pages; they took me back to the little cottage in Cross Lane. I had never realised how funny Mammy could be but when she wrote about the gossip in the town, she had a way of saying it that made me laugh.

I knew that it was Agnes that wrote the letters for Mammy – she always had – but it was Mammy's voice I heard as I read them.

Mrs Healey, from down the quay, had a baby and she not a day under fifty! Mr Healey strutted around town like Rudolph Valentino for weeks. Old Mulligan died, Rose, and there wasn't a tear shed for him, now isn't that sad? It turned out he had a nephew in America who inherited the whole lot, the shop

as well. That's where Agnes is working and she loves it there.
She has a best friend and it seems to have taken her out of her
shell. Kathy has a new feller every week, I never know what's
going to come through the door next. Of course, none of them
last, poor devils. You'd have to knit one to her own pattern to
satisfy her. She has broken hearts strewn along the length and
breadth of Ballykillen.

The biggest news was that my little sister, Bridgy, had won a scholarship to the Loretto, where the posh girls went. Mammy held a party for her in the cottage and she had her picture in the paper. *I was that proud of her, Rose, but I had to keep it to myself, for isn't pride a sin against the teachings of the Lord? But oh, I was, Rose, I was.*

And so that was how I spent my days – lying in my bed, reading letters and longing for home.

I was brought to my senses by Sarah. We'd been cuddled up on the couch when she'd pulled away from me. 'Rose?' she said.

'Yes, darling?'

'You smell awful bad.'

I was mortified. 'Do I?'

'Yes, Rose, you do. I think you should have a wash. I think you would smell better if you had a wash.'

I nodded and smiled at her. 'I think you are right, my darling, clever girl. That is exactly what I shall do.'

'Tommy Duggan at school smells and no one wants to sit next to him. Shall I tell him to have a wash too? Because he might not know that he smells.'

'I don't think that's a great idea, it might hurt his feelings.'

'Have I hurt your feelings, Rose?'

'No, Sarah, you've done me a favour.'

'So why wouldn't I be doing Tommy Duggan a favour? He smells like fish and he might be glad to know it.'

I grinned at her. 'Maybe Tommy Duggan likes smelling of fish.'

'Well, I wouldn't like to smell of fish.'

I went into the bathroom and looked in the mirror. The face looking back at me was the face of a forty-year-old, not the twenty-two-year-old that I was. I felt ashamed that I had allowed myself to become like this. Well, I was going to do something about it – Tommy Duggan might like smelling of fish, but I didn't.

From then on, after seeing Sarah off on the school bus, I walked. Whatever the weather, I walked. I discovered parts of Brooklyn that I had never seen before. I leaned on the wall and watched the ferries going backwards and forwards across the water to Staten Island. I wasn't brave enough to buy a ticket but maybe one day, me and Sarah could.

On one of my travels, I found myself in front of a tall, red-brick building with 'Brooklyn Library' written in black letters over the arched doorway. I hesitated at the bottom of the steps, feeling nervous to go in on my own. It had started to rain, that soft spring rain that smells of flowers and fresh grass, but which soaks you through in minutes, so without another thought I ran up the steps and pushed open the door. My nose was at once filled with a sweet musky smell, like damp laundry, mixed with must and dust and paper. I breathed it in and looked around. Wooden shelves, filled with hundreds of books, reached almost up to the ceiling. Motes of dust danced in the shaft of light streaming in from the long windows that took up the whole of one wall. I ran my fingers along the spines of the books, just as I had seen Alice do, so long ago. I'd often thought of that day and Alice's words to me, as she'd held a book up to her nose: *'It smells so delicious that I want to gobble it up, every page and every word, so that it is part of me forever. Wouldn't that be wonderful, wouldn't that be the most wonderful thing?'* Now I knew what she'd meant, for I felt the same myself.

In front of me was a beautiful staircase leading up to the next floor. The place seemed deserted; I couldn't see a single person, or hear a sound. I wandered around until I came to the children's section. I picked a book and curled up in an old armchair. The book I chose was *The Railway Children*. It had been one of Alice's favourites and was now one of mine.

Someone touched my shoulder and I nearly jumped out of my skin. 'Oh, I'm sorry I frightened you, dear.'

Looking down at me was a woman. It was hard to tell her age as she was on the plump side. Mammy always said that if a woman carried a bit of weight, it was hard to put an age on her as she has fewer lines on her face. The woman standing in front of me had startling red hair and, God love her, a startlingly large nose – but a lovely smile, which made you forget the hair and the nose.

I closed the book.

'I couldn't tell you how many times I've read that book,' she said. 'Isn't it a lovely story?'

I smiled up at her. 'It is.'

'I don't remember seeing you in here before, are you a member?'

I put the book down. 'Oh, I didn't know you had to be a member.'

'You don't,' she said, smiling. 'You can come in here anytime you like and read the books but if you were a member, you could take books home with you.'

'If it's all the same to you, I think I'd like to read them here, it gets me out of the house.'

'You come any time you like and next time we'll have some tea.'

I put the book back on the shelf. 'That would be lovely,' I said. 'Thank you.'

'You are very welcome and I hope to see you again soon.'

'You will,' I said.

I hadn't been around people much since leaving the tailor's shop and it had been lovely to speak to her. I would come again.

When I walked out of the library, the rain had stopped and the sky was blue. Everything smelled fresh and clean. There was still an hour before Sarah was due home from school, so I headed to the park. I walked over to the bench and sat down. It was the bench that David and I had sat on. The white snowdrops were back again and the purple crocuses were as beautiful as they had been when I still had David beside me, that day when I still had a wonderful life ahead of me. I would never forget him, or Martha and I would never forget Alice and Raffi, but I had to move on for Sarah's sake. The future I had hoped for was gone; it was in the past and I had to look forwards not backwards, or I would go mad. Right now, it was Sarah who mattered. It was time to tuck all those wonderful memories safely away in my heart. It didn't mean that I would forget them, I never would, but it was time to let them go for now.

I left the park and started walking again, this time towards the tailor's shop. It was a day for saying goodbye, for putting old ghosts to rest and this was another one. I stood outside the little shop and thought about the Lyns. I prayed that, wherever they were, they were safe and well. Life would have been so much easier if I'd still had Hanna; she would have helped me come to terms with losing David and Martha, she would have helped me make sense of everything. The little shop was boarded up and looked sad and abandoned. It looked the way I felt.

I started walking back home, with my head held high. Something inside me had changed. I didn't question what it was but I was just going to embrace it with open arms and be grateful. Maybe God was feeling guilty and was trying to make it up to me. I felt a cloud lifting from my shoulders. As I approached the brownstone houses, I could hear laughter and cheering and as I got nearer, I could see people were hugging each other. I smiled at a young woman who was dancing and twirling on the pavement.

'Is it someone's birthday?' I said.

She stopped dancing and gave me the biggest hug. 'Haven't you heard?' she said.

'Heard what?'

'The war in Europe has ended. Germany has surrendered.'

I burst into tears and was immediately surrounded by people hugging me and laughing and kissing my wet cheeks. 'The war is really over?'

'Yes, it really is,' said the girl. 'This is indeed a wonderful day.'

'Oh, it is, it really is.'

I said goodbye and started running and running until my heart was pounding in my chest.

I ran until I came to Saint Rosie's. I was going home and it was time to forgive yer man upstairs.

PART FOUR

Chapter Fifty-Four

COMING HOME

1945

The boat was packed to the gills and most of the passengers were Irish. Not only had Bruce arranged our journey home, he had also booked first-class cabins. And what a difference money made. We were treated like royalty; there was even a separate gangplank for first-class passengers. I suppose I should have been impressed with the extra attention but I wasn't. Everyone deserved to be treated with kindness and respect, not just people with money. After all, weren't we all going to end up on the same gangplank?

Mr Carty had come to the house one morning. 'There are a few things that I need to talk to you about, Rose,' he'd said.

'Nothing bad, I hope.'

He smiled. 'Nothing bad.'

'Then I'll get us some tea, Mr Carty, or would you prefer coffee?

'Tea would be lovely and please call me Bruce.'

I filled the kettle and leaned on the sink, waiting for it to boil. I suppose he wanted to tell me that I'd have to leave the house, now that Martha was dead. I'd been expecting that but as I was going home, it didn't matter.

I carried the tea in and we sat opposite each other. He took some papers out of his briefcase and put them on the table.

'David came to see me before he went away. He needed to change his will in case the worst happened.'

'And it did,' I said.

'Sadly, it did,' said Bruce. 'But he had the sense to put his life in order before he went.'

I nodded.

He leaned forward. 'Rose,' he said, 'he has left everything to you.'

I frowned. 'To me?'

'Yes, Rose, to you.'

'But what about Sarah?'

'Martha and David came to my office together. Martha has left her house to Sarah. It will be sold and the money put in trust. Martha has also left five thousand pounds to you, Rose.'

I stared at him, feeling as if the wind had been taken out of me.

'So, you see, my dear girl, between the pair of them, you are a wealthy woman and although the circumstances are not what we would have chosen, I am delighted for you. I shall arrange for you to receive the money monthly so that for the immediate future you can rent a house that is suitable for you and Sarah. This will give you time to find a forever home and it will also pay Sarah's school fees.'

'Can she not go to the convent?'

'That will be entirely up to you, Rose. You are now her guardian and must do what you feel is best for her. I know you will make the right decisions, as did David, or he wouldn't have entrusted her to your care.'

I sat there trying to make sense of it all. What in the name of God was I supposed to do with all that money? What would Mammy say? What would everyone in Ballykillen say? I would be treated differently; the money would set me apart from my neighbours.

'Do I have to take it, Bruce?'

'Take what?'

'The money?'

Bruce laughed. 'It's yours, Rose. What you do with it is up to you but it's not something that you can give back.'

*

I leaned on the railings and stared at the grey water. In that moment, Martha's words came back to me: *'The young girl who left Ballykillen is not the same girl who will return.'* Martha would have known about David's will and in her own way she was trying to prepare me for what was to come.

Well, Martha had got it wrong. Money wasn't going to change who I was inside. It wasn't going to make me all high and mighty. What was money but bits of metal and paper? It wasn't flesh and blood and it wouldn't keep you warm on a cold night. I was Rose Brown from Ballykillen and that was who I would always be. If I was stuck with the money, then I would use it wisely and maybe do some good with it.

There were lots of children on the boat and to Sarah it was a huge adventure and she was loving it. I watched her playing hopscotch with a little girl she had befriended. Sarah was growing like a beanstalk and she was beautiful – a miniature Alice but without Alice's frailty. She would make her own decisions and walk her own path without having to lean on anyone else to hold her up.

Martha had said that Alice marched to her own drum and in a way, she had been right, but only if she had the rest of us marching right behind her. Alice was the most complicated person I had ever met. She was like a rare exotic bird, with wings so wide that she left the rest of us in her shadow. I had never really understood her until the night she had walked away from her baby. She had walked away without a backward glance because her own needs had come first. That was the moment the veil lifted and I saw her for who she was. Beautiful, kind, caring and utterly selfish.

Alice and myself couldn't have been more different and I wondered what had made David fall in love with me. What had he seen in this simple, uneducated girl after loving Alice? Whatever it was, I thanked God for it. Our time together had been short but I would never, ever regret it.

On our last night on the boat, we went down to the third-class accommodation, drawn there by the music. We walked along the narrow corridors, following the sound of laughter and song. When we pushed open the door, I smiled; it was like coming home. The laughter stilled as a rich deep voice started singing, 'The Wild Colonial Boy'. We stood in the doorway until a woman beckoned us across to her table. 'Sit yourself down here, love,' she said, in a strong Irish accent. 'Would your little girl like a mineral?'

'Sarah?' I said.

'What's a mineral?'

The woman laughed. 'A lemonade,' she said.

Sarah smiled at her, 'Yes, please, I like lemonade.'

'Connor,' said the woman. 'Get the young one a lemonade.'

'And what about yourself?'

'I'd like one too,' I said.

'Make that two, Connor.'

'Right, Mammy,' said the boy.

'I haven't seen you on the boat,' said the woman.

I didn't want to tell her we were in first class, so I said the first thing that came into my head.

'I've been awful seasick,' I said, hoping that Sarah wouldn't say anything and, God love her, she didn't.

We had the best time and I wished we'd come down here before. We sang the songs I'd grown up with, the rebel songs and the sad ballads. The Irish loved to sing about their heroes and their mammies. We even joined in the dancing, me and Sarah, holding hands and spinning round the room. These were my people and this was where I felt comfortable. It made Ballykillen seem that much closer.

Bruce had wired Mammy to let her know that I was coming home but I asked him not to say when. I didn't want to be met off the boat. I wanted to take Sarah home to Ballykillen on the Thrupenny Rush. He had also had the presence of mind to tell her that I would be bringing Sarah with me.

The next morning, I stood on the deck, watching the green hills of Ireland emerge from the mist. My heart was bursting with happiness, I couldn't believe this day had come. I would soon be in the arms of my family, in the little cottage in Cross Lane.

Chapter Fifty-Five

Sarah knelt up on the seat, watching the countryside flying past. She had her nose pressed against the window, taking everything in. She kept turning round and asking, 'Are we nearly there, Rose? Are we nearly there?'

'Not long now,' I said, smiling. 'Not long now, my darling girl.'

My tummy was in knots. I couldn't wait to see them all. My sisters would be all grown up, not the children I remembered. I wondered how much they had changed and would they see a change in me? But there was one thing that I knew would never change and that was our love for each other. The outside might be different but not the inside.

'The sea!' shouted Sarah, suddenly. 'It's the sea, Rose!'

I watched as the lighthouse came into view. 'We're home, Sarah, we're home.'

I took down the two bags, which was all I'd brought with us. Bruce had arranged for the rest of our belongings to be sent over.

I stood on the little platform and breathed in the smell of the sea, the smell of home. Nothing had changed in all the years I'd been away and to top it off, here was Billy Ogg walking towards me.

I smiled at him. 'Hello Billy, long time no see.'

'Hello yerself,' he said, as if he'd seen me the day before.

'How are you?'

'Don't you be asking me how I am, Rose Brown,' he almost spat at me.

'I was just making polite conversation, Billy.'

'And don't ask me how Minnie Ogg is, do ya hear me? I don't want her name mentioned on my platform.'

I wondered what on earth Minnie could have done to have brought this on. 'I wasn't going to, Billy,' I said.

'Yes, well, don't.'

Sarah had been staring wide-eyed at Billy. 'He owns the platform?' she said, as we walked away.

I grinned at her. 'He thinks he does, Sarah, it's just that no one has informed the railway. Now, let's get ourselves home.'

Home, I thought, *what a wonderful word.*

I held Sarah's hand as we walked through the town. There were times in Brooklyn when I had thought this day would never come. If this was a dream, I never wanted to wake up.

'This is Ballykillen, Sarah.'

'I think it's very nice, Rose,' she said.

'I hope you'll be happy here, my love.'

'Of course I will, silly.'

I laughed. 'Yes, of course you will, silly me.'

I wanted to run but I didn't want to make a show of myself. I could just hear the gossips. 'Did you see Rose Brown, tearing through the town like an eejit? And her a grown woman.' I laughed out loud at the thought. They'd live on it for months.

Sarah looked up at me. 'What are you laughing at, Rose?'

'Myself,' I said, grinning.

Just then someone called my name. 'Rose,' she was yelling. 'Rose Brown?'

I turned around and saw Orla Feeny flying towards me. She had a huge smile on her face. Jesus, I'd never seen Orla Feeny smile in all the years I'd known her. She threw her arms around me and hugged me as if she never wanted to let me go. 'It's so lovely to see you, Rose,' she said.

I smiled back at her. Well, it looked like some things had changed! 'It's lovely to see you too, Orla.'

'Oh, Jesus, I've left the baby outside Mulligan's. I'll pop across later and we'll have a catch-up.'

'Is the baby yours, Orla?'

'Jesus no, I'm minding her for a friend. Oh, I'm so glad you're home, Rose.'

I watched her running back down the street. Her mother must be delighted after wearing out her poor knees, praying for Orla's redemption.

'Is she your friend, Rose?' said Sarah.

'Looks like it,' I said, grinning.

More people were saying hello as we walked along. Jesus, we would never get home at this rate.

We passed the bottom of Windmill Hill. 'That's where my best friend lives, Sarah. Her name's Polly.'

'Are we going to visit her?'

'Not yet.'

'I wish I had a best friend,' she said.

'You'll have loads of friends here. Sure, they'll be only queuing up to be your friend.'

'Will they?'

'They will, of course.'

As we walked up Cross Lane, I had an awful big lump in my throat. I was home and I would never leave again, not ever.

Before we went in, I put a finger to my lips. 'Not a sound, Sarah,' I whispered.

'Because it's a surprise?' she whispered back.

I opened the door and walked into the little room as quietly as I could. Mammy had her back to me. I dipped my finger in the holy water front. 'God bless all here,' I said, loudly.

Mammy turned around. She didn't speak, she just stared at me, and then I was in her arms and we were both sobbing. 'Oh, my darling girl, is it really you?'

'It is, Mammy, I'm home.'

'Why didn't you let us know?'

'I wanted to surprise you.'

'And you did, you surely did.' She held me away from her. 'Let me look at you.'

'Have I changed, Mammy?'

She smiled. 'Not a bit. You are still my beautiful Rose.'

Sarah hadn't moved from the door, she just stood there looking around the room.

Mammy walked towards her and knelt down. 'So, you're Sarah?' she said gently.

Sarah nodded.

'Welcome home, my love.'

Sarah frowned. 'This isn't my home,' she said quietly.

I didn't know what to say. I hadn't expected this. I'd talked a lot about the cottage to Sarah, maybe I'd made it sound better than it was. I felt so bad, as if I'd let her down by bringing her here. Martha had warned me that it wasn't going to be as simple as I thought it would be. Sarah's bedroom was bigger than the little room we were standing in.

'What's wrong, my love?' I said.

Tears were streaming down her little face. 'You have a mummy. Rose, why haven't I got a mummy?'

So, it wasn't the size of the room that was upsetting her. 'You can share mine, Sarah. Would you like that?'

'You can't share a mummy; mummies aren't for sharing.'

I didn't know what to say and my heart was breaking for this beautiful little girl who deserved to have a mammy of her own.

Mammy was still kneeling in front of her. 'How about a grandma, Sarah? I would love to be your grandma. Would you like that? Because I would like that very much.'

Sarah didn't speak. She stared at Mammy and then put her little arms around Mammy's neck.

'There now, my little one,' said Mammy, dabbing at her eyes. 'You have made me very happy.'

Just then, the door was flung open and a young girl almost fell into the room. She was wearing the brown and yellow uniform of the Loretta and she was beautiful. 'I bumped into Orla Feeny in town and she told me you were home. Oh, Rose, is it really you?'

'Bridgy? My little Bridgy?'

'Not so little,' said Mammy, laughing.

'And who's this?' she said, smiling at Sarah.

'I'm Sarah Townsend and this is my grandma. Do you have a grandma?'

'No, I don't, Sarah, and do you know what?'

'What?'

'You are a very lucky girl, for you have the best grandma in the whole world.'

'Of course I have, silly,' she said, which made us all laugh.

Next in the door was Agnes. 'Rose,' she said, flinging herself at me and almost knocking me to the floor. 'I bumped into Dermot Casey and he said you were home.'

'Does the whole of Ballykillen know I'm home?'

'Of course they do,' said Mammy.

'Oh, Rose,' said Agnes. 'I can't believe it's really you.'

I suddenly realised that Agnes was talking out loud and not whispering. 'You're speaking,' I said.

'And she never stops,' said Mammy, smiling.

'I am,' said my shy little sister.

'And did a miracle happen?'

'It did,' said Mammy, 'and the miracle's name is Ruth.'

'She's my friend,' said Agnes. 'I met her at work.'

'And what has she managed to do that the rest of us couldn't?'

'Ruth is deaf in one ear and she couldn't hear what I was saying, so I had to find my voice because I really wanted her to like me.'

'I'm sure she would have liked you anyway.'

'She might have liked me,' said Agnes, grinning, 'but she wouldn't have heard a word I was saying.'

'Well, thank the Lord for sending her to you.'

'Amen,' said Mammy.

'And you must be Sarah?' said Agnes. 'I've heard all about you.'

'And I've heard all about you too.'

Agnes smiled at her. 'Well, there you are. We know each other already.'

Sarah grinned at her. 'Yes, we do.'

Last in the door was Kathy, followed by Polly.

I held them both in my arms. They might all have been older but to me they were the same as they had always been.

'We met Saint Orla,' said Kathy and she told us the news.

'What happened to the girl? Did she have an apparition?'

'She did indeed,' said Mammy. 'She saw the face of Christ in a piece of toast and she hasn't been the same since.'

I was laughing so much, I could hardly speak. 'In a piece of toast?'

'In a piece of toast.' Mammy was laughing and then we were all laughing, even Sarah, who didn't know what we were laughing at.

'To be fair,' said Agnes dabbing at her eyes, 'the toast did have a look of him.'

Oh, how I had missed all this. The face of Christ on a piece of toast? It could only happen in Ireland.

Chapter Fifty-Six

Me and Polly were sitting on the flat rocks, looking out over the sea. I'd been imagining this moment for so long and I couldn't get enough of it. The green hills across the water, the silence that felt as if I was in church and that particular smell of home.

'Are you happy to be back?' said Polly, linking her arm through mine.

'Oh, I am, Polly.'

'But won't you find Ballykillen a bit dull after America?'

'America isn't as exciting as you think. I mean, it was lovely and I have wonderful memories that I wouldn't have had, if I hadn't gone, but it wasn't home. I learned that people are more important than places.'

'I'm sorry about David, Rose, you must have been only heartbroken.'

'I still am but once Martha died, I had to step up and look after Sarah. I had to put her first. But it was hard, Polly.'

'I think you were very brave to go through all that with no one of your own beside you.'

'I didn't have a choice, did I?'

'I suppose you didn't.'

'Now, what about you, my friend? Are you still walking out with Jimmy? And isn't it about time you had a ring on your finger?'

Polly lifted her eyes up to heaven. 'Aren't I the biggest eejit to have fallen for Jimmy Coyne?'

'But you love him.'

'I know, isn't it desperate?'

'Is it?'

'Of course it is. I'll be stuck in Ballykillen for the rest of me life, surrounded by a pile of bloody kids. It's not what I wanted at all.'

'He's a lovely lad, Polly.'

'But he has no prospects and I'll never be swanning around in a swanky car with Jimmy Coyne at the wheel.'

I wanted to say that love was more important than a swanky car but I had a feeling that was not what she wanted to hear. 'Life has a way of working out, Polly.'

'Well, if I marry Jimmy Coyne, I know exactly how mine is going to work out.'

'I wouldn't be so sure of that. I thought I had mine all worked out, but I was wrong.'

'Oh, I'm sorry, Rose. There's me blathering on when you're heartbroken.'

'Let's go to the hotel and have a grand cup of tea. The tea in America is desperate. They put the milk in first, can you believe that? It would turn yer stomach.'

We walked across the road and went into the hotel. Mary Coyne was at the desk. 'Well, if it isn't Rose Brown, back from America. Come here 'til I hug ya.'

'You're looking well, Mary,' I said, as she put her arms around me.

'You're looking well yourself, girl. Is it a holiday, or are you home for good?'

'She's never leaving these shores again,' said Polly. 'Unlike meself,' she added.

'Sit down and I'll bring the tea over.'

We sat down at a table and waited for the tea. I looked round the room. 'I thought things would have changed while I was away but everything is exactly the same.'

'I wish it would bloody change. Ballykillen is stuck in the eighteenth century and it always will be. The only changes around here are folk dying and folk giving birth.'

'That's called life, Polly, and sure, I wouldn't want it any other way.'

'I would.'

'You think you would.'

'It's alright for you, Rose, you've seen a bit of the world.'

'And it's not that different to here.'

Mary came across with the tea. 'There's a feller looking for you, Rose.'

'A feller?'

'Yes.'

'What did he look like?' said Polly.

'I didn't see him, the manager did. All he said was that there was a feller looking for Rose Brown and he wanted your address. Oh, and he said he wasn't Irish, he had an accent.'

'What sort of an accent?'

'I'm sorry, Rose, but I haven't a clue.'

'How exciting,' said Polly. 'Have you any idea who it could be?' I shook my head.

'Do you think it's that sailor boy you were canoodling with, out at Temple Michael?'

'Polly Butler! We were not canoodling.'

'Well, you were kissing and in my book that's canoodling.'

'Well, it can't be Erik, for didn't he come to my house? He wouldn't be needing to ask anyone for my address, would he?'

'I thought for a minute he'd come to claim you and carry you back to Norway over his shoulder.'

'And why would I be wanting to go to Norway? I've only just got home.'

'Well, it must be someone who's only desperate to see you.'

'Shall I tell the manager to give out your address if he comes in again?'

'I wouldn't,' said Polly. 'He might be an axe murderer.'

'She's right, well enough,' said Mary. 'You can never be too careful. I'll tell you what, if he comes in again, shall I set up a meeting here at the hotel? And then if he's an axe murderer, he'll have us to contend with.'

'And I'll come with you,' said Polly, 'as your bodyguard.'

As we walked back through the town, we were both wondering who the feller might be.

'It would help if we knew what accent he has,' said Polly. 'Now I'd say if he isn't yer man from Norway, then he's going to be either English or American. Did you have a fling with anyone else in America? Or England, come to that?'

'No, I didn't. I haven't a clue who he could be.'

'Well, I can't wait to find out.'

We didn't have to wait long because that evening, Mary Coyne turned up at the door.

'God bless all here,' she said, dipping her finger in the holy water.

'Amen,' said Mammy. 'Oh, it's yourself, Mary. How're you doing?'

'I'm grand, Mrs Brown, and how's yerself?'

'I'm very well, thank you, Mary, and even better since Rose came home.'

'Have you come with news of the mystery man?' said Kathy. 'Rose told us all about him and we're only dying to know who he is and what business he has with Rose.'

'You're the only one who's dying to know, Kathy,' said Mammy.

'No, I'm not, we're all curious.'

'When are you getting married, Mary?' said Agnes.

'We want a place of our own first. I don't want to start married life with my parents or Liam's.'

'That's wise,' said Mammy. 'You have to build your own nest and not squash into someone else's. Will you take a cup of tea, Mary?'

'I won't, thank you, Mrs Brown. I'm just popping in with some news.'

'About the feller?' said Kathy.

'Yes.'

'Bridgy?' yelled Kathy.

'What?' shouted Bridgy from upstairs, 'I'm doing my homework.'

'Mary Coyne is here with news about the mystery feller who's after Rose.'

'I'll be down,' shouted Bridgy.

'He's not after me,' I said.

'Well, he's after something,' said Kathy.

Bridgy ran downstairs, jumping the last couple of steps and landing in the room.

'Fire away,' she said, grinning, 'and shouldn't Polly be here?'

'Jesus, Bridgy,' I said. 'Perhaps you should go out in the lane and make an announcement.'

She grinned. 'Do you want me to?'

'Enough now,' said Mammy. 'You have the floor, Mary Coyne.'

Chapter Fifty-Seven

The next morning, Polly and I walked through the town towards the hotel. I felt sick in my stomach and I didn't know why. Mary had set up a meeting with the mystery feller, who had come back into the hotel just after we'd left.

'I'm not sure this is such a great idea, Polly,' I said.

'I'm not sure, either.'

'I thought you'd be all for it.'

'Well, I was, but now I'm not. I mean, he could be anyone.'

'Well, he's obviously someone.'

'But he's a stranger. Did you ask Mary what accent he had?'

'I didn't and I was only kicking meself after she'd gone.'

'Aren't you an eejit, Rose Brown? It would have narrowed things down, if we knew what accent he had.'

'Mary said that he was nice-looking though and very polite.'

'A polite axe murderer, I'm thinking you don't get many of those in Ballykillen.'

'I just can't think who it could be, I don't know any strange men.'

'Well, whoever he is, he's desperate keen to have gone back to the hotel a second time.'

As we walked into the hotel, Mary greeted us with a smile. 'That's him, over there in the corner,' she whispered. 'Will I introduce you?'

'Now why would you be wanting to do that, Mary Coyne? Sure, he must know her, or he wouldn't be here.'

'I never thought of that,' said Mary.

'Jesus, he's gorgeous!' said Polly, as we walked towards the table.

The man stood up and held out his hand. Polly was right, he *was* gorgeous. He was tall and blond and he reminded me of someone. He reminded me of Erik.

'Christy Larson,' he said, shaking my hand and then Polly's.

We sat down at the table and waited.

He stared at me. 'Rose?' he said.

I nodded.

'You are just as my brother described you.'

Polly was looking at the two of us, her eyes out on stalks. 'I'm Polly,' she said. 'Rose's best friend.'

'It's a pleasure to meet you, Polly.'

So, he was Erik's brother, but that didn't explain why he was In Ballykillen.

'Thank you for meeting me, Rose,' he said. 'You must wonder why I am here.'

Mary came across with three teas and some buns. 'Is everything alright, Rose?' she said, placing them on the table and winking at me.

I nodded.

'Well, if you need anything, just yell.'

I grinned at her. 'I'll do that.'

'Fine so,' she said, walking away.

Christy didn't speak for a bit and then he said, 'I'm afraid I have some sad news for you, Rose. My brother Erik died at the beginning of the war.'

I could feel my eyes filling with tears, remembering that lovely boy and the short, special time we spent together. 'I'm so sorry.'

'My condolences,' said Polly.

'Erik spoke of a young girl called Rose Brown and of a magical day, sitting on the banks of a river, behind a haunted abbey. I think my brother fell in love with you that day, Rose, and when he said goodbye, I believe he left a piece of his heart behind him. His one wish was to come back and tell you so, but sadly, that dear boy never got the chance so I have come in his place and I hope you don't think me foolish but I wanted to do it for Erik.'

'Isn't that desperate romantic?' said Polly, biting into a bun.

I wiped away the tears that were running down my face. Christy reached across the table and held my hand. 'I'm sorry I've upset you, Rose.'

I shook my head. 'I'm happy you came.'

'Oh, I'm so glad, I'm so very glad,' he said.

'So am I.'

'I would like very much to go to the place he talked about. Would it be asking too much for you to take me there?'

I smiled. 'Of course not, I would be very happy to do that.'

Christy talked about Erik and about his family in Norway and we arranged to meet up the next day.

'Do you want me to come with you?' said Polly, as we walked back through the town. 'I mean, you don't know the man and it's awful isolated out there. Anything could happen. It might be best if I brought Jimmy as well.'

'Jesus, Polly, why don't you invite the whole town? It's hardly likely that he would come all the way from Norway just to murder me.'

'I'm only thinking of you, Rose.'

I smiled at my friend. 'I know you are, Polly, and I'm grateful for your concern but I'll be fine.'

'Maybe bring a knife just to be on the safe side.'

I laughed. 'Have I ever told you that I love you, Polly Butler?'

'Mmm, you might have done,' she said, grinning.

We were laughing as we linked arms and walked home.

Chapter Fifty-Eight

We were silent as we walked through the woods towards Temple Michael but it was an easy silence. It had been autumn when I'd walked here with Erik and now it was summer. The trees had been so beautiful that day, reds and browns and yellows, falling around us and crunching beneath our feet as we'd walked. Today, sunlight dappled through the lush leaves, the tree branches leaning into each other, creating a magical walkway with a dense green ceiling above our heads.

'I have imagined this so often, Rose,' said Christy. 'Erik described it all so vividly, I felt as if I was walking beside him. I feel him beside me now.'

'You must miss him,' I said.

'Every day. We were very close. As children, we did everything together, he was my best friend.'

'He talked about you, Christy. He told me how you would help the fishermen unload their catch and how your mother would make you strip off at the door before she'd let you into the house.'

Christy laughed. 'And we didn't blame her, for we smelt very bad. There was only a year between us in age but I always looked up to him, I wanted to be just like him. He had this warmth of spirit that drew people in. Everyone fell under his spell, Rose, especially children. He seemed to understand them without patronising them and they could sense that. He would have been a great father and that is the saddest thing of all.'

I remembered how kind and gentle he'd been with my sisters, how he'd spun Bridgy around and how he'd noticed the shyness in Agnes. 'I would like to have known him for longer,' I said.

'Your time together may have been short but he never forgot you, Rose. He carried that memory of you in his heart.'

'I just wish we had had more time.'

'Maybe time has little to do with love.'

We emerged from the wood and followed the path, between high grasses, towards Temple Michael.

'The abbey,' I said, pointing to the crumbling, grey building ahead of us.

Christy stopped walking and looked around him. 'No wonder my brother never forgot this place, it has a magic about it.'

'I've always thought so,' I said.

'And it's haunted?'

'Well, I can't say for sure. I've never seen anything to make me think it is – in fact, I've always found peace here.'

'So perhaps it is just hearsay, created by the old ones to pass down to the next generation.'

'Well, Orla Feeny swears she saw the vision of an old monk but then again, she swears she saw the face of Christ in a piece of toast, so I have my doubts.'

Christy laughed. 'In a piece of toast?'

I grinned. 'That's what she says.'

'I've heard it all now.'

'Mind you, she was the spawn of the devil before the toast episode and now she's a changed woman.'

We were laughing as we walked amongst the ruins of the old abbey, through the graveyard and down to the river.

'This is where we sat,' I said.

'Then can we sit here too?'

'Of course.'

We sat on the bank and watched the River Blackwater flowing past. I wanted Christy to love this place as much as I did. I wanted him to find the peace that I always found here and I wanted him to like me. It suddenly seemed important that he liked me.

'It's beautiful, Rose,' he said, as if he could read my mind.

We sat quietly, looking across at the big house and at the humble cottages that seemed to tumble down towards the water. I had been coming here all my life and I never tired of it. My sisters and I would picnic here beside the river when we were children and then we'd play chase around the ruins.

'Who owns that?' said Christy, pointing across the water.

'Old man Mulligan,' I said. 'Well, he used to, but he's dead now.'

'It's a splendid house.'

'Which is more than can be said for old Mulligan.'

'Would you like to live in a house like that, Rose?'

I shuddered. 'I'd hate to live there. I'd say that it would always have the spirit of Mulligan, roaming round the rooms like an angry old ghost. He'd be awful put out that someone had the nerve to live in his house. He nearly caught me scrumping apples once. He was tearing towards us like a mad man.'

'Scrumping?'

'It sounds less sinful than stealing,' I said, grinning.

'So, you wouldn't want to live there?'

'No, I shall find a cosy little house for me and Sarah and it will be nothing like that great mausoleum of a place.'

'You have a child?'

'Oh, I'm her guardian, not her mother. Her name is Sarah and she is six years old.'

'There must be quite a story behind that.'

'There is.'

'Would you tell me, Rose? For I'd love to get to know you better.'

And so, as the Blackwater River flowed past, I told my story. I told him about Raffi and Alice, I told him about the ship being torpedoed and I told him about the little tailor's shop and about the Lyns being taken away in a lorry and yet, I didn't tell him about David and I knew why. It would change things between us, even though there was nothing between us to change.

'How long are you staying here?'

'I'm not sure. My plan was to see more of Ireland before I go back to Norway but I'm in no hurry. I would like to spend more time with you, Rose, if that's what you would like.'

I looked into his eyes that were the same bright blue as Erik's.

'Yes, Christy, I would like that.'

He reached over and tucked a stray piece of hair behind my ear. The touch of his hand against my skin made me feel warm, made me want more. *Jesus, Rose Brown*, I thought to myself, *you've only known the man for five minutes and here you are behaving like a hussy.*

'You are as lovely as my brother said you were, Rose.'

And you are lovely too, I thought.

Chapter Fifty-Nine

Me and Polly were sitting on a wall down the quay. 'He left you all his money?' she said.

I nodded. 'And five thousand pounds from Martha.'

Polly nearly fell off the wall. 'Jesus, Rose, you could buy the whole town with that. What are you going to do with it?'

'Well, the first thing I must do is find a place for me and Sarah. We're bursting at the seams in Cross Lane but as for the rest of it, I really don't know. In fact, I was all for handing it back.'

'You were going to hand it back? Are you mad altogether, Rose Brown?'

'You're the only one I've told.'

'You haven't told your mammy?'

I shook my head.

'Well, you'll have to tell her sometime, you can't keep a fortune like that hidden forever.'

'When we came across on the boat, we travelled first class. There was a separate gangplank for first-class passengers and that's how I feel about the money – like I will be on a different gangplank to my family and friends.'

'Well, I wouldn't mind being on a different gangplank,' said Polly, sighing.

'And anyway, it still doesn't feel like mine.'

'Well, it is, Rose, so you're going to have to find a way to live with it.'

'I know.'

'You can treat me to an ice cream if you like, I have no worries about spending the money.'

'Come on then,' I said, jumping off the wall.

As we walked along the strand, I decided that I would tell Mammy about the money when I got home. Knowing my mammy, she wouldn't care what gangplank I was on and it wouldn't change her love for me. I felt ashamed for thinking such a thing.

'So, tell me about the date with yer man. You're keeping awful quiet about it.'

'It wasn't a date, Polly, it was just…'

'Just what?'

'Friendly and nice, he's easy company, it was nice.'

'Easy on the eye too.'

'I can't deny that.'

'Does he have a girl back in Norway?'

'Now how in God's name would I know? I was hardly going to ask.'

'But you like him and it would be handy to know whether he's available before you find yourself falling for him.'

'Who said anything about falling for him? Sure, we've only known each other five minutes.'

'Have you never heard of love at first sight?'

I laughed. 'Do you know what you are, Polly Butler?'

'No, but I expect you'll inform me.'

'You're a born romantic.'

'Always have been,' she said, laughing.

'So, when are you and Jimmy tying the knot?'

'Don't be talking about it.'

'That was what Billy Ogg said when I asked him how Minnie was.'

'Have you not heard? It was the talk of the town.'

'That's exactly why I haven't heard, ya eejit. I haven't been in the town, have I?'

'Well, wasn't she after being whisked off to England by a stranger.'

'Minnie Ogg?' I said, amazed.

'I swear on my brothers' lives.'

I laughed. 'And would you swear on your mammy's life?'

Polly grinned. 'I would not, but it's true all the same, Rose. She was swept off her feet by an Englishman.'

'I still don't believe that anyone would sweep Minnie Ogg off her feet. What was an Englishman doing in Ballykillen, anyway?'

'He was looking for his ancestors up at the graveyard.'

'And that's where he met Minnie Ogg?'

Polly nodded. 'Minnie was tending the grave of her long dead grandmother. Mind you, it might not have been her grandmother at all, because as the whole town knows, Teddy Collins, who minds the place, is a desperate drunk and he buries bodies all over the place.'

'And he was taken with her?'

'He was taken by her voice. I'm not sure that anyone in their right mind would be taken by Minnie Ogg. She's hardly love's young dream. She was singing, "When Irish Eyes Are Smiling". It was her granny's favourite. Mind you, she was probably singing it to someone else's granny. But anyway, he was smitten with the voice and he told her that he would make her famous and off she went, without a thought for Billy Ogg. The poor man was heartbroken.'

'Well, he didn't sound very heartbroken, he sounded as if he wanted to kill her in cold blood.'

'And to top it all off, they left on the Thrupenny Rush and he had to blow his whistle and wave his flag and watch his wife disappear into the distance.'

I couldn't help but laugh, thinking of poor Billy waving his little red flag. It occurred to me that I hadn't done much laughing since I left Ballykillen. Nothing would make me leave home again, not ever.

Chapter Sixty

The more I got to know Christy, the more I liked him. I saw him as much as I could and I looked forward to those times. I found myself taking care with my appearance, wanting to look nice for him. These feelings left me confused. I still loved David but because of Christy, I found that the pain of losing him was getting less. Sometimes when I thought about David, it was Christy's face that came into my mind.

Everyone liked him except Sarah and that bothered me, because I had to put her first. Sarah would stand in the bedroom, watching me getting ready to go out. She would lean against the door with a scowl on her face and when I'd get home, she would sulk and not speak to me.

'She's just a child, Rose,' said Mammy. 'A child who has lost everyone she loved and now she's afraid of losing you. Give her time, she has to feel secure in the knowledge that you are not going to leave her.'

'Of course I won't leave her, Mammy. Anyway, Christy and I are just friends. He's done nothing to make me think that we are anything more than that.'

'Then you are blind, Rose Brown, for the rest of us can see very clearly what his feelings are. Sarah may only be a child but she senses it too and she needs lots of reassuring. It has been just the two of you for a long time and now she is having to share you and she doesn't like it. Take her with you sometimes, include her. Let her see that just because you have a new friend, it doesn't mean that you love her any less. It's a balance, Rose. You have every right to spend time with Christy and I am happy for you. Sarah will come round, my love.'

'I hope so, Mammy.'

'What she needs is friends of her own age. She needs to be running the fields and lanes as you did when you were a child and then she'll be too busy having fun to be worrying about what you're doing, or *not* doing. Have you decided on a school yet?'

I'd told Mammy about the money, so she knew that I had the fees for the private school.

'The money feels like a bit of a burden, Mammy.'

'All I can say, Rose, is there's a lot of people in this town who wouldn't say no to a burden like that.'

'And Polly is one of them,' I said, laughing.

'What school would her father want her to go to?'

I had no doubt which school David would have chosen for his daughter. 'He would have wanted her to go to a private school,' I said. 'But his lawyer said that it is up to me to do what I think is best for her.'

'Agnes and Bridgy were both happy enough with the nuns but Sarah hasn't been brought up in the Catholic faith and it may set her apart from the other children. Bridgy loves the Loretta and the emphasis is more towards the reading, writing and numbers than on religion. I think that it would be a better fit for Sarah but as yer lawyer feller said, it's up to you.'

'The Loretta it is, then. I shall go there tomorrow and see when she can start.'

'I think that's a good decision, Rose.'

Christy and I had planned a picnic and I decided that I would take Sarah with us. Mammy was right; the child was feeling left out and I wanted her to know that Christy wasn't some ogre who was going to take me away from her.

Christy came to call for me at the cottage. 'It's a beautiful day for a picnic, Christy,' said Mammy, handing him the basket of food.

'Indeed it is, Mrs Brown,' he said, smiling.

'There's a blanket in there as well, in case the ground is a bit damp.'

'Right,' he said. 'We'll be on our way then.'

'Sarah, we're going,' I called.

Sarah came running down the stairs. 'Have I ever been on a picnic, Rose?' she said.

I thought about it. 'I don't think you have, darling, are you excited?'

'I'm very excited but I wish we had a dog, Rose. If we had a little dog, we could take him with us.'

'Would you like a dog?'

'I would like a dog very much. My friend Sonia had a dog called Freddie and I liked to pet him.'

'And what would you call your dog?' I asked her.

'Mmm, I'm not sure. What would you call *your* dog, Granny?'

'Let me see now,' said Mammy, smiling down at her. 'When I was a child, we had a little dog called Buddy. But you know what, darling? I think that the naming of a dog is a very big decision and only you can decide, because the dog would be yours.'

'I'll think about it,' said Sarah, very seriously.

I'd noticed that Christy hadn't said anything during this conversation. In fact, he didn't look very happy. 'Sarah is coming with us?' he said.

I nodded. 'I thought it would be fun for her.'

'But didn't you say you were going to show me the hill? Wouldn't that be too much for a child?'

'I'm not a child,' said Sarah, glaring at him.

'She'll manage,' said Mammy. 'Sarah has a strong pair of legs, haven't you, my love?'

'I have, Granny, and I'll get up there quicker than *he* can.'

Sarah had emphasised the word 'he' without even a glance at Christy. *Dear God, I was going to have my work cut out here.* 'Right then, let's be off.'

'Is *he* coming with us, Rose?'

'Of course he is, it will be fun.'

Sarah frowned. 'I thought the picnic was just for the two of us.'

As we walked out the door, I heard Christy mutter something under his breath. It sounded awful like, 'So did I.'

'I think we should go to the beach,' I said. 'There'll be more for Sarah to do there.'

'As you like,' said Christy.

As we walked through town towards the strand, almost everyone we passed said hello.

'Do you know everyone in this place?' said Christy.

I laughed. 'It's a small town.'

We walked onto the beach and Christy spread the blanket on the pebbles. 'Can you find me a stone in the shape of a heart, Sarah?'

'Of course I can,' she said. 'I'll take it home for my granny.'

'That's a lovely idea, darling.'

'I wanted to talk to you about something, Rose,' said Christy.

'Sarah,' I called. 'Try and find one for Agnes and Bridgy as well, I think they would like that.'

'I will,' she said, running off.

'Are you listening, Rose?' said Christy.

'Sorry, yes, of course I am.'

'Would you come to Norway with me? I'd love to show you my own town and introduce you to my parents.'

I was taken aback at what he was suggesting. 'I'm sorry, Christy, but Sarah is only just beginning to settle. I couldn't take her on a journey like that.'

'I wasn't thinking of the child,' he said. 'I meant just you and me.'

'No, I couldn't leave her.'

'But your mother would look after her, wouldn't she? I couldn't help noticing that the child calls her "Granny".'

Something was shifting inside me. He couldn't even manage to call Sarah by her name. I remembered Erik. I remembered his kindness and his gentleness with my sisters. I had fallen a little in love with him and maybe for a while I'd thought I was beginning to feel the same for Christy but Christy wasn't Erik. He didn't care about Sarah, in fact he wanted nothing to do with her and Sarah, God love her, had seen something in him that I hadn't seen. If there was ever going to be someone else in my life, it would have to be someone who loved Sarah as much as her daddy did, otherwise I would be content to spend the rest of my days alone.

Christy reached across and held my hand. 'I am trying to say—'

Just then, Sarah ran up to us, holding out a handful of pebbles. 'They don't look exactly like hearts, Rose, but I think they are very nice pebbles and I don't think that Granny and Agnes and Bridgy will mind, do you?'

Before I could answer her, Christy snapped at her. 'Can't you see that Rose and I are trying to have a conversation?'

Sarah's little face crumpled and I took her in my arms and kissed the top of her head. 'I think they are the nicest pebbles that I have ever seen, my darling girl, and I think Granny and Agnes and Bridgy will love them and do you know why they will love them?'

'Why?'

'Because you collected them.'

'Can I finish what I was saying?' said Christy, impatiently.

'No, you may not and I think you should go.'

'Go where?'

'I don't care where, just not here.'

'But—'

'Please go, Christy, please go now.'

'What have I done?'

'It's what you *haven't* done. Now, let us part on friendly terms and not make this any more awkward than it already is. You wanted to see more of Ireland and that is what I think you should do, because we won't be seeing each other again.'

'You are a fool, Rose,' he said, standing up. 'I was offering you more than this backward little town ever could. I was going to relieve you of the burden of a child who is not even yours.'

'The "child" as you call her is not and has never been a burden. Sarah is a gift, the most precious gift that I have ever been given. It's you who are the fool if you can't see that. Goodbye, Christy.'

He didn't answer, he just strode away up the beach. I watched until he had disappeared from sight.

Sarah, who had been cuddled into me, lifted her head and grinned. 'Eejit,' she said.

I laughed. 'Well, it didn't take you long to become a little Irish girl. Eejit, indeed!'

Chapter Sixty-One

I thought that I was going to miss Christy but I didn't. I had been a fool, the worst kind of fool.

He had been nothing more than a sticking plaster over an open wound. The trouble with sticking plasters is that they eventually peel off, leaving a place underneath that hasn't healed and is just as painful as it ever was. When we were children and we'd hurt ourselves, Mammy always said, 'There is no point covering it up, you have to let the air get at it.' But that was what I had been doing. I had been covering up my grief with a bit of plaster, instead of letting it heal in God's own good time.

I didn't blame God, in fact I thanked Him for bringing me to my senses. It seemed that myself and yer man upstairs had come to a sort of understanding and decided to rub along with each other. I would put my trust in Him now and not in a bit of plaster. I even felt grateful to Christy for bringing me to this place.

Polly and myself were in the town running some messages for her mother. 'He was awful good-looking though, wasn't he?' said Polly, as we started to walk home.

'I'm learning that looks aren't everything, Polly. Christy was like a book with a beautiful cover but with no substance inside its pages.'

'You're getting awful wise in your old age, Rose.'

'It's a pity it took me so long to get there.'

'Ah well, better late than never, for he turned out to be a gobshite.'

'I thought he was nice, Polly. I thought he was like his brother but he wasn't.'

'Well, I have to say, Rose, that I had my doubts.'

'Why didn't you say anything?'

'You were happy and I could have been wrong but I just had a feeling about him.'

'So did Sarah.'

'Wise little dote.'

'She is. Christy wanted to take me to Norway but he didn't want her with us. It was then that I knew he wasn't the man for me.'

'You had a lucky escape, Rose.'

'So it seems.'

'Did the pair of you kiss?'

'Funnily enough, we never did and I'm glad we didn't now. That's why I was surprised that he wanted to take me to Norway when we'd never done more than hold hands and that was only the once.'

'Now that's strange, Rose.'

'I thought so.'

'Maybe he thought that once you saw Norway, you'd fall into his arms and never want to come back to Ballykillen.'

'Well, he thought wrong.'

As we turned into Windmill Hill, we could see a crowd of people gathered outside the cottage.

'There must be something wrong with Mammy,' said Polly, as we started to run.

There was a ladder leaning against the wall and Jimmy was balancing on the top of it.

'Jesus, Jimmy,' shouted Polly. 'What are you doing up there? Are you wanting to break your neck?'

'I'm trying to rescue Finn McCool,' he shouted back.

Various people were shouting instructions up to Jimmy. Dermot Casey seemed to have elected himself as spokesman. 'You need to climb onto the roof, Jimmy, and make a grab for him.'

'Don't you be climbing up onto that roof, Jimmy,' shouted Polly. 'And don't you be encouraging him, Dermot Casey.'

'It's the only way to save the cat,' said Dermot.

'I can get another cat,' said Polly. 'I can't get another Jimmy.'

'Well, make sure it's not a blind one this time,' said Nora Connell, who lived next door. 'I've had enough of him staggering into my house and banging his head off everything in me kitchen.'

'This is no time to be telling someone who is about be bereaved what sort of replacement cat to choose,' said Dermot.

'Bereaved?' screamed Polly, clutching onto my arm.

'I was just trying to be helpful,' said Mrs Connell. She was about to stalk off when her foot caught the bottom of the ladder and it started sliding down the wall, cracking into two pieces as it hit the ground, leaving Jimmy clinging to the guttering.

'Jimmy,' screamed Polly.

'Hang on there, man,' shouted Dermot. 'Don't let go.'

'I wasn't planning to,' shouted Jimmy.

'He's going to fall, Rose. I know it, he's going to fall,' said Polly, 'and he'll be paralysed for life and have to spend his days in a chair.'

Just then, Mrs Butler hurried up the hill, pushing Sean in his pram.

'What in God's name is Jimmy Coyne doing, swinging off my roof?'

'He's trying to rescue Finn McCool,' said Dermot.

'Polly, get the good blanket off my bed, we'll catch him. Hurry now.'

'Yes, Mammy,' said Polly, running into the cottage.

'Good call,' said Dermot.

Finn McCool had now sniffed his way across to Jimmy and was sitting on his head.

Polly came out with the blanket and we all took hold of it. Ballykillen hadn't had this much excitement in years.

'As tight as you can now,' said Dermot. 'Okay, Jimmy, let yourself fall and we'll catch you.'

'Brace yourselves,' said Dermot as Jimmy and Finn McCool came flying down from the roof. Jimmy was light and he landed in the middle of the blanket with a big grin on his face.

'It's a good job it wasn't Billy Ogg up there,' said Mrs Butler. 'He would have gone straight through my good blanket.'

'Oh, Jimmy,' said Polly, kneeling beside him and holding him in her arms. 'I thought you were going to die and I couldn't bear it if you died, for I love the very bones of you.'

He smiled at her. 'Does that mean you'll consent to marry me at last?'

'Oh yes, Jimmy. I will.'

A cheer went up from the crowd and everyone started clapping as Finn McCool strolled off without a care in the world, banging his head on the ladder as he went.

Chapter Sixty-Two

Ballykillen lived for weeks on the story of the cat on the roof and as the story went on, it got more and more fanciful. Some said that the spirit of Christ himself had entered the soul of Finn McCool, just to bring Polly to her senses and make her realise how much she loved Jimmy Coyne.

Mrs Connell was now actively encouraging Finn McCool into her kitchen, so that the neighbours could come and pay homage to him. Mammy said it was a wonder she wasn't charging them. She even hinted that Finn McCool had regained his sight and that he should be canonised, which was a load of rubbish because he was still banging into everything.

I was feeling calmer these days. I could never regret having met Christy because for a while, he had soothed my broken heart. I'd grabbed onto him like a drowning man. Mammy was right, it was healthier to let my sorrow get some fresh air and not try to deny it by putting it out of sight. I even began to feel sorry for Christy because, God forgive me, I had unknowingly used him for my own ends.

One evening, when we were sitting round the table eating our dinner, there was a bang on the door. This was unusual because in Ballykillen, people would just walk in and not bother knocking. Bridgy got up and looked out the window, 'There's a grand car outside, Mammy,' she said.

The door banged again and Kathy jumped up to answer it. I could hear her speaking to a man.

'It's for you, Rose,' she said.

I went to the door to find a young man standing there. Beside him was a large trunk.

'Delivery for Miss Rose Brown,' he said, smiling.

'I'm Rose,' I said, smiling back.

'Sign here,' he said, handing me a piece of paper.

I wrote my name and the man carried the trunk into the room.

'Good day to you,' he said, tipping his hat and walking towards the door.

'Wait,' I said, running upstairs. I came down and put some money into his hand. 'For your trouble,' I added.

He tipped his hat again. 'Thank you, miss.'

'You are very welcome,' I said.

Once he'd gone, we all sat on the floor and stared at the trunk.

'What d'you think's in it, Rose?' said Agnes.

'I haven't the slightest idea,' I said. All mine and Sarah's clothes had been delivered already, so I knew it wasn't that.

'Well, the best way to find out,' said Mammy, 'is to open it.'

I undid the straps and then opened the lid. I will never forget the looks on my sisters' faces as, one by one, they lifted the beautiful dresses out of the trunk – velvets and silks, satins and crepe, in blues and reds and greens, each one more beautiful than the next. Kathy held a black sequined evening gown against herself and spun around the room.

'Where did they come from, Rose?' said Mammy.

I could feel my eyes filling with tears when I thought of my beautiful friend. 'They were Martha's.'

There must have been at least twenty dresses in the trunk.

'Are they ours?' said Bridgy.

'It looks like it,' I said.

'There's a letter,' said Agnes, handing me an envelope.

'Read it out to us, Rose,' said Bridgy, holding a green velvet dress against her cheek.

I opened the letter and started to read.

Darling Rose,

I hope that these dresses will give you as much joy as they have given me. Each one has its own story to tell, of those golden days when I lived in France and Italy. Those days when I smoked Turkish cigarettes from an ivory holder, when I drank champagne out of crystal glasses and ate caviar by the spoonful. They speak to me of artists and gigolos, gypsies and clandestine affairs in the dark alleyways of Paris. They speak to me of life and love, of meetings and partings. Wonderful, wonderful memories that I thought would last forever, only to realise that the first hallo is already racing towards the last goodbye but of course when you are young, you think that you have all the time in the world.

I still think of myself and my darling Alice dancing around the room in our finery. She so loved dressing up in these beautiful clothes. It's a memory that I cherish. And so, I say to you, Rose and Kathy, Agnes and Bridgy and your wonderful mother: wear them, enjoy them, feel the sensation of silk and satin against your skin, don't let them hang in a cupboard as I did. Wear them when you are washing up, wear them when you are cleaning windows, but wear them.

My love to you all, especially to you, Rose and Sarah. May you all have happy lives, with the odd bit of excitement thrown in. Embrace change and strive for individuality. Be the best version of yourself that you can be, but above all, never harness yourself to someone else's wagon; find your own. Don't waste your time longing for someone who can never be yours. It is only through our mistakes that we find wisdom, so take a deep breath, cry if you must but move on, for there will be better things waiting around the next bend in the road if you only look for them.

Oh, and read books, read lots and lots of books. It's the only way to find Wonderland.

Think of me sometimes,
Martha Xxx

Chapter Sixty-Three

Mammy and I were alone in the kitchen, drinking tea at the table. 'There's something I want to do, Mammy,' I said.

'And what is that, darling?'

'I would like some sort of celebration for the lives of Alice and Raffi and David. A service of remembrance. Do you think that Father Luke would be agreeable, even though they weren't of the Catholic faith?'

'Aren't we all God's children, whatever faith we follow? I think it would be a beautiful and fitting thing to do, Rose, and I'm sure that Father Luke would be very honoured to do it.'

Mammy was right and although I had thought it would only be a small gathering, news had filtered through the town and St Mary's church was packed. It was a simple but beautiful ceremony.

Candles flickered on the stone ledges beneath the windows and people placed flowers on the steps of the altar. Alice and Raffi and David were strangers to them and yet the people of Ballykillen honoured them as if they were one of their own. I was touched by their kindness.

When the choir sang, 'For Those in Peril on the Sea', I felt Sarah's hand slip in mine as tears ran down my face. I thought of Alice and Raffi and David and I felt, at last, a sense of peace wash over me. There would never be a grave to kneel beside, but their lives had been honoured and I felt that maybe now I could let them go. I would make sure that Sarah would always know that once she had a mammy called Alice, a daddy called David and a brother called Raffi. They would never be forgotten while I was here to keep their memory alive.

On the morning that Sarah started school at the Loretta, Mammy and myself watched her walk hand-in-hand with Bridgy, down Cross Lane, wearing their brown and yellow uniforms. My eyes filled with tears as I waved from the doorstep, remembering the baby that I had held in my arms on that cold night, not knowing whether we would live or die and here she was, a bright, beautiful little girl at the start of new adventure. I was so proud of her and I couldn't have loved her more if she had been my own child.

I watched until they were out of sight and walked back into the house. I'd been feeling restless since I'd woken up and now I didn't know what to do with myself. I was pacing up and down the small room, getting under Mammy's feet.

'Get yourself out for a walk, Rose. Blow those cobwebs away, for you have me brain mashed with your wanderings.'

I laughed. 'Sorry, Mammy, but I'm all over the place. Yes, I think a walk is exactly what I need.'

Summer had turned to autumn and there was a chill in the air as I walked towards the hill. I pulled my coat closer around me and started climbing. I was glad that I had never brought Christy here; this was my special place and I didn't want the memory of him to spoil it.

I was boiling by the time I reached the top, so I took off my coat and spread it on the ground. The sea was calm today but I knew how easily it could turn into something wild enough to toss a little boat into the air and slam it back down again into the cold raging waters.

I turned my back on the sea and looked instead on my beautiful Blackwater River. This river had always brought me peace. There was something calming in the way it moved, gently and smoothly, as if it had nothing to prove and being itself was enough. The sea was different; it seemed always to be in a hurry, rushing towards some destination. Changing, always changing, never stopping long enough to enjoy the shore that it was rushing towards, never staying long enough to notice the beauty of the smooth pebbles that it dragged back into the ocean.

I realised that was how I had been, since losing David. I had never given my heart the time to really take in what had happened. I had blocked him from my mind because the pain was so huge that I was afraid of it. That was why I had turned to Christy. I had turned to him as my saviour, when the only saviour I needed was myself.

Mammy once said that you don't get over someone you have lost, you learn to live with it, for if your love was true, then they deserved your grief.

Alice used to read quotes from books that she liked. I could sit for hours listening to her. I recalled one that for some reason had stayed with me.

She was no longer wrestling with the grief.
But could sit down with it, as a lasting companion
And make it a sharer in her thoughts.

It was written by a woman who wrote under the name of George Eliot.

That is what I would do, I decided: I would make friends with my grief. I would sit beside it and I would remember the love David and I had for each other and not be afraid. I would take it slowly like the river. I would give myself permission to cry, I would allow myself to scream if I needed to. I would not look outside my heart for someone to fix it. I would accept that some things just can't be fixed.

I hoped that Sarah was having a lovely time at her new school. I hoped she would find a special friend, someone she could have adventures with, someone who would always be there for her, as Polly had always been there for me. But what would I do with my life, now that Sarah was stepping out into the world? I had to find somewhere for us to live but what then? Polly would marry Jimmy and God willing, have children. Things were bound to change between us, even if we didn't want them to.

I sighed and looked down at the river. Everything was moving on without me, even my beloved Blackwater. Everything and everyone had somewhere to go, except me. Maybe I wasn't supposed to go anywhere, maybe just being here was enough.

When I thought about the journey I had been on and the people I had met, it felt more like a dream than reality – as if it had never happened at all, as if I had never left Ballykillen. My fingers closed over the aquamarine crystal around my neck. This was real, this was solid, but the people I had met and loved were more like characters in one of Alice's books, not real people at all. Alice used to say that even if a book wasn't to your liking, you will always have learned something from it. So, what had I learned, now that I had read the last chapter and closed the book? I suppose I had learned that I could be strong and perhaps even brave. I had learned that even a broken heart can mend and I had learned that grief doesn't kill you. I had found love in unexpected places and that love would live in my heart forever. I had my memories, even if they were now no more than shadows that drifted in and out of my mind, but most of all, I had learned that I could survive.

I lay down and closed my eyes. I felt at peace as I drifted off to sleep.

When I woke, I was cold, the sun had gone in and the wind was sharp. I stood up and looked down the hill. There was a figure walking slowly towards me. I rubbed my eyes and stared. I wanted to run to him but I couldn't move, because I couldn't believe what I was seeing. I couldn't believe that it was him. And then he was standing in front of me, tears running down his cheeks, and then I was in his arms. I felt his shoulder blades jutting out from beneath his thin jacket but he was alive, he was real, as real and solid as the crystal that hung around my neck.

'David?'

He held me away from him and gently touched my face.

I was laughing and crying as I looked into his beautiful eyes. 'You came back to me.'

'I will never leave you again, my Rose. I will never leave you again.'

And as the River Blackwater flowed gently below us I knew that, at last, I had truly come home.

A Letter from Sandy

Dear reader,

Thank you for choosing to read *The Irish Nanny*. I do hope you enjoyed it. I would like to thank all my readers, for your ongoing support, messages and amazing reviews. I have really enjoyed hearing from you, and I will always respond to your messages. It would be great if you could take a moment to post a short review; these reviews are very helpful to a writer.

To keep up to date with the latest news on my new releases, just click on the link below to sign up for my newsletter. I promise to only contact you when I have a new book out and never share your email address with anyone else.

www.bookouture.com/sandy-taylor

Thank you again for all your support and encouragement. I really do have the best readers and I really do appreciate you all.

Sandy x

SandyTaylorAuthor

@SandyTaylorAuth

Acknowledgements

So many amazing people to thank. My wonderful daughter Kate and son-in-law Iain. My beautiful grandchildren, Millie, Archie and Emma, who bring me such joy.

To all my family here and in Ireland, who mean so much to me. Mag and Paddy, Marge and John, I am so lucky to have you in my life.

Where would I be without all my wonderful friends, who have always been there for me, especially during the last two years. Thank you for the fun and the laughs we have had when I doubted that I would ever laugh again.

Special mention to dearest Louie, who means the world to me. To my dearest friend and soulmate Wenny. To my very talented friend, fellow writer and general sounding board Lesley. To Angela, Lis, Anne, Bren and darling Clive. To the teapot club and the cabana girls. Can't wait to hug you all again.

To Izzy and Allie, two very special people who have just fought their own battles and come out of them as beautiful and brave as ever. I am so very proud of you both. I haven't mentioned everyone, but you know who you are and you know that I love you.

To the amazing team at Bookouture. Claire, Natasha, Noelle and Kim, who have been so supportive of my writing. To my lovely editor, Emily, you have been wonderful. I feel privileged to be part of this very special publishing house.

And last but never least, my friend and agent Kate Hordern. Thank you for everything you have done for me.

To my son Bo and my friend Linda, who I will always carry in my heart.